CHASING

INNOCENCE

John Potter

Published in Great Britain in paperback in 2012 by Creative Crow

Copyright ©John Potter 2012

A CIP catalogue record for this title is available
from the British Library

Paperback ISBN 978-0-9570870-0-2

Creative Crow
www.creativecrow.co.uk

Cover Design by Richie Cumberlidge at Daniel Goldsmith Associates
Typeset in 11.5/13.5 Adobe Garamond Pro by Daniel Goldsmith
Associates, Cheshire
Printed in the UK by Lightning Source UK Ltd, Milton Keynes

For You

Some things are lost before we realise they are precious

Sometimes they are taken

Sarah Sawacki checked her watch against the clock on the dash and returned to her vigil. Her eyes fixed on the bungalow, moving tirelessly from the door to each window. An ordinary bungalow in an ordinary street, a low brick wall topped by a low hedge.

Her car was silent save for the occasional shift of her body, her shallow breathing. Seconds ticked by and minutes passed. She checked her wrist and the dash again. She opened the door and climbed out, pulling her bag with her. A big open-topped bag, gripped so tight it made her knuckles white.

She walked the sixty-two steps along the pavement to the bungalow's gate, a journey she had taken each hour between ten and five over the last two days, her hours of opportunity while Adam worked unaware. Her days here, this vigil, was for her.

A grainy picture in a newspaper had led her here, to this street outside this bungalow. The picture was of a nine-year-old boy, the boy would be a man now, probably about twenty-four, just like her. She had known the boy back then. They had stared across the playground at each other, their shared nightmare acknowledged without ever speaking a word. The newspaper said the nightmare was now released and free.

The picture had been three months ago. Since then she had sent endless emails and signed up for countless website subscriptions, waiting on letters, spending an eternity in records offices and looking hopeful across desks, using her curse, coercing detail. Men rarely refused and women sensed her burden, bonded, were seldom reproachful.

The nightmare had moved but not that far. Her pursuit narrowed to a partial postcode, to this once-village, now consumed by the sprawl of London. Her days then were of criss-crossing streets and the aisles of local stores. Three days ago she had seen him, loading shopping into a car. His profile correlated from memory in an instant. She followed him here, to this ordinary street, and then returned home to prepare.

Sarah pushed the bungalow gate open with her hip and walked the final six steps to the door. Using the edge of her fist, five sharp hard sounds followed by silence. Just like every other time, every hour of the last two days.

She counted down from ninety and repeated the five sharp knocks. Stood and waited, a statue on the doorstep, one hand in her coat pocket, the other clutching her bag tight to her side. Sometimes sensing sound within, a moving shadow through glass, the grey day now heavy as if rain were in the air.

She waited and counted and knocked again. Forcing herself to stay still and not run, ignoring her mind's incessant gabbled warnings. The effort it required, of climbing from the car, the sixty-two steps, was wearing at her sanity. *Would it be this time?* Part of her hoped he would never open the door, imagined herself forever keeping vigil because she could not imagine anything else. The consequences of her actions, for what she intended doing, were unconsidered. Her other life was distant. Her determination to face him drove her. Her life now was this door. She heard a latch fall and a lock click and the door opened.

Three days ago she had known it was him without registering any particular detail. Now he was real and looking at her. Those thin lips set within that neat greyed beard, those piercing blue eyes, her five foot and inches dwarfed by his six foot and inches, more so now he stooped a little.

'What is it you want, banging like that?' His voice was tense, worn now, but it threw her back fourteen years. For a moment she was ten again.

'I would like to talk,' she said.

He replied, 'Do I know you?'

For the first time she noticed him unsteady on his feet, saw beyond the beard and eyes of her memory. His weight was supported on a walking stick and his face had aged more than fourteen years. He should be in his sixties but looked closer to eighty.

'Yes,' Sarah answered. 'You used to teach me gym, when I was at school. Private lessons, seventy-seven weeks.' The detail that defined her.

He shook his head. 'I don't recall, I taught lots of children.' He started to close the door.

She stepped forward, using her foot and free hand to stop its motion. She leaned in.

'Please, it's important to me. I need…I need closure, I just want to talk. You know why. Five minutes, please.'

She stared up at him, widened her eyes and let nature do the rest.

Could see it working, that curse of hers. That fire in his eyes rekindled by the innocence on his doorstep. He would settle for five minutes in her company, his eyes roving, seeing past the clothes to her naked as a child. He nodded and moved his weight on the stick. And with her skin crawling, the voices screaming for her to run, she stepped into his house.

He led her into a living room, sparse and frayed, propped the stick against the wall and made his way carefully to the kitchen. Sarah examined the room without moving then sat on the edge of a sagging sofa, her bag on her lap, knees together, grateful for trousers although she always wore them.

After a few minutes he returned and handed her a cup on a saucer, taking his own and easing himself down into a matching armchair.

'Out with it then,' he said, staring at her over his cup with those eyes. He drank from it and swilled noisily, as if testing a vintage.

She watched the fall and rise of his throat, considered her own cup and what might be mixed with her milky drink. Did not want him seeing what she was thinking, needed him to see her innocent. So she drank a mouthful of the hot liquid and stared back at him.

'Do you have guilt?' she asked. Not the question she had rehearsed.

He nodded without pause and they sat in silence. Eventually he spoke. 'Every day it's there as I wake. Then I shut it out. My needs are part of who I am, as is my guilt.'

Sarah felt disorientated, light-headed, knocked sideways. Not from the drink but from her mind's desperate attempts at rationalising this room, for her being here. The voices screamed at her, for what his body could do, had done to her. Those strong arms from which she never escaped.

She sat still with her bag on her knees, hands resting on top holding the cup. In the bag was the knife she had stolen from her mother's kitchen, fourteen years ago. A carving knife with a six-inch blade, once gleaming but now rusted and pitted. She had stolen it after sixteen of the seventy-seven weeks. She had survived his lessons by escaping to her imaginary world and because of the hope the knife gave her. For what it promised. Although she only ever hoped, could never bring herself to that promise. Until now, but now felt all wrong.

'Would you say sorry to me, apologise for what you did?' She placed her cup on its saucer on the floor.

'Unreservedly,' he said. 'I wish…I wish…I am sorry.'

3

'Just like that?'

'What else?' He shrugged. 'I cannot take it back. I have served my time.'

She leaned in a little, frustrated at her inability to conjure vengeance, her wrists resting on her bag, her knees pressed together.

'You said it was my fault, that I caused it.'

'You did, in a way,' he answered. 'But you weren't to know. You were too…too hard to resist. You still have it you know, that innocence that children lose.' He licked his lips and drank more tea.

'You haven't paid your debt,' she said. 'You served time for what you did to someone else. What you did to me is unspoken. You changed what I was. Changed what I was meant to be and made me something else. My…life.'

Her voice trailed away and she mentally crept back into herself. With every minute in this room her determination, so strong in getting her there, was seeping from her. She was still the child to his adult.

'I am sorry,' he repeated. 'Is there anything else?'

She shook her head and faded more. They sat in silence. She stared at the carpet around his feet, could picture those feet bare in the shower. It was all wrong. She had rehearsed this conversation a thousand times, a constant rerun in her mind as she watched from her car. Except now she was here there was no momentum for redemption. She felt defeated in the face of reality. There was no changing anything, making anything better. He was an arthritic old man with a walking stick. She had so wanted him to know her pain.

She stood and self-consciously smoothed her coat, waiting as he slowly rose. She stepped aside as he passed her, following him to the hallway. He pulled open the front door.

Sarah had thought this moment through with every other. She did what she had planned because the plan was all she could think to do. She stepped towards the door and turned, put one hand up on his shoulder and on tiptoe kissed that horrid stubbly cheek. She whispered, '*Thank you for apologising.*' The tea churned in her stomach at the sudden memory of that beard, of being that close. Her hand inside her bag, her fingers tight around the leather-bound handle.

He looked touched and surprised and for a moment she saw a glimmer of the monster behind his eyes. Her opportunity, but in that unguarded second her hand refused to move. With the evidence of her memories locked away her conscience would not pass sentence. No matter how much she willed her arm to motion, for all she had pent up inside, her hand stayed buried at the bottom of her bag.

He held the door open wider and a breeze rolled through the doorway, brushed against her legs and swirled around them both, washing the smell of his body across her face. A hard smell that jarred like a violent impact, bubbling free the memories so carefully locked beneath a dark ocean. The sound of a child's confused sobs, the pain, his ever ceaseless hands, fingers pushing inside her wherever they could. Thin lips that touched all of her skin, that scratchy, stubbly beard. Her struggle to breathe and her panic as he forced himself into her mouth, the searing pain inside her stomach as he thrust over and over.

She heard the cry as if from a distance, a wail that turned to a scream and then a primal snarl. Aware she was moving, punching forward, so hard she stumbled as her fist bounced off his chest. The force of the blow knocked him backwards and unsteady, down on to one knee, then on to the floor. His face contorted, not from shock but horror at what he saw in her face. Unaware of the blade buried to the hilt in his chest, crimson spreading across his shirt as his head hit the floor.

Sarah watched him gasping at the ceiling, for seconds, possibly minutes. Then she pulled her phone from her pocket and dialled with trembling fingers as she walked back to her car.

ONE

The Present

Adam Sawacki did not need to open his eyes or reach out a hand to know he was alone in bed. That was a given. Just as the shower was always the first sound he heard each morning, his first thought to imagine Sarah beneath the cascading water.

A sudden heave of plumbing heralded silence. Opening his eyes he blinked at the light shining through yellow curtains. Gradually he focused and looked beyond the rise of duvet over his feet to Sarah's dressing table. It was seven fifty, Saturday morning.

The bathroom door opened, creating a draught that chased through the apartment, bossing the curtains. He heard the light pad of feet.

'Tea?'

'Please,' he answered, imagining the towel captive on her waist and hips, her bare skin goose-pimpled, the smell of talcum, listening to her clatter crockery.

He shifted his focus to the three pictures on the wall beside her dressing table, holiday snaps printed to canvas. At the top a glittering translucent sea, at the bottom a close-up shot of flowers. His and hers. In the middle a concession by her for what she could not be for him. A picture of her topless on the beach, with a tentative smile and hopeful eyes, ponytailed hair bleached by the sun and tugged by the wind, her body adolescent save for a woman's poise.

He turned on his side and watched as she closed the door with her foot, placing his drink on the floor beside the bed. Then awkward seconds laced with expectation, usually broken when she stepped across to her dressing table.

But today, as she very occasionally did, she simply took a step back. Just out of reach. Her cup held between both hands, her arms covering her chest, a tentative smile and her deep brown eyes, a quality beyond the physical. It was everything she was, fragile and lithe. A heavenly creature. Her curse she said, his irony.

'What're you gawping at?'

'Some kind of beautiful,' he answered. It was the truth, but what he usually said for fear of tipping the balance.

'You always say that, I know what you want,' she said, a little playful, shifting her weight from one hip to the other, a shy nipple making itself known as she moved her arm. She did not step away. He relaxed. Her need outweighed her fear.

'Why don't you come here Mrs Sawacki, maybe this man can make you happy.' He gave her his biggest grin.

She could not help snorting as she laughed. 'You're stupid.'

He exaggerated nodding, watching her hopeful eyes. 'I promise to be on my very best behaviour.'

'We haven't got time. We need to get ready.'

'We've got all weekend to go shopping. Come here,' he repeated.

'I'll make the sheets wet.'

'I hope so.'

She hesitated, caught between decisions. 'You're changing them.'

He nodded.

'Promise?'

He nodded again and immediately forgot. Her desire and his expectation hardening him beneath the sheets.

'Then you have permission to touch,' she said, although she did not really like being touched, at least without invitation.

She placed a knee on the edge of their bed and leaned towards him. He placed a hand gently on her shoulder, tracing the curve of her back through damp trails of water as she kissed him closed mouthed, which was how she always kissed without compromise. She reached across and placed her cup squarely on a coaster, then sat back and tugged free her towel, revealing a bikini shaped triangle of white flesh and neatly trimmed pubic hair. She pulled the duvet from his body, revealing him naked. Her fingers closed around the shaft of hard flesh, squeezing, an eyebrow cocked as she looked at him with a nervous smile. As intimate in the realm of foreplay as she ever got. She crawled onto all fours and kissed him again, whispered into his ear.

8

'Please me husband, and please be gentle.' She rolled onto the bed beside him, onto her back, eyes wide and watching.

He let his fingers drift, creating a slow pace in her mind while replenishing the tactile memory of her body in his. He kissed her shoulder and tried not to loom over her, drifting his mouth down across her chest, lingering at her nipples, down to her stomach, letting his breath roll warm across her skin. Her body lay rigid.

He eased open her legs and as his tongue found moist flesh, the first tremor of pleasure rippled through her body. He resisted his own need to push her legs wide, to satisfy his own want rampaging inside, letting her relax to the trusted touch of his tongue, calves tapping against the back of his arms, resting on his shoulders, gradually opening her legs wider as she lost herself.

His tongue danced and nurtured the tension, building a fire that marched a blush breathless across her stomach, up her chest and to her neck. Holding her on the brink, tantalising as her body writhed, fingers locked in his hair, pulling him into her restless groin, holding her in the moment until she could stand no more, reaching her gasped tremulous conclusion. It was the only way he could pleasure her, and he immediately wondered how long before the next time, with her legs open with breathless abandon. Weeks, sometimes months.

He fought again the need to push into her, to take from her what he needed. Instead he kissed the inside of her thigh and moved slowly forward, feeling the damp promise of her flesh on the tip of his. Then her eyes flared to wide panic and she jacked her palms against his chest, rolling him aside. He immediately bottled his frustration, taking a deep breath. A moment's silence was usually followed by her quiet apology, a tension that took days to dilute. Except this time she eased him back and climbed onto him, taking him aching into her hand, lowering herself down. He felt her flesh warm as it eased over his, encompassing, then very slowly rising up and down in turn.

These moments made up for almost everything. He revelled in the sensation, Sarah moving to an increasing rhythm, with flushed cheeks and earnest eyes, the visual and tactile beauty of her body a priceless feast. The repeated friction of pelvis on pelvis gradually turning her earnest face to determined. She placed her hands flat on his chest, pulled her legs up to a squat and leaned back with her hands now on his thighs. Opening her legs decadently wide for him she thumped down hard.

Adam's sense of delirium immediately burst, giving himself to the unstoppable as her movement slowed and he pumped then ebbed into her. Bottling his frustration again, he managed a contented sigh as she half clambered, half fell onto the bed, effecting a giggle as she did. Then, crawling forward, she gently kissed his darkly stubbled chin. A kiss of love and apology that she held longer than he expected. She laid a hand on his chest and her head beside her hand, studying him with those innocent eyes. He winked and was rewarded with a smile that bounced his heart on elastic, watching her watching him as they caught their breath. Then she swung her legs off the bed and pulled open the curtains.

He closed his eyes, his mind restlessly flitting from thought to thought, listening as she headed to the shower, the heave of plumbing. Collecting her tea when she returned, she sat at her dresser. He kept his eyes closed, picturing the play of muscle across her narrow back. Struggling as he always did, to imagine her plunging a carving knife into any man, let alone an old man.

It was nearly four years since the police had found her, sitting shaking in her car outside the old man's house. In a world subsequently turned upside down, the reaction of parents had been the biggest surprise to him. Sarah was vilified for dragging the past horrors suffered by their children into the public domain. It had forced them to move halfway across the country.

Her lawyer said she was lucky. The old man had survived a punctured lung and a heart attack, and the judge had been sympathetic. Adam had never considered six months in psychiatric care, and many more of debilitating tests and evaluation, any kind of lucky. Not when you considered everything else.

TWO

Simon Thompson waited in the quiet of his car, parked beside the park beneath a row of high trees, waiting for the girl.

The girl's name was Andrea. Simon felt sorry for her. She was driven from Northampton every other Friday, just her and her dad, asleep when she arrived and carried into the dreary flat. After a trip to the pool on Saturday mornings, she was left alone all Saturday afternoon while her dad worked the door of pubs and clubs, picking her up and taking her for something to eat between shifts, before abandoning her alone in the flat to spend all night by herself, watching TV and falling asleep on the sofa.

Saturday mornings after the pool she waved farewell to her dad, walking through the park to the library where she stayed until it closed. Who could blame her for not returning to that flat? The afternoon she spent drifting in and out of shops and returning to the park, where she sat on her coat reading a book. If it was raining then she would tuck herself in the corner of a coffee shop, counting her money for the shake and big cake, studying her puzzles and busy writing her hopeful stories.

Simon knew her routine better than she because she did not comprehend routine. He knew what she would choose to do in any given circumstance, after weeks of watching her, studying the streets of this market town, the ebb and flow of the people, their attitude and attention to detail. Planning his routes of escape, his long journey home.

A pink figure appeared in his rear view mirror and slowly grew. Her hair was wet from the pool. He watched her walking along the path, expectation slithering inside as she scuffed past, those weary boots kicking through leaves. This was not the place. Like the flat there was always someone watching and too much he could not control. He knew where though. Andrea collected her dad's prescription on Saturday afternoons and waited for him in the mouth of the alley.

THREE

Adam waited as Sarah locked her car, draping his arm across her shoulders as she drew level. They walked through the open car park to a narrow alley, its dirty red brickwork curving away to shadow, empty bags drifting in small circles at the entrance.

'Where to first, Mrs Sawacki?' he asked her.

She looked sideways up at him. 'The Pine Store, we need somewhere for all your books and magazines.'

He groaned. 'A bookcase! Where on earth would we put it?'

Sarah gave his question serious thought, as if she had not already measured and knew exactly where it would go. 'In the corner, behind the armchair.'

'Is there space?'

'I think so.'

'Maybe we could check out the estate agents first?' he offered hopefully.

She stopped, stunned. 'Adam, you're kidding? We're not buying somewhere bigger just because you don't tidy. The last thing we need is a move.'

'I wasn't thinking move away, just somewhere…'

'Like a house,' she finished for him, studying his face. 'You've thought about this?'

'A little.'

She pushed her hands into her coat pockets, not sure what to think. 'I don't want change, not yet. I love where we are, not just Hambury but the flat, our life now. We're anonymous here, just faces in the crowd.'

Perplexed, she walked away, still talking, 'What would be the point, can't we just be happy in this life a while?'

They emerged from the alley into the High Street, a busy human tide surging in all directions.

'You know I want the same things, Sarah, but...'

'But what Adam?' She knew of course what the *but* meant, that you put more than books into houses. Families lived in houses, a topic they almost always silently avoided.

Adam was not about to provoke an ice age. 'OK! I'll do you a deal. We take a peek at the estate agents and I'll be your obedient shopping buddy.'

'We simply can't afford...' Her voice trailed away, her eyes on his, calculating. 'OK, let's check your estate agents. You have any in mind?'

'There's some by the station.' He was wary at her sudden turn. 'You sure?'

'Yes, Adam, if it's important to you. We're only checking them out. Then we can go buy the bookcase, and I need a new suit for work. Then we'll feast in the market square and you can tell me all about that surprise you've been going on about all week.'

Which now felt far from the gleaming beacon it had. She reached up and affectionately swept the hair back from his forehead. 'Cheer up.'

He smiled back and they started towards the station.

FOUR

Several estate agent brochures were now buried at the bottom of Sarah's bag. The bookcase had been chosen over coffee from a shortlist compiled as they filed between stores. It was being delivered Tuesday. Adam had then spent an hour waiting outside various changing rooms while Sarah toiled over trousers and loose suits, all part of her ceaseless quest to break the pull of eyes to her body. A difficult illusion, always undone when she moved.

It was after two by the time they were seated in their favourite pizzeria. Adam's menu lay on the table. He rarely varied his choices. Sarah was studying hers, tapping a finger against her chin, as if its contents were entirely unknown to her. He shifted his attention from her considered expression to the dynamics of those around them, couples and parents and excited children, barely-contained teenagers, sun-dried grandparents and pink-cheeked babies. The cacophony was laced with shuffled cutlery, the crash of stacked plates, and espresso steam. He craned sideways to see if two men were holding hands.

'Five o'clock.'

He jumped. 'Sorry?'

'Five o'clock,' she repeated.

He turned in his chair, following her gaze to the door. A thirty-something woman was communicating with a waiter using expressive hand gestures.

Adam turned back. 'Wow.' He sneaked another look as the woman took her seat by the window.

Sarah leaned in. 'Who's she meeting?'

'You first,' he returned.

She studied the woman. 'That's a polished look, but she's out for the day, not meeting a man.'

'Really?'

'Yup,' Sarah said confidently. 'Definitely not meeting a man. Possibly a girlfriend but that's a lot of razzmatazz. I'd like to see the girlfriend.'

Their waiter arrived, his pen poised. Adam ordered and then, after further consideration, Sarah made her choice. They were soon alone again.

'Your turn,' she said.

'Hang on.' He gave the woman another look; her elbows were on the table, her chin resting on steepled fingers as she stared out of the window.

He looked back at Sarah. 'It has to be a first date, maybe a second.'

Sarah groaned loudly and heads on adjoining tables turned in their direction.

'Sorry Sarah, I didn't hear you?'

She reached across and smacked him on the shoulder. 'You're embarrassing me, Adam.'

'I'm embarrassing you? I thought you were doing quite well by yourself.'

Smiling, Sarah rested her elbows on the table, mirroring the posture of the window woman. 'So you think she's meeting a man?'

'All that effort isn't going to be wasted for no reason.'

'No, Adam, you would dress up to go on a first date. Maybe the second, if I recall correctly, but then you'd revert to type.' Delivered imperiously. 'But that whole look could be a misdirection, all that mechanism in her appearance could be designed to hide something.' Sarah paused and contemplated. 'Maybe a scar or something.'

'Phew, that's a lot of deduction from glossy hair and sparkly earrings.'

She grinned at him and took a sip of her wine. 'In fact there's something a little sinister about her, don't you think? She's deflecting attention from something.'

'Possibly.'

They both leaned back as their food arrived. Sarah picked up her fork, using it to re-arrange the aubergines on her plate. They ate in silence, lost to individual thought while listening to the ebb and echo of the restaurant.

'So what's this big surprise?' Sarah eventually asked, idly pushing her last piece of torn chicken around the plate.

The question completely wrong-footed him. He spent seconds grasping at the plausible rationale he had rehearsed.

'Well, it's not really that important.'

'Really?' She looked at him, wide eyed. 'It's been the big secret all week.'

'I know, but it can wait.'

'It bloody can't, tell me.'

'I'll tell you when we get home.'

'You will tell me now or lose me forever.'

Her eyes were sparkling, her mouth soft and smiling. Her obvious ease in the moment gave him a fool's hope.

'Well, you know how work gave me a new client?' he began, cautiously.

'The bank?'

He nodded. 'They also offered me more money.'

'Really, oh Adam that's great.' Then she leant forward and whispered, clandestinely, 'How much?'

'Twenty.'

'*Thousand?*'

He nodded, and the air in her lungs escaped in one long burst, washing warm across his face with a hint of Valpolicella.

'God, Adam, that's amazing. That's almost what I earn in a year. What made them do that?'

'They hadn't given me a rise for three years.'

'I know, but from nothing to that, after so long. There must have been a reason?' She studied his face, expectant.

There was a reason, of course, which was the detail he was worried about. He had thought about lying, but he considered lying to Sarah to be on par with taking money from children.

So he breathed in and told her. 'I resigned.'

'You did what!'

Heads turned in their direction. He lowered his voice, attempting to compensate for the rise in hers. 'I resigned; but it's cool. I knew they would come back.'

'But...our flat.' Scarlet crept up her neck for a second time that day as she tried to hold on to the moment. 'What if they hadn't come back, Adam?'

'But they did, Sarah. It's not like I'm unemployable if they hadn't.'

17

'You risked everything without saying anything to me?'

'Sarah, I didn't risk anything. I knew they would offer me a rise, they as much as told me so and I wanted it to be a surprise. I thought you might be happy.'

'I am, it's just, well, Adam!' She looked away, then realised the obvious. 'So this is why the interest in estate agents?'

'Well kind of, I'm not trying to pressure you…' He reached forward and drank some of his beer, making sure he got the next bit right. 'It just seemed this was as good a time as any. We could check what's out there, no rush or anything.'

Sarah stared at him thoughtfully. 'You're throwing me off centre, Adam. I'm perfectly happy where we are. We finally get ourselves settled after all that mess and you want to change everything. We don't have to spend the money, we could save more.'

All that mess! He thought to himself, he knew she meant more the aftermath.

'There's a little more, kind of,' he said.

'There is?'

'They also offered me an extra day working from home.'

Sarah rolled her eyes. 'What is your fascination with not going to work, you should go out and meet people, you know.'

'I meet plenty of people, Sarah.' Frustration was eroding his reserve. 'If I only have to commute twice a week that's good with me. Besides, one day we might be grateful one of us can be home during the week.' As soon as the words left his mouth he wished he could have pulled them right back.

Sarah went very still. 'What's that supposed to mean?'

Having placed himself on the precipice it was now crumbling. 'Well, you know, if we ever…'

'Started a family. That's what you're going to say, isn't it?' Suddenly she had difficulty knowing where to put her hands. 'You know I won't, Adam, I can't, not a child. Not into this world.' She gestured as if the evidence surrounded her. 'I just can't. Why would we want to change what we have now, after everything? You said you were indifferent about kids.' Her last comment was loaded with hurt, as if he had lied about the one thing she valued above all.

It had been a hard day skipping around his wife's frailties. 'I was indifferent then, Sarah, but that was five years ago.'

18

'There is no way I'm bringing a child into this world. Not me, Adam.' She scraped back her chair and stood, her arms hanging awkwardly at her side. Her mouth opened as if she were about to say something else, but she stopped herself. Instead she grabbed her bag and turned to the toilets.

FIVE

Adam spent most of the following minutes wondering how the conversation had gone so bad. He watched Sarah walk back to their table, her movements now devoid of their usual poise and fluidity. She rested her hands on the back of her chair.

'Look, I'm going to go and cool off.'

'Sarah, sit down, I'm sorry.'

'No Adam, you're fine, we both know who's the fuck-up in this relationship.' Her voice was raw and full of emotion.

'That's nonsense. Sit down, please!' He tried keeping his voice quiet but they were increasingly the focus of surrounding tables.

Sarah shook her head. 'Give me an hour or so.' She checked her watch and pulled on her coat. 'I'll meet you outside the alley at four thirty.'

He looked blank, so she elaborated. 'The alley next to the car park, Adam, beside Boots!'

'OK. Sarah?'

She did not answer, lifting her bag as she left, the door slowly closing behind her.

Sarah turned left outside the restaurant, heading across the square with no particular purpose or destination in mind. Just walking, hoping momentum would ward off her thoughts. She threaded between the stream of shoppers, went past the church and over the bridge, drifted along the High Street before stopping and turning back to the bridge. She climbed down the steep steps to the towpath, passing bars that backed on to the canal and a chorus of leering cheers. She entered the park, which was almost empty, only a man and a young boy untangling a kite and a mother with a monster pram heading at speed towards the town.

Sarah flopped down on a bench facing the canal, losing her thoughts in the water and the overcast sky reflected in its ceaseless movement. A few swans showed interest before realising a lost cause.

She was tired, exhausted from combating this gnawing torment at every turn. The fear and anger was always coiled inside, waiting to be set free. Why did Adam have to push now? Just as she was relaxing into this new life. She and Adam were good together. The men in her previous relationships had quickly grown frustrated by the need she created in them that she could not satisfy. Adam struggled, she knew that, but his nature was too caring and gentle to pressure her. He was the constant and reliable presence in her life that she gravitated around. Except the same qualities she cherished the most were now leading him towards wanting a family. The thought of a child petrified her, the fear that her child might suffer even a small part of what she had been through. She could never live with herself. She would never let it happen.

Intermittently she checked her watch, letting her anger and resentment flow into the chill air, slowly taking back control. Eventually she stood and walked back across the park.

In the High Street she shaded her eyes and peered through the shop window, squinting through reflections and the books on display. She could not see Adam inside, so she wandered towards Boots and stationed herself opposite the alley, the street lights and failing daylight casting it deep in shadow, the autumn day now turning towards the night ahead. Children were everywhere, all in restless vivid colours, sometimes without chaperone in small groups.

She watched an old woman approach Boots and pull open the door, holding it open and smiling at someone inside. A young girl emerged, smiling back as she stepped onto the street. The girl looked around hopefully, as if she was expecting someone to be there.

Sarah's breath caught and she took an unconscious step forward. The girl was about ten, pretty, with mousey hair falling to her shoulders. She was wearing a short jacket and jeans, a pink T-shirt and weary Emu boots that drooped back almost to the floor. Sarah blinked; she was a child who stood out in a street of children, small and fragile although her poise carried something more, of the woman she might one day be, as if she already knew some of this life's burden. Sarah's heart beat erratically. It was like watching video of herself from a life before.

The girl opened a blue bag and dropped a small white bag inside it. Then she waited, her eyes searching the crowd, realising she was being watched. She looked across the street through the people. Their eyes met and they exchanged uncertain smiles. Then the girl's attention shifted back to her search, shrugging and casually wandering into the mouth of the alley, out of the way, partly consumed by shadows as she knelt and attended to her boots.

Sarah restrained a powerful urge to go over and say hello. *To what end?* She was on the verge of walking over anyway, but instead she forced herself to look away, checking through the shapes and colours for Adam. *Where was he?*

When Sarah looked again the girl had vanished. She took several faltering steps towards the alley. *Where did she go?* But only the deep shadows remained.

SIX

It was easy because of what he knew, easier even than he had imagined. He waited through the day, moving through the small market town, looking for some discord, for a ripple at odds with the usual weave of humanity. He saw only the bustle of busy minds. And then it was time. He stood the sign at the mouth of the alley, facing out to the car park. A big red triangle: *No Entry, Chemical Cleaning.* Beneath the words a symbol depicting liquid corroding a hand. Even kids backed away from that.

It was then about waiting those last minutes in the shadows, leaning against the wall. Five of his long steps from the High Street, seven for anyone else. More for a child. The box was ready and folded. A flick of the wrist and small latches locked it open, a reinforced base, plywood sides. Just big enough for a foetal child if you folded the limbs tight to the body. Outwardly it looked like he had just bought a hi-fi.

Sourcing the right product and size had been difficult; over time it had evolved. Just like the contents of the syringe in his hand. Learning the basics of anaesthetics had been easy, he'd read the books. Getting the drugs and the mix right was not. He used two syringes. The first was powerful and quick acting, the second lay waiting in the boot of the car, less potent but longer lasting.

For Simon it was all about preparation, to the simple end of passing unnoticed in the minds of strangers. He was not inconspicuous if discovered now, but guiltless. He waited patiently for the girl to appear, always working through the scenarios and what might go wrong. But she arrived just as every other time, adjusting those boots. He called her by name. 'Andrea?'

She turned and took two distracted steps towards him, then another, uncertain.

'How do you know my name?'

'Your dad sent me, Andrea. Brian sent me to pick you up.'

Knowing her father's name placed him within the realm of credibility, just long enough. Confused she walked right to him, puzzling the nice-looking man who knew her father. And then he moved, fast. Clamped his hand over her mouth and pulled her into him. The white exposed skin of her neck spattered with a squirt of liquid as he cleared the needle, then plunged it into her flesh. Her innocent eyes were now wide with a sudden fear, her mouth working beneath his hand, her body squirming against his leg. Her struggle was brief. He lifted her as a father would, the syringe hidden back inside his jacket, and moved further back into the alley. Ten seconds and counting. He flicked open the box with a twist of his wrist, hearing the reassuring sound of the latches locking. He folded her inside, shielded from the street by his broad back. It took fifteen seconds more and then he lifted the box in both hands and calmly walked to the car park, laying the sign flat on top of the box as he stepped from the alley and towards the Rover.

SEVEN

W<i>here did the girl go?</i> Sarah took a step towards the alley, looking down the street and back to the alley, but the girl had vanished. She walked across the street with shoppers sidestepping to avoid her, squinting into the shadows but seeing only a quiet dark. She stepped across to Boots and peered around advertisements into the store, hands like a visor over her eyes, edging sideways to look down the aisles. No sign of the girl. Her mind clawed for an obvious answer.

She looked back to the street, her eyes darting from one shape to the next. Hundreds of legs danced the shopper's hoedown but none were clad in those small weary boots. She looked to the alley again. *It was the only place.* She took one and then two steps, venturing between the high bricked walls and their shadowy embrace.

'Hello, are you all right?' Her voice faded into the dark. She chastised herself for being scared, took a deep breath and stepped fully into the alley. It was empty. She walked its full length to the car park.

It was open here and brighter from natural light, the car park half full, her Toyota several spaces from the exit. She looked through each plausible space, out to the snaking line of brake lights. Still no sign of the girl. She could feel a numbing cold crawl across the back of her skull.

There were a few people. A thin man in muddy cycling gear was fastening a bike to a roof rack. A tall man, shifting a box between his arms, maybe a microwave, unlocked the boot of his car. Two children chased a Labrador in circles, their mother waiting by a car, hugging dry cleaning. Sarah circled, uncertain, wondering if the girl might be in the car. She was not.

'Can I help you?' The mother's expression was aghast beneath heavy make-up. Sarah's attempt to see into the car had taken her right next to it.

'Sorry, I was wondering if you'd seen a girl walk past, maybe ten or eleven, so high?' She demonstrated the girl's approximate height with the flat of her hand.

'She's not yours then?'

'Sorry?'

'The child, not yours?'

'No, we're out with friends, their girl has wandered off.'

The woman did not look convinced but called for her husband. Grey hair bobbed up over the roof of the car, shaking his head at the same question. He ushered the children away from a departing Rover patiently idling, the man with the microwave. The cyclist was now leaning against the rear of his car changing shoes.

Sarah thanked them and reluctantly walked back to the alley, checking through all spaces and pathways, the queue of traffic. There had been no time for the girl to completely vanish, surely? Something was wrong though, some elusive detail she had seen but not yet realised. The numbing cold at the back of her skull was now spreading across her shoulders, moving down her spine. She felt increasingly disorientated, her brain instinctively trying to slow her down, having already unconsciously processed that detail.

She walked back into the alley, pacing out the seconds and the girl's possible movements. *How long had she looked away for?* She stood on the verge of the High Street. There was still no sign of Adam and no sign of the girl. The detail was still elusive, the tension reaching across her back and pulling the muscles tight. She looked at her watch impatiently, realising she was early more than Adam was late. Then the detail did wriggle free, and with realisation came a starburst of fear for the girl. She threw a quick glance into the street, hoping Adam might magically appear. She forced stiff limbs to action, turning into the alley and trying to make herself run, but her body would not obey her. Her legs felt heavy like concrete. She stumbled and fell against the wall and down onto her knees.

Sarah could have missed the girl. She might have been lost to the busy street or disappeared amid the aisles of Boots. She knew that, but it did not matter to her. The elusive detail was the weight in the box. A microwave would be heavy for her but *not* for the man lifting it into the

26

Rover. He was tall and broad. The box he lifted looked like something heavy was inside, something heavier than a microwave.

Only this mattered to Sarah, now verging on panic at her inability to stand. She could feel her legs but had no control over them, aware of every passing second. She could only think of the girl's future, she did not need to imagine it. The images exploded in her mind, and with the images came anger, adrenalin surging and fury thumping through her veins. Sarah dug her nails into the palms of her hands, drawing blood as she pushed up through her legs, her eyes fierce. Managing to stand, using the wall and her shoulder, willing her legs to move, step over step. Gritting her teeth she was now walking awkwardly, accelerating to a clumsy jog into the car park and checking each of the cars queuing. The Rover was at the junction. She unlocked her car as she approached, glancing her head painfully off the doorframe as she climbed in, unsteady. She reversed with a quick look over her shoulder. The couple with children watching as she accelerated out of the car park, her Toyota's suspension protesting loudly as she bumped onto the road just as the Rover turned and disappeared from sight.

It would take precious minutes to queue at the junction, so she sped past the stationary traffic on the wrong side of the road, engine screaming. Straight over both mini roundabouts, ignoring the shocked and angry looks of those queuing. She almost made it, coming to a screeching halt as a car turned into the road. She shouted and pounded on the horn, oblivious to the instant fury of the driver. She edged forwards, urging him backwards with frantic hands, forcing her way to the main road through sheer belligerence. The Rover was gone.

She accelerated to the next roundabout still on the wrong side of the road, pulling in at the last second and braking hard to a chorus of angry horns. She had two choices. Go right through the suburban stretch or left to the motorway. She lurched forward through red lights and a sudden scream of rubber clawing for traction, a red car and an open-mouthed woman to her right. She fluttered an apologetic hand and flattened the accelerator, working through the gears, veering across the road to sweep around a Volvo, along the stretch of dual carriageway towards the motorway. And still no sign of the Rover. She followed the road around, scanning the lines of traffic waiting at the junction, breathing loud with relief. The Rover was two cars from the front. She was sure it was *the* Rover because it had two yellow signs in the rear window, *Baby on board!*

Child on board! which she had thought was odd as she watched it leave the car park. She had never seen a car with both before.

Taking advantage of the red lights she pushed her phone into its cradle, brushed the hair back from her face and settled into her seat, trying to calm her wild heart with deep breaths. The lights changed and she followed the Rover onto the westbound motorway. Already the voices in her mind were gabbling incessant warnings and doubts.

EIGHT

Adam arrived opposite Boots just after four thirty and immediately felt uneasy. Sarah was not there and Sarah was never late. He waited, just in case, the sense of unease growing with every minute, cursing that he had left his phone at home on his desk. Eventually he gave up waiting and started searching the likely places Sarah might be, ending in the park. Then out of desperation he returned to the restaurant and finally to the car park at the end of the alley.

It was the last place he checked because Sarah leaving without him was the last thing he imagined her doing. Whimsical tantrums were not her style even if she had been upset, although it was a relief to find that Sarah's car was not there. It meant she was probably driving it. He just had no clue where. Which led him to the small matter of *why*? There would be a reason. He needed his phone, so he jogged to the square and into a cab.

Sarah's car was not at their apartment either, although he had hoped it would be. He wearily climbed the steps to their apartment and retrieved his phone from the study, then went to the living room. Three missed calls. He unlocked the balcony door and stepped out onto the balcony, the garden spotlights now pushing back the half-light of evening.

He dialled his voicemail and listened to the messages. Sarah's voice was competing against the drone of her car, each word weighing him down. There were three messages that were fragments of a whole. Her first call had been cut off, on the second she hung up, lost for words. The third gave most of the detail. Sarah was following a car. A car she thought had a box in the boot with a child stuffed inside. Which was about one on the list below his worst-case scenario.

Returning to the living room he listened three more times, writing

29

the details onto a notepad, running his hands through his hair. Sarah had given him the car's model, colour and all but the last two digits of the number plate, lost to noise. Dialling Sarah's mobile he got an out of service tone. He redialled over and over until it rang, finally hearing her voice for real when she picked up. The noise in her car sounded like she was next to a waterfall.

'Adam, thank God.'

He closed his eyes and tried to make his voice calm, 'Sarah, where are you?'

There was a short pause before she answered, 'Junction 17.'

'The M4?' His voice rose in pitch.

'Yes.'

'Christ Sarah! That's, that's bloody Bristol!'

'Adam please don't shout at me.'

'What?'

'I said, don't shout, please.'

Her desperate tone disarmed him. 'Look, sorry, but Bristol! I looked all over for you.'

'You didn't have your phone, Adam, why don't you ever take your phone?'

He just never thought about it at weekends, having been glued to it all week. 'How much petrol do you have?'

'I filled up yesterday like I always do.'

'OK...' He thought hard. It would be almost impossible to deflect her.

'So you're just going to keep following this car to God knows where. Then what?'

'I haven't thought that far ahead.'

'I bet you haven't.' He could feel panic taking hold, his mind already playing different scenarios and consequences, irrespective of whether there was a child in the boot of the car.

'Sarah, think about this, when the car pulls over what are you going to do? Ask this guy if he's just kidnapped a child?'

'Please, Adam.' Despite the fluctuating static he could hear the tremor in her voice, misreading it as uncertainty.

'Sarah, think about this. You have the licence number, we can just give this to the police. You could turn around at the next junction.'

She snapped back. 'You know what I think about that. The police

30

won't do anything until it's too late. I need to follow this car, stop it before it happens.'

'Stop what precisely? How do you pro…' He heard a loud, warped shout from Sarah and then just the waterfall effect. Seconds passed, during which he reached a hundred worried conclusions, then her voice came back, but distantly.

'Adam, he's turned off, I almost missed it. It must be Delamere services. I'll call back.'

'Sarah?'

The call disconnected and all he could hear was a deafening silence.

NINE

Sarah had been concentrating on their conversation and hadn't noticed the Rover signalling to pull off the motorway. She desperately pumped at her brakes as she tried to make the turn. The sudden deceleration dislodged the earpiece, dropping it into her lap as everything slid off the passenger seat into the footwell, her heart hammering as she crossed white lines and cat's eyes and made the turn, working hard then to keep the car under control and not ram into the back of the Rover.

The Rover pulled to a stop away from the services and to the right. Sarah continued around, parking at the opposite end near the exit. She pulled the key from the ignition and turned around, sitting in silence, watching as a distant silhouette climbed from the Rover, moved around to the boot and lifted it open. She watched the silhouette lean inside, waiting with bated breath. He closed the boot, locked the car and walked towards the bright façade of the services. She waited, watching him pass through shadows and pools of light, up shallow steps to the entrance.

As he disappeared through the doors she pulled her phone from its cradle, lifted her bag from the footwell and climbed out. She took stock of the scene. It was busy. People were everywhere, trailing to or from the services, or levering children and the infirm into and out of vehicles. She headed away from the building, moving between and around cars. Walking with purpose but not obviously towards the Rover, she hoped.

She approached the Rover in an arc, her senses straining for any noise, lengthening her stride and slowing, but there was nothing. Just the tick of a cooling engine, no movement or sound that could be construed as a cry for help. The Rover sat insolently quiet. She peered through the windows but there was nothing on the passenger or back seat. It was completely empty. She walked around to the boot and tried opening it, just in case. It was locked. She bent down, pretending to pick up something she had dropped. She banged the boot with a fist, five sharp hard sounds. Waiting on one knee for as long as she dare, fiddling with her bag, hoping for some response. There was nothing. She stood and walked towards the large revolving advertisements either side of the entrance.

The bright interior was busy, echoing with the chatter of disparate groups, snippets of sentences and conversations suspended in the air. She walked the length of the services to a queue for bagels, looking for the Rover driver. She picked him from the crowd as he disappeared into the toilets. He was big, tall and broad but not bulked like a body builder. His movements flowed, full of self-assurance, from being bigger than everyone she guessed. She bought two coffees out of habit, which mostly convinced passing Romeos she was not alone. Then she found a seat among the corralled tables, a vantage point with a full view of the open-plan stores and the bustling concourse.

The Rover driver was gone for eleven long minutes. The worry she might have missed him almost took her back outside. Then he emerged from the toilets and walked directly into a store, browsing through magazines. She picked up her coffee and sipped it, watching him over the top of the cup. He looked to be in his early thirties, with short brown hair, highlighted as if he spent a lot of time in the sun. He wore dark jeans and a faded T-shirt and a light jacket, apparently favouring purpose over style, although they looked good on him. People flowed around him like water around rock, seldom was anyone tall enough to clear his shoulders. He pulled a magazine from the rack and she pulled the phone from her bag, flicking through the address book and dialling Adam's mobile.

The call connected. Adam answered on the fourth ring.

TEN

Brodie Larson and Duncan Morgan had been best friends since Brodie's mother was moved to the council flat next to Duncan's, twenty-one years ago. Their friendship grew in the corridors and stairways of their tower block, where they had decorated their first elevator together at the age of five, and at nine were together expelled from school after abusing the deputy head one time too many. From the age of twelve, they were frequently incarcerated in various care homes through to the magic age of eighteen. At which point Brodie, short and dark haired and outwardly angelic, and Duncan, rectangular and ginger and possessed of a Cheshire grin, were launched upon a largely unsuspecting society.

As adults their primary craft was misdirection and sleight of hand. Following the car auction trade at random across England, they worked large public venues and sprawling service stations. Always dressed smartly and working as a team they criss-crossed car parks and through groups of people, acquiring bags, phones, wallets and all manner of electrical goods.

Which was how they came to be leaning against a row of slot machines in Delamere services that Saturday evening, drinking from bottles of Coke while studying the flow of humanity. They had already spent a profitable ten minutes in the car park and were now planning an equal time in the main building. It was looking good, almost nobody was paying them any attention.

'Where to first?' Brodie asked, staring along the main concourse.

Duncan scanned the bustling throng. 'Reckon we just get cracking, sweep to the bagel bar and back down. Do the same over and see if anyone's ripe for my charm. Couple of lasses just disappeared into Smith's and there's one over there I'd pay all night for.'

Brodie followed his gaze. 'Her with the two cups on that table?'

'Aye,' Duncan confirmed. 'Look at her, quick grin and she'll pop like champagne.'

'My friend, even I'd pay for that. You seen a boy sittin' with her?'

'Nope.'

'So what's the bet the other cup's still full?'

Duncan considered Sarah and the two cups. 'A cert I'd say. I'll walk by on the way back up.'

Brodie nodded. 'Reckon a lass like her'll have a big fat purse with lots of cards, maybe a wad of cash.'

'And some good naked piccies on her phone.' Duncan winked, flashing a portion of his Cheshire grin. 'Girls like her always got a fella trying to get naked piccies. Bet she even takes 'em herself.'

'Guaranteed. There's always some from the holiday. Nice and hot, running around with no top on. Maybe even get some good ones of her and the boy.'

Duncan placed his Coke on a slot machine. 'Let's get going then, who's leading?'

'Me first,' Brodie answered. 'Don't want you scaring the natives.'

'Right on my friend, lead the way.'

Brodie pushed off and Duncan pulled off his jacket, folding it over his arm. Setting the bag on his hip, making sure it was open and not snagged, he then pushed off himself.

The first pass netted one wallet on the first hit. The man bounced off Brodie and patted his right jacket pocket. Duncan relieved him of the burden two seconds later. The second hit just scowled absently, giving Duncan no choice but to guess and guessing wrong. The final one was a disaster, so surprised at Brodie's contact she lost her footing and collapsed with a short scream. Brodie helped her up and apologised, catching up with Duncan who had walked on past.

'That was bollocks.'

Duncan nodded affirmation. 'Aye, and now the masses have clocked you. What to do?'

Brodie checked the concourse for security, but everything remained as it had. 'Not get tagged, we still have the stuff from the car park.'

'So?'

'One more sweep, then check out that girl. If she's good, do her and shoot.'

'I'll lead.' Duncan readied his jacket and the bag, handing them to Brodie.

The second pass went better. Brodie was pleased with himself. The man forgot where his wallet was, first patting his trousers then realising and patting his jacket. The unconscious smile was all Brodie needed, shifting his balance mid-stride. Close to perfect.

Duncan watched his approach. 'Do well?'

'Aye.' He looked across at Sarah. 'She's still there, talking on the phone. Has to be her mum or the boy.'

Duncan held out his hand. 'Give me the bag and I'll give her a rattle. Maybe give her a reason to get going.'

He made his way to the seating area and through the tables, using momentum to swing the bag from side to side. He let it swing out as he neared Sarah. Spinning around as he felt contact, grabbing the cup and flashing her a megawatt Cheshire grin. Distracted, she glared up at him.

Brodie waited by the slot machines. 'So?'

'Man! No problem, she's on another planet. Looks like she's seen a ghost or something. My charm didn't even register.'

'You're fat and losing it, that's what. Look like she's leaving?'

'Was giving the boy sweet nothings.' As Duncan answered Sarah stood, dropping her phone into her bag.

'We good?'

'We are my friend.'

They walked in separate directions, Duncan to the entrance, waiting on Sarah. She stepped onto the main concourse and he turned towards her, Brodie in step a few yards to the side and behind her.

Duncan counted down, three, two and he looked sideways, turning as he stepped forward and directly into Sarah's path. She bounced off him and stumbled sideways. He reached forward and grabbed her arm, his other hand on her shoulder then waist as he apologised. At the periphery he saw Brodie move in. Then it all went horribly wrong.

ELEVEN

'Where are you?' Adam's voice was almost frantic when he answered Sarah's call.

'Delamere, Adam. I'm watching him, he's browsing through magazines.'

'The Rover driver?'

'Yes.'

'You're watching this guy?'

'Yes, what else?'

'Jeesus…' Then silence.

She imagined Adam sitting on the sofa or leaning against the counter in the kitchen, running his hands through his hair, something he always did when stressed. Her gaze wandered. She watched a group in matching football scarves pass by, then a couple of stiff-legged bikers carrying helmets and coffees. She made eye contact with a young man who looked away, disinterested, walking straight into a woman. The woman collapsed with a short scream; there was a brief commotion as he helped her up.

'What're you going to do?' Adam's voice brought her back to the moment.

'What was that?'

'I said, what're you going to do, Sarah?'

'I don't know, just keep following him, I guess.' Her attention was now back on the Rover driver.

'Are you sure?'

'Of what I saw? Of course not, I've been questioning myself constantly. I keep coming back to the box, there was definitely something wrong with it.'

'You're sure about that?'

'Yes, it was like a microwave or something. Just a square box, but whatever was inside was too heavy, the weight was wrong.'

There was a silence as he tried to imagine it. 'Maybe the box was just something he used. Maybe he was picking something up, was just using the box to carry an engine part, a heavy ornament or something?'

That idea had not even crossed Sarah's mind. Her stomach knotted. Her breath rolled in short bursts across the handset. She reached across and picked up her coffee.

'Adam.'

'Yes?'

'I trust in everything I saw.' She sipped the drink and set it back on the table, watching the young man who was now talking to a ginger-haired man. 'How about I report I heard a child shouting in the boot.'

Adam answered straight away. 'In the Rover? Accuse some guy of kidnapping a child? How do you think that will look if you're wrong?'

'What if I'm not?'

'You don't know anything for sure, Sarah, the last thing you need is more headlines in the papers. Remember it's you who doesn't want to move again.'

Which was a point well made. The Rover driver paid for a magazine and walked into the food hall.

Adam continued. 'I'll go to the police with what you have, please just come home, Sarah.'

She almost laughed. 'OK, so I come home. Then we hear a girl is missing and she's never seen again. Or her body turns up in a field or something. How do you think I would deal with that?'

Not well was the answer on the tip of his tongue. She had trumped any argument he had.

Sarah felt his defeat, watching the ginger-haired man walk towards her. She groaned inwardly. His bag knocked the table as he passed, toppling the spare coffee. He caught it and gave her a wide cheeky smile. She glared back at him.

'What was that?'

'Nothing Adam, just some clumsy bloke. Almost knocked over your coffee.'

'Mine?'

'It doesn't matter.'

'You OK?'

'He didn't knock it over, no spillage.'

'No Sarah, I mean are you OK? You need to be careful!'

'I know.'

'Look, I'll go to the police. If you're right this girl will already have been reported missing, don't you think?'

'Possibly.'

'Do you have the number plate?'

'I told you that.'

'You did but I couldn't make out the last two digits for the noise.'

She reached for her bag but pictured the notepad in the footwell of her car. 'I don't have it, I'll tell you when I get back to the car.' The services now felt like the wrong place to be, she felt too exposed.

'Adam, look, I'm sorry. You know me, know why better than anyone. I'll call you from the car.'

She disconnected and brushed away tears with trembling hands. She took a last sip from her coffee and dropped the phone into her bag, stepping down from the seating area and towards the entrance. She caught a glimpse of ginger and then someone knocked hard into her. Stumbling she felt hands on her shoulder then her arm and her waist.

Sarah did not like being touched, at all. Especially without invitation. She reacted instinctively, punching out the heel of her hand. It was the ginger-haired man, that same stupid grin, his hands roving. Her palm scuffed up off his chest and hard under his chin, his teeth clomping closed with the force. Simultaneously she felt a tug on her bag, turning as Brodie wrenched it free. Duncan ran and Brodie followed. Except Brodie ran into a human wall. Sarah looked up in disbelief. It was the Rover driver.

He effortlessly lifted Brodie as if he were a mannequin, plucking free Sarah's bag. Then a casual shift of his wrist sent Brodie sprawling and sliding across the floor, frantically scrambling away. The driver watched him race through the doors, then stepped across, holding out Sarah's bag. He smiled self-consciously.

'He ran into me.'

She looked up into the face of her nemesis. He was really quite good-looking. Not in an angular jawed way, more boyish, with a natural blush that added to the impression. Still in shock she reached forward and took her bag. 'Thanks, I mean thank you. I really appreciate that.'

He looked at her, concerned. 'Are you OK? You look like you should sit down.' He moved forward as if to help her and Sarah stepped back.

'No, I'm fine. It's been one of those days.'

'Tell me about it,' he replied.

She wrenched her eyes from his, looking into her bag. Her mind was racing. 'I don't think there's anything missing.'

'That's good then.' He paused as if unsure what to do next, turning to leave.

'Sarah,' she said, stepping towards him, holding out her hand.

He turned back and smiled politely, engulfing her hand in his, but lightly, as if he knew how fragile she was.

'Simon,' he said. 'Safe journey.' And then he walked away.

Sarah stood still, a stationary figure amid the flow of people, ignoring the questioning looks from those passing her. Her overriding impression was that he smelt like…like walking on the beach. Warm eyes that contained nothing malign. A trace of an accent but nothing she could place. He was softly spoken, maybe northern with the hard edges smoothed out. She propelled her limbs into action, scanning the floor for anything she might have dropped. Then she followed Simon out through the doors, doubting herself all the more.

TWELVE

dam's taxi edged through the market square, through the traffic
lights and past the train station, over the bridge spanning the
tracks and came to a stop by a long low building. Two Volvos
were parked outside, clad in luminous blue and yellow squares. A sign
above the building's glass door read *Hambury Police Station.*

The door swept open and he stepped inside, not sure what to expect.
He found himself staring at a ticket machine. He pressed the red button
and after a pause the machine dispensed a blue ticket.

The main waiting area was large, the floor a worn linoleum. The walls
were covered in posters and government issue paint. Bolted to the floor
were rows of chairs facing clear perspex booths. A mix of people were
dotted among the seats. Sitting front centre was a soldier of fortune type,
complete with downward curling moustache and green combat jacket.
Adam chose a seat several spaces along. The soldier of fortune did not
look like he wanted company.

A buzzer sounded and a display in the ceiling flashed *533.* Adam's
ticket read *536.* He watched a large woman stand and make her way to
the booths. He pulled out his phone. There were no missed calls or
messages. He pressed speed dial and waited with an addict's breath in
his lungs. It went straight to voicemail. Reluctantly he slid the phone
back into his pocket.

The large woman started crying and returned to her seat. The buzzer
sounded and another woman, smartly dressed and slim, headed towards
the vacant booth. Nobody moved for the following buzz, so the display
flashed *536.* Adam stood and walked across the room.

Shatterproof was etched down one side of the perspex screen, although the ragged scratches and deep chips indicated many had tried disproving the statement. A white-shirted officer, with compassionate eyes and short grey hair, sat the other side. His pen was poised over a yellow form, a tray stacked full of them on the table beside him.

'I think a child has been kidnapped.' The only statement Adam could think to make.

The officer's gaze flicked up over Adam's shoulder and then back down to the sheet of paper in front of him. Then he put down the pen and sighed.

'You *think* a child has been kidnapped?' he asked.

'Yes, my wife is sure a child has been abducted.'

'Why is your wife not reporting this?'

'She…she followed the person she thought abducted the child, in her car.'

'You said she was sure?'

'I am. She is sure.'

'So how can she be sure?'

'She was sure a box loaded into a car had the girl inside. She is sure of this.'

The officer looked at the yellow page, centred it with a finger. Looked back up at Adam. 'Where is your wife now?"

'Watching the driver of the car. I haven't heard from her since.'

The officer opened his mouth then closed it. He told Adam to wait and disappeared through a door. He returned minutes later.

'I will take a few details. Then my colleagues will take a statement.' He picked up his pen.

'Sure,' Adam replied and they rattled through the everyday semantics of Sarah's life. When they were done the officer directed him back to the seats. The soldier of fortune was now gone, so he sat in his place, which was still warm. Adam checked his phone again and watched the display in the ceiling flash through a succession of numbers. People walked to and from the booth. The acoustics meant little of the detail remained secret. He watched a tracksuited teenager head towards the booth as a heavy door swung open on his right. A female constable appeared, wearing a combat vest and a bulky belt.

'Mr Sawacki?' she called.

Adam followed her through the heavy door into an office. The floors were covered in coarse grey carpet tile, the walls painted a cool blue. The only difference from a *real* office was in the wall art. Here modernist prints were swapped for posters with big knives, guns and innocent faces. The constable ushered him to a corner office, leaned in and flicked on the light. It had floor to ceiling glass on one side, closed blinds and beech-coloured wooden chairs around a matching table. An ordinary meeting room in another world. He pulled out a chair and sat down.

'Detectives Boer and Ferreira will be with you soon.'

The door swept closed, rattling the blinds and playing with the posters. *We want your gun, not you.* And behind him, *Know your neighbour? Terrorists live among us.*

He tapped his fingers on the table and resisted the urge to check his phone.

THIRTEEN

Francis Boer dropped his keys and phone onto the coffee table, loosened his tie and stepped into the kitchen. He mentally braced himself for the clink of bottles and looked past his overbearing need. He opened the fridge door and pulled out a plastic bottle of water. He poured himself a glass then went back to the living room, flicking off the lights as he did.

He was too tired to get undressed. He savoured two mouthfuls of the water then set it on the table, easing himself into his chair. He released the footrest and winced through the pain, reclining far enough to take the weight from his stomach but was still able to look through the patio doors. Not that he could see much at this time of night, just outlines and shadows, the bushes and treetops. It did not matter. He filled in the detail from memory. The sun shone and the garden bloomed, the yelps of children splashing in the pool, his wife in cutoff jeans with limbs brown from the sun. He could smell that paddling pool.

Closing his eyes he let the images play. And slowly another memory sidled into the frame, of a popping cap and the glorious hiss, a bottle cold in his hand and then between his lips, the bitter taste into his mouth.

Twenty years ago mortality had been a distant destination for Boer. Twenty years that passed with no thought for time. Now his mortality loomed, an ever-shifting shadow flowing through his blood and reaching out from within, carnivorous and uncaring. Just like that. One day worrying if that strain would ever heal, the next searching for flexibility in the meaning of *terminal*.

He had not thought fifty-three any age to wave goodbye despite knowing better people that had died younger. He was not being singled out, this was just how it was. The six-month countdown had been two years ago. Now at fifty-five he was living on unexpected time. Time explained by the white-coated with talk of secondary and primary causes, the malign forces in his blood suffocating those spreading within. A body almost too ill to be ill.

Francis Boer was not a man who believed in hope by divine fingers, but he did believe in hope itself. His life had been his career and his career had been crime, or at least tracking those who committed crime. Along the way it had cost him his marriage and contact with all but one of his three children. As an eager constable he had believed he could make a difference, a belief diminished through time and the endless cycle of human flaws and desires. Too many were the innocent faces that filled his thoughts. Boer's hope was built on a need to claim redemption for one more. Not to suffer the frustration of a system that relied on bodies to find the guilty, but to save an innocent. Then he would be done. A life for a life. A sentimental hope, he knew, and selfish, a hope almost used up at that.

He took another drink of the water, imagining that bitter taste, laying his head back on the leather and closing his eyes, revelling in the silence and his good memories. Holding the bad ones away. Somewhere between unconsciousness and the sound of playing children he heard the ringing. He eased himself slowly forward and reached across to the table, flicking open his phone. 'Boer.'

'Sorry to disturb you, sir, but everyone else is out, I wouldn't have rung otherwise.'

He swapped the phone between hands, pressing it against his good ear. 'What's the problem, Sergeant?'

'Missing child, sir, report came in a couple hours ago from the father. Then we had a male walk into the station, believes his wife witnessed a child abduction.'

Boer picked up his keys. 'You've called Helen?'

'Yes, sir, DS Ferreira is on her way.'

'You still have the man there?'

'He's waiting for you in one of the offices, sir.'

'Excellent, Sergeant, I'll be there shortly.'

Detective Inspector Boer closed the phone, pulled on his jacket and checked the time, ten past eight. He'd been home for less than an hour.

FOURTEEN

Sarah realised her phone was missing when she climbed into her car. She spent frantic seconds rummaging through her bag and in desperation emptied its contents on the seat. The two pickpockets had not left empty handed after all. Now her dilemma was what to do next?

She considered running back into the services for a pay as you go phone, but her problem was time. Simon in his Rover could only go west but the next junction was not far. So she stayed in her car and scooped everything into her bag as the Rover rolled past. She followed behind, for just fifty yards.

The Rover pulled into the petrol station and Sarah hastily diverted to the lorry park, parking behind a thin line of trees separating the two spaces. She dismissed the idea of refuelling for fear of coming face to face with Simon again, or the risk of being caught in a queue and losing him. Nor did she want to assume her phone stolen only to find it later under a seat. But despite looking in the unlikeliest places she could not find it. She tried to keep calm. She organised her bag and folded her coat on the back seat. She made herself comfortable and waited. There was nothing she could do about it now. She watched Simon through the trees as he walked back across the forecourt then followed him down onto the motorway.

He pulled off at the next junction and turned north, her Toyota tracing the same path seconds later. Her heart beat fast and full of hope. Leaving the motorway might mean the end of the journey. It was a hope far from reality. They drove on through narrow country lanes, often in procession amid a weaving line of brake lights, passing through empty landscapes and prim village streets of grey-bricked buildings, brightly lit pubs with windows glowing.

She started arguing with herself over the semantics of the box. The sound of her voice a soothing antidote as the two cars ploughed through the dark. Then the Rover's brake lights suddenly flared and grew large. She realised with sudden panic that he was stopping. Simon immediately climbed out, but instead of waving her down and confronting her, he stepped onto the verge, aiming a thin glimmering arc into the ditch. Then he was lost to her rear view.

She began searching for somewhere to pull over and wait, spending nervous seconds expecting lights to appear from behind. Seconds that seemed like minutes. The trees eventually gave way to angular silhouettes and a number of large outbuildings set back on a rise, a farm, she thought. She reversed up the rough track as far into the farm as she dared, stopping beside the first outbuilding and turning off the engine. The dark immediately encroached and Sarah realised a need of her own, quickly climbing out and around to the back. She pulled down her jeans and managed to balance with her fingertips on the dusty boot, alone with the creaking trees and the breeze rustling dry leaves. The cold busily foraged over her bare skin, up beneath her shirt and set goosebumps across her stomach. Her eyes never moved from the road. She hoisted her jeans when she was done and climbed back into the car.

To her left was a corrugated barn that blocked her view of the Rover's approach, hiding her car by the same measure. She would not see the Rover until it disappeared into an alley of trees to her right. She slid down into the seat, listening to the tick of the cooling engine. Time slowed. Two cars passed. She realised as her fingers reached for the ignition that neither were the Rover. Five minutes turned to ten. The heat slowly seeped away into the night and the cold reached in. She deliberated the consequences of turning back to check what he was doing.

From her right something hard crashed against the door, rocking the car and clawing at the window. Screaming, she jumped violently, almost fully into the passenger seat. Instinctively but fearfully she looked back and saw a golden face with large black eyes, hot breath steaming the window and a pink lolling tongue. The golden retriever was immediately joined by a twin face, pawing the glass together, then the wrinkled inquisitive gaze of a woman appeared.

Sarah extracted herself from the handbrake, feeling dizzy from the rush, her heart thumping. She lowered the window by a fraction.

'Are you all right in there dear? Sorry to startle you.' The woman peered through the gap as the dogs tried to pull themselves through it. The woman pushed them away and clapped her hands, and they both raced back into the farmyard. Sarah lowered the window, the cold air welcome on her flushed cheeks. She stared wide-eyed at the woman. The low light was not doing the woman's features any justice. She looked no more than sixty, with short blonde hair and a kind, creased face, wearing a long ribbed cardigan.

'I'm really sorry, I felt tired and this looked like a safe place to park for a few minutes. I hope you don't mind?'

The woman's eyes were piercing blue diamonds. 'Mind! I wish just half the scallywags was a'pleasant, my love. Why don't you come in for a cuppa? You look like you could do with a drink.'

The invitation seemed unimaginably appealing. 'That's so considerate,' Sarah answered, one eye on the road. 'But I don't have much time. I thought I would just stop here and close my eyes for a few seconds?'

'Not a problem at all m'love. You hunker down there as long as you like. Where you headed?'

Sarah had no idea. She had a vague notion they were driving north but she had long since lost sight of distance and direction. She offered Birmingham as a hopeful answer.

This earned her a puzzled look. 'Birmingham you say? You're certainly taking the scenic route! Do you know where you are?'

Sarah shook her head.

'Well if you head left out of here, if I recall that's where you came from, you go through Stratford. Right will take you to Warwick. Was you heading for the M40? There's no junction near here, you know.'

'I really am out of the way, aren't I?' She tried to sound flippant and think of a plausible explanation. 'I have to admit I was a little lost. There don't seem to be any signs here?'

The woman laughed, a musical sound. 'Well of course not, this is the country my dear. They all got ripped up when Hitler did his thing, s'pose nobody bothered putting them all back. You keep on this road and you'll end up in Coventry though. My advice is keep eyes out for the M40. You'll see signs when you get to Warwick, it'll double you back but you'll get there. Got some way to go though.'

'That's so kind, I appreciate that.'

'Is no problem.' She looked into the empty spaces of the car and then back to Sarah. 'I'm surprised such a pretty thing doesn't have some man in tow. Need them to do all the worrying you know.'

'Well, I have, but he's at home and I lost my phone.'

'Oh you poor love, no wonder you look at your wits end.' She delved into a pocket. 'Why don't you give that boy a ring. Arthur makes me take this when I walk the dogs.' She held out her hand. Sarah had to blink several times. A mobile phone. She could not have been more surprised if large luminous wings had suddenly unfurled from the woman's back.

'You don't know how much this means.'

She took the phone and the woman smiled wide and knowing. 'Oh I think I do, don't you worry. Talk as long as you like, I get all kinds of free minutes. I need it back mind, just leave it on that gate there.' Sarah followed the woman's gaze to a gatepost across the track. 'I'm away now to run a little heat from those dogs.'

With that she whistled and the two dogs came hurtling past. 'You take care now.' She followed the dogs down towards the road.

Sarah held the phone in her hand as if it were a bar of gold. It was similar to one she had owned several years ago, weighty and thick, the sort that only did texts and calls. She pressed keys and the screen blinked on, throwing a glow across her face. She watched the dogs dart across the road and disappear through a gap in the trees, the woman following behind. And then Sarah let out a groan of despair – she could not remember Adam's number. She was so used to her phone's address book, only half his numbers appeared jumbled in her mind's eye. Her fingers hovered over the keys. Their home number she recalled with instant clarity. As much as she desperately tried, Adam's number would not come.

With this lifeline, not being able to hear Adam's voice felt like a gift snatched away. Feeling heavy with frustration she reluctantly called home, hoping he might be there. The line connected and the answering service clicked on. She tripped over where to start and then began to talk.

FIFTEEN

Adam peeked through the blinds at a constable busy alternating glances between a keyboard and screen. It had been thirty minutes and there was still no sign of anyone. And still nothing from Sarah. He moved back to the table, trying not to imagine the worst.

Outside he heard a male voice, then seconds later the door swung open, the blinds and posters waving in unison. A dark-suited man leaned in, resting his hand on the door handle.

'Mr Sawacki?'

'Yes?'

The man nodded and stepped in, pulling out a chair. As he did a woman followed, closing the door and placing a notepad on the table. She sat next to the man, their movements separate but synchronised. Adam lifted his chair back a pace and the man rested his forearms on the table, the buttons on his jacket sleeves clicking against the veneered surface.

'Some introductions.' His open hand gestured towards the woman. 'Detective Sergeant Helen Ferreira will be leading this interview.' Warm brown eyes looked up on cue, her mouth widening to a friendly smile.

'And I am Detective Inspector Francis Boer. I will ask questions if need be, probably more at the end.'

Adam nodded and they both waited as Detective Ferreira organised papers. Then she looked across the table at him.

'You believe your wife witnessed a child being abducted. Is that correct?'

'Well, not exactly witnessed. She is sure a child was kidnapped.'

Ferreira's pen tapped her notepad, then her attention back at him.

'Ideally we would like to speak with your wife. When was the last time you spoke with her?'

'We talked while she was at Delamere. She was meant to ring when she got back to her car.'

'Your wife was at Delamere?'

'She followed the Rover there.'

Detective Boer gave his partner a sideways glance. She took the prompt. 'Why don't you rewind to the beginning?'

Adam was in the process of thinking where the beginning was when it dawned on him. 'I could play you the messages Sarah left me, her voicemails, if you wanted?'

Ferreira nodded and watched him lay the phone on the table, listening to his messaging service and then a brief silence. Then Sarah's voice and the waterfall effect filled the room. A voice from a life that felt increasingly distant to Adam. Ferreira asked him to play the messages four times in total, her pen skipping across the page. Adam's attention shifted from the table to his interviewers.

Detective Boer's eyes were dark and sharp, set in a deeply lined face. He looked to be in his early sixties. A moustache stretched the entire width of his mouth, curving down each side. Like his hair it was thickly dark with a mix of grey. He was wearing a once-smart suit, now creased as if it had not seen a hanger in days.

In contrast Detective Ferreira looked mid-twenties, stylish but understated in a dark blouse and olive suit, her tiredness evident around her eyes, darker and at odds with the latte colour of her skin. Her dark hair was centre-parted and tied back in a thick ponytail. The phone fell silent. He reached over and disconnected the call, seeing something of Sarah's dilemma reflected in both their faces.

'Thank you.' Boer placed his fingertips on the table. 'You talked while she was at Delamere?'

'Yes, but she hasn't rung since. She was watching the driver in the services.'

Boer slowly hoisted himself to his feet using Ferreira's shoulder as leverage, looking down at the notepad and back at Adam. 'Did you confirm the rest of the number plate?'

'No, that was one of the things she was going to call about.'

'And your wife's vehicle details are correct?' He slid the yellow sheet into the middle of the table and turned it around.

Adam checked and nodded.

Boer looked from Adam to Ferreira. 'I'll get a car over there.'

The blinds and posters saluted as Boer left the room. Ferreira smiled across the table. 'If you don't mind, Adam, I would like you to tell me about your day. What you were both doing, where you were doing it. Your wife's state of mind?'

Adam fidgeted. 'Well, it's, well we…'

She stopped him. 'This is a witness statement Adam, so relax. If you were a suspect we would be in a different room, and I might not be so nice.' She smiled again. 'Now tell me what comes to mind. Start with realising your wife was missing and work from there.'

So Adam did, beginning with his arriving opposite the alley, his search and going back to their apartment, skipping the detail of the calls they already listened to. He told her of talking to Sarah at Delamere and everything he could recall of their conversation, to his sitting in that room.

Ferreira caught up with her notes and looked at him. 'Why were you separated?'

The word *separated* jarred. 'Sorry?'

'Why were you not together when Sarah disappeared?'

Adam's pupils flared and his hands moved restlessly in his lap. He looked to his right and back at her.

'Sarah had a few things to get, she left me in the restaurant. We had a meal you see, just before.' He felt as if Ferreira's eyes were burrowing into him, reaching inside.

'Would you say Sarah was emotional when she left you?'

'Upset? I find women often are.'

Which earned him a raised eyebrow and a broad smile. 'I would say you might be right.' She let the silence play, rocking her pen between index finger and thumb.

'It's complicated.' Adam said, trying to avoid this shifting around to Sarah's state of mind.

'Complicated? So Sarah might have been emotional when she saw the girl abducted?'

This got a snapped reply, as it was meant to. 'Look detective, yes, Sarah was emotional. Do I think it would impact her judgement, of course. But only to heighten her awareness. If she thought something happened then it did, I can't say much more than that.'

52

She leaned back and looked at him apologetically, and suddenly two truths dawned for Adam. There was a missing girl and Sarah was a suspect.

'There's a girl missing isn't there?'

Her gaze met his. 'We don't do anything without purpose Adam.'

Which he took to mean yes. 'Sarah would never harm a child. Trust me on that front.'

Ferreira centred the notepad in front of her, deciding to wait on Boer's return before pushing any further. 'Let us step back through the detail we have. Once we're sure I will fill out the statement. I suspect Detective Inspector Boer will want a few words when he gets back.'

Adam leaned forward, elbows on the table, waiting for the first question. The process took another thirty minutes, in which she cross-examined every detail. At one point Detective Boer came back into the room. He placed a folder on the desk and wordlessly listened.

SIXTEEN

Adam read through the statement and signed, flipped the form and skimmed through the personal detail. He signed again then slid it back across the table.

'We done, sir?' Ferreira asked, knowing they were far from done.

'A few questions, Helen.' Boer pulled across the statement.

Adam had been preparing to stand. He slumped back into his seat, watching Boer's mouth move beneath the moustache as he silently read through the detail. *Who still had moustaches like that?*

When Boer finished he handed Ferreira the statement and set his hands flat on the folder on the desk. Looking directly at Adam, his eyes gleamed bright like something new was illuminating them.

'Sawacki, now that's a name you don't hear often.'

'I wouldn't have thought so, Detective. It's Polish, my great-grandfather came here during the war.'

Boer nodded acknowledgement. 'Sarah Sawacki has a ring to it. Don't you think?'

Adam's heart beat a little faster.

Boer continued, 'That name's been bouncing around my head since I saw that report sheet. I got to thinking, I know that name. So I got the constable out there to tap it into the computer. Amazing things, hooked into all sorts. About ten seconds and your wife appeared on the screen.'

Adam sat still as Boer opened the folder, sliding a printed photo of Sarah onto the table, which Adam had never seen. It was Sarah and it was not. His wife stood against a white background. It was her face but her eyes were somewhere else.

Boer tapped the photo with a bony finger. 'Straight away I

remembered that face. It's what struck me at the time. It's like a face that says innocent but doesn't fit with what she did. I remember that. So I got her case file printed as well. What do you think about that?'

Adam felt cornered, almost frozen by the power Boer now seemed to possess. Ferreira sat back and watched.

'Tell me Adam, fill in the detail. What did your wife do that stuck in my mind so? That made me wish I could shake her hand. That's what I recall thinking, but I couldn't shake her hand could I? Because it didn't go well for her, did it?'

Adam was torn between talking about Sarah's past and what it might bring to life, and equally in need of sharing the burden.

'It's not what she did Detective, it's *why.*'

Ferriera blinked several times and Boer smiled. 'Start with the *why* then, son.'

Adam drew small circles on the table then looked up at Ferreira and then Boer. 'Sarah had gym lessons when she was ten, private lessons in a local school at night, that lasted eighteen months. They weren't chaperoned. When Sarah refused, her mother forced her to go, her father worked overtime to pay for them. Nobody even knows what happened, save for Sarah and the instructor. She literally can't verbalise any of the detail, the words just won't come out. I can't even begin to imagine the horror. I guess you two may know?'

Boer and Ferreira nodded slowly in unison, both sets of eyes staring back at him.

'And the *what?*' From Boer.

'The day after our first wedding anniversary, four years ago. Sarah had found where the gym instructor lived, by now he was a pensioner. He'd been jailed for something else and released with a different name.'

Adam paused, his mouth dry. Boer waited patiently and Ferreira laid her pen on the notepad. Adam continued.

'I look back and there were small signs but nothing that hinted at what she was doing, or was planning to do. I had no clue. Having tracked this guy down she talked herself into his house. She asked him to apologise and he did. She thanked him, hugged him and buried a rusty carving knife to the hilt in his chest. We're talking Sarah, forty-five kilos last Christmas and five foot two in bare feet. You can imagine the force it would have required.'

Ferreira absently nodded. Boer looked like he was trying to recall some distant memory. 'She didn't kill him?'

'No, she punctured a lung. She called the police from her car. He had a heart attack, from the shock I guess. The paramedics said another ten minutes and he'd have been dead. Sarah always maintained it was never about killing him. She just wanted him to know her pain. She kept saying that over and over.'

Boer drummed his fingers against the table. 'My memory isn't what it was. It went to court, what happened?'

'Could I get some water?' Adam asked. His mouth felt like it was cotton-lined.

Ferreira pushed her chair back. 'I'll get some. Detective?'

Boer nodded.

She returned with a brown round tray and six small plastic cups, sliding the tray onto the table. They all reached forward, picking a cup each. Adam knocked the first one back and reached for another. Boer sipped his slowly, savouring each mouthful as if it possessed a quality Adam had never discovered in water. Ferreira's sat untouched by her notepad.

Boer placed his cup on the table. 'It went to court?'

Adam turned the cup in his hands. 'Sarah was charged with attempted murder and we went through six months of hell for all the wrong reasons. The local press created a lot of bad feeling. Sarah was never known as a victim of the old man. She had been in trouble as a teenager. She assaulted a teacher and later two boys from her school. Then she was expelled for carrying a knife in her gym bag. The same knife, as it turned out. The press focused on her, raked up her past and cast her as some psychotic harlot. She'd struggled in relationships, she's so…so damaged about intimacy. She never stayed in any for long. The most trouble though was from the parents of children who'd been taught by the old man. When it all came out Sarah was vilified for bringing the past back into the spotlight. Can you imagine men and woman in their fifties spraying graffiti on our house and car?'

Boer wiped a hand across his mouth. 'Nobody knows guilt better than a parent, Adam. Discovering your child might have been a victim of brutal abuse, that you might have put your child in that situation, it creates all kinds of reactions. Many parents deny it and go to extraordinary lengths to maintain the illusion. Sarah threatened that illusion. Now tell me, she avoided prison, the judge did something?'

Adam nodded. 'They wanted Sarah to testify against the old man but no matter how hard she tried she couldn't. They tried hypnosis but she blacked out, they couldn't bring her round and she spent a night in hospital. I think that really hit home. The judge ruled the case against Sarah was not in the public's interest. The charge was dropped and she was found guilty of GBH in a closed court. She got a lifelong restraining order, three years' probation and spent six months in Culpho Psychiatric Hospital, then another nine as an outpatient. She was really ill by that time.'

'Then you both moved here?' asked Ferreira.

'I relocated just over three years ago while she was in Culpho,' Adam replied. 'With the local reaction the judge suggested we consider a move, he was very understanding.'

Boer laughed, a harsh sound in the room. 'I would say so, a guy with a carving knife stuck in his chest written off as GBH, that's a very understanding judge.'

Ferreira reached forward and took a sip of her water. 'So tell me, Adam, why you think your wife is not being irrational, is not off chasing shadows.'

'Sarah is not irrational, detective. Stabbing the old guy was for her, punctuation for a time in her life. She can't escape what he made her, it is what she is. She doesn't chase shadows though, because mentally she can't afford to.'

Boer studied him. To Adam it felt like radar searching for the anomaly in his character.

'I'm not going to take much more of your time, Adam. So answer me one more question honestly. Do that and you might save me a lot of wasted time and perhaps even a young girl's life.'

Adam waited for the question and Boer asked, 'In your opinion Sarah would be following a child she saw taken in the High Street. Rather than, say, having seen the child, taken her because the child represented something Sarah lost, that she thinks the girl can give back to her?'

Adam was shocked that was even on the agenda. 'Sarah and I argued before she disappeared, detective. It was because I want a family and she doesn't. She is petrified even part of what happened to her might happen to a child of her own. That's what I'm worried about. It's not whether she would harm a child, it's the opposite. She'd follow the girl to hell to protect her, with no thought for herself. She just won't stop.'

Which was what Boer had already concluded, having read through Sarah's case notes and psychiatric evaluation. Although a second opinion was always useful.

SEVENTEEN

Having said all she could think to say, Sarah left the phone on the gatepost just as the woman had asked. Then she spent anxious minutes waiting, trying to fathom why Simon was taking so long. She debated whether to turn back, maybe he had turned around. Or something even worse. Then headlights illuminated the road and the Rover swept past. She held back from turning the ignition as long as she dare, then rolled down onto the road as the first fat drops of rain burst across her windscreen.

The rain quickly became a downpour that offered a welcome veil of anonymity as she followed the Rover through endless weaving lanes to a busy glistening junction, the two yellow signs working their way through the succession of lights onto a dual carriageway and then a motorway. The doubting voices in Sarah's mind now spitefully changed tack. They no longer tempted her with whispered pleas to turn around, instead they warned her away with intricate flashes and promises of what might lie ahead.

The south fell away and the northern shires made themselves known. Towns and cities counted down. Thirty-five, fifteen and one and then they were gone. Names she knew, places she had never been. A single wearing question constantly clamouring for attention: *Where?* The uncertainty of not knowing was exhausting. *Are we there yet?* Child voices in her mind.

The oncoming headlights endlessly flared across the rain-spotted windscreen and the rhythm of the wipers became cathartic. Each blink of heavy eyes was an excuse for them to stay closed. Twice they had, jolting open to a surge of adrenalin. She opened the window but the rain peppered the side of her face and crawled down her neck. She settled for the air-con blasting cold across her body, uncomfortable but vital. The fuel gauge was now hovering precariously above the short stretch of red. Soon the amber light would glow on the console and her journey would be thirty miles from its end.

A glimmer of hope as the Rover indicated and they finally left the motorway, turning down a slip road to a roundabout and onto a dual carriageway, her hands tightly gripping the wheel, shoulders hunched and eyes wide. The road's surface changed, making the percussion of the tyres almost deafening

The gauge dipped into the red and the console flashed orange as they crested a rise and Sarah's destination did finally open before her like a vista from science fiction. A horizon of glowing sky made dirty pink by the dense landscape of shimmering lights beneath it. A line of high towering funnels spewing thick smoke that merged pink as it reached the cloudy haze. The vista grew in her windscreen, the funnels growing to giants before the Rover finally turned off. She indulged in closed eyes as they waited at lights beneath the arches of a viaduct. It was over two hours since the farmhouse and four since she'd left Delamere.

Her Toyota was now one car behind the Rover as they edged through late night traffic, passing bars and restaurants into outlying suburbia, lone pubs on street corners, dormant warehouses and shuttered shops covered in graffiti, a brightly lit petrol station with a high red canopy. They filtered right and down a shallow descent beneath a bridge and out the other side, into streets of houses that led to streets of houses, winding roads, speed bumps and silent schools. They came to a T-junction and Sarah's heart tripped giddily. She watched the Rover turn left and immediately right, passing a pub on the corner. She waited as the car in front dithered turning right. She pulled out and then right, past the pub, seeing his brake lights up ahead. He signalled and turned right again and she followed. Thinking to herself, this must be it. The car ahead turned onto a drive, but already her mind was registering something wrong. Sarah passed and pulled over several houses along, immediately turning in her seat to watch for Simon's profile.

A woman, short and round and partially lit by a porch light, climbed out of the car. A newspaper held above her head as she trotted to the porch. Where were the two yellow signs? They were gone, this was not a Rover and that was not Simon. She screamed loud and hard, punched the wheel and screamed again. The sound shrill and despairing, filling the car and trailing away, lost to the rain tapping chaotically on the roof.

Something inside Sarah swung free, momentarily knocked loose. It was the same feeling as opening a newspaper and seeing a grainy picture of a young boy's face, the same sense of disconnection she felt after the news of her mother's unexpected death. She closed her eyes, dizzy with exhaustion and utter frustration. She had lost him.

In some part of her mind the sound of rain reminded her of tap dancing, a long distant memory from a childhood before, thinking of home, of going home. Simon was going home. She would not be defeated, not by simply losing her prey. She forced herself to be calm. He had to be almost home, you would not weave through those annoying turns and speed bumps if you had no need to.

She tapped her fingers in time to the rain, playing the last minutes through her mind's eye. She had turned left and then immediately right, passing the pub and following the brake lights. Had she seen any other cars? She did not think so. So he must have turned again after the pub. She hoped.

Sarah swung the car around and then turned left at the junction back towards the pub. There was a street opposite she had not seen before, it had to be where the Rover had gone. She turned into the road and peered into every drive, doing her best to ignore the amber light on the console. There was no sign of the Rover. Following her instincts she turned right at the end, into a road lined by grey brick terraces and then into a square. If she could not find the Rover here she would go back to the petrol station, refuel and buy a local map. She would then cross-section the whole area – even if it took the whole night.

She drove around the square, passing a row of shops, all dark and shuttered save for a brightly lit takeaway. She did a complete circuit but there was no sign of the Rover. She turned into a cul-de-sac.

The cul-de-sac arced to the right and slightly uphill with cars parked on both sides. She cruised as if casually looking for a space and then she saw it. She almost missed it, did a double take. It was parked on a drive on the left, edged close to a garage door, darkly green and beautiful, stationary and empty. *Child on board. Baby on board.* She drove to the end of the avenue, which bulged to a semi-circle, turned and back to the square.

She parked and checked the time. It was now ten past ten. She studied the fuel gauge, now completely below the red. She turned the key in the ignition and the engine fell silent, wondering how much fuel she had left, would there be enough even to start the car? She turned the key again, the dashboard lit and the engine started. The rev counter jerked up as she pressed the accelerator. She turned the key a final time and all went quiet.

There was at least enough fuel to start the car and get going, although she had no intention of doing that just yet.

EIGHTEEN

Adam stood in the rain outside the police station. He was not ready to go home, not to their home so carefully created by Sarah. So he started towards the town centre. Across the bridge, over parallel gleaming tracks and down to the station, the street lighting and station entrance reflected in the wet pavement. At the periphery of his vision a moving shadow, then a hand from nowhere on his coat and a disorientating punch into the side of his head. He felt fingers around his wrist, pulling and twisting it back on itself and an excruciating pain leapt from his elbow to his shoulder, allowing him to be marched around into iron gates that rattled in protest. His arm was pushed harder up his back, the weight of his attacker pinning him against the gate.

The pressure of the bars against his face forced his mouth open. He could smell a fustiness not suppressed by the rain. He relaxed his body, coiled all his strength inwards and burst backwards, but it made no difference. It was like pushing against a wall. His arm was ratcheted higher, the pain causing him to shout out.

'What do you want?' The sound was muffled, his mouth unable to properly shape the words.

'You were in the police station!' The man's voice carried a hard edge. Not just of anger but something else, it was almost desperate.

'So?'

'Tell me about the girl.'

'What girl?'

'THE GIRL. The one you told the police about.' The weight pushed heavier into his back, his face jammed harder against the gate. His initial reaction beside shock had been to assume he was being mugged. He quickly re-appraised.

'God, the girl, look I was in there about my wife.' He made a wild guess. 'Are you the girl's father?'

Seconds passed, the silence filled by Adam's laboured breathing and the sound of rain. The weight shifted but there was still no give.

'Look, if you are bloody let go and we can talk! I have nothing to hide from you.'

'What about your wife?' The same hard edge to the voice.

'My wife, she, she saw a girl kidnapped. She followed the kidnapper and I haven't heard from her since. I was reporting it to the police.'

Frustration and anger pumped adrenalin through his body. He bunched his muscles, but was totally at the mercy of someone stronger and much more adept. Instead he vented through words. 'For fuck's sake let go of me!'

'Not yet. What did you tell them?'

'I told them everything my wife told me. She was following some guy in a car, he had a box. She was convinced a girl was inside it.'

More empty seconds of rain, then the weight finally relented and his arm was released. Behind him he heard boots step back. Massaging his shoulder, he turned. For a moment the dark profile and the partial features floated at the boundaries of familiarity, and then he remembered. It was the soldier of fortune. The guy sat in the front row at the police station.

Adam waved his arm in small circles. 'So you're the girl's father?'

The man nodded.

'So why not just ask? Instead of this?' He glanced at the gate to demonstrate his point.

'Because guys like you don't talk to guys like me.' The voice was now calm and matter of fact.

'All you had to do was say who you were. Why would I not?'

The man said nothing, just watched Adam, still totally in charge. He had short dark hair, a softness to his features. There was something almost vulnerable masked by the set of his jaw and the moustache that curled down around the corners of his mouth. It put Adam in mind of Boer's. The man's eyes were his most striking feature. They possessed a quality, as if they had seen more than anyone should in a lifetime. His wet combat jacket hung open, underneath he was wearing a plain T-shirt and jeans. And then the man stepped forward and held out his hand.

'Brian Dunstan.'

Adam was so shocked he stepped forward without thinking and they exchanged a wet handshake.

'Adam Sawacki.' He remembered his frustration, brushing past Brian and back into the rain. 'You've got some way of introducing yourself.'

They now faced each other. The man's smile made the moustache lopsided. 'Charm has never been my thing. And like I said, guys like you. How about you buy me a drink.'

'Buying you a drink is the last thing on my mind.'

The man shrugged. 'I don't have any cash, otherwise I'd buy you one.'

Adam's instinctive answer was to say no but the thought of Sarah stopped him. She was probably following a car with this man's daughter stuffed in the boot.

'Where?'

'The Locksmith,' the man answered. 'It's a pub across from where I work. It's near.' He glanced at his watch. 'I have thirty minutes before I clock on.'

NINETEEN

Sarah pushed her handbag under the passenger seat then stepped onto the wet, uneven pavement. She yawned and stretched as the cool breeze foraged beneath her shirt, busy rejuvenating her senses. Sea air, it occurred to her.

It was an area not unlike the one she had grown up in, maybe a little bleaker here, more worn down and ominously slick in the night rain. The square was set around an expanse of grass half the size of a football pitch. At one end were swings, a roundabout and slide. *No Ball Games* hung on a post leaning almost horizontal. The row of shops included a launderette, newsagents and bookmakers, a Chinese takeaway. A corner store with a man silhouetted, waiting on shutters slowly rattling down. Three dark shapes detached from the swings and headed towards her.

Sarah popped the boot and tugged free Adam's fleece, giving it a shake over the pavement then pulling it on. It was impossibly large over her body but she wanted to wear something Simon had not already seen. She folded her coat into the boot as the three shapes ambled to a stop a few steps away, two boys and a girl. The boys were in their early teens, wearing baggy trousers and tops, the girl younger and taller on the right.

'We'll look after your car for a bag of prawn crackers,' said the boy in the middle. An accent like Simon's but harsher.

Sarah was in no mood for light conversation. 'I'm not here for food, I'm also very busy.'

The boys fidgeted and Sarah made a show of closing the boot. She locked the car and turned as if to walk away.

'What're you doing here then?'

'None of your business.'

'Why is your top so big?' The one on the end spoke this time, the girl remaining impassive.

'Sorry?'

'Your top, it's way too big.'

'Look, I've got to get going.'

'It looks like a man's top, you a boy?'

The girl momentarily came to life. 'Jay, shut up!' She was slender and pretty, her hands pushed into a short anorak with a fur-lined hood.

'You look like a boy.' The boy at the end again.

'I'm not, and I don't have the time for this.'

The middle boy asked. 'I bet you're looking at them houses for sale?' He nodded over Sarah's shoulder.

She followed his gaze to the cul-de-sac and looked back at him, quickly reappraising. 'You're very clever, how'd you guess?'

'You look the sort,' he said, pleased with himself. 'You know, too much money. My dad says anyone'd be fucking crazy to. Buy one that is.'

'So you live here then?' She looked at the girl but it was the middle boy who answered.

'In Eve Hill, at the end. They're all out down the pub.'

'All who?'

'Mums and dads, down the pub.' He nodded slyly at the girl. 'We're going back for a bit of spit roast, ain't that right Cat?' He skipped backwards, dodging a punch from the girl.

'Mattie! You're gross!'

The boy laughed and bounced back, pushing into the girl.

'Look I really have to get going, lots of houses to see and all that.'

'Show us your tits then, before you go.' The boy at the end this time. The girl groaned.

Sarah reacted instinctively, angrily stepping towards him, almost nose to nose. 'How about you go home before I really lose my temper.' It was a gamble at best. He was slightly taller than her but took a step back, glancing at the other boy for support. The middle boy stepped between them.

'Can't wait for you to move in,' he said, directing the other boy away. 'Be nice to pretty up the neighbourhood.' The last was thrown over his shoulder as they walked towards the cul-de-sac.

The girl offered a hushed, 'We're going to watch a movie.' She jogged to catch up with the boys, casting a glance back as they disappeared into the street.

Sarah caught her breath, checked she had her keys and walked across the road to the Chinese takeaway. Two men and a woman stood outside, idly watching as they blew smoke into the night air. She offered them a friendly smile and looked up at the printed menu, sliding her hands into her jeans and counting off the seconds. She gave the children enough time to get to the end of the street twice. Then she turned and walked past the corner store towards the cul-de-sac.

Eve Hill Way was a more recent addition to the square. The squiggle at the bottom of a capital *Q*. Cars were parked on driveways and on the street, lamp posts illuminating all with a sallow light. Almost every front garden contained piles of bricks and concrete slabs. All the houses were semi-detached, symmetrical twins with attached garages either side of a narrow alley. Estate agent boards dotted the street.

Sarah picked a house for sale just past and opposite the Rover. Resisting every urge to run, she walked as if she really were a late night house hunter, stepping with purpose onto the pavement and then with relief into the alley. She took a deep breath and leaned against the concrete garage wall, cloaked in shadow, looking back across the street. She could feel pin pricks of sweat on her neck, a cold sensation spreading from the back of her skull. She watched the house, the Rover unmoving on the driveway, a downstairs light on behind drawn curtains. From the shop end of the street headlights illuminated the rain and cast reflections off windows. Simon's front door opened.

He had changed. It was him without a doubt, reminding her just how big he was, now wearing a loose T-shirt with football shorts and flip-flops. He scuffed over to the rear of the Rover and lifted out the box Sarah had first seen a lifetime ago. He closed the boot and carried it into the house, the blue sole of a flip-flop flashing as he kicked closed the front door. She was right, there was definitely something wrong with the weight in the box.

She blinked rain from her eyes, her gaze intent and calculating, shifting from the Rover to the front door, to the alley and back again to the Rover. She slid back the sleeve of the fleece. It was ten thirty. She pushed away from the garage and walked across the street and into the alley beside the Rover and once more into shadow.

TWENTY

The Locksmith pub faced an Indian restaurant and a club. The club's pink neon sign shone above a fluttering awning and a queue of huddled people, the occasional shout and laughter. Adam noticed Brian exchange nods with the dark-coated bouncers.

Inside, the Locksmith was small, a fruit machine, a few figures at tables or against the bar, a woman stacking glasses. Adam slid two whiskeys across the table and sat opposite Brian.

'I take it you don't work as a waiter then?'

'What?'

'You said this pub was across from where you work.'

Brian nodded. 'Going to be a fun night. Everyone wet and cold and impatient. So tell me your story, Mr. Swanky.'

'It's Sawacki.'

'I know. Tell me about your wife and what she saw.'

'Can I ask you something first?'

'Like?'

'How do I know you're the girl's father?'

Brian pursed his lips, pushing up his moustache. 'You don't.'

'So?'

'So what?'

'Maybe your daughter's at a sleepover and you just forgot or something?'

Brian looked hard at Adam, swirling whiskey around his glass before lifting it to his mouth. He swallowed. 'Andrea's a good girl. I get her two weekends in four. Saturdays we go swimming in the morning, or to the park. I work Saturday afternoons so she goes off by herself. She picks up my prescription from Boots along with a few bits and pieces and I usually get there just after four thirty. She's never late, always early. Today she wasn't waiting.'

Brian moved his right hand on the table, covering it with his left. Adam was sure it had been shaking, although he very much doubted it was nerves.

'So that's why we have the same problem,' Brian finished. 'Now you're going to tell me if that matches what you know.'

'It does. Sarah was outside Boots. I should have met her but I was late.'

The fruit machine played a tune and Brian picked up his drink with the right hand. 'So what else do you know?'

'Not much,' Adam lied, considering what he would say. He told Brian the detail that encompassed Sarah's initial three voicemails, up to her driving along the M4. He omitted the number plate and the detail of Delamere, summarising Boer and Ferreira in the briefest terms.

Brian listened intently without interrupting. When Adam finished he leaned back in his chair, chewing his lip, the moustache moving like a small animal. 'So did they say what they were doing about it?'

'The police? No, they just said they will contact me when they have news, or need to talk again.'

'You haven't heard anything?'

'I did only leave the station thirty minutes ago.'

Brian's dark eyes fixed on Adam. 'Your wife, that's some woman. Nobody follows anyone like that. Most people would convince themselves nothing was wrong, would rationalise it and walk away. I bet you could repeat that scenario a thousand times and nobody would jump in a car and follow a stranger.'

'Do you think so?'

'I know so, people don't pay attention anymore. They're too scared of what might happen if they step outside their own world. Yet your wife is off and running.'

'She saw the box, it...'

Brian stopped him. 'That's not what I'm on about. I mean it takes something to actually follow a stranger, given what she thought the guy just did. It takes something else to keep following. That or you'd have to be crazy.'

For all his rough edges Brian had whittled the detail down to the fundamental issue as quickly, if not quicker, than Boer and Ferreira. Adam laughed nervously. 'What can I say, she's a motivated woman when she gets going.'

'You got that right.' Brian set his glass on the table. 'You haven't heard from her since?'

'Nope.' He decided not to say anything else. Thirty minutes had to be up soon. 'So your last name is Dunstan,' he offered, trying to move focus away from Sarah.

'Sure is.'

'So, Andrea Dunstan. That's a cool name, kind of makes her sound like a Saxon princess.'

Brian drained the remainder of his drink before answering. 'Pity that's not her name then. Her mother didn't give her my name. I'm only on the birth certificate so she can shaft me for child support.' He looked down at his watch and then back at Adam. 'I gotta go, where do you live?'

Adam was shocked. 'What, I…um, why?'

'We still have things to talk about.'

'We do?'

'Of course. For a start you haven't told me everything, but I'm not going to hold that against you. I wouldn't have either. Me and you have a lot in common though.'

'What's that?'

'Something missing, of course. Andrea is a small ray of light in a world of fucking dark. I've let her down. So I'm going to think a few things through, factor in what you just told me. Might as well do that at work as anywhere. Then I'll head over, then we're going to decide what's to be done about it.'

'Do, done what?'

'Your address?'

'But, the police. They are…'

'Just give me the bloody address, Adam, it's not like I'm asking you to hand over the sodding keys.'

Adam stammered but relented, as much from not having a viable reason to say no.

Brian hoisted his wet coat as he stood. 'See you later then.' He walked out of the pub and across the street. By the time Adam finished his second whiskey Brian had re-emerged outside the club in a smart white shirt, dark trousers, and the obligatory long overcoat. Adam checked his phone, no missed calls or messages. He was still reluctant to go home but where else could he go? He walked back into the night and the rain, nodding in reply to Brian's wave and heading towards the deserted taxi rank.

TWENTY-ONE

The entrance to the alley was lit by street lighting that quickly faded to inky dark, with a line of trees silhouetted at the back of the houses. Sarah stood in shadow beside Simon's garage. Breathing shallowly, trying to stay the tremor in her hands, the fluctuating beat of her heart, her eyes slowly adjusting to the gloom while she listened to the changing rhythm of the night. The voices in her head all screamed *turn around!*

Another five steps and she stopped between two gates, the rain resonating off a million different surfaces. She reached up to the gate on her right and on tiptoe peered briefly into the neighbour's garden. White light suddenly flooded the expanse, exposing garden furniture, a baby slide and a collection of children's plastic toys. She ducked back down. Nothing happened. No back door pushed open, no shouted voice. Seconds passed and then minutes and then the light blinked off. She turned and stared at Simon's gate.

She took the handle in one hand and used the palm of the other to push. There was some give but the gate stuck at the base. She shifted her stance and levered it upwards, pushing and turning the handle. It gave a little more. She leaned in with her shoulder, using all her forty-five kilos and the tired wood cracked open. Rusted hinges protested and the gate opened wider. Sarah stepped through into a long narrow garden.

On her left was a small greenhouse of clear plastic panels, distorting light and the shapes within. To her right, open grass ran to the trees at the rear. She turned her attention to the back of the house. She had read you could evade security lights by moving in small increments towards the light, but she had no desire to spend all night doing that in the rain.

Instead she poked her head around the greenhouse and ducked immediately back. Nothing happened, no white light. So she popped her head back and took a good look.

A narrow patio stretched the full width of the house, the slabs at the right illuminated by light escaping through curtains and twin patio doors. Set to the left of the doors, a square window obscured her view inside with a roller blind, a pot of utensils and washing liquid between the glass and blind. Above on the first floor a bathroom window and its bubbled glass. To the left the house gave to the garage.

She kept to the left, passing the greenhouse in a crouch, to the back of the garage and a single dirty window. Rising slowly, she used the cuff of the fleece to wipe away grime and rain, and then peered through. She could make out faint outlines that made the space inside seem empty and clean. Tools hung from a wall shared with the house, beneath them sat a work bench. At the far end light seeped from beneath a door, probably the hallway. From somewhere inside, upstairs, she heard a loud bang that made her flinch, sounding like a door slammed by the wind, except there was no wind. Whatever caused the noise doused the light at the end of the garage. She waited through tense seconds, ready to run, her jeans by now wet through, her hair clinging damply to the side of her face.

With little to be seen inside the garage she crouched low and scuttled beneath the kitchen window to the edge of the patio doors. She set herself against the wall and craned sideways, looking through the gap between glass and curtain. Inside was a dining room, a stairway on the right, double doors opposite leading to a living room. She smelt the rich aroma of a neighbour's takeaway and her stomach rolled with hunger. She moved across to the next door and peered through another narrow gap between the frame and curtain, a thin sliver that allowed her to see more of the dining room. She saw the box on the floor, and squinted, forgetting to breathe. It was a hi-fi box, not a microwave after all.

She wrapped her fingers around the door handle, ready to see if it was locked, when Simon ducked into the dining room and scooted the box to the middle of the room. He leaned over it and did something inside that made the sides fall away. Sarah's heart skipped a beat and she gasped out loud. A smudge of pink and mousey hair, a small body in a tight foetal curl. The girl appeared asleep, her body limp as Simon lifted her and hoisted her carefully over his shoulder and back into the living room, away from view.

73

Sarah stayed crouched for several seconds, thinking what to do. There really was only one thing to do now. She stood, turned and saw a vague stocky outline, not much taller than she was. In one hand he held a white bag, a Chinese takeaway it occurred to her. She didn't see the other hand, coming from the right. She turned straight into it, the force of the blow spinning her around and into the patio doors, her head bouncing with a resonant thonk off the glass and she slid unconscious onto the wet patio floor. Defeated in an instant. Then there was only silence, save for the sound of the rain.

Hakan stood staring at Sarah's body for long seconds. She was definitely a woman, although he had not been sure initially. The large top she wore made it difficult. It had left him with a moment of dilemma until the gasp, which left him with no choice. They had been lucky this time. Simon was getting careless. *Who was she?* Nobody local would even dare come into the garden, not *his* garden. He used his keys to unlock the door, with his free arm scooping up Sarah, using the other hand to pull open the door, the white takeaway bouncing off the frame as he stepped in. He closed the door, scuffed his feet on the mat and called out. 'Simon!' His voice was accented, Nordic, with the sound projected from the base of his throat. There was no answer. He repeated, 'SIMON!'

Simon appeared, standing just beyond the dining room door, wiping his hands on a cloth, his hairline obscured by the frame. His expression annoyed. 'What?'

Hakan wordlessly carried Sarah into the living room, making Simon step aside. He dropped her onto the sofa. Simon's eyes following, mouth agape.

'Jees, where'd you find her?'

'In the garden watching you, that is where. You have been sloppy, she must have seen.'

'No way, nobody would around here. Nobody could have anywhere. It went perfectly. Nobody could have seen.'

He leaned over the sofa and looked at Sarah, brushing the damp strands of hair from her face. 'Hambury went just as expected, Delamere checked out, nobody followed me, nothing happened.' He moved her head from side to side, examining her face. A realisation dawned.

'Fuck!'

TWENTY-TWO

Brian's head ached but all things considered it was worth it. There had been a time when jumping the queue outside a club validated instant retribution. Nowadays the rules dictated bouncers escort troublemakers off site, and if they came back you escorted them away again. Aggression, especially outside MadHatters, was the absolute last recourse.

Which had been Brian's intention as he walked with Paulo to the queue, to extract three guys jumping the queue. He had even asked nicely three times as per the local police directive. When that had failed he put one of them into an arm lock ready for the short walk across the road. Paulo did the same with one of the others. He deliberately avoided the short stocky one, the one most likely to put up a fight, as per the directive, which dictated you remove the supporting cast and you removed the threat. It sometimes worked and sometimes not. On this occasion it did not. The short stocky one had pushed him, quickly followed by a brief flash of metal.

Technically the push was a punch and Brian knew instantly the knife was little more than a couple of inches long, probably a fishing knife by design, now an accessory for posturing. The kid was holding the damn thing all wrong. That annoyed Brian more than anything, reduced now to disarming idiots with no comprehension of consequences. This, along with the hopelessness he felt of the day, the guilt he felt for Andrea, provoked his reaction.

He twisted the guy he had away, howling, into the street while blocking the incoming knife with his left forearm. Immediately grasping the wrist and snapping it around, opening up the guy's body as he stepped forward with his weight rolling from heel to ball, using the power through his shoulders and neck to drive his forehead forward. He connected with the bone just above the stocky guy's left eye. There was blood but no crunch, just a sound not dissimilar to fresh coconuts crashing together. The stocky guy went straight down, a cut freely bleeding above his eye. A reminder not to jump the queue at MadHatters the next time he looked in the mirror. Apart from a few screams that had been it, over in less than two seconds. Brian wiped the blood from his forehead and ten minutes later watched the three forlorn figures climb into a police van.

That had been over an hour ago. Now it was one thirty and most of the overspill had gone home or were already consumed by the thumping bass behind. A burst of static filled his ear, then nothing. He pulled out the earplug and gave it a flick, pushing it back in again. Another burst and he made out a voice. 'Brian…wants…office … Dmitri.'

Which he translated to mean Dmitri would be replacing him outside and he was wanted in the office. Which was not good. He turned and looked into the club, as the massive frame of Dmitri pushed through the double doors towards him.

MadHatters was the building's second incarnation as a club. Before that it had been Hambury's one time cinema, which meant it had a lot of stairways and narrow corridors. The walls were painted dark mauve over ancient wallpaper, the floors and stairways covered in the same industrial carpet of dark swirls and curls. The *office* was the old projection room and the base during business hours of Ali, the club's owner and only surviving son of first generation Nigerian immigrants.

Brian knew the legends around Ali's financial standing, the stories of drug running, protection and extortion, internet scams and ongoing investments in the online porn industry, were just myths, mostly of Ali's creation. They were propagated with the high turnover of staff and compounded by the machete Ali kept on the wall behind his desk, and the long necklace of pickled human ears he kept in his drawer. Brian had known Ali for over a decade, they had served together. He had never seen Ali do anything outright illegal.

He knocked twice and stepped into the office, pushing the heavy door closed behind him. The deep bass of the club faded to a distant thump, the occasional strobe of lighting the only evidence of the masses dancing below. Ali was sitting behind an oak desk wearing a fitted blue suit, waistcoat and white shirt. Taller than any man Brian had known and not carrying that much excess weight. Opposite the desk was a sofa and sat on the sofa was one of the dancers, all lean glistening limbs and a dark fringe cut straight across her forehead. Brian only knew her name was Yana, and that she and Dmitri were seldom apart outside of the club. Ali gestured Brian to a chair, two long steps from the door.

Brian did not move. 'I'll stand if you don't mind boss.'

Ali nodded as he pushed his large frame back into his protesting chair. 'You OK there Brian?' His voice was deep and measured.

'So, so, you know boss.'

'I do. It's been a quiet night, everybody hunkered down at home. Nobody likes the rain, do they Brian?'

'No boss, a lot of bad tempered people out tonight and they don't like queuing.'

'They don't, that's for sure. And Brian?'

'Yes boss?'

'Cut the boss crap will you, I hope you're not showing off for the good lady here.'

Brian glanced across at the girl. She returned a smile that flashed jade eyes and freckles. Ali's deep voice pulled him back to the matter in hand.

'For such a quiet night it's good to see at least one of my staff has been busy. I hope your head is not too sore, my friend.'

Shifting his weight, Brian leaned back against the door. 'Holding up, you know.'

Ali nodded. 'I do.' He stretched long legs beneath the desk, two parallels tipped with shiny brogue shoes. The fingers of his right hand splayed on the arm of his chair. 'I assume, Brian, you are going to tell me why you assaulted one of my customers?'

'They weren't customers Ali, you know that. They were looking for trouble.'

'And in you they found what they were looking for, didn't they?'

Brian nodded towards a row of small screens on the far wall. 'I did everything I should have, the guy had a knife and used it. You know that, Ali, because you watched it all happen on one of those screens.'

'I did, Brian, and you know what, I can also watch the whole fucking thing in glorious slow fucking motion replay if I want. That doesn't change a damn thing, does it?'

'The guy had a knife.'

'So what, Brian? These guys are nothing to what you're used to, you disarm and two of you escort them away. If they keep coming back you escort them away again. Using your head as a blunt instrument, as much as it's suited to the task, happens a long way down the line. You know that, Brian, why do you keep testing me?'

Brian moved away from the door but could not stand at ease so he shifted back. Ali did not wait for his answer.

'I have guys standing out there watching you week in week out, wondering why the fuck I don't fire you! And you know what that kind of wonder breeds Brian?'

'Indiscipline.'

'Yes, Brian, it does. Before I know it I have bouncers knocking lumps out of customers and each other and I wave goodbye to my 6 a.m. licence.' His fist clenched, like a big black mallet but only butted the top of the desk lightly. Collecting his anger.

'So what's wrong?' He looked Brian up and down and then looked him in the eye. 'You're looking rougher than normal, you got problems?'

Brian pushed his hands behind his back and leaned against them. 'Well you know. Life can be tough.'

'I do know. So what're you into, nothing that will come back to me I hope?'

'No, nothing like that.'

'What then?'

'Well, you know, family stuff. It can get on top of you.'

'It sure as hell can. Isn't Andrea down this weekend? Is she OK?' Concern now in Ali's voice.

'She's good. Still telling me what to do. You know Andrea, ten going on thirty.' The words caught in his throat, coming out uneven.

The dancer on the sofa looked up at him, reassessing.

'Look boss, I better get back.'

'You'll go back when I'm good and done, Brian. You're sure there's nothing wrong with Andrea. Her mother still sucking the life outta you?'

'No, well, yes. Liz is Liz, vengeance is her game but nothing new. I got a few things I need to sort, is all.'

'Things, serious?'

'Ali, are you going to fire me?'

Ali blinked at him, holding on to his answer a beat too long. His lips parted and closed again, he seemed to grow just a little bit smaller.

'Not this time Brian, but this really is the last time. I'd want you at my side in any fight. You know that, we done that. But we're not fighting wars, Brian, not anymore. Sort your shit out my friend, find a way. I can't have you knocking my customers about. If you want to keep burning then fine, but you're not taking me with you.' Both men looked across the room at each other, the only sound the distant bass. 'You got that, Brian?'

Brian nodded, turned and reached for the door.

'Hold your horses, for fuck's sake.' Ali heaved himself out of the chair. 'Jeesus Brian, come here.' Ali's frame filled the room, reaching into his trouser pocket and coming out with a rolled wad of notes. He licked the tips of his fingers, his pink tongue a contrast against the dark skin of his lips. He counted off three notes. Looking at Brian he reconsidered, counted off another two and then held the notes out.

'Here.'

Brian hesitated, conflicted by pride and need.

'Take it. Call it a bonus, off the record for old times' sake. Take Andrea out tomorrow. Get her something nice and maybe even treat yourself, get some new clothes even.' He grinned. 'But make sure you let Andrea choose them.'

Brian reached forward. 'Thanks, Ali.' He curled the notes into his palm.

'Now get out of here, get changed and go home. You just used your last life, my friend. Think about what you need to do, not just for this job but in life. We all had to adjust. Now make sure you get Andrea something nice, say hello to her for me will you.'

Brian pulled open the door, taking a last glance at the dancer and then back at Ali.

'I will,' he said, and left.

TWENTY-THREE

Brian walked out of town, his heavy boots ringing a hollow echo, around roadworks with lights at a constant red, past untidy rows of terraced cottages and through the leisure centre, jumping across a ditch and wading through long wet grass, finally stepping over the decrepit barbed-wire fence at the back of his flat.

Inside the flat was clean as it usually was two weekends a month. He left the lights off, trying to shut out Andrea's attempts at dispelling its bleakness. Reminders of Andrea were everywhere. From her pictures on the walls to the arm covers and cushion she made for the ancient sofa, the mobiles of painted glass hanging from the window. She had tirelessly followed the light, refracted red and green during the summer, the colours shifting across her jubilant face.

Stacked on the carpet beside the sofa were her books, her diary and puzzle book, her pencil case on top. On the sofa his neatly folded sleeping bag and a duvet he used as a mattress. A sheet of paper lay square on the sleeping bag, a picture she had left for him. He could make out shapes and words but dared not go over, not yet.

He would get home at dawn on Sunday mornings and she would be there, sprawled pink cheeked and asleep on that duvet, the sleeping bag either by her feet or on the floor, every light on. She hated sleeping in his bedroom while in the flat alone.

Brian walked through to the kitchenette and retrieved a half bottle of whiskey, rinsing a glass and sitting in his chair, savouring the harsh taste. Andrea would wait for that first mouthful to wash down, as if waiting for some silent signal, raising her head and peering at him through bleary eyes, climbing off the sofa and onto him. Then he would feel the weight of her body as she curled into him, her head on his chest, a few mumbled questions, the draw of breath into and out of small lungs. It was his favourite time. He knew he was not the dad he was supposed to be, knew he fell a long way short. This was a time though, when he could hold his daughter and not worry about it being enough. Her body warm beneath the palm of his hand and so fragile as he stroked the hair from her face, marvelling at her ability to love him regardless. Constantly hopeful and ever trusting.

But not tonight. He poured another drink, looking across at the sofa and the sheet of paper, ignoring it for now. He drained the glass and got on with the job in hand, preparing for what he used to do best. He walked through to his bedroom and pulled his old kit bag from the creaking wardrobe. The bedside clock ticked past three as he packed everything he knew would be useful into the bag. The bottle of prescription tablets dropped in last. Then he carried it back to the living room and poured himself another measure, staring at the sofa until the glass was empty. He steeled himself and stepped over, plucking the picture from the sleeping bag.

Andrea loved drawing fairies and angels. A large collection adorned the walls of the hall and his bedroom. Each picture had a purpose which she would earnestly explain. This one did not need explaining. It showed herself at one side of the page, her hair hanging either side of a round smiley face. She was standing on a green-coloured surface he assumed was the park, an outlined white shape by her feet with a long neck and orange beak. She had drawn him stood at her side holding her hand, looking like a caveman in a green jacket. Just the limitation of a child's artistic skills? He suspected not. As always with Andrea there was an angel. She had drawn gigantic wings that emerged from his back either side of his jacket, so big they disappeared off the page. The bottom corner was filled with little blue kisses. He could hear her voice. *Daddy's burns look like angel wings.*

A ceaseless, child's hope, to see something good in something so debilitating. She saw good in him when he was too weary of life to even look anymore. A maladjusted ex-soldier discharged from a world he had thrived in, handed a medal and a disability pension and thrust into a civilian world he cared nothing for. Until now.

He pushed the folded picture into the kit bag and took a last slug of whiskey, screwing on the cap and dropping it onto the sofa. He flicked through her neat stack of books, stopping at her dog-eared favourite, recalling the numerous times she had tried reading it to him. He slid

81

that into his bag as well. He contemplated her diary, picking it up and skimming through the pages, half afraid of what he might find of himself reflected in her words. He dropped it onto the sofa next to the whiskey. The police would find better use for it.

Brian closed the front door and stepped again into the night, moving back across the field and through the town, down onto the tow path, through the park and past the bench overlooking the canal. The night was still and quiet save for the persistent rain beating against trees and evergreen leaves, the canal a chaotic dance of expanding ripples.

Twenty minutes saw him pause as the bordering trees gave way to a wide lawn and modern apartments. Soft spotlighting highlighted the slanting rain and three joined buildings with Edwardian façades. He walked across the wet grass to a gravel car park, checking the three entrance doors. Number five was in the first block, probably the middle flat on the first floor. He walked around to the back and looked up at the first floor balconies, each with black painted metal railings.

A collection of small toys had been neatly stacked against a wall. He picked a knee-high plastic slide and positioned it, testing his weight. It would probably hold. He pulled the strap up over his head so the kit bag hung from his back and took two steps back. He clenched his fists and opened them and launched himself forwards. The slide cracked loudly as he propelled himself upwards, clamping his fingers over the edge of the balcony floor, swinging for a second and scrabbling to get leverage. He caught his breath, looking through a ground floor window and straight into the wide impassive eyes of a cat. He then pulled himself over the railing and onto the balcony.

The garden lighting cast his shadow long, through the windows into the dark apartment. He could make out a leather sofa faintly outlined, Adam stretched on the sofa, a glass on his chest.

Satisfied he was in the right place, Brian moved one of the two plastic chairs beneath the partial cover of the upstairs balcony. He would let Adam sleep a while, the peace before the storm. Sarah Sawacki was his lifeline. Andrea had vanished to thin air. Sarah had left a trail. Waiting went against his every instinct but experience had taught him patience now would save him wasted time in the next days. This was the time to focus and let his mind work through the detail. Besides, being in the open reminded him of the good times, of hunting demons. He pulled Andrea's favourite book from his bag and started reading.

TWENTY-FOUR

She blinked twice but it was dark. Something was wrong. Not just physically, it was wrong inside her head. She was there but deep inside. A small glowing firefly surrounded by shards of memories and broken images, all knocked loose and switched about. The probing pathways that once connected smells to colours, colours to emotions, shapes to faces and images to places, had been disconnected or misplaced, realigned on the dial of recollection.

She blinked again but it was still dark. Where was she? Where was Adam? Who was Adam? She had dreamed, dreamed of herself as a child before. *Before what?* Dreamed of herself as a child crouched down over herself, could feel her hot hands, tears wet and warm on her cheeks. Just like her own world, her escape world where the rain was always warm and the fields rolling green. It felt like home, she had been there so many times. To escape from what? Where was the horseman? There was always a horseman. Warm rain on her face and the sea crashing onto a beach, the sound soothing and repetitive, vivid blue. She could feel the sun hot on her skin, the sand burning her feet and his arms around her shoulders. Simon? Real happy smiles as a plane buzzed across the sky, a large banner trailing: *You've been drugged.* Why couldn't she remember? What is my name? I can't remember my name? A face, pale, dark hair and sad. Was that Adam? Who was Simon? Was she married yet? She could hear her mother's voice. *Time to stop screwing around.* If only she knew, why can't I get clean? Erase it. Surely she must know? Must have guessed. But guessed what? She closed her eyes and opened them again.

He had a grey beard, had been a winner. She so wanted to please him. Guilt, what had she done wrong? Why her? She could see herself as a child. The warm rain. Who was Andrea? Why can't I wake up, WAKE UP! *You're already awake sweetie.*

She tried reaching out from inside, to move her arms and legs, but there was nothing, no feeling. Just the intention to move a leg, but nothing back that said *Moved leg as requested.* Could she feel anything? She could feel but the dark made it hard to place the component parts floating on the salty sea. Her arm was curled around her head, but stuck and cold like dangling from a car window. Her other arm was bent at the elbow, pushed against something hard. Was it a door? She was lying on a hard floor. Could she hear something? Something move outside? Outside where? Something small, breathing. Something pushing against her elbow; or had she moved her elbow? Could she hear voices? Distant, a conflicted sound. And then close by, soft and almost pleading *Are you awake?* Little more than a child's whisper. Was she talking to herself? Something warm on her arm, a small hand feeling in the dark. The conflict a little closer. She couldn't speak, wanted to say; *I'm awake, who are you?* But her mouth refused, so she tried with her fingers. Imagined them moving, willing her fingers to life. Contact! A little shriek then something warm shuffled closer. *You are awake, are you OK?* A girl child.

For some time there was nothing more, just that sense of something small and feral on the verge of panic beside her. Then something heavy moved and she could see a thin vertical sliver of light, growing wider to the sound of heavy stone moving. She tried turning her head, drawing up her legs, but they refused to move. Her eyes struggled to focus, seeing the contrast but not the shapes. The light blotted out as something large moved in. *Don't, I won't go.* A small voice pleading next to her. *Stop him, please stop him!* Lifted from beside her, thrashing. Her mind screamed. *Stop, stop, stop!* But she could not move and an instant fury, anger, slashing, blood-stained, standing in the expansive field. Feeling the warm rain on her upturned face. And then the light grew thin and disappeared to the heavy sound of concrete over concrete. Alone, silence but for the blood pumping inside her head, her heart, the glow larger inside her mind, reaching out and slowly reconnecting. Sarah, she was Sarah.

TWENTY-FIVE

A dam was not in the mood for bed when he got home, not for their bed neatly made and minus one. Everything in their flat was Sarah, from the colour of the walls, the sofa, the pictures on the walls. He turned off the lights and lay on the sofa, stretched out with a long measure of Jack Daniels in a glass on his chest, playing through the events of the day. Their argument in the restaurant. Wondering what he might have done to cheat chance and have Sarah sleepily peering around the door, a naked shoulder and hip on show. Wanting to know when he would come to bed.

Everything was chance. He slept in short bursts, dreamed she called to say she was coming home. He woke in starts. The clock on the wall marched past twelve and two and on. Nudging towards five when he suddenly opened his eyes and remembered he had not checked their home voicemail. He juggled the drink as he stood, managing to catch it as the remaining liquid sloshed in the glass. Then two things happened in quick succession. He realised there was a message and as he pressed the button and turned to listen, he looked out through the balcony door, almost shouting with fright when he saw Brian looking right back at him.

He let Brian in without thinking. Then his dilemma was how to listen to Sarah's message in secret, which was now impossible. So he just got on with it, playing it over several times with pen and paper in hand. Brian stood sentinel by the patio doors, his kit bag still hanging from his shoulder, listening to Sarah's voice with eyes cast intently on the floor.

Sarah's message contained every detail from the moment she left Delamere. Of her bag being taken and Simon retrieving it, telling her

85

his name, that she had followed him for almost two hours and of her waiting in the farmhouse. That she used the woman's phone to leave the message. She detailed where the woman said she was and where the Rover might be heading, a description of the farmyard. Her voice was a monotone throughout, save for emotion at the end and then Sarah had disconnected.

For Adam the message was initially hopeful. The hope quickly turned to dread when he considered a lot of time had since passed. It was now five in the morning, a different day, it was Sunday. And there were no new messages.

For Brian the message was confirmation this woman genuinely believed she was following a car with a child in the boot. Andrea. The message also held a whole lot of new information that started with Delamere. Its location would be important in relation to Hambury and where Simon was heading. All Brian had to do now was prise Adam out of his cosy little nest.

TWENTY-SIX

The gurgling slowed to intermittent bursts then stopped altogether. Adam pulled the pot from the hotplate and poured the coffee, taking both cups in search of Brian. He followed the smell of musty clothes through the hallway, past his empty study and, incredulously, to the bedroom. Brian was stooped, peering at the picture beside the dressing table, of Sarah topless on the beach.

'Christ, Brian, what're you doing in here?'

Brian straightened and took the offered cup. 'Just looking around, trying to see what sort of woman your wife is. Get an idea for how she thinks.'

'You seen enough to reach any conclusions?' He failed to keep the indignation out of his voice.

'Yup.' Brian grinned back at him. 'Your wife is hot with a big fat capital H. How'd you pull a bird like her?'

'That's totally out of order. I'm a good match for Sarah.'

Brian shrugged. 'Bet you spend your holidays warding off a beach of hard-ons.'

'You're so crude, of course I don't.' Adam faltered at his partial lie. Brian had cut straight at his Achilles heel. Adam was tall and decent looking, but photos of Sarah's previous boyfriends or those he met had always daunted him. Six years on and he was now almost immune to the stares she attracted. He knew she valued who he was above all else. And then he realised the important detail in what Brian had said.

'Why would you want to understand how Sarah thinks?'

'I'd have thought that was obvious.'

'Not really, enlighten me.'

'Understanding how your wife thinks will help us find her and my daughter.'

'Us, find? Aren't the police doing that?'

'Sure they are, but you're not going to sit on your hands and do nothing are you?' Brian stepped across to the bedroom door.

Adam stared incredulously at his uninvited guest. 'What could I do that the police can't?'

'A lot. We pull on our thinking caps, there's a lot *we* can do.'

'I'm sorry but the best people are already looking for Sarah and your daughter, the police. Where would we start, what would we do?'

Brian did not immediately answer. Instead he looked over at Sarah's picture, the hopeful smile and those eyes, the body. He walked through to the hall, pausing outside Adam's study.

'It's a shame,' he said, looking into the study. 'I was thinking, all this expensive kit and pretty furniture you'd have something more about you.'

Adam followed, wrinkling his nose. 'There is, but unsurprisingly it doesn't include finding missing people, and I won't be made to feel stupid because of that!'

'I didn't say you were stupid, you're obviously not. You're just not thinking straight. Remove the emotion and finding your wife is just a puzzle to be solved. The police have an advantage but they're also slow and crippled by bureaucracy. We can do things and go places the police can't.'

'You mean like break the law?'

'No, I mean like do whatever it takes to find your wife. You do want her back?'

'Of course!'

'Well that's a relief, for a minute there I was wondering.'

'That's not fair, there's nothing I want more than Sarah here.'

'So stop feeling sorry for yourself. I'm going to find my daughter. You can come with me and help put things straight or sit here and face the alternatives.'

'Which are?'

Brian turned and faced Adam, leaning against the study doorway. 'For a start I'm not hanging around to be one of those haunted fathers at a press conference, begging for some nutter to let his daughter come home. No chance of that. I'm not going to have everyone staring at me thinking I messed with my own girl. Do nothing and this whole fucking country will be watching our sad little faces over their TV dinners. It'll be the big game, guessing which one of us is the bad guy. No way.' His eyes briefly flared, scared.

Adam walked through to the living room, thoughtful. 'Which one of us? Why ever would anyone think I was guilty?'

'I guarantee you the police will think your wife took Andrea.' He followed Adam. 'When they realise that's not the case, your wife being missing will put you in the spotlight.'

'Then I have no desire to make things worse. Besides, and I repeat, I don't track missing people for a living.'

'So what do you do?' Brian dropped down onto the sofa.

'Digital security.'

Brian looked thoughtful. 'What's that?'

'Mostly it's about companies paying us to break into their computers and security systems, to make sure their competitors can't. We profile staff, do background checks and the like. Almost everyone has a digital footprint these days. You'd be amazed.'

'So you're like a computer investigator?'

He shook his head. 'Not at all, a large chunk of what we do is testing internal security. More often security is compromised by the people using it. The important point is I don't have the first idea how you would find a missing person.'

'If you can break into a company's computers you can go a long way to finding your wife. You just have to start thinking straight.'

'And you are?'

'I'm what?'

Adam blinked theatrically back at Brian, mostly to give himself chance to think. He had underplayed how good he was by some margin. Twenty grand pay rises were not given to the ordinary, even if he had needed to resign to get it. All he wanted was to deflect Brian's attempt at recruitment. 'Are you thinking straight?' he answered. 'What qualifies you as being the straight thinker over me?'

'I didn't say I was. You don't need to worry about me, I'll pull my weight.'

'You're a bouncer, Brian!'

'I wasn't always a bouncer.'

Adam looked at his unwanted and unwashed guest on the sofa, wondering what Sarah would have to say about that. 'The police are best placed to find my wife and your daughter. And I'm going to be right here just in case there's anything else I can do to help.'

Brian sighed and pinched the skin above the bridge of his nose, creasing his forehead. He gestured to the armchair across from the sofa. 'Sit down.'

Adam shook his head. 'I don't see there's much to discuss. I'd rather stand.'

'You're starting to piss me off, Adam, sit down before I lose my temper, you stubborn fuck.'

Adam remained still. He wanted to be alone and to get his bearings. Looking at Brian he realised just how exhausted the man looked, his right hand shaking as it had the night before. He stepped across to the chair and sat down.

'Your wife is missing and you're going to wait here for a call?'

'Yes I am.'

'Then wake up, open your eyes!' Brian placed his empty cup on the floor and glared across the room. 'The reality is you and me are the best chance Andrea and your wife have.'

'No, the police are the best chance they have.' Adam's voice was higher in pitch than he would have liked.

'So tell me, good citizen, how often do you see stuff like this end with smiling faces?'

The realisation spread across Adam's face.

'I didn't think so. What're you going to do, get up every morning and wait for news that two bodies were found in some muddy copse, or washed up on some beach? Before you know it you'll be standing over Sarah's battered body in a morgue, wondering how that body could have got so messed up. Imagining what must have happened and doing that for the rest of your life. A life wishing you had tried, had actually done something.'

It felt like a punch in the face, flashing vivid images through his mind. It made Adam angry and indignant. 'Don't go unloading your guilt on me. You're the one that started all this. If you hadn't left your daughter to roam the streets none of this would've happened.'

For a moment Brian looked like he might physically react, then he looked away and used the pad of his thumb to smooth his moustache, gazing through the patio doors at the emerging morning. They sat in silence for almost a minute. Adam spoke first.

'You don't know Sarah or me and have no basis with which to make judgements. So stop pushing me, as if I am the one at fault here. It's not fair.'

'Fair!' Brian suddenly turned on him, almost snarling. 'Fucking fair! To think I spent ten years fighting for this country and people like you. You march about with this sense of self-righteousness, wasting your time with decisions on fucking hair wax and shades, what up-your-arse car to ponce about in. As if you've a divine right and deserve everything. Fucking fair! I expect you think bad stuff only happens to bad people and they might even deserve it. Well wake up, because the real world just came knocking on your door. Nothing is fair.'

'I'm not like that.' Adam struggled to say anything more expansive.

Brian expelled the air from his lungs, his whole body deflating. He slowly pushed himself up off the sofa.

'This is getting repetitive. You're obviously smart but you're deluded. I'd hoped there might be something about you, the same get up and go your wife has. Seems I was wrong.'

He hauled up his kit bag that lay like an oversized draught excluder by the balcony door. Inside metal clanked against metal, a noise like a ratcheting chain.

'When I find your wife I'll be sure to send her your love. I'll use the front door if you don't mind.' His heavy boots reverberated across the laminate as he stepped from the living room into the hallway and out of sight towards the front door.

The blood thumped through Adam's head, ceaseless and roaring. Images of Sarah flew through his mind's eye, a frenetic slide show of smiling pictures punctuated by washed out greens and a broken body on a morgue table. His mind pin-wheeled, imagining the detail. He was not even sure where the words came from.

'You were a soldier?'

Seconds ticked by with only Brian's motionless shadow visible on the hallway wall. Then Brian reappeared in the doorway.

'Fuck me, Sawacki, I thought you were letting me leave!'

He ignored the comment. 'You were a soldier?'

'The best kind. Two Para.'

'And you really think that qualifies you?'

'Qualifies me? No, this qualifies me.' He tapped the side of his head. 'The training comes in handy.'

Adam drummed his fingers against the arm of the chair, working on regaining order in his mind. 'Soldier or not, you're totally out of order, spouting off your bullshit psychology.'

'I'm not putting anything on you that you haven't already put on yourself.' Brian took a step into the living room. 'Andrea's missing and yes, part of that's my fault. But someone set her up and someone took her. There was nothing I could do about that. But I do intend finding her and I need your help.' He swung his bag onto the floor and sat back down.

Adam glared at him. 'You're some piece of work.'

'It has been said.'

'So we've come full circle. Where would we start?'

Brian rubbed his right shoulder and placed his left hand over the shaking right hand. 'Where do you think the police will start?'

'I told you, I have no idea?'

'Think.'

'I don't know, I really don't know!' Then a thought occurred to him. 'You said somebody set your daughter up?'

Brian smiled at him. 'Of course. Who sits in an alley off a busy high street and snatches a child without anyone but your eagle-eyed wife noticing?'

'Someone who knows what they're doing?'

'You got that right, probably not the first time either. So what's the next big question that really stands out?'

Adam shrugged. 'I don't know?'

'Think about it, a random child might be with friends or with parents. How would he know she was alone? It can only mean one thing.'

It took a few seconds for Adam to figure what Brian was getting at. 'You mean this guy picked her, specifically? He knew her routine?'

He got a nodded response.

'So when did all this occur to you?'

'About half an hour after Andrea failed to show last night. When I had ruled out all the other possible reasons. So ask yourself what else is obvious, Mr Sawacki, now we know this guy knew Andrea's routine?'

Adam's mind was now slowly clicking into motion. 'I guess the question is what made him choose your daughter?'

'Bingo! So why?'

'Well, I guess he could have scouted about and your daughter fitted the bill.'

'Unlikely, someone desperate might but this was too planned and too calculated. Desperation and long-term planning don't go together. Andrea was selected and not at random.'

'So who knew you leave your daughter alone Saturday afternoons?'
He loaded meaning into the last, which Brian ignored.

'Well that's the thing. Four people that I know of. The first is my boss
Ali, we're not so good now but we go back a long way. The second is my
ex. She works in Boots and handed Andrea my prescription just before
four thirty. She was the last person I know who saw her. I'd ruled her
out by five.'

'How come?'

'I asked her some meaningful questions. She didn't have a clue and
she wasn't lying.'

'How can you be sure?'

'For a start she has two kids of her own she's bringing up by herself.
She juggles shifts in Boots with working escort to pay the bills. I drive
her sometimes. She can't afford to be telling me lies.'

Adam shifted in his chair. 'An escort, you mean like a hooker?'

'Well, she can be a little touchy on your choice of titles but sure. A
few of the girls at the club do as well.'

'Hookers in Hambury!'

'Like I said, open your eyes.'

Adam let the palms of his hands drop onto the arms of the chair. Not
an aggressive act, just one of resignation. 'So who are the other two who
knew Andrea was alone?'

The end of Brian's moustache did the upwards thing as he smiled.
'That would be me and Andrea.'

The words hung in the air, the seconds marked by the clock and the
sound of birds outside greeting the morning.

'Which leaves only you then,' Adam stated. 'Unless of course Andrea
masterminded her own kidnapping.'

'I'd be the obvious choice.'

Now Adam was confused. 'So if not you, it had to be random, unless
Andrea told someone, a friend or something?'

'That's the thing. Only a few people know what she gets up to here
because I have to work nights, I can't afford to broadcast it.'

'What do you mean, broadcast what?'

For a second Brian's face changed to guilty and then back again. 'I
work odd hours. I leave Andrea home alone Saturday nights. I work the
door at MadHatters, it's the worst shift. Ali has a late licence, the extra
cash is what I live on. Even if I could get a sitter for those hours, I

couldn't afford to pay them. If her mother knew I left her alone she'd crucify me and set the social services on me for good measure. I'd probably not see Andrea again until she was eighteen.'

This was all going from bad to worse. 'So you leave your daughter alone Saturday nights and she keeps to herself for fear someone will find out? That's rubbish.'

Brian did not answer and Adam let the silence play before continuing. 'Maybe your boss isn't the buddy you thought.'

'No chance. Ali's real pissed at me but this isn't his style. He doesn't know any details, just that she's here every other weekend. Andrea's a smart kid, she knows the score. She wouldn't tell anyone.'

Adam could not imagine trusting any friend of Brian's. Hookers! That had been missing from the Hambury website. There seemed only one reasonable course of action. 'We should give the details to the police, let them do the rest.'

'Sounds like the right thing to do, doesn't it?'

It dawned on Adam that he might be missing the point. 'But?'

'The police are going to head straight towards suspect primo, the damp loser sat on the sofa. I'll be no good to anyone sat in a holding cell. Finding out who set Andrea up is for the police, we track your wife and I guarantee we find…'

Brian's eyes closed and his mouth pinched tight, his whole body rigid as if dealing with some vicious internal pain. Then he breathed out and continued as if nothing had happened, '…find more pieces of the puzzle.' Both his fists unclenched.

'You all right?' Adam asked.

'Sure, just suffering a bit is all. I'll take a couple of tablets, it'll be fine.'

Adam hesitated. 'What will be fine, what kind of tablets?'

'Prescription type tablets.'

'For your hand?'

His question was rewarded with a thin smile. 'For my back. It's a long story.'

Adam felt like driftwood pulled along by a fast flowing river. 'That image of Sarah in a morgue…'

Brian nodded. 'We need to get moving. Simon probably used Delamere as a base, the location will be important.'

A thought occurred to Adam. 'You have any transport?'

Brian shook his head.

'So you were going to hitch a lift?'

'If I had to. The world's full of cars and careless owners. I'd have borrowed one, there's a few nice ones downstairs.'

Adam sighed and fetched a cup of water from the kitchen, waiting for Brian to dig a bottle of tablets from his bag before handing it to him. 'If we're going to sit in a car together you need to shower and change. You can borrow some of my clothes. You're a little shorter but broader, they should kind of fit.'

He walked through to his study and tapped a key on the keyboard. He used a local car hire when he needed to drive. The only time he'd used them this early was when Sarah's mother died. Ten minutes later he received email confirmation the car would be ready for them in an hour.

TWENTY-SEVEN

Her memories of before were recalled as composites of a time. Short flickering images that gave a sensation of the moment without ever pointing to any particular one. There were images and sensations of playing hopscotch but not of any individual games. She could recall hours whiled away in the back garden but not one occasion. All the individual moments lost to a child's routine of getting up, school and gym and home and bed.

Sarah could not recall the first moment she had met *him*. She had memories of a life before and then he had been there. Her first recollection was of Sunday lunches. She had an image in her mind of *him* sitting opposite, framed by the window and the colours of the garden. In this snapshot he ate with his mouth open, roast potatoes and beef thrown about like clothes on a slow spin. The stubbly beard moving in small motions, his pale skin and permanently pink cheeks. Those ghastly thin red lips. He stretched out his legs beneath the table so she had nowhere to put hers, other than to rest against his. She had thought *him* selfish. There was plenty of room beneath the table. Later she learned the Sunday lunches were part of her mother's recruitment of *him* as a tutor for her talented but distracted child.

Then the lessons started. Even these were lost in time, her first impressions of the empty school at night overrun by the subsequent dread of later visits. It must have started well because the trophies soon appeared. There had not been any trophies before, just glowing school reports of potential.

Sarah did recall he was a very good instructor, his hands shaping her body through every movement, his drills giving her confidence and discipline. The routines before had felt hurried in her mind as if her body was constantly racing to catch up. With his direction everything happened in slow motion. She was in total control, practised and prepared with just her ability defining the quality. And she had no shortage of that.

Then she had won the regional finals. To this day the trophy held pride of place in her parents' living room, although it was now layered in dust and only watched over by a bewildered father. Her mother's voice echoed wistfully. *To think what you might have gone on to achieve!* Could she really have been that blind?

It started with a hug. Sarah could not recall much of that either. Just the long drive and being at the competition, the regional finals, the large gymnasium full of squealing children and throngs of gabbling parents. She was nervous before such a large audience but knew she had done well. Then someone announced third and second place and then first and her name was called. She exploded with utter joy, leaping up and down in her leotard, screaming with arms aloft. The excitement inside was more than any physical action could manifest, it had nowhere to go. She screamed louder and then leapt into his arms. He was simply the nearest person she knew, it was after all because of *him*. She had screamed so hard she forced all the air from her lungs as she clamped onto *him* and hugged so tight.

Everything that happened over and over during the following seventy-seven weeks, he justified in that moment. Saying it was the feel of her body as she held on. Her breath as she kissed his cheek. He told her she must be grateful to be learning the lessons of life as a child. To be learning from someone experienced. He was saving her from all that pain when she was older, all that uncertainty. Boys would like her better. One day she would be grateful. It was meant to be. He was preparing her for life as a woman, she must be grateful. Don't cry, be grateful.

Sarah opened her eyes. She blinked through the memories to the here and now. It was dark. Her heart felt heavy and her brain was busy sounding an alarm. What was wrong, where was she? She blinked again and nothing changed. It was dark and there was no sound, nothing but the furious mechanisms of her mind. Why could she not move? She fought the rising panic. The images shifted in the kaleidoscope of recollection, realigning to an ordered sequence. Faces were matched to places and emotions to people, the reality of now and the memory of the journey, of getting to this moment, slammed home. The panic ran free, a dark stain spreading across the fabric of her mind as the fear clawed for escape.

But Sarah knew the consequences of surrendering herself to that fear; she had walked that road and knew where it led. She reined it in and worked on maintaining control, and gradually with control an awareness of her body. She was lying on her back, arms at odd angles. One above her head pushed against a hard surface, a smooth wall, the other lay beneath her body. Moving resulted in a searing pain, but they did move, they were not broken. Focusing on her right arm she moved it down slowly, a painful groan as cramped muscles protested. She eased her body to one side and freed the other, letting the blood flow with fingers kneading palms.

Her legs were folded, almost foetal but twisted to one side. She stretched them outwards and touched the opposite wall. She was in a very narrow space. The fear clawed frantic, the air thick and heavy. She waved a hand in front of her face. She did it again and again but there was nothing, no shadow over shadow, nothing but endless dark. Was she blind? She needed to breathe, to know where she was. How to get out? Her head spun. The dark was all consuming and heavy, pushing in at her from all sides. Her heart thumped uneven. Her mind conjured frenetic gnashing teeth and whispered voices. *His* voice full of need, *his* gnarled fingers reaching out for her, scratching at her face and tugging at her hair, pulling at her clothing, probing, his breath like sour milk. She could feel *him* move closer in the pitch dark, all around and looming over her, hands on her head, forcing his flesh inside her mouth, hard and pulsing, thrusting with a groaned ecstasy. The bitter taste of *him* pumping warm that she gagged and choked on, spat out. He was everywhere, hands reaching from all directions, an endless queue of thin red lips and jutting flesh waiting their turn at the feast. The fear ripped a jagged hole and clawed free. Sarah screamed and screamed.

The screaming was at first a submission to the fear, a noise that defined the horror. A noise she had to escape from. She dived into the ocean, the ocean that bordered the imaginary world of her childhood. It was aqua blue and shimmering full of sunbeams, swimming as far as she could and ever down to a peace within the great void, the sounds of the real world distant as she fought for a foothold on her mind. Fighting with the determination of a wilful child who did endure each week. The adolescent who did survive, who did step around the sanctuary of suicide, the woman who knocked on *his* door. Sarah had spent her whole life surviving and she had done a lot of it here, treading water in the vast sanctuary of the ocean as she slowly took back control. And then when she was ready she kicked towards the surface, back to reality and the screaming.

She clamped her mouth closed and pushed back the fear. There was nowhere to go, right now there were no fingers feasting on her body, nothing in her mouth save for her own tongue and this thick air. There was no danger now. She must think, breathe and take control. She lay still. Her hurried breaths became a shallow control, calibrating and working at keeping that control.

She very carefully pushed herself up until she was sitting, running through a systems check of body parts, all accounted for and responding. She had a tender jaw and a throbbing head. She ached and was exhausted but her body was operational.

The floor was hard, a carpet over concrete. She reached out with her left hand and found a third wall but only emptiness on her right. Fight the fear. The air was stale like attics and sheds. There was no sound other than her own breathing and the friction of her body against the carpet. Utter dark, utter silence. On all fours she moved blindly into the empty space, fearful for what she might touch as she reached forward. The tips of her fingers landed on something smooth, wood she concluded, cautiously feeling the object in her hands. A small footstool. She put it to one side, reached out again and touched a soft material. A small mattress pushed against the final wall. A very small space. Fight the fear. Her hand glanced off something cold on the floor, knocking it over. It was round, slightly smaller than a football. A curling shape protruded from one end, a bulb. She found the cord, then the switch and pressed it. Light filled the space, timidly at first, a tepid orange glow that grew brighter with each passing second.

Sarah was in a room she could not stand in. A small rectangle no more than four foot by eight. The carpet was old, a worn rusty colour with dark swirls. She could see no door, but there had to be one. She reined in the panic. The room was walled with wide strips of plywood, including the ceiling. She perched on the edge of the mattress and drew her knees close.

There were two old shelves of tatty books, a motionless extractor fan in one corner. On the floor beneath the shelves, where she had just lain, was the footstool, ancient and pitted. Tacked on the wall above the mattress were two creased posters of fairies. Sarah shook her head, they were grotesque in this context. She was in a prison designed for a child, a girl child. She looked closer at the wall beside the bed at a random cluster of scratches, the scrubbed traces of stubborn pen marks. She did not dare think now of those who had been here before.

Thrown into the corner on the mattress was a thick red blanket. Sarah reached over and pulled it towards her, revealing a light blue bag that triggered a memory of the girl outside Boots. She resisted the urge to look inside, instead spreading the red blanket over the mattress. Then she shuffled around the room on her knees, rapping hard with her knuckles across every space of the four walls and then the ceiling. There was no sound that gave any indication of an exit.

She consoled herself with the knowledge that if she had got in, she must be able to get out. For now she knew all about the room she could know. Now she had to steel herself for what would come, she could not afford to be weak. She had to be in control, be rational and be ready. She would be none of these things if she gave in to fear and panic.

Sitting back on the mattress Sarah closed her eyes. She firmed her resolve and took two deep breaths. She turned off the light and suppressed every urge to turn it straight back on.

TWENTY-EIGHT

Helen Ferreira shifted the thick wad of folders between her arms and buzzed the intercom. It was early Sunday morning and quiet save for the drip of rainwater from trees and guttering. A shape emerged through the thick glass, wearing a voluminous white shirt. To her surprise it was Boer. Not because he was in, he was always in, just seldom downstairs. The lock clicked and he pulled open the door.

'Helen.'

'I take it you did go home, Fran?' She stepped inside.

'I did, couldn't sleep. Can't get the Sawacki woman out of my head. I came in to chivvy things along, see if we can get a head start.'

He held out his arms. 'Give me some of those, just stack them up.'

Ferreira hesitated.

'Come on now, I'm not a write-off yet.'

She shifted the files onto his arms and then followed him, passing the post room of wire-framed pigeon holes and the kitchen, sparsely clean. He stopped at the vacant duty desk, stacked her folders onto the desk and perched himself on the edge.

Ferreira paused. 'And why precisely are you downstairs covering the duty desk?'

'I asked the sergeant to find me a fresh case file.'

'And why would you want one of those?'

'Because I want something to put all the detail of this case into. Something I can actually hold on to and browse through without battling through bloody screen savers and no end of passwords.'

She smiled as the sergeant returned, handing Boer the empty file – a thick blue hardback with a wide spine edged in a dull metal. He stacked

101

it on top of the folders and carried them up the stairs.

The office was a stark contrast to the bustle of the week. The phones sat silent and the chairs were empty, the occasional desk neatly tidied amid the general clutter. A long window cut horizontally along one wall, covered by partially closed blinds. Boer's dark jacket hung from the back of his chair, as it did most days of the week. It was surrounded by sheets of paper laid on the floor, some piled on his desk, their desks the last two on the right facing each other beneath the window. Ferreira looked at her watch. It was not yet seven thirty. 'Exactly what time did you get in this morning?'

'Early. A lot of the stuff we requested got printed remotely overnight. I got in and found it all over the floor. I've been sorting through it.'

Ferreira took her folders from Boer and he took his file from the top.

'I take it you got through to the Chief Inspector?' she asked, moving the folders to the floor beside the radiator and dropping her bag on top.

'Yup, she's setting up an 'all ports' and kicking the media team into action. Depending on what we find today she'll decide tonight on what kind of media. If this is what it appears, the circus will start tomorrow. She sounded positively upbeat.'

'She's very photogenic. Was she OK with us on *this*?'

'Of course.' Boer looked across at Ferreira, a frown creasing his forehead. 'Although she made it clear this was her case. We're to head up the localised investigation while she runs the wider show.'

Ferreira sighed. 'Dear Chief Darling. And in your considered opinion what does *this* appear to be?'

'Abduction of a child by non-parent. Family Liaison are in Northampton with the mother now. She was at a church function with a raft of witnesses yesterday, and the stepfather was in Harrogate surrounded by technicians. The girl's father was minding the door at Banjo's until four thirty. He was the one who reported her missing.'

'Did we find out if she had a mobile?'

Boer nodded. 'The mother doesn't allow her to have one, same story with a computer. They only use the stepfather's laptop and never on their own. We're trying to get hold of that.'

'And you're sure the abduction by non-parent is not abduction by Sarah Sawacki?' she offered.

'Are you?'

'Didn't say that Fran, just putting it out there.'

'Anything is possible, Helen, but I just don't see it, not with the data we have.'

Ferreira watched Boer lower himself to the floor, one knee at a time, a hand on the desk for support, his concentration morphing his expression to a grimace. Whenever she asked him to describe the pain, he said it was indescribable. He was also royally proud, so she left him sorting sheets of paper into piles on his desk. She turned on her computer, pulling the keyboard towards her as she waited to log in. 'I'll print the rest of these reports, then we can work out where to focus.'

Ten minutes and the printer was busy spewing paper, Boer clipping pages into his file like a schoolboy intent on a project. She opened a new case file on her computer and pasted in the digital versions of the same documents, her preferred method, neatly ordered alphabetically and cross-referenced by topic, each word indexed. By eight thirty she was almost finished. She left the computer indexing and placed both hands on the desk. 'Coffee?'

He looked up. 'Tea. I'll go, it must be my turn.'

'Stay there, Fran, I need caffeine in the next ten minutes, not this afternoon.' Her voice was tender and amused. He smiled and she retrieved her purse, resting her hand briefly on his shoulder as she walked to the double doors.

Outside the pavements and roads were slick, the blue sky reflected in varying sized puddles. Yellow tape fluttered in the morning breeze, cordoning off the alley. A constable stood sentry, raising a hand in acknowledgement. Another would be stationed by the car park exit. Often forensics in open places, especially public places, felt futile. Occasionally something was discovered that changed their whole perspective.

She resisted the urge to take a look and catch up on gossip, carrying on into a narrow café favoured by station staff and taxi drivers for the strong coffee. She ordered two *skinny* muffins, a large tea for Boer and a large filter coffee for herself. She was passing the train station on her way back when her phone started vibrating. But with a bag dangling from her left hand and a large cup in each, she let it ring. As she neared the bridge it started vibrating again. Someone needed to talk but there was nothing she could do about that, except walk faster.

Back at her desk she put the cups and muffins to one side and immediately checked her phone. Three missed calls from a mobile she did not recognise. She called the number from her desk phone and to her surprise Adam Sawacki answered. He told her of Sarah's call the night before, summarising the detail and giving Ferreira the pin number to his home voicemail, pre-empting her request to come over and listen. All she had to do was dial his home number, punch in the code and she could listen to the message.

She thanked him, dropped the handset into the cradle and clicked on the loudspeaker, checking the number on her notepad as she dialled. The fact Adam was jittery had registered, but she put that down to a sleepless night worrying about his wife. She got Boer's attention and they waited in silence, listening to the ringing. She imagined Adam at home, tempted to pick up the call anyway, in the hope it was Sarah. When the messaging service announced itself Ferreira keyed the code and readied her pen.

She played the message over until she had every word, taking the best part of thirty minutes. Finally she accepted the voicemail's offer of calling the caller, hoping she would be connected to whoever owned the phone Sarah had used. The number was withheld. Boer sat with his elbows on the open casebook throughout, waiting for her to disconnect before he spoke.

'Your thoughts on Sarah Sawacki now?'

Ferreira considered her answer, placing Boer's tea and muffin next to the case file. 'She's been slipping down my list of suspects since we heard the messages last night. Either that or she needs an Oscar nomination.'

'And some,' he agreed. 'She got his name. That's pretty impressive. Warwick gives us a few geographic possibilities.'

They both looked across at the UK map. There was one almost floor to ceiling each end of the office, a multi-coloured demographic of Berkshire crime tacked on the side. They checked off Hambury below Oxford, to the left of Reading, tracing the path from Hambury to Delamere horizontally west, then deviating diagonally north east to Warwick. The path created a shape like the bottom of a Z.

'What does it tell you?' he asked.

Ferreira leaned back in her chair, pulling the lid from her coffee while studying the map. 'He seems to have followed a fundamental escape philosophy, run in the wrong direction and then turn and run home.'

'Where does the line end if you keep going?' He leaned forward and squinted.

She traced the imaginary line, continuing north and east to the coast.

'Hull, if he didn't make any other turns.' She looked back at Boer. 'The fact Sarah even followed him to Delamere means he wasn't paying attention.'

Boer agreed. 'His main point of risk was taking the girl in the alley. After that he knows the odds are in his favour and getting better with every minute. If it wasn't for Sarah we would've wasted days combing through the local countryside and dredging that damn canal. Except Sarah walked right under his radar.'

'Or she did,' said Ferreira, drinking from her coffee. She watched him over the top of the cup.

He stopped, his mouth open mid-thought. 'Yes…twelve hours is too long. Her luck ran out.'

'So now we have two victims and are none the wiser.'

'We are wiser, Helen. Simon didn't take the child to kill her, at least not straight away. And I doubt any man's first instinct is to kill Sarah Sawacki.'

'Four days?' she proffered.

Boer lay his hands flat on the case file. 'Two at least. We need to get busy. That probably starts with Warwick.'

Ferreira nodded, looking back at the map. 'Warwick is fairly central. I can't see him going south again. He must have thought he was home free. So he either went straight on north east with the furthest equation being Hull. Or … if he turned north west we have Blackpool. Or God knows where else.'

Boer started flicking through pages in the case file. 'Let's see if the partial number plate matches any of those geographic areas. I'll race you, paper versus computer.'

She swung around, placing the coffee on her desk. 'I'm not playing your silly games, Fran, just tell me.' She picked at her muffin and impatiently tapped a finger against the keyboard, checking the computer's progress on the index. Less than ten per cent. Boer moved backwards and forwards between pages.

'There are seventeen possibles based on colour and the variables on the number plate. They're spread across the UK.' His finger traced across the pages. 'And none registered to a Simon.'

'Which means the car was stolen or he just bought it.'

'Yes.' Boer spent several seconds scanning through the list of addresses, then looked up at Ferreira. 'We need the CCTV from Delamere and the rest of that number pl…'

A long intrusive tone cut through the conversation. An internal call to his desk phone. He reached over and answered, giving Ferreira a concerned glance as he pulled across a notepad. By the time he replaced the handset he had turned a shade greyer. She waited.

'West Midlands just called in Sarah's car. The fire brigade were called to a vehicle fire in West Heath at four this morning. Totally burnt out. The plates were missing. They ran the engine's serial number and got us via the lease hire.'

'Did they find anything inside?'

'A body type anything, no. Forensics are waiting for our lead. I gave them context, they'll get a proper look this afternoon when the Chief signs it off.'

'We already knew the twelve-hour gap wasn't going to bring anything good.'

'Yeah, I know.'

They both fell quiet, processing the extra information.

'You know what?'

He looked up enquiringly.

'Sarah Sawacki's car tells us Simon isn't working alone.'

He sighed. 'To be expected. There's usually some other misguided individual lurking in the background.'

'So where to first, boss?'

'The beginning. Dazzle me, Helen.'

'Right.' She pulled across her notepad, clicking her pen. She had thought this through while waiting for sleep the night before. 'Our first port of call has to be opportunity. She had to be targeted.'

'Not a desperate predator and a random child?'

She shook her head. 'This was planned and methodical. Someone knew a lot about her.'

'How?'

'A friend of Andrea's? Possibly of the family. Although judging from Brian Dunstan's statement the mother can't know what goes on while Andrea's here, or she'd never let the girl come back. He's hardly at home.'

Boer moved with the intention of retrieving Brian's statement but his stomach convinced him otherwise. 'Who took his statement?'

Ferreira plucked it from the pile and handed it to him. 'Warren and Natasha. They said he was a mess, aggressive as well.'

Boer looked through the transcript. 'I'm not surprised, I'd be too if my daughter was missing.'

'No, a mess like in what he wore, what he was like. We need to talk to him.'

'We do. When did you last drive to Northampton?'

'Northampton?' she said, surprised. 'Ricky and I went earlier in the year, it took about ninety minutes. You want to talk to the mother first?'

He nodded. 'Nobody will know Andrea better, what she's like and who her friends are. Who else might have known her routine. We find out what the mother knows about Andrea's visits to Hambury and it'll give us a better perspective on Brian. The mother gave Andrea her own surname and not Brian's, you know that?'

She shook her head, finishing the last mouthful of her muffin before replying. 'I'll arrange an interview with Brian's ex here and get the duty sergeant to chase up the Delamere CCTV, it should be in Reading by now.'

'They're probably waiting for the Chief to sanction Sunday overtime.' Boer failed to keep the frustration from his voice.

Ferreira was used to this when it came to Boer's relationship with CI Anne Darling. She gave his untouched muffin a predatory look. 'You going to be OK in a car for three hours? That's a long time and you've already put a day's shift in.'

'To the cause, Helen. There'll be less traffic on a Sunday. Should be quicker. I want to check out the stepfather as well. If I sleep in the car, all the better. I certainly wouldn't at home or here.'

She stacked loose papers and slid them into a drawer, checking for her keys and phone. 'We'll get Brian Dunstan picked up on the way back.'

'Sounds like a plan.' He eased into his jacket, completing a similar check for his keys. He clasped the case file under one arm and his tea in his free hand. 'Would you like my muffin, Helen? I'm afraid I'm not hungry.'

'No, I'm fine Fran, you eat it. You could do with the calories, I couldn't.'

'Helen, take it, I'm not hungry and you probably didn't get breakfast.'

She waited a beat and then took it. 'Only because I'm following direct orders, you understand.'

As they walked across the car park a thought suddenly occurred to Boer. 'Did you have anything planned for today?'

Ferreira shook her head and smiled. 'After last night I cancelled everything including church, Tesco's, ironing and trash TV.'

'Your dedication is commendable. How is Ricardo?'

'Lonely.'

'Really? I'm sorry, Helen.'

'Don't be, Fran, I was only joking. Ricky probably won't realise I'm missing until he gets hungry, the fridge is full so that won't be until four at the earliest. He's on the home straight for his PhD.'

'What's he doing this time?'

'Industrial Psychology.'

'Wasn't that what he did last time?'

'No, part of his masters was Cognitive Psychology, we did it together. He's focusing on engineering now. His plan is world domination and five children.'

'Five!'

'What can I say, we're both Catholic. Anything under four is considered a poor show.'

TWENTY-NINE

Adam took Brian's instructions with a nod and walked away, merging with the crowd. Brian waited and looked around. Delamere was busy. The car park was full of four-by-fours and family cars, camper vans and low-lying coupés. Inside it was even busier. People were everywhere.

Brian felt good, the cutting pain across his back now suppressed to a needling ache, although wearing Adam's hand-me-downs he felt like a dog in a collar for the first time. He checked to make sure Adam had not turned back then stepped across the concourse to a door marked *Staff Only*. He tried the handle but it was locked, so he knocked and waited, not expecting it to open although you never knew. It stayed closed. So he tracked back outside and around the building, stepping from the pavement over shrubs and through shingle. There was always somebody out back and today was no exception.

The guy was big, once he might have been muscled big, now it was more Humpty Dumpty. He was wearing a neatly pressed white shirt with dark shoulder loops, a matching tie held in place by a golden pin, the shirt neatly tucked into dark belted trousers. Brian wondered at that; if you were overweight and took the time to look smart, surely you would take the time to lose a bit of weight.

The guard looked up, took a last long drag on a half-finished cigarette and moved back inside. Brian caught the door just before it closed. He affected a polite, enquiring tone.

'I wondered if I might trouble you with some questions.'

The guard stopped as he reached for a door opposite, turning without moving the lower half of his body. 'If you're from the local press you're wasting your time. Nothing's happened here.'

'I'm not from the press.' Brian stepped fully into the small space, taking a quick look at the gold badge on the guard's chest.

'I just need a minute of your time, Steve, that's all.'

The guard's eyes followed the door as it swung closed behind Brian and the lock clicked. The small room was now lit by a dim bulb above. 'You're not allowed in here. Now you've gone and let the door close. It can only be opened from inside the control room.'

'Is that a fact?' said Brian. 'Maybe we could have a quick chat then, just as long as it takes you to get the door open. Then I'll be gone.'

'You can't come inside. We have our security systems in here. Wait there.'

The guard pulled a chain from his pocket, shuffling keys. Finally he pulled the door open and backed through, warily watching Brian, who waited until the door was almost closed then took one long quick stride. He wrenched it open, immediately stepping through and slapping both hands hard on the guard's fleshy chest, forcing him backwards, off balance, feet working double time to catch up. After that it was simply a matter of maintaining momentum, marching into a brightly lit room. For a moment Brian worried Steve might go straight through the partitioned wall and sprawling across the concourse. The wall bowed, a two-way mirror shimmered and Steve came to a stop as a thin man in a similar uniform leapt up from his chair.

'What the fuck!'

Brian angled himself between the door and the two men. 'Now keep cool there guys. I'm not here to hurt anyone or cause trouble. I will though if you start fucking about. I've a few questions and I'll be on my way.'

The second guard was young, wearing an oversized uniform. His big eyes glared out from beneath a black turban. A silver name tag stated his name was Sachgian. His voice was high pitched and edgy.

'All I gotta do mister is press that button there and the police will come running, then we'll see about some questions.' He looked meaningfully at his desk.

Brian smiled widely back at him. 'You go for it.'

The young guard's body swayed and his expression shifted to uncertain. Brian took a quick glance around the room and then from one guard to the other.

'You've got a lot of kit in here. I take it those screens are recording everything that happens?'

Both guards blinked in unison and then Sachgian answered. 'It's not the screens that do the recording, they just shows the pictures.'

'Is that right, so where're the tapes from last night?'

The guards both blinked again. Steve answered.

'The police, we gave the recordings to the police.'

'That so?' Brian took a step towards Steve.

'Yup, s'pect you could ask them, I'm sure they'd lend them to you.'

'S'pect they would, Stevie boy, especially if they keep shop like you two slackers. Now tell me, what do those boxes under the tables do?'

'They're computers,' Sachgian answered.

The two-way mirror bowed as Steve straightened his shirt and rearranged his belt. 'And there's nothing on them you're getting your hands on. We're just going to stand here and wait. Let us know when you want to leave and we'll show you out. We'll then hand the CCTV of you to the police.' He nodded over Brian's shoulder. 'If you feel like getting a bit rough that works as well, if you could be so kind as to hit me first. I'm not allowed to initiate force.'

Brian re-appraised Steve and took a step back, looking over his shoulder at a camera mounted above the door. He turned back. 'You know, I came in here being all polite and all you guys had to do was answer a few questions.'

'We're answering no questions. Not to you.' Steve said.

'Is that so, you fat fuck, you and I both know that camera is nothing but a toy.'

'If that's what you'd like to think, feel free. Makes no difference to me.'

'I know that camera's just for show, Stevie boy, because you guys don't want anybody knowing what you get up to here. I know a bunch of guys like you. They spend their lives cooped up in holes like this. It's why I was being polite, they're mostly OK guys. But they're always scheming to make a few extra quid, just can't help themselves in a place like this.'

Both guards glared back at him.

'So what is it, knocked off DVDs? A camera in the ladies? Maybe you're on a retainer, looking after the girls working the hotel. Recreational drugs on the side? There's always something and I couldn't care less what it is. All I have is a few questions, then I'm gone and you'll never see me again.'

'What do you want to know?' Steve drew in a long breath and blew it out hard, launching himself towards Brian with one large arm arcing around and upwards, a silver knuckleduster clasped in his hand.

On the whole Brian considered it an impressive move, no over-emphasis by moving his legs or dropping a shoulder. All the power came from balance. With the addition of the knuckleduster, it was a sure-fire lights out Brian Dunstan. Except Steve's problem, despite his technique, was generating power and disguising the movement. The energy rippled across all that fat and gave Brian all sorts of time to react. He went passive, stepping back and sideways, deflecting the blow with his open palm. The impact forced Steve's hand open, sending the knuckleduster flying over Brian's shoulder and clanging noisily off a desk and wall and pin-wheeling back into the air. By the time it thumped onto the floor he had wrenched Steve's arm around and turned it back on itself, the pain forcing him to the ground. Brian gave Sachgian a completely unnecessary back-off stare and focused his attention on Steve, now gasping and scrabbling for leverage against the floor and wall.

'Now look here Steve. This is not what I want. I admire your attitude but I repeat, I'm not here to hurt you or ruin what you've got going. So, are you going to stop fucking me about because next time I won't be so gentle.'

Steve nodded and patted the ground like a defeated wrestler, rolling on the floor as Brian released him. He slowly heaved himself up with the help of a chair and immediately brushed himself down.

'You're not a nice person, you know that?'

'Yeah, well, thanks for the scoop. Now sit in that chair and don't go making any sudden movements.' Steve stepped over to his desk and sat down.

'Now are you two going to answer a few questions?'

Steve nodded slowly.

'Good. For starters I suspect you guys spent a lot of time today talking to the police.'

Steve nodded at Sachgian. 'He has. I did the early shift yesterday.'

Brian stepped over to Sachgian who looked at him fiercely for a handful of seconds and then stared down at his feet. 'What were they asking about?'

'They…they wanted to know if there'd been any disturbances. What coverage our cameras have. Said they were looking for a woman and a young girl.'

112

'Did they?' Brian looked out through the two-way mirror, looking for Adam as Sachgian continued.

'Yeah, they wanted copies of everything we had on the car park and inside from five last night to midnight. We had a couple of pickpockets doing the rounds as well.'

'Part of an organised crew?' His attention back on the young guard.

'Nah, we saw them once last year and twice this month. Only difference was they tried taking this woman's bag, some passing beefcake came to her rescue. We never saw no young girl. Not one with the woman. The police were right interested in her, wanted footage of everything, took up almost a whole DV...' His mouth clamped closed.

'DV what?' Brian asked, unfolding his arms.

Sachgian looked sideways at Steve, then fixed his gaze on the wall behind Brian. Brian took a good look around the room, the shelves and stacks of plastic cases.

'DVD, is that what you were going to say? Thought you said it was on tape?'

'No,' Steve said from his chair. 'You asked where the tapes were, we didn't correct you.'

'So which is it?'

Sachgian answered. 'Security systems haven't used video for years, the quality isn't good enough. You can have someone bang to rights and they'll still deny it's them and there's nothing anyone can do.'

'So DVDs like in movies you rent?' Brian asked. '*Happy Feet* and all that?'

'I suppose so, if that's your thing.' Sachgian scratched at his chin. 'Each camera takes a single high-definition picture every second and stores that on disk. We pick out the required timeline and burn it to DVD.'

Brian smiled and clapped his hands together. 'Excellent, I'll take two copies like you made for the police. Stevie boy can do that. And make sure you don't mess me about because if you do I'll be back to haunt this place. Same goes for calling the police when I'm gone.'

Without acknowledging him Steve slowly stood and reached up to a shelf, pulling down a stack of DVD cases.

'While you're doing that I have a few more questions for young Sachgian here, about last night.'

THIRTY

Simon leaned over the slumped body of the child. She was so peaceful and innocent and so beautiful, even with a tear-stained face and red splotches around sore eyes. She was so small, yet already something of the woman she might be. His need shifted inside of him, a craving that he fought in the prolonged dark of closed eyes. But the need won and he reached out, stroking stray hairs from her face, his fingers across the soft skin of flushed cheeks.

'Stop that, Simon, there will be time enough.' Hakan picked up the syringe from the floor. 'She is ready?'

'She is.' Simon stepped back from the sofa. 'She's very loyal to her father, but in time she'll have no choice but to believe us, we know too much about him.'

'Good, then you'd better get the woman. It is time to cut off the loose ends.'

Simon carefully scooped the child into his arms, shifting her head onto his shoulder and her weight onto his forearm. He carried her through to the hallway and out through a doorway into the garage.

Hakan pulled his phone from his leather jacket, keying in a number and watching the screen. He began pacing an elliptical path around the living room, turning the syringe over and over. He was tired, none of them had slept. For the first time in a long time Simon was giving him problems.

'Halloo Baldur.' He did not pause for pleasantries, nor did he bother to switch into Baldur's native tongue, which was different from his own and from this English language that he could not abide. 'What is your status?'

Hakan's momentum around the room slowed as the remote voice

answered at length. Resuming his pacing and smiling, he listened to the voice explain all it had just finished doing.

'And her bag, the coat?' Hakan asked. '…Back in her flat! Good.' He chuckled to himself. 'You are very inventive. The husband is not there?… OK, then he's probably still with the police…Is that right? In the bedroom? Very much the modern woman. You have done well, what about the car?…No, not that, the Rover. It cannot bring police here… No, I do not care. We need that document, that address is all that ties us…Yes, it was a mistake for Simon, but it was the least of them. If not for this woman it would not have mattered…Then do what you do best Baldur, I want that path erased. If someone looks hard enough, I do not want to lose what we have here. Understand?…Excellent my friend, thank you.' He snapped the phone closed.

Just one piece of paper and one troublesome woman stood between Hakan and untroubled sleep. And he would deal with the woman right now.

THIRTY-ONE

Adam stacked the bags of maps on the table and sat down, watching the throng of people flow through the main concourse. He tried to imagine Sarah here, less than a day ago, maybe sitting at one of these tables, possibly even the one he was at now.

The image of Sarah on a morgue table now haunted him almost permanently. It kept him with Brian on this fool's errand, although doing something did keep his emotions at bay. Brian also seemed to offer some hope, but Adam could not imagine what they would learn by being here. What would anyone remember? What could they find? Putting everyone into a headlock would take a while.

He pulled a large atlas from one of the bags, absently watching a door open on the far side of the concourse. To his surprise Brian emerged, stepping around people and up the steps. He dropped into the chair opposite and placed two DVD cases on the table. He tapped his index finger against the plastic.

'Guess what they are?'

'Neil Diamond in Vegas?' Adam ventured.

Brian ignored him. 'CCTV footage on DVD. How about that?'

'Really, from last night?' Adam was shocked and a little impressed.

'Sure, two copies. From five in the afternoon through to midnight.'

Adam looked at Brian. 'How'd you get that?'

Brown eyes gleamed back. 'I asked nicely. Security were only too pleased to help when I explained why. Ran me off two copies there and then.'

'And that was it?'

Brian nodded.

'Cool,' Adam said. 'I'll get my computer.' He looked down at the atlas on the table and back to Brian. 'I got this and about fifteen cities from Birmingham upwards. Marker pens are in there as well.'

Five minutes later he returned with his laptop bag bouncing off his hip. Brian had the atlas open at the UK map, using a marker pen to draw an upside down triangle with a corner each touching Blackpool, Hull and Warwick.

Adam cleared a space for the laptop as Brian closed the atlas, scuffing his chair around. They both waited for the computer to load the first DVD. Several small images appeared on the screen. Brian leaned in closer, almost with his chin on Adam's shoulder.

'How're we supposed to make anything out?'

'It's a contact sheet, Brian. There are seven cameras.' He expanded the first folder and clicked on the first image. It filled the screen, showing the slip road from a vantage point high atop a lamppost. The road wound around to the car park, illuminated by several globes lighting the approach, the occasional splotch of green. The date and time were stamped in yellow numbers on the bottom right of the screen. Adam pressed the spacebar and advanced the image, but nothing changed save for the time by an increment of one second. He repeated the process until the time had advanced by fifteen seconds. Apart from the shifting shadows and leaves everything remained static.

Adam leaned back in his chair. 'With seven cameras, each with sixty pictures a minute, that's over three thousand images per hour per camera. We could be here for days. On top of that coordinating the timeline between cameras is going to be a nightmare.'

Brian looked blankly from the screen to Adam.

'I tell you what,' Adam offered. 'Why don't you get some drinks and I'll see if I can download something. We can't be the first people that needed to check through multiple CCTV feeds.'

To Adam's surprise Brian wordlessly pulled a handful of change from his pocket. 'What do you want?'

By the time Brian placed two coffees on the table and resumed his co-pilot's position, Adam was busy pressing keys and flicking between images. He waited for Brian to settle.

'The file structure is fairly standard for CCTV. There were lots of programs we can use, I downloaded this one because it's simple to use.'

Adam pressed a key and the images started advancing. Seconds passed with only the yellow numbers and shifting shadows changing. Then the screen flared and a car emerged from the slip road, arcing around in short jerking movements.

'The software works like a normal video player.' He demonstrated fast forward and rewind. The digits were now accelerating like a stop watch, cars appearing as momentary flares on the screen. He pressed pause.

Brian looked from the screen to Adam. 'Seems simple enough but what about the other cameras?'

'That's the clever bit, watch this.' Adam pressed a key and the image switched to a bird's-eye view of the car park, from a camera mounted high above the services entrance. The time stayed the same. He moved through the different cameras, the next inside above the main services doors, looking along the main concourse. It showed the corralled area of tables on the left and the shops on the right, the image frozen with bodies mid-motion. The next camera faced the line of shop entrances. A third camera pointed back along the main concourse to the entrance, the shops on the left, the seated area on the right. The final two feeds were blank screens with the time stamped at the bottom. He switched to the camera covering the shop entrances.

'How come the picture is so clear?' Brian asked.

'It's the quality of these cameras and the lighting. I could make a fair guess at the branding on that woman's handbag if I wanted. They probably rely on the quality to make convictions.'

'The blank screens are dead cameras?'

'Yup, the computer stamps the blank image anyway.' He switched back to the car park slip road.

'Very good.' Brian reached across to his drink. 'So we step through this until Sarah's car shows up.'

'Exactly.' Adam fast-forwarded through the images, a brief glare on the screen heralding the headlights of each new car. They watched through to 17:45. 'I called Sarah about this time,' Adam said, concentrating on the screen. 'She was approaching Delamere.'

The images played on, the time marching forward. Then the screen flared and Adam paused the image at 17:49. The green Rover was frozen on the screen as it turned into the car park, a smaller silver car right behind. 'That's it, that's Sarah and the Rover!' They both leaned in.

'Christ, Adam, she's not being very discreet, could she have got any closer?'

Adam studied the image, hypnotised by the small silhouette of Sarah inside the silver car. 'The Rover turned off the motorway unexpectedly.'

'Take it back a couple seconds,' Brian instructed. 'Think we had the number plate there.' He produced a small worn notepad and a very short pencil from his back pocket. The image skipped back several seconds and then froze. The lettering of the number plate was clearly highlighted against the luminous background. Brian wrote it down. 'That a match for the one she gave you?'

'It is, except before I wasn't sure on the last two digits. We are now. Detective Boer will be pleased about that.'

'Yeah, well we won't get too excited just yet.' Brian looked at the screen. 'Jump to the other camera and see if you can zoom in and get a look at him.' Adam switched to the bird's-eye view above the services, showing a much smaller image of the Rover pulling into a space at the far end of the car park. Sarah's car continued almost completely around, parking diagonally opposite and closer to the services exit. Adam froze the image when the Rover door opened and zoomed in. The Rover grew to a quarter of the screen's size.

Brian fidgeted impatiently. 'Is that as close as you can get?'

'Yup, at this distance the camera has limits like your eyes do.' He zoomed closer and the image broke down into square blocks of colour. He zoomed out and centred on Simon, his head and shoulders above the top of the car door, pink and dark smudges but no defined features. He let the footage play, pausing again as Simon opened the boot, but they were at the wrong angle to see anything. They watched him grow on the screen as he moved towards the camera, into the bright circle of light spotlighting the entrance. Adam paused the image, filling the screen with Simon's head and shoulders.

'Bingo!' he said. 'That's the difference we get with him closer. The only detail we can't see is the colour of his eyes.' They both stared at the face.

Brian spoke first. 'Let's hope Sarah's following the right car, this guy looks like butter wouldn't melt in his mouth. Big though, hard to take down. Follow him inside.' Brian copied the time stamp into his notebook, 17:53:37

Adam switched to the inside camera. The top and rear of Simon's head appeared, walking straight over to a mini arcade on the right. He positioned himself and turned so he could look back at the entrance.

'Stop!' Brian instructed. 'Guess he is the right guy.'

'There's a doubt?' Adam asked.

'There's always doubt. No point us tracking the wrong guy because he caught Sarah's eye at the right moment. So we make sure, and that my friend,' he nodded at the image, 'is pretty damn sure.'

Adam studied the screen. 'He looks like he's waiting for someone?'

'He is, he's waiting for someone to search him out as they walk through the entrance. Keep your eye out for Sarah.' Adam nodded and fast-forwarded. The time ticked to 18:01:47. Simon stepped from the arcade and into the services, moving through the crowd.

'Must have thought he was in the clear. Take us back outside to the main camera, see what your wife's been up to.' He looked down at his notes. 'Back to the mug shot of Simon.'

Adam flicked between cameras to the car park, playing the images in reverse, people walking fast backward. He stopped at 17:53:35 and then set it playing. They both watched Sarah's stationary car, partially blocked by the yellow time stamp. After a few seconds a small shadowed shape emerged, moving away from the services around the edge of the car park.

'Christ, what's she doing?'

'Checking out the Rover,' Brian stated. 'She's got nerve, that's for sure.'

Adam watched Sarah peer into the Rover, then disappear from view behind it, as if she were kneeling, and then seconds later she stood and walked towards the services. 'I told her to be careful,' he exclaimed, plaintively.

'You should pay attention. She's doing what she had to.'

Adam let this pass, mostly because a building sense of dread rendered him mute. They were looking at images from over twelve hours ago. He paused playback as Sarah emerged into the light of the services. He zoomed in and centred on his wife's head and shoulders, the light picking out her features. A chill crawled up his spine. She was looking directly into the camera, through time, right at him. There was nothing hopeful in her eyes any more, just narrow determination.

Brian struggled to pull his eyes from her face. He saw more than determination. To him she looked driven and haunted. Sarah Sawacki was a very interesting woman.

Adam forced himself to switch to the third camera inside, looking back towards the entrance. They watched Sarah walk towards them, tracking her progress through each internal camera, to the bagel bar just as Simon disappeared into the toilets.

'He didn't even see her,' Brian said. 'He wasn't even looking. Fast-forward to when he comes out.'

'What exactly are we looking for?' Adam asked.

'Anything at all. Anything that might tell us more about this guy, anything.'

Adam fast-forwarded to the point where Simon re-emerged. 'Was that almost ten minutes he was in there?'

Brian compared times. 'Eleven minutes twenty-eight seconds to be precise.'

'What was he doing?'

'I dunno. Taking a dump? Can you see anything different, same clothes?'

'It all looks the same.' Adam rewound to a full image of Simon emerging, illuminated by harsh light outside the toilets. 'I can make out detail on the T-shirt, like a faded logo.' He filled the screen with Simon's chest and the faint outline of a logo, changing the colours of the image, darkening and lightening, moving slowly between different contrasts and hues, the logo sometimes clearer and then fading.

Brian tilted his head. 'Is that three lions?'

Adam nodded. 'Looks like it. The light's picking out old glue or discolouration in the fabric. You might not notice stood next to him. That's about the best I can do right now.'

'Three lions isn't going to get us far. Where'd he go after?'

They watched Simon turn from the toilets back to the main concourse and into a shop, switching cameras and seeing him stand by a rack of magazines. Adam paused the image as Simon reached for a magazine.

Brian scuffed his chair closer. 'What magazine is he picking up?'

Adam jogged the image backwards and forwards, Simon now frozen with the magazine in hand. It gave them an angled view of the cover. He enlarged it on the screen, a blue cover centred with two smudged shapes of white. One letter of the title was clear enough to guess at.

They both leaned in, shoulder to shoulder. 'Is that a bird?' Brian squinted.

Adam did the same. 'Not sure, looks more like a boat, maybe a yacht if that letter is an H.'

Brian sat back and blinked. 'I think you're right. A yachting magazine?' He pulled open the atlas. The top two points of his upside down triangle were Blackpool and Hull. 'I guess they'd have marinas. Let's see what else he picks up.'

Simon kept looking at the same magazine. Adam let the images run in real time but it was difficult to see whether he was flicking through it or actually reading. Then Simon stepped across to the till and paid for the magazine and then immediately exited into the food court.

Brian closed the atlas on his lap. 'Swing over to Sarah, see what she's up to.'

Adam did, finding Sarah hunched over a table with a hand to her ear. Two cups of coffee and her bag were sitting on the table. The time stamp was now 18:18:22. 'She must be talking to me.' Adam said, watching a ginger-haired man pass beside her table, then two frames of him reaching across it and then away.

'Pause that.' Brian said, thoughtfully. 'That must be one of the guys that took her phone.'

Adam forwarded through the images. 'She said some guy knocked her drink over.' It occurred to him as he watched that this was their last conversation. The time stamp now read 18:23:01. They watched Sarah stand and step onto the main concourse.

'Switch to the camera above the entrance.' Adam did. The seats were now on the left, the shops and arcade on the right. The first frame showed a smudge of ginger at the bottom. As they stepped through the images it moved towards Sarah.

'Slow it down. There's another one somewhere, probably behind her.'

'What's happening?' Adam asked.

Brian looked sideways at him and then back at the screen. 'Must be where she lost the phone.'

They watched the ginger-haired man walk into Sarah, then a dark-haired man pull free Sarah's bag. He ran straight into Simon and then spreadeagled on the floor. Simon handed Sarah her bag.

'Now that's interesting,' Brian said.

Adam was incredulous. 'Are we really sure he's the right guy?'

The images kept playing and Simon turned away. 'Oh Christ!' Adam said, watching Sarah and Simon link hands. She looked so small next to him.

Brian grinned. 'I guess this is where she got his name, she doesn't mess about. Jump back outside and fast-forward.'

Adam's finger paused over the key and then he switched to the bird's-eye view outside, watching Simon make his way to the Rover. The headlights came on and the car reversed. It looped around the top of the screen and down the right side, passing behind Sarah's car then off the screen. Her headlights blinked on and she followed.

Adam began rewinding the images. 'I'll see if we can track the pickpockets.'

'Don't bother.' Brian stood, stuffing the maps into the bag with the atlas.

'But…'

'But what?'

'They attacked Sarah, we should see where they went.'

'Leave that to the police. It's not important. Time for Warwick, Mr Sawacki.' He held out his hand. 'Keys.'

'Keys?'

'The car keys, come on.'

'You're not insured, Brian, I can't let you drive.'

Brian laughed out loud, the sound echoing into the ceiling. It was the first time Adam had heard him laugh.

'What's so funny?'

'Adam, you're going to be busy going over every square inch of every image we just looked at. And then checking that T-shirt logo some more. And then you're going to do the whole lot again and then again.'

'But, you aren't insured.'

'This isn't your neatly ordered world, remember? It's the one where the good-looking Samaritan drove away with my daughter stuffed in his boot and your wife following in hot pursuit. I promise to drive carefully.'

THIRTY-TWO

S arah heard a distant metallic sound and then the close rumble of heavy concrete in front of her. It was the only wall, she had decided, where a door could be. A thin sliver of natural light crept into the small space and she pulled her legs back and shifted into a squat on the mattress. The door was two breeze blocks thick, edging further into the room. The gap between each block was filled with hardened foam, the same between the blocks and the plywood panelling. For soundproofing, she imagined. The door stopped and a thick arm moved into the space, pushing the block sideways, the muscles in the arm taut with the effort.

The block came to rest and Simon's large frame filled the entrance, almost as formidable as the concrete door. Then he moved back, disappearing from view, leaving a square of open space. She was looking into the garage, *but where was she?* She fought every instinct to run for the opening, forcing herself to stay where she was. He reappeared with the girl in his arms, ducking then shuffling through and towards her. He kneeled and leaned forward, lowering the girl onto the mattress.

Sarah tightened her grip beneath the blanket, around the leg of the small footstool. She lifted it a little so the blanket fell free and then with every ounce of strength, swung it around in an arc defined by the low ceiling, aiming at the back of his head. Her fury exploded with the physical action, the effort forcing a low growl. Simon shifted his weight too late in reflex to the sudden movement, the stool catching the side of his head, raking his ear and bouncing hard off his shoulder. She immediately swung back around, aiming another blow, eyes wide, the growl turning to a scream. That was stopped short by the flat of his hand as it pistoned outwards, smacking into her chest and sending her sprawling across the room. She thumped into the wall, books from the shelves falling around and onto her.

Winded, she sucked in air, desperately looking for the stool. But he was already moving towards her, narrow paths of blood winding darkly down the side of his face and the stubble on his chin. She braced herself for a violent reaction but there was no evidence of anger in his eyes, just an incredulous curiosity that verged on compassion. He leaned in, his shadow moving over her body. He studied her, taking the whole of her in.

'Sarah Sawacki, why did you have to follow me?' A statement more than a question, asked in the same soft accent.

She blinked back at him, her white shirt rising and falling as she collected her breath. He wiped blood from his chin and continued. 'In four hours last night you created more problems for me than I've had in the last four years. That is something to be admired, at least by me. Sadly not by anyone else here. You're lucky the brothers are busy, fixing the problems you have created. Hakan is not much better though, not so much a lover of pain, just of answers.'

Sarah breathed in as if to say something, but he stopped her with an index finger over his own lips. He picked up the wooden stool and looked back at her. 'I really wish you had not followed me.' And then he shuffled back to the gap and ducked out. Seconds later his face reappeared. 'You can come out by yourself or I can come and get you.'

She did not move. He had not laid a single speculative finger on her, nor had she seen the realised opportunity chase across his eyes. She had seen something, was it regret? Panic bubbled heavy in her stomach as she thought through her options, long enough for him to stoop back down and only then did she move, slowly crawling towards him, past Andrea asleep on the mattress in the corner.

The door was part of the garage wall, opening into the room from beneath the work bench. She had to crawl through the opening and out from under the bench before she could stand, realising the space must somehow be claimed from the kitchen. She brushed herself down and watched Simon, keen to know how the door closed in the vain hope she might figure out a way to open it from inside. He leaned over the bench and pulled free a metal cable attached to a hook on the wall. The wall was also home to saws, lines of screwdrivers, spanners and various other tools. She liked the idea of a saw, but to reach them she had to get past him. Otherwise, save for a stack of yachting magazines, the garage was clean and empty. Cleaner than any garage she had ever seen.

Simon glanced at her as if assessing her intentions, pushing his hand into a thick glove and pulling the metal cable towards him, as if doing a bicep curl. The muscles in his arm and across his body bulged, stretching the material of his T-shirt, now stained with blood from his head. The door slowly inched back across the opening and then towards them, finally dropping into place with a heavy thud. If she had not just watched it close, she would never know it was there.

'You're so clever,' she said.

He smiled thinly and laid the glove and cable on the workbench, before ushering her out of the garage, through a hallway and into a living room, closing the doors behind them. The living room stretched away further than it was wide, a brown sofa on the right. On the left white vertical blinds reflected most of the daylight back out to the day.

In the middle of the room was a plain wooden chair, on the carpet beside the chair a bag of black plastic cable ties. Her stomach turned and she stopped. Simon's hand clamped on her shoulder and directed her around and down onto the chair.

'You can struggle,' he said, 'in which case I will hold you down. Or you can just let me do this. Either way it's going to happen.'

She felt a sob rise and checked it, she wanted to howl and fight but she could do neither. She let Simon do his work, wincing as he pulled the plastic ties tight, the whole time looking at the sofa and the short man who sat on it.

At first she did not recognise him although she knew the kind of man he was in an instant. He was white, with broad shoulders in a dark leather jacket. His hair darkly dyed and balding, his face square and pinched and heavily creased, his small eyes roving up and down her body. He was a complete contrast to Simon in every way. And then she realised he was the man who had found her outside. He could not be more than five foot five. The man Simon called Hakan.

Simon finished with the cuffs and walked out through the double doors. Moments later she heard a tap running, imagining him washing the blood from his face. It gave her a fleeting sense of satisfaction.

'What is your name?' asked Hakan.

She kept her mouth closed, trying to flex her ankles and wrists to attain a level of acceptable pain.

'What is your name?' he repeated.

'You know my name.'

'Do I?'

'Yes you do. Your pet knows it, so must you.'

He scratched at his eyebrow, his eyes on her. 'But I want you to tell me.'

'I will not.'

'I think you will.'

'I will not.'

Hakan pushed himself off the sofa and stood. He took one step towards her and brought his open palm around hard across her cheek. The blow snapped her head around so hard she felt a pain in her neck, her eyes rolling past unconscious and back again. She tasted blood in her mouth and he sat back down.

'I think you will Sarah.'

She stared at him with defiant eyes, but defeat sat just behind them. She did not want to be hit again, not like that.

'My name is Sarah, Sarah Sawacki.'

'Good Sarah. That is good. Of course I knew your name. Now we both know the rules and the consequences for not following them. You must understand I have learned a lot about you in the past hours. You do not know what I know. So you must pay careful attention to the truth.'

She gathered the blood and saliva in her mouth and spat it onto the carpet in front of her. Then carefully watched his fingers shift along his thighs. He did not stand, which she was grateful for.

His eyes moved from the carpet to her face. 'You will tell me everything I want to know, Sarah. If you do you may see the next hour. I understand you want to go home, to see your husband and live your life. This may be possible with the truth.'

She probed her tongue carefully around her mouth, checking all teeth were accounted for. 'I have no interest in going home, not without the girl.'

He shook his head, a slow dramatic movement. 'Then I am sorry for you Sarah. This will not happen. The child is going away to live another life. One where she will be cared for and looked after. She will be the focus of attention and much regarded. She will have a better life than she has now, and we know a lot about the life she has left behind.'

127

Her sense of futility and his talk of Andrea's wonderful future built an anger inside her despite her best efforts to close it off. A hatred for this man that she fell short of expressing. 'You're a sick man.'

He smiled as if receiving a compliment. 'Quite possibly. Now tell me, Sarah, why did you follow Simon? What did you see, Sarah?'

Despite her anger, her desire not to be hit again and the relevance of the information moulded her answer.

'I didn't see anything. I followed him on a hunch. The girl disappeared into the alley. I went into the alley and saw *him*.' She nodded at the double doors. As she did Simon reappeared, holding a damp towel to the side of his head. His eyes dropped to the small splatter of blood at her feet. He looked at her and Hakan and then with the corner of his mouth upturned he kneeled, using the towel to clean the carpet.

Hakan waited until Simon had finished before he spoke again. 'So, Sarah?'

'So I followed him.'

'That is it?'

'The box he carried was wrong. It just looked wrong. It was too heavy for what should have been inside.'

'And do you follow any suspicious persons?'

'No, not any person.' She paused, realising her thirst. She looked across at Simon, now leaning against the door frame, and then to Hakan. 'Can I have some water? I don't feel well.'

'I am not surprised. I think we can manage some water in return for cooperation.' He nodded and Simon returned with a full glass, patiently holding it to her lips as he tipped it slowly into her mouth. She gulped it down, some of it escaping down the corners of her mouth, running down her neck onto her shirt. It tasted like nectar. When the glass was empty Simon stepped back and sat on the arm of the sofa.

Hakan continued. 'Now we shall proceed. You followed because you had no better explanation for where the girl could be. And you did not see our friend here until you saw him with the box.'

'Yes.'

'Good, Sarah. Hambury has many car parks. Why was your car parked in this one?'

'We always park there. It's why I was waiting at the end of the alley.'

'You then followed my friend to the services. Who did you ring, Sarah, who did you call on your way to this services and what did you tell them?'

She hesitated for a second, weighing again the value of the information over its cost to her.

'I rang my husband, of course, I told him the Rover's number plate.'

Hakan smiled. 'Of course you did, Sarah, and what was he to do with it?'

She answered honestly. 'Go to the police.'

'And did he?'

'I sincerely hope so.'

'You do not know?'

'No, I lost my phone.'

'Ahhh yes, the missing phone. How fortunate we have an eyewitness in this very room. Can you tell me, Sarah, why your husband would be off reporting number plates to the police and not jumping in his car to rescue or even stop you?'

'He doesn't own one.'

'He does not have a car? You do not strike me as a woman who attracts a poor man, it is impossible to think he would not have a car.'

'He just doesn't, he catches the train or works at home.'

'Works at home?' He turned to Simon, adding drama to incredulous, and back again to Sarah. 'What a comfortable cosy little country this is. What a lucky man.'

'He is, but then he is a good man. People trust him.'

'Any man deserving of your trust must be good, he must also be a man who makes good money. These men all have nice cars, in this country for sure.'

'He used to have a car, he sold it.'

'Did he now. Sold it to give you the home you wanted. The loyal man. Do you find, Sarah, that men do as you ask? Do you expect us to fall for your wide eyes?' He shuffled to the sofa edge and planted his foot on the floor. 'Do you think you can be the woman and turn our minds?'

She was confused, unsure what he was getting at. Then she saw the movement of his arm, bracing herself for the blow. This time there was real venom in the strike, rocking the chair precariously back on its rear legs. Spotted white filled her vision, blotting out the colour and then everything went black.

When she opened eyes she was staring at her lap, blood dripping onto her thighs.

'You understand, Sarah. I have no patience for a woman's tricks and

129

with Simon you are barking at the wrong tree. It is not women his eyes seek. So if you need something you will ask, the answer will be yes or no. We do not like the woman's tricks here. Understand?'

She didn't, not really. She moved her head up and down anyway, small careful movements while staring at her lap, tears diluting the splotches of blood on her jeans.

'Good.' Hakan did not return to the sofa. Instead he began pacing slow anti-clockwise circles around the chair.

'So now we know your husband is the loyal man, off talking to the police. You know not what happened, he did not call to tell?'

'No, I lost my phone.'

'After the police, he would do what in your absence, knowing you have not called for so long?'

'He, he would wait at home for me to call.'

'You are sure of this?'

Sarah licked the blood from her bottom lip. 'I'm certain.'

'He would not play the hero and come looking for you?'

She shook her head. 'He wouldn't know how. He would do what he can for the police and wait.'

Hakan slapped his hands jubilantly against his thighs. It made her flinch.

'Then it seems your husband must still be with the police. I hope he is entertaining them with his pleas of innocence.'

'What do you mean?'

'Well, your husband is not at your home because my two most reliable colleagues have been there. They took a good look around your cosy place and the fine things you have there, especially the nice picture of you on the beach. But no sign of Mr. Sawacki. If we are to believe you there is only one other place this loyal husband can be.'

The thought of Hakan or anyone he knew in her home repulsed and angered her, then it dawned on her what Hakan was saying, that Adam must still be at the police station. It made her feel relieved that he was safe and out of the way.

'So now, Sarah, that leaves us with the small matter of why you really followed my friend. Why were you really outside the alley? Why does a woman come so far on a hunch?' Again Hakan paused for effect, enjoying his drama. 'You must tell the truth Sarah, it is not just your own future you must now consider but your husband's too. I can easily set my friends in search of him if you do not.'

THIRTY-THREE

The journey to Northampton brought Boer and Ferreira to a freshly built suburbia of three-storey houses, the wide drives and brown brickwork complementing bright painted fascia and double garage doors. Boer carefully sat himself on a low wall and watched Ferreira as she knocked and moved between neighbouring doors. Eventually a figure lingered in a doorway longer than it took to glance at a badge and shake their head. Ferreira asked questions Boer could not hear, but knew were focused around *Where are the family in number fifty-two?*

Ferreira thanked the neighbour and walked back across the wide road, her olive jacket flapping open. She rested a hand on her hip as she stopped in front of Boer. 'What're you looking at?'

He gave her an embarrassed smile. 'Something in my eye. What did they say?'

She kept her eyes on him for a second and then took a look at her notes. 'They're at church, they go every week.'

'Really?'

'Yep.' Ferreira checked her watch. 'Only the mother and kids though. The husband works away a lot, at least that's what the neighbour seems to think. They should be back any time.'

Boer scraped his heel across the pavement. 'I don't get that.'

'What don't you get?'

'You get two constables banging on your door Saturday night and you find out your daughter is missing. So the whole family decamp to church the next morning?'

She let her breath out slowly. 'Faith is important at times like this Fran, you know that.'

Boer shook his head but said nothing, a large car pulling their attention to the road. Both watched hopefully as it approached, gleaming in the midday sun. They looked back at each other as it passed by.

'What else did the neighbour say?' he asked.

'Not much. They keep to themselves, occasional conversation. A couple of the local girls sometimes babysit during the week. The mother sings in the church…'

The throaty throb of an engine chased along the street, drawing their attention to a dark shape turning into the road.

'What the hell is that?' Boer asked.

'No idea, it's big, some kind of truck.'

It drew closer and a window buzzed down. The female driver leaned over and called down, her voice competing against the engine. Boer looked at Ferreira. 'What did she say?'

'I think she wants us to move our car, we're blocking her drive.'

They both looked at their car and then at the drive. Ferreira had left space enough for a lorry to reverse in. She pulled the keys from her handbag and raised an eyebrow at Boer.

He followed the truck into the drive, watching as the double garage door smoothly opened and the truck came to a stop centrally inside. Silence flooded the space and a woman jumped down. The word prim sprang to Boer's mind. She deposited a young girl onto the garage floor and was about to reach back when another child leapt down onto the concrete, this one older, maybe seven or eight, with eyes only for Boer. She marched straight towards him, ignoring a half-shouted rebuke from her mother.

'Hello, my name is Emma. I bet you're a policeman. Have you found my sister yet? Mummy says Brian made her run away. Brian is my sister's daddy but he's not mine.'

'Emma!' The mother clamped a hand over the girl's shoulder and flashed Boer a fraught smile. 'I'm sorry, bold as can be.' She stroked the child's head. The smaller girl clung to her mother's leg, shyly watching Boer while gnawing at a small toy.

He glanced across at the garage. 'Hell of a truck you have there. Bet you get a lot of respect on the road.'

'It's not a truck, actually, it's a Hummer. And yes, there are some amazingly bad drivers out there. My children's safety is of the utmost importance to me.' She gave the approaching Ferreira a studied look and then did the same for Boer. Her mouth did not entirely conceal her assessment. 'And who might you be?'

He pushed a hand into his jacket and produced his ID, which she took from him.

'I'm Detective Inspector Boer and my colleague here is Detective Sergeant Ferreira. We're here to talk with Elizabeth Smith, would that be you?'

She studied the ID, flipping it over before handing it back. 'Yes it would. If you're here about my daughter then I have already spent a considerable amount of time talking with the police, last night and this morning.' A thought suddenly occurred to her, she looked at him hopefully. 'You have news?'

'I'm afraid not. We're hoping to get a first-hand understanding of your daughter. Anything we can learn about her habits. What she is like, her strengths, her state of mind. What she does when staying at her father's, her friends there?'

The woman blew out her cheeks in a half laugh. 'I take it you've spoken to her father?'

Boer shook his head. 'We will talk to him later. It would be very helpful if we could get your perspective.'

'That's a shame. Andrea's just like her father, almost as stubborn and just as wilful.' Her eyes wandered to the windows of her immediate neighbours. 'You'd better come inside.' With that she flourished a hand at the garage and shepherded the two girls towards the house. Boer watched the garage door slowly descend and turned sideways, winking at Ferreira as they both followed the mother into the house.

THIRTY-FOUR

Simon shifted his weight on the arm on the sofa, watching Hakan pace around the chair, pulling and picking at the truth, his arms cutting small movements through the air. He was not sure Hakan's intention had been to kill the woman but it looked that way now. After the next blow she would trip in and out of consciousness. If he hit her while she was unconscious the force would snap her neck.

Simon did not share Hakan's ease with death. Not from any emotional or moral standpoint, but simply because he did not like killing. He didn't have time for ghosts or gods, but each time he had killed it felt as if something fluttered free and became part of the burden he carried. He was in no hurry to do so again.

Now he was witnessing the woman's last minutes. He should probably leave but could not. Was there a flicker of regret? There was something. She presented a challenge he had not known for a long time. There was something in her relentless desire to follow him that neither of them could comprehend. What had it taken for her to sit in the dark of that small room, to take her fear and mould it into a weapon? He had seen it in her eyes, she was not trying to knock him out with the stool, but erase him. That took a certain state of mind.

Hakan stopped and slapped a hand on his thigh, the woman flinched and Hakan reversed the direction of his pacing, increasing his speed, questioning her over and over. The woman's eyes wide with anger and apprehension at the prospect of a sudden descending hand.

Neither of them believed she had seen anything, she could not have. Her opportunities were limited. His planning and attention to detail had been meticulous. Baldur had sourced the girl and had been ingenious in

134

his methods. He'd given Simon the detail and there had been a lot of it. Taking the girl had been simple because of what he knew. Except now it was not.

At Delamere the pickpocket ran into him, what was he to do but give the woman back her bag? He had forgotten her before climbing into the Rover, oblivious throughout the journey. It had been difficult though not to take a look at Delamere, to not touch his prize. By Stratford the nagging need had turned to writhing want and he could not help himself. To feel her breath on his fingers and her beating heart beneath his hand, so beautiful. How was he to know the woman was parked in some farmyard making calls? How had she managed that, to find a phone in the middle of nowhere?

However you looked at it, everything added up to chance and nothing more. They had problems now but Baldur and his brother were solving them. Sarah Sawacki was certainly not part of some organised front attempting to prise away Hakan's high-earning commodity. That had been tried and viciously defeated on two occasions. Sarah Sawacki was simply unlucky. There was something about her though, that pulled at something inside of him.

Hakan looked over at him, smiling and shrugging his broad shoulders. The woman was now crying, her tears adding to the damp patches on her shirt. The questioning moved to the detail of the call at the farmhouse, covering the last of the angles. For a few seconds she looked confused in the haze of pain, trying to recall how they might know and then remembering the indignity of her home and life laid bare.

From somewhere deep inside of him a voice whispered a tentative *Stop*. But what could he stop and why? If Hakan did not kill her then Baldur would. Once you moved beyond the question of what brought her here, what was there? She was still a woman.

He shifted again on the arm of the sofa, impassively watching. Hakan was now chasing the final details, the woman mumbling, barely comprehensible, made to repeat the answers again and again. They knew all they needed to know. Hakan was just biding his time. His hand descended as he stepped around her, the movement disguised. She might have thought the shift in tone meant the ordeal was over, it caught her unaware. The blow was the hardest so far, the chair and the woman spinning and toppling onto the carpet. Hakan grinned at him as he lifted the chair upright, the woman's chin rolling onto her chest. Hakan ran his fingers through her matted hair, taking a fistful and pulling her head back. He opened her eyelids and looked at dilated pupils. She would never know consciousness again.

Stop, said the voice again, louder this time.

But why? She was of no lasting interest. *Was not the challenge she presented interest enough? Look at her! Something innocent, no conceit. Something of what you used to be.*

Hakan let her head drop to her chest and flexed his fingers as an athlete might before a prize-winning feat. He swung the palm of his hand around in an arc for the final time, angled upwards as if batting a home run.

'*STOP!*

Hakan looked around and up at Simon with wide-eyed disbelief, the expectation of death raging in his eyes, Simon's hand wrapped around his wrist. 'What are you doing, Simon? Let go of me immediately.'

'Stop this Hakan, enough.'

'How dare you!' Hakan swung his free fist around at Simon, but he was off balance and a foot short of being a physical threat. Simon locked his arm under Hakan's and used the palm of his hand to push him down onto the sofa.

'She will die, Hakan, but not like this, I will take her out on the boat. I still have tests to do.'

Hakan looked back up at him. 'You are a crazy man, Simon. You would not do this with the brothers here. She has been nothing but trouble and you want to keep her alive?'

'It'll just be for a day.'

Hakan let his frustration ebb before coolly pushing off the sofa, making Simon step back. He straightened his jacket.

'I see my faith in you needs reappraising. There have been too many mistakes here already. We will talk about this before you leave. If your needs get the better of you, remember you will have the child for three months when you sail. I do not need her screaming this place down. Understood?'

Simon nodded and without further word Hakan brushed past him to the front door. For several minutes after the door closed Simon stood still, contemplating what he had done, thinking through what it meant for him and Hakan. Still puzzled by *why?* It had been an impulse, driven by some buried instinct.

He walked through to the kitchen, retrieved a small knife and carefully cut through the cuffs. He let Sarah slump forward into his arms, lifting her with her head rested against his chest, carrying her through the dining room and up the stairs.

THIRTY-FIVE

The reception room contained two decadent sofas that matched the room's calming hues of earth brown and cream, the sofas facing each other across a tree stump now sculpted and polished into a table. Boer lowered himself onto one of the sofas and Ferreira sat beside him.

'Wow! One day I'm going to find me a rich man and have a house like this.'

'I thought you didn't attract rich men?'

'I don't. I'll abandon my Catholic ways, change my style of dress, show a little more cleavage.'

Boer nodded silent acknowledgement.

She directed his gaze to the wall. 'What do you think that cost?'

They both stared at the large rectangle of canvas that dominated the room. To Boer it looked like someone had spent hours hand-writing notes on lined paper, set them on fire, thrown water on them and then stuck what was left onto the canvas. And then splattered red and yellow paint on top.

'God knows, a lot probably.'

From the kitchen they could hear the distant echo of plates and crockery being pulled from a dishwasher. The insistent high pitched voice of a pleading child eventually cut off tersely by the mother, followed by hushed rapid fire dialogue. Two sets of light feet tramped up the stairs and across the floor above.

'You want me to lead?' Ferreira asked.

He nodded. 'I need a few words at the outset.'

'OK.' She retrieved her notepad and pen from her bag, crossing her trousered legs. They both waited in silence, their eyes moving from neatly ordered curtains to polished surfaces and rows of framed smiling faces. One of the pictures caught Boer's eye. He struggled to his feet and picked up the photo.

'My God.'

'What?' asked Ferreira.

He showed her the photograph. 'Who?'

'Well, my super detective powers say she's not one of the girls here, I would say that has to be Andrea.'

He frowned back at her. 'Look harder.'

Ferreira stepped over to him and took the picture from his hand, studying it. She handed it back. 'Sorry boss. I'm struggling.'

He looked at the picture. It radiated from the eyes. 'Don't you see?'

Ferreira shook her head, then frowned. 'You mean Sarah Sawacki?'

'Yes, look at it. Sarah saw Andrea and saw herself…'

The faintest noise from the hall diverted their attention. The mother stood in the doorway with a tray held in both hands. 'Sawacki?' she said as she stepped into the room. 'I haven't heard that name before?'

Ferreira gave Boer a meaningful look that he avoided, carefully placing the photo back onto the polished surface. He and Ferreira sat down in unison, waiting on the mother as she distributed cups and a glass of water for Boer. She finally folded herself with precise movements onto the sofa opposite.

'Your daughter Emma,' Boer began, 'seems to think Andrea has run away. I have no idea how that came to be but I want you to know before we go any further that nothing points to your daughter running away.'

'But she cou…'

'No, Mrs Smith.' Boer's voice was harsh. 'We have an eyewitness who saw your daughter just before she disappeared.'

'You do?'

'Yes, we are not sure of a good many things but from what the eyewitness saw, Andrea running away is not a consideration.'

The mother sat motionless, staring round-eyed at some space through and beyond Boer, before focusing back to the moment. She made as if to stand but slumped back onto the sofa. 'My baby has to come back.' Tears glistened in her eyes and immediately spilled onto her cheeks.

Ferreira cut in. 'Mrs Smith. I am so very sorry. It was careless of us to assume you had been told the circumstances of your daughter's disappearance. Doubly so that you should receive this information so bluntly. I apologise on behalf of us both.' Ferreira let the pause and the woman's sniffing drag on long enough for Boer to register her annoyance.

'The fact is, the eyewitness story has been attested by several sources and we are well on our way to making fast progress.' Ferreira waited to see whether the mother's tears would abate but her shoulders started to shake. She leaned over the arm of the sofa, produced a box of tissues and started dabbing at her eyes.

'So if we could possibly ask you to tell us anything that might be useful about Andrea and her friends, her habits and her relationship with her father, that would be incredibly helpful.' Ferreira stopped talking and waited, too angry with Boer to give him the satisfaction of a glare.

The mother kept dabbing at her eyes, the sniffs abated and she slowly pulled herself together. She leaned forward with her forearms resting on her knees, her mascara a little smudged, tissues hanging from her hands.

'He's a complete mess, you know that?'

'Pardon me?'

'Brian, Andrea's father. He's a complete waste of space. I wouldn't be surprised if he was involved somehow. He seems to have little regard for his daughter's welfare. You should speak to him. You will learn more that way than wasting your time with me.'

Ferreira tested her pen on a corner of her notepad and noted the date and time in the other corner. 'What do you mean, "he was involved"?'

'Well, I don't mean exactly. But somehow I bet his lifestyle and the people he mixes with have resulted in all this.'

'You can't be more specific?'

'No, I don't know,' her voice faltered.

Ferreira decided to change tack. 'What about when you first met? He must have caught your eye at some point.'

'Sorry?'

'When you first met Andrea's father?'

The mother snorted. 'I was young and extremely naive. When I look back I'm amazed I saw anything in him. But I grew up in Colchester, it's teeming with soldiers. Paratroopers are the best of the best, a real catch to an innocent seventeen-year-old. Brian was a paratrooper. Did you know that about him?'

Ferreira nodded and started drawing a small circle on the left side of the page.

'Well, one thing led to another. If you got married you got a house. I fell pregnant straight away. Andrea was almost six weeks premature.'

Beside her Boer stifled a cough and reached for his glass of water. Ferreira drew a bigger circle around the one she already had.

'But it didn't work out?' Ferreira asked.

The mother laughed, a short sound that rose quickly in pitch. 'Do you know what he did?' Ferreira shook her head although the mother was not cueing on her reaction. 'Well I'll tell you. He woke me up in the middle of the night with Andrea still a baby in her cot. He told me he couldn't give me the life I wanted, that he would do his bit for Andrea and then left. The life I wanted! Just like that, pulled on his jeans and walked right out the front door. In the middle of the night, can you believe a man would do that?'

Ferreira looked sympathetically back at her. 'He has at least kept his word regarding Andrea.'

'What do you mean? He's a disaster. I don't recall the last time he kept his word, to me or Andrea.'

'I mean he has always provided for her. Our records show he has missed only two support payments in the last nine years. And those missed payments were in the six months following his discharge from the army.'

'Yeah well, there's a big difference between regular payments and contributing. I've applied for a full financial declaration four times in the last two years. But each time I get a letter back saying he has been correctly assessed.'

She looked at them as if they were meant to be appalled.

'Which means?' Ferreira asked.

'Well it is obvious, he's lying of course! I expect his black buddy is fiddling the books somehow. I'd bet he blows the rest on drink, he has a problem you know.'

'Did Andrea tell you that?'

'The alcohol, no. She never tells me anything about him or her weekends in that place. And to be honest I'm probably better off not knowing. It takes me almost an hour to disinfect her when she comes back, you know. He seems to think children love passive smoking and grow healthy and strong purely on a diet of sweets and pizza.'

'So you can say you know a little about what Andrea does while staying with him?'

'I suppose so, she's usually very guarded. I'm sure he warns her against me. I pray to God he watch over her.' Ferreira's pen busily moved across the page.

'You pray to God that Brian watch over Andrea?' Boer asked. 'Or you pray that God watch over her?' He took another sip of water.

The mother looked at him, puzzled, her mouth curled down at one end. Then she returned her attention to Ferreira.

'So it would be fair to say, Mrs Smith, that you have little knowledge of your daughter's routine yesterday or at any time during her visits.' Ferreira's pen was poised.

The mother nodded. 'She was with her father and that's about all I know. He turns up Fridays after school in his stupid little security car and brings her back Sunday tea time.'

'His security car?'

'Yes, Ode… whatever security or something. It's owned by the black buddy. Ali, that's his name. There were three of them that served together, thick as thieves. Brian and Mike were always in trouble. Ali was the father figure, keeping them in line. It's why Brian now lives in Hambury. Ali is just about the only person that will put up with him.'

'And Brian's friend Mike?'

'Got himself killed in Helmand. Brian was injured at the same time. It's why he was discharged. He gets disability in addition to the pension, you know.'

Ferreira caught up with her notes, trying to imagine what Boer was thinking next to her. 'So they served together in the Paratroop regiment?'

'Two Para, yes. They used to tell the most amazing stories. It all seemed perfectly likely back when I was younger, but you just think to yourself they made it all up to charm innocent girls like me.'

Boer stifled another cough but found himself sipping an empty glass and struggling to keep the cough under control. He shifted himself to the edge of the sofa, gasping. For a few painful seconds both women sat watching him before the mother whisked the glass into the kitchen, quickly returning with the glass frosted and full of water.

'Sip this, the cold will help.'

It did, soothing his throat and spreading a welcome chill down through his stomach. 'Thank you. That was very kind.'

She folded herself back onto the sofa. 'You really ought to see a doctor about that cough, you know, you don't look well at all.'

'I know. Can't seem to shift it. But thank you, this has helped.'

Ferreira waited for Boer to get comfortable and then continued. 'Can you tell us anything more about this Ali?'

'Not much. You'd know him if you saw him in the street, the sort that blocks the sun. Nigerian parents I think. From what I hear he has a finger in just about every pie.'

'What does that mean, every pie?'

'Well you hear all sorts of stories. And like I said he's almost a father figure to Brian, so it's difficult seeing the wood from the trees. Popular thought is he made his money in internet porn and prostitution.'

'How did you hear about that?'

'Friends of friends. I still talk to people back home. The regiment is a close community even after you move on, word gets around.'

'It certainly does.' Ferreira glanced around the room. 'At least now you seem to have built a good life here.'

'Yes, although there's always more to be achieved of course.' She followed Ferreira's gaze and appraised with a measure of satisfaction, 'Kevin is a wonderful husband. Our faith and hard work has taken us a long way. But that's not to say life is easy.'

'It never is, Mrs Smith. Your husband is something to do with IT?'

'He runs his own company with twenty men working for him.' The mother's answer was heavy with pride. 'It's mostly networks and cabling, media systems and the like. With so many jumping on the bandwagon it's twice as competitive. He has to work all hours.'

'Your husband is working away this weekend? When will he be back? We would like to talk with him.'

Uncertainty briefly shifted across her face. 'I told him to stay put.'

'But his stepdaughter is missing?'

'I know, but it has taken him a long time to get this contract. It would be jeopardised if he left now. I have faith, Detective. My daughter will come back to me, she has got to.'

Ferreira tried to contain her shock. 'Mrs Smith, your husband might be able to help, tell us of conversations with Andrea, things he might know about her.'

'Detective, nobody can tell me anything about my child I do not already know, certainly not Kevin. He loves her like he does his own two but I run this house and those girls' lives. Anyway, if there was something important he would have told me himself, he tells me everything.'

Ferreira searched for the right words. 'My intention is not to be accusing and there is no obligation for Mr Smith to be here now, but we will need to talk to him, sooner rather than later.'

The mother gave a short nod. 'He should be home later tonight. We can re-evaluate tomorrow.'

Ferreira's pen moved rapidly across and down the page.

'OK, maybe we should move on to Andrea herself and what she is like…' A loud crash above was followed, after a short hush, by a child screaming.

'Right on cue,' the mother said. 'Why don't you come up and take a look at Andrea's room while I tend to the wounded.' With that she unfurled from the sofa and left the room.

THIRTY-SIX

The gentle movement down the side of her face felt safe so she opened her eyes, to a natural light that filled the room from above and behind. In front of her Simon was crouched, looking intently not at her but at her cheek. He was using a damp cloth to wipe away blood, the wet material in short strokes attentive to her face and neck. His other hand easily rebutted her attempt to push him away, supporting her as she swayed, unbalanced from the effort.

She slumped back against the cistern, hard against her spine, suddenly aware of being in a bathroom. She thought about screaming but the effort required meant the intent never passed from thought. Her eyes wandered. His T-shirt lay crumpled on the floor, his bare skin smooth and tanned, gleaming with a soft radiance that pulled her along the contours of muscles moving thickly across his shoulders.

'Where's he?' The effort of forming each word was a difficult journey in itself.

'Gone.'

'Coming back?'

'Not for a few days.'

It took her a while to put the span of a day into context. A day seemed some distant definition of time, a few days an eternity she could no longer comprehend.

'My… Adam. What about him?'

'You've caused us problems, Sarah, but you're not the threat we thought you were. Hakan will not waste time on your husband.'

'Why'd he go?'

'That's none of your business.'

'No, I thought…'

A faint smile pulled his mouth wider and the focus of his eyes shifted to hers. 'You thought you were going to die. So did I.'

'I am…here.'

'You are.' He reached across to the sink and ran cold water onto the flannel, rinsing it and pressing it against the side of her face.

'You…stopped him?'

'Hakan?' He shook his head.

'I…imagined…'

Simon did not answer, resuming his study of her face. He cupped her chin in his palm, carefully turning her head from side to side. 'You have a small cut on your cheek. It's going to bruise and swell a little, although most of the blood has come from cuts in your mouth and you have bitten your tongue. Considering the alternatives, not a bad return.'

He reached around, picked up his T-shirt and stood, a physical motion complemented by a ballet of muscle that made the movement majestic. He turned on the tap and dropped the flannel and T-shirt into the sink, kneading them in the water, using a hand to steady Sarah as she toppled sideways. He gently pushed her against the wall, poured bleach into the sink and wiped his hands on a towel.

'Guess that's you about done, Sarah Sawacki. Need a hand?'

She opened her eyes and stared at his offered hand, ignoring it. She shuffled to the edge of the toilet seat, her hair falling around her face as she moved her weight on to legs that immediately buckled. Simon caught her as she crumpled and effortlessly lifted her body into his arms.

They swept along a white balconied landing, passing closed white doors and down stairs to the familiar. Through the living room past the chair and into the hallway, into the empty garage. He set her on the floor, propped against the wall. She watched as he retrieved a mat. Her eyes closed and then it was just dark.

THIRTY-SEVEN

They both listened to the mother's footsteps climb the stairs. 'You go ahead,' Boer said. 'I'll follow you up.'

Ferreira gave him a rough approximation of a scowl. 'You had better not go stealing any pictures.'

'Me?'

She looked sternly at him then followed the mother up the stairs. Boer waited for her to reach the landing before pushing himself up. He took another look at the photos on the polished wood. There were none of the stepfather, at least not here.

He walked along the hallway and into the living room, hearing the muffled voices above. This room was much the same as the first, the same sort of opulence except in a bigger space. Varying sized ornaments and sculptures were strategically placed. More photos by the window, this time several of a square-faced man with short dark hair, the stepfather. One picture placed centrally and bigger than the others, showed the man standing proudly atop a hill, a young girl dangling from each arm, the smallest around his neck. Boer looked around the room. Another rectangular canvas featured on one wall, this one entirely comprised of thick strokes in all shades of grey, save for a smooth white circle at the centre. A wide flatscreen television was placed centrally on the room's largest wall.

He walked in his socks through double doors into a large dining room. A long wooden table ran the length of the room, chairs for at least ten were set around the table, a manicured lawn visible beyond French doors. The only decoration here was a large wooden crucifix fixed high on the wall, a detailed metal Jesus hanging from it. It dominated the room.

The kitchen was functional. Dark worktops contrasted with white cupboard doors and gleaming saucepans hanging over a spotless breakfast bar, a matching utility room with a stack of neatly folded washing. He walked back into the hallway and mounted the bottom step, hearing from above the sniffs of a recovering child and the mother soothing while investigating the semantics of tears.

Boer reached the top step out of breath, his left hand pressed hard into his stomach. The mother, draped in the smallest girl, appeared in a doorway, concern and assessment drawn across her face as she watched him.

'Andrea's bedroom is down here, Detective.'

He followed her to a room opposite a large bathroom. The older of the young girls fell in beside him, matching his faltering step, looking up at him with a happy smile on her face, a trace of Andrea in her features.

'When I grow up I want to be a policeman like you.'

'Do you?' He managed a caricature of surprise that triggered a distant memory of laughing children. 'But I am old and soon I'll spend all my time gardening.'

She did not seem put off. 'But you look like a policeman who catches bad people.'

'In here detective.' The mother gestured to the bedroom, stopping the girl before she had a chance to follow. 'Feel free to look around, if you have more questions we'll be downstairs,' which caused an outburst of high-pitched pleading that trailed away with the mother.

Boer stepped into Andrea's bedroom. The floor was covered in raspberry carpet and the walls were painted an off-white pink. The clutter of childhood neatly ordered with a place for everything and everything in its place. Covering a good part of the wall space were pictures and posters featuring fairies and angels, either drawn by the girl or bought for her. He wondered how long it would be before they gave way to spotty boy bands and celebrity faces he would never know.

Ferreira thanked someone on her phone then flipped it closed. 'Come and look at this.'

He stepped around a shaggy white rug and joined her beside the bed. They both looked at a postcard-sized picture on the bedside cabinet. The picture was of a beaming child wrapped in the arms of green-jacketed man. 'Seems you have some competition in the unruly moustache stakes.'

'Funny. Brian Dunstan?'

'Yes, confirmed by the mother.'

He studied the photo, which showed a man in his early thirties with short brown hair, the moustache partly obscuring a youthful face. Boer tried without success to avoid seeing Sarah Sawacki in the girl's eyes. 'Your thoughts, Detective?'

'I would say your average well educated, sentient, pre-pubescent girl child. Reads a great deal.' She nodded at two low bookcases either side of a desk. 'She is trusted to do her homework alone because doing homework is something she has always done. Very creative judging from the artwork.'

'A diary?'

'Takes it with her when she visits her father.'

'What about an address book, or anything she might have written in?'

'There are notepads in the bookcase she uses for homework and doodles from what I can see, and in those blue-backed folders are the stories she writes.'

Boer stepped over to the bookcase and pulled one of Andrea's stories at random, scanning through the pages. Each page was full of neatly written text, the occasional doodle in the margins, mostly of wings. He read a few lines. The doodles matched the content, a boy and an angel.

'I think it's time to pull in the father,' he said. 'The real one. Make sure we pick up the diary and anything else they can at his house.'

Ferreira patted her pocket and the phone. 'Being done.'

He nodded agreement. 'Could you have a word with the mother. We need a team to go over every inch of this room.'

'She's not going to be happy, she's still convinced the girl's going to magically show up.'

'Despite my best efforts to force the reality home?'

'Despite your clumsy efforts at forcing the point home.'

He scratched the tip of his nose. 'I guess that's the nature of the mother's faith summed up right there.'

'What do you mean by that?'

'In the face of all evidence she continues to believe the improbable.'

'Is that faith, Fran, or hope?'

'I think the first feeds off the later. She should stop wasting our time messing about in church and bleating on about the girl's father. Faith isn't going to bring back Sarah Sawacki or the girl. That's going to need a lot of hard work by a lot of people. And even then it probably won't be

149

enough. So if you could, let the mother know there will be a team here tomorrow morning to take apart the bedroom. If she resists let her know in no uncertain terms the paths we can follow if we want to.'

'You're the boss. I'll get a picture of the girl, save you stealing one.'

'That would be good. I'll be down in ten.'

He waited until her footsteps faded, letting his eyes move from one space to another around the room. When he heard distant voices he stepped over to the first of the bookcases and eased himself down onto his knees, then sat cross legged on the floor. He pulled the first book from the top shelf, flicking through the pages, holding each by the cover and shaking loose anything pushed inside before sliding it back and moving to the next. He worked along and down shelf by shelf, then shuffled across to the next bookcase, repeating the process before moving to the desk, checking the books stacked on top, then in and under the drawers.

By the time he had shaken free the last book he had a collection of five bookmarks designed for child minds and a small pile of scrap paper covered with doodles. More wings – the girl was obsessed. He placed the paper and bookmarks on the top of the bookcase and moved to the white, wooden-framed bed. He wasn't sure what he was looking for, but then he never was until he found it. He pushed his hands under the mattress, fingers bumping over the wooden slats. He shone a small torch from his key chain under the bed, from one end to the other, seeing only a few dustballs against the skirting, a lost sock and some tissues. Next he pulled out the drawers of the bedside cabinet, checking beneath both and under the cabinet with the light. There was nothing.

His eyes moved to the white shelves of plastic storage boxes on the far wall, but he did not move towards them. Instead he sat on the edge of the bed, looking at the walls, the bookcases and back to the bedside cabinet. He picked up the photograph of Andrea and Brian and flipped it over. He pushed back the metal clips and eased out the wooden backing, a thin sheet of paper advertising the frame's manufacturer, the photograph, the glass, and a small creased piece of notepaper hidden behind the picture.

On the paper was a phone number with a Hambury area code, written in the same style he had seen through the rest of the room. He placed the paper on the bed and re-assembled the picture, placing it back on the bedside cabinet. He studied the paper for a long time, contemplating the possible reasons that brought the paper and picture together. Finally he pulled his phone from his pocket, dialled 141 and then the number. The call connected and was answered almost immediately by a deep voice that said two words. A first name he knew after a heartbeat of recollection, the second a surname he did not even comprehend. He disconnected and slid both the paper and mobile into his jacket pocket.

He let his eyes wander from poster to picture around the room. He stopped at a drawing above the headboard, the drawing surrounded by framed images of fairies and nymphs. It was a child's drawing of a man in army uniform, a big smile beneath a big moustache. Initially Boer puzzled over the odd shapes coloured yellow in the background, until he realised they were yet more wings, splayed outwards from her father's back. Leaning forward he pulled the bottom edge away from the wall and peered up at the back. *Get well soon Daddy* was written in large letters with a lot of love and kisses. The paper was creased as if it had been folded and used as a card.

Boer stood and smoothed down his trousers and then the bed, casting one last look around the room and then made his way downstairs. He suffered several minutes of glares from the mother while fending off questions from the older of the two girls. Ferreira finally brought their visit to a close, both of them silent for most of the return journey, busy ordering the detail and thoughts of the last hour in their minds.

THIRTY-EIGHT

The next time Sarah opened her eyes it was to the glow of artificial light and the sound of the concrete door coming to rest. She was immediately aware of not being alone. Her eyes finally focused and she felt a pulse of exhilaration. The girl was sitting in the corner of the room on the mattress, knees drawn up to her chin, wide eyes fierce.

'Hello,' Sarah said.

The girl's bottom lip trembled but her mouth remained firmly closed. Tears forced themselves onto cheeks already streaked white amid a torturous day's grime. Sarah's instincts pulled her towards the girl, but her attempt to crawl failed. Her head spun and she fell sideways onto the floor. With little ability to coordinate her limbs she managed to slowly shuffle around so she could lean against the wall. Exhausted from the effort she let her arm flop onto the foot of the mattress. She tried to think of words to say but nothing seemed to fit. 'You OK?'

'Stay away, I'm not talking to you.' The girl's small pink lips clamped closed. She drew her legs tighter into her body.

The context of the words did not register at first as Sarah tried to centre her thoughts, the girl's anger reminding her of a small animal cornered.

'I saw you in the alley,' Sarah said. 'I came here to help you.'

The girl chewed her lip and her mouth remained obstinately shut. When she eventually spoke the words came out in a rushed torrent. 'I know who you are, you're with them. I saw you in the street, they told me all about what you did to help them, I know you're here to make sure I behave.' She breathed deeply and looked defiantly back at Sarah.

'I am here for you, they have been…pretty horrid to me.'

Silence again as the girl's need to speak fought her desire not to. 'My dad wouldn't do this, not to me.'

'Do, this?'

'They said he won't pay the money he owes. So they took me instead. He wouldn't, not my dad.' The tears easily bubbled through the thin shield of anger, quickly giving way to sobs.

Sarah watched, unable to act on the girl's anguish, desperate to comfort her but physically incapable of moving an inch closer. In part it felt like looking back through time at a previous incarnation of herself. Seeing the cruel world of men emptied onto a child's unaware sense of reality. She felt every heave of the girl's chest and of those fragile shoulders and arms racked with a misplaced guilt. A young life ripped from all it holds precious. Unaware the worst was yet to come. The girl's crying continued in Sarah's mind long after her own eyes closed, through the hours of fitful sleep.

THIRTY-NINE

Adam pulled out his phone as he wandered down the sloping track and past the hire car Brian had bumped onto the verge. He dialled home as he stepped onto the quiet country road, full of trepidation and hope. There were no messages.

He looked up and down the road and saw no sign of Brian. He had been gone for over an hour. This location had taken them hours to find, the frustration increasing with each hour of criss-crossing the countryside. Brian was sure Sarah had made her last call from here and that made the location important in Brian's eyes.

Adam's phone started ringing and Boer's name flashed on the screen. He had programmed both the Detective's numbers from cards they handed him the night before. He had no desire to talk, certainly not to Boer. He needed more time to think how he would explain what he was doing, mostly because he was not really sure what that was. He waited for the call to end and switched the phone to silent.

He walked back up the slope to the disused farmyard and a large plateau of uneven mud, flanked on the right by imposing oaks and sycamores, the trees overlooking the yard and open fields at his left. At the far end of the yard the shell of a farmhouse sagged grey and exhausted from inattention. He walked to the broken fence, his shadow long and descending in front of him, scanning the outlying fields now golden in the afternoon sunlight. His eyes skipped from ploughed mud and bordering hedges to brown and yellow trees, a distant church spire and dotted houses. Eventually he spotted a small figure jogging in a rough parallel, growing in size as Brian came around and towards the old farm, finally labouring up the shallow embankment and climbing up over the

154

fence. He blew hard as he made the yard, bending over with both hands on his knees.

'Fuck me Sawacki! I used to be able to do that all day.'

'Do what?' Adam asked.

Brian looked at him, taking several more gulps of air. 'Reconnaissance.'

'Reconnaissance for what precisely?'

Brian gradually caught his breath, standing with his hands on hips, his chest rising and falling.

'This has to be the right place, although nobody knows an old woman who matches what Sarah described, certainly not one that brings her dogs for walks through here.' He gestured in the vague direction he had come from. 'There's a few young couples in converted cottages, a farm with barns full of vintage cars, a deserted pub and a rundown vicarage. I've done a complete circuit.'

Adam was confused. 'What use would talking to the woman do anyway, she's hardly likely to know where the Rover was going?'

Brian scowled back at him. 'You're a negative little shit. Anything we can take to narrow our choices from the west coast or east, I'm going to take.'

'But…' Adam opened his mouth and closed it. 'So what next?'

'Is that your phone?' They both looked down at Adam's phone flashing through his pocket.

'It's Detective Boer, he's been ringing for the last ten minutes.'

Brian looked thoughtfully at the phone and then at Adam. 'Why don't you answer, he could be calling about something interesting. What's he like?'

'Boer? He's old, got a dodgy moustache like yours, thin as a rake and grouchy. You'd probably get on.'

'I meant does he sound like he knows what he's doing?'

'Totally, he's one of those old timers who knows what's what. Hooked into everything. He knew there was something about Sar…'

Brian waited on the rest of the sentence but Adam just looked startled and pursed his lips together. 'Something what about Sarah?' he asked.

'Nothing, he was just really good.'

'Spit it out.'

'It's long and complicated and I don't want to discuss it.'

'So give me the quick version.'

'I can't.'

155

'Jeeses Sawacki, I won't tell anyone. Cross my heart and hope to die.'

Adam ran a hand through his hair. 'Well, Sarah has a bit of history. She assaulted some guy a few years back who turned out to have done all kinds of stuff to her as a child. Boer remembered her.'

'Boer remembered her? That must have been some kind of assault.'

'There was a carving knife involved.'

Brian quickly re-calculated his appraisal of Sarah. She went up several notches in his estimation. 'Anything else about the Detective?'

'He didn't look like he would suffer fools.' A realisation dawned on Adam. 'Why, what's on your mind?'

'I guess it's make or break time. Give me your phone.'

'Why, what are you going to do?'

'Talk to Boer of course, one of us has to.'

'But why?'

'Well he's ringing you for a start, which means he wants to talk. So if you're not going to, I might as well. He certainly isn't going away. You never know, he might help us.'

'But he won't, he'll think we're on the run or something.'

'He will if he doesn't talk to us, which is why one of us has to answer that phone. You can do it if you want.'

'But we have nothing to say to him, do we?'

Brian sighed, long and frustrated. 'Can you tell me what new and revealing information your ongoing review of the surveillance has produced?'

'You know the answer to that. The logo just looks like three lions. It might be part of a larger logo.'

'And we're both in agreement that three lions isn't necessarily going to narrow our investigation by much.'

'Of course. I need internet access to start cross-referencing logos, maybe find one that looks similar.'

'And apart from the road to nowhere down there, which may narrow our search to the east coast, what else do we have?'

'Nothing.'

'So trust me, Adam, we need to talk to him. You never know.'

'But he's a policeman, he'll know I'm with you.'

Brian wiped his palms on his jeans and held out his hand. 'Give me the damn phone.'

Adam reluctantly handed it over.

Boer had hung up. Brian dialled the number.

FORTY

'If that's not Adam who is it?' Boer asked.

'It's Brian Dunstan.'

There was a short pause before Boer spoke again. 'So you now have coercion and kidnapping to add to the long list of things we need to talk about.'

'I do hope you're not implying I kidnapped my daughter, detective, because that could piss me off. If you're referring to Mr Sawacki, he's here of his own volition.' Brian glanced across at Adam.

'Where might here be?' Boer asked.

'Somewhere between Stratford and Warwick. Probably at the site where Sarah Sawacki made her final call last night.'

At the other end of the phone the background noise faded and he heard a muffled command. Then the detective's voice returned.

'And what do you have, Mr Dunstan?'

'Right now, CCTV footage from Delamere showing the Rover driver making sure he wasn't being followed. We have a full mugshot of the guy. He missed Sarah because she was busy checking out his car. Sarah talked to him and followed the Rover out of Delamere, which you already know. There's nothing in the footage to indicate where they were going.'

'What else?'

'What else? How far are you into reviewing the CCTV, all that Sunday overtime been sanctioned yet?'

Boer ignored the comment despite its accuracy. 'Tell me what else you have.'

'Not much. We're here trying to get a handle on where he might have

157

been going. Why the Rover came down this road. It's mostly used by locals travelling between villages, it doesn't even feed onto the M40.'

'Part of a misdirection or part of the route home?' Boer asked.

Brian liked Boer's directness. He thought the question over, scanning the countryside and the cathedral trees that marked the road's passage. 'Both, I would say. It's part of the misdirection in that he doesn't want anyone knowing he came this way. Which means he was probably heading home.'

'Excellent. Mr Dunstan, wait a second please.'

Brian heard muffled sounds then Boer's voice returned. 'What about the number plate?'

'What about the number plate?'

'Don't mess me about Brian.'

'I'm not, the camera was broken.'

'No, it wasn't,' Boer answered. 'So let's try that again. What is the number plate?'

'What would I get in return?' Brian countered.

'It's about time you realised the gravity of your situation, Mr Dunstan. There is no bargaining point here.'

'I am fully aware of the situation, Detective, which is why I'm not still twiddling my thumbs in Hambury. But I can't afford to give you all I have with no return.'

'Give me a minute,' Boer said, and then silence.

Brian wandered to the edge of the farmyard, looking out across the vista of fields beneath the autumn sun. Boer came back.

'I'll give you the address of the Rover's registered owner if you give me the number plate.'

'I don't believe you.'

'Take it or leave it,' answered Boer. 'I want to find your daughter and Sarah Sawacki, just like you do. Alive is my preference, trust me on that front.'

Brian turned and faced the sun, feeling the warmth on his face. He told Boer the number plate and Boer's voice faded again, as if he was talking with someone while turned away from the mouthpiece. Brian felt a wave of pain pulse out across his ribs and his back. He embraced it.

Boer's voice returned again. 'Thank you, Brian. As for the address, Adam can give you that.'

'What's that fucking mean?' But Boer had disconnected. Brian turned to Adam and took a step at him. Adam took a step back.

'What?'

'The number plate?'

'The Rover?'

'Yes the fucking Rover.'

'So?'

'You can find out the Rover's registered address?'

Adam thought for a second and then shock and realisation spread across his face. 'But…I can't.'

'What do you mean you can't?'

'I can't, I could get fired.'

'Fucking fired.' Brian took another step forward and Adam took another step back.

'I don't want to encroach on your cosy world or anything but there's the small matter of your missing wife and my missing daughter. Now explain to me the full meaning of "I can't".'

'I could lose my job…' Adam's voice failed, realising the futility of the statement. 'I just didn't think, it never even occurred to me.' He looked utterly defeated, his eyes wide and almost panicked with the realisation.

'Your wife is missing and it never occurred to you, what planet are you on?'

It simply hadn't, suppressed by that part of him still hoping Sarah would call and say she was home, that this nightmare would be over, suppressed by that part of him programmed not to lose his job so he could pay their mortgage. And now Brian's disdain seemed to magnify the inadequacy he felt for everything, the responsibility he felt for Sarah being in the wrong place at the wrong time. Everything that had been simmering inside of him the last day now boiled over. The anger exploded outwards, he stepped forward and threw everything he had into the punch.

And Brian let him do it, realising Adam's conflict in the half second before the punch was thrown. He moved his body so the first punch landed against his shoulder, the second harder into his side and then Adam was on top of him. An elbow glanced across his cheek, then Brian turned beneath the next blow and kicked Adam's feet away. The momentum spun Adam onto his back and he hit the mud hard, knocking all the air from him. He immediately rolled away, coughing and spluttering.

Brian stepped across and pinned Adam to the ground with a knee on his chest, batting away his furious attempts to knock him free.

'Stop it and listen.'

Adam did after a while, his eyes full of anger and tears.

'I'm sorry if I was hard on you, but I really need your help here. Now what do you need to access that information?'

'Internet access,' Adam wheezed. 'We need somewhere with a mobile signal and GPRS or better.'

'Speak English, Adam, what's that mean?'

'There's mobile signal here but no internet carrier. We need to go somewhere that does.'

'Good.' Brian stood and held out a hand. Adam ignored it and stood by himself, glaring at Brian as the sun disappeared behind tall trees, the shadows reaching out across the fields. Brian held his right arm.

Adam broke the silence. 'You're not an easy person to like, Brian.'

'Yeah well, I get that.'

'Did I hurt you?' Adam asked.

Brian laughed. Adam did not. The shadows reached further across the fields.

'Tell me what's wrong with your arm.'

'It's not my arm, it's my back, the nerve endings are all messed up.'

'How come?'

'I had a run in with an RPG and lost.'

'A rocket? When you were in the army?'

'What's with all the questions?'

'Because I need to trust you, Brian, and to do that I need to know at least a little about you.'

Brian relented. Adam was a little earnest but he kind of liked him. 'I served in the second Paratroop regiment. We were in the Eden they call Helmand. Full of nasty little fuckers.'

'What did you do as a Paratrooper?'

'In the regiment you all muck in, my primary role was target acquisition.'

'Target acquisition?'

'I was a sniper, Adam.'

Adam was not expecting that, he imagined Brian closer to the action. 'A sniper?'

'Sure, and a good one. I could take out the engine block in a moving vehicle at twelve hundred metres and my longest kill came in just under two klicks, although she was sat nice and still. The nerve endings in my back are so messed up now, I can't pull a trigger and be sure I'm not going to blow my own foot off.'

'You shot a woman?'

'They have two eyes and ten fingers, Adam, can press buttons and pull triggers just like any man I ever knew. The tricky bit was not hitting the kid. She had it strapped to her, they do that.'

Adam shook his head and Brian was not in the mood for moral dilemmas. He turned and headed back down the muddy track, passed a crumbling outbuilding on the left, a gatepost without a gate and to the car. Adam followed a minute later.

FORTY-ONE

Boer dropped the phone into his jacket pocket and leaned his head back against the headrest. He closed his eyes.

'You want me to take you home Fran? You could do with a rest.'

'I'm fine, Helen, just thinking.'

She tapped her index finger against the steering wheel and looked at the clock on the dash. They were running out of day. They had arrived back in Hambury just before three to find Brian Dunstan was not in custody and nobody knew where he was. So they had checked in on the search of his flat. Sparse was not the word. It looked like Brian Dunstan had packed and was not expecting to come back. Andrea's books and neat piles of clothes indicated she thought she would be. Her diary was now their prize and on its way to the lab in London. Sometime that evening they should get photographed images of the pages. They had left the forensic team in the flat checking through the hidden and microscopic detail.

They had then driven across town with the intention of talking to Adam Sawacki. They were now parked on the gravel outside his apartment. The fact Brian Dunstan was missing was half expected. Ferreira even suspected Boer put off pulling him into custody for that very reason. But discovering Adam Sawacki was now off their radar was a surprise. To now find Adam and Brian together, neither she nor Boer would have envisaged that. And now Boer was treading a very fine line.

'That could go horribly wrong.'

'I know.' Boer kept his face angled at the car roof, his eyes still closed.

'You've given Dunstan key information relating to a criminal investigation. You have seen his record, he's not reliable.'

'He's certainly not a reliable citizen, although a Military Cross might indicate he was a good soldier. At the end of the day I haven't told them anything. I'm sure it would have occurred to Adam eventually. He's a smart kid even if he is still in shock. As for Dunstan, I'd rather he was out looking for his daughter than in a cell. He could be useful.'

'He needs to be in the station talking to us, Fran! Not chasing down our bloody leads. The Chief Inspector will want to know what we have on Brian and we have a whole lot of nothing.'

'I just talked to him, he sounded like an OK guy.'

'Francis, you're an arse!'

Boer rolled his head sideways and looked at her through heavy eyes. 'I want to find Andrea and Sarah, and I want them alive, Helen, not to waste days and weeks hoping someone finds their bodies so we can harvest forensics. I want them alive and Brian improves our chances of that happening. He looked at the CCTV hours ago, tech are only just looking at our copy.'

'But the Chief…'

'I'll give Anne what she needs. Don't you worry on that account.'

'But she's going to want him front and centre with the mother tomorrow.'

'Has she confirmed that already?'

'Yeah, she called while we were driving back. You were asleep.'

'No I wasn't.'

'Yes you were, Fran, your chin hit your chest just before the M40 and it didn't come up again till we came off the A34. You were out for over thirty minutes.'

'I was thinking. I wasn't asleep.'

'OK Fran, whatever way you want it.'

'Why didn't she ring me?'

'You never answer her calls.'

Boer returned a shallow nod in acknowledgement. 'What did she say?'

'Press conference midday tomorrow. We haven't wasted a week here hunting through the local hotspots, she's going national straight away. With Sarah's background and a pretty girl missing the media will be all over it. It could be her big break.'

'God, Helen, you're starting to sound like me.'

'So, do you want the good news?'

'She wants you sat right beside her?' he said.

'No, me and you.'

He groaned. 'What does she want me there for?'

'I guess she sees this as your last big tango. She wants you right next to her so she can bask in the glory.'

'What glory?'

'You're one of the most decorated officers outside London, Fran, legitimately decorated and you've never used your influence to get a seat upstairs. You work in Hambury when you could have gone anywhere. We look up to you and she wants some of that.'

He grunted. 'She's going to be pissed when I don't show then.'

'Francis…'

'No, I mean it Helen. We're trying to find a kidnapped child and a missing woman, not work on our TV portfolios.'

'That's going to look bad for both of us.'

'You can handle yourself. Everyone knows what I'm like. Chief Inspector Anne Darling can kiss my bony arse. Besides what's the worst she can do, fire me? I could be dead in a week.'

'Come on, Fran, don't be like that. You've been managing. There's been no change for almost a year, has there?'

'It's different now. I'm tired of it all Helen, this constant rat race of people going all out to get more for themselves and not giving a damn what they do and who they do it to. I'm just about done and glad of it.'

'Done with the job, or done with life? Because if it's the latter Ricky wants your TV.'

Boer laughed and pushed himself upright. 'That's my girl.' He pressed the palm of his hand into his stomach. 'It's time for you to step up, Helen. If anyone ever told me the best partner I'd ever have would be a woman, I'd have struggled with that. But a lot has changed these last twenty years. This is not my world anymore, it's yours. You sit beside Anne with my best wishes. I won't be there.'

'Thanks!' she said. They sat in silence.

'Where to next then, boss?'

'The station. I think we've wasted enough time today. We need to get someone over to the Rover's registered address. I'll be lucky if that's done before tomorrow. Should give Brian time enough.'

Ferreira reached for the ignition.

'And I want you to check this out for me.' She stopped and watched him produce a piece of crumpled notepaper from his jacket.

'What's that?' She took it from him. There was a phone number neatly penned across the middle. 'This is Andrea's handwriting. Where did you find this?'

'Questions, questions.'

She stared hard at him. 'You old dog, you found this in her room. Where was it?'

'Behind the photo of her and Brian.'

Ferreira slapped the palm of her hand against the wheel and let out a long low frustrated groan. 'Don't die just yet, I obviously still need you. Whose number do you think it is? We should call it.'

'Did that already.'

'You did, who answered?'

'Ali.'

She thought for a second. 'Brian's boss? What did you say?'

'I hung up.'

She stared out of the window trying to imagine the various scenarios. 'Brian's boss!' She said again. 'What do you want to do?'

'I don't know, that's what I was thinking about. I didn't want to jump to any wrong conclusions.'

'Like what?'

'Like immediately assuming this number means Ali's involved. There's a lot of reasons for this number being in that picture frame. I think I have most of them figured.'

She looked from the paper to Boer and back down. 'I'll dig up what I can.'

Boer clicked his seat belt into place. 'You focus on that number and I'll start chasing down loose ends. You never know, we might even have the diary by the time we get back.'

FORTY-TWO

Adam found the internet signal he needed as they entered Warwick. Brian pulled over and turned sideways in his seat, watching intently as Adam logged into his company's web portal. His nerves led him to hit all the wrong keys and two attempts to log in. Two attempts that would be flagged on some log that may or may not come to the attention of a human. Just as the government bureau maintaining the databases also ran audits that had to be quantified against sanctioned requests. If they ever flagged this one the penalty was a large fine and his job.

He paused and concentrated and typed the correct password, clicking through the screens. He was finally presented with a search box and a blinking cursor. His moment of truth. And now it was here it seemed irrelevant. So pointless. He was sat in a car surrounded by looming medieval buildings, connected via a wireless signal to a distant faceless computer. He typed in the number plate and seconds later he was looking at an address in Peterborough. Feeling a little jubilant he turned the laptop so Brian could see.

Three hours later they were standing in a village street, in the dark, a few miles north of Peterborough's main suburban spread. The village was on the verge of countryside, the street full of former council houses now neat and prim. Brian parked at the end of the street and they both walked to the house, the registered address of the Rover's owner. A battered Mondeo was parked on the drive, beside a concrete path that led down the side of the house to darkness. Green light glowed through closed curtains at the front of the house.

Brian stepped up to the front door and knocked. When there was no answer he knocked again and they waited. There was little sound save for the distant drone of the main road. The night air was cold, their breath misting. He stepped onto the lawn and rapped on the window. Still nothing.

'Maybe he's gone out?' Adam offered.

Brian turned to him. 'Eight on a Sunday night, a place like this. I doubt it. Everybody's cosied down thinking about work tomorrow.'

He stepped around Adam and along the shadowy path beside the house, stopping at the back door. He knocked and waited and when nobody answered he tried the handle. The door opened. Adam half whispered, half shouted a rebuke as Brian stepped inside.

Three things occurred to Brian as he moved fully into the kitchen. First, the place had been ripped apart. Just about everything that had been in the cupboards was now on the floor, including most of the cupboard doors. Second, he could smell gas, not strong but distinct. Third, he could also smell burnt flesh. A smell he was never going to forget. Adam stepped into the kitchen behind him.

'Stay there,' Brian instructed, keeping his voice low. 'Lock the door. If anyone runs at you just get out the way, I'll be right behind them.'

He stepped through the clutter on the floor into the dining room, finding the same carnage. A table on its side with chairs scattered around it. A broken laptop in the corner with a boot-sized hole in the screen. There were drawers on the floor with paper everywhere, spaces on the wall where pictures once hung, now lying broken on the floor. He walked through to the living room and the same chaos. Someone had been looking for something and they had really wanted it. The cloying smell of burnt flesh.

He tracked back through the kitchen, past Adam looking questioning, and into the hallway, finding a hissing Calor bottle in the middle of the floor. He shut off the valve and stood and listened. He could hear the groan of central heating, the tick of a clock. His own shallow breathing. He looked up the stairs, stepped onto the stairs. One step then two and up onto the landing, the smell overpowering, now mixed with the heavy odour of excrement and petrol. He checked through each room, finding the same chaos in each. Then he moved into the spare room, which he had saved for last because he had a pretty good idea he knew what was in there.

It was impossible to tell the man's age by his face. Brian had thought him sixty plus from the photos downstairs. He was naked on a chair that matched the others in the dining room. The man's legs and arms were bound to the chair using grey industrial tape, which was also stretched across the man's mouth. His body was covered in burns, but that was far from the worst of it. He heard Adam's tentative steps up the stairs.

There was a hobby table to one side. On top lay a bloody knife and a blowtorch still with a vivid blue flame. The trigger was taped down. The blowtorch was connected to a dirty rubber hose that wound across to a propane cylinder. The blowtorch would have looked benign if not for the evidence etched across the man's body. Brian looked at the man as he peeled the tape from the trigger and shut off the flame.

The man was dead, that was for sure. His last hours had not gone well. Death, Brian guessed, was probably caused by a heart attack, the tape across his mouth to stop the screaming. There would have been a lot of screaming.

On and all around the chair were faeces and blood mixed with urine, burnt flesh cut free. Cuts and burns not only covered the man's body, they delved into it. Long valleys of burnt flesh stretched along each limb, deep cuts slashing across his chest and stomach. Two charred holes had once been his eyes, burnt right out of his head, the same with the flesh and gristle of his nose and ears, just not there anymore. The smell.

Brian heard Adam step into the room, a gurgled moan, then a second of total silence. Then Adam stumbled back out to the landing.

FORTY-THREE

Sarah woke with her head resting on her arm, her arm on the mattress. At some point she must have slid sideways as her body was curled on the carpeted floor. She could feel something else draped over her; the red blanket.

She looked up. The girl was in the same position in the corner, now with her legs crossed and a large book open on her lap. Her mouth moved in small motions, her teeth grinding; biscuits from the sound of it. Sarah pushed herself up and pulled the blanket down into her lap. 'You did this?'

The girl kept chewing, then her chin dipped in acknowledgement. She swallowed. 'You were shivering and groaning. I thought you were cold.'

The girl pulled another biscuit from a small packet and pushed it whole into her mouth, manoeuvring it into position, with a brief look of concentration as she bit down.

'That was sweet, thank you.' And then it dawned on her, *biscuits!*

Her eyes fell on a collection of new shapes beside the light, an open box full of biscuits wrapped in plastic, a bottle of water. A glass bowl of red grapes pulled from the stalk and a large empty porcelain basin.

'Him?' She asked.

The chin dipped again and the mouth kept working.

For a brief moment Sarah considered refusing the food but her stomach's need propelled her forward and onto all fours. She forced herself to take a drink of water first – a beautiful taste and a welcome sensation that reached out through her whole body – trying not to gulp it down. She screwed the cap back on.

The grapes were soft and the biscuits past their sell-by date but she did not care. She scooped a handful of packets and grapes into her arms, walking back on her knees to her spot at the end of the mattress. She dropped the grapes into her lap and ripped open the first packet, aware of the girl's eyes following her every movement, calculating.

Sarah ate five packets, each containing three flat biscuits made largely of seeds and nuts. She could have kept eating but forced herself to stop. Instead she popped the grapes in turn into her mouth, the taste sharply sweet but still a forgotten luxury for the senses. When she was finished she dusted the crumbs from her trousers onto the carpet, a small act of defiance but in reality there was nowhere else for them to go. She looked across at the porcelain basin. 'Is that what I think it is?'

Another dip of the chin. Sarah screwed her face in disgust which prompted a slightly more vigorous nod of the head. Then the girl realised and studiously averted her attention back to the book.

'Have you slept?' Sarah asked.

No response.

'What book are you reading?'

No response.

'Is it good?'

No response.

'How old are you?' With this last Sarah placed her hand on the edge of the mattress.

The defiant face looked up. 'Stay away!'

She tried to recall the children of friends, how to win over child minds, but the reality was she made an effort not to be near children. Her only point of reference was herself. She had loved silly stories as a child.

'We have to help each other, don't we? To be in this horrid place together and not be friends would be worse than being here alone, don't you think?'

Still no response, but she could see something of what she said had hit a nerve. She kept talking, not sure where the words came from, making it up as she went.

'Maybe you're not a girl after all?'

No response.

'Maybe you're a troll and I mistakenly thought you were a girl.'

No response, but she could see the girl was no longer focused on the book.

170

'A mute troll, with a big fat nose and eyes like saucers.'

The girl looked up. 'I know what you're trying to do!'

'You do?'

'Yes, you're trying to make me talk, I'm not stupid.'

Sarah continued, 'The cleverest troll there ever was with ears like cauliflowers and little teeth that gnawed at rocks. Munch, munch, munch.'

No response.

'They would say, "Who is that troll over there making all that noise?" And everybody would shout at once, "Why that's the cleverest troll ever was. Just like her mother." "Mother troll?" they would ask. And everybody would shout, "Yes, you know, old Mrs Cleverest down the road."'

Still no response but now a smile forced itself onto the girl's face.

'"Old Mrs Cleverest, she can't be her mother. This one's far too grumpy and mean and munchy and mute to be one of hers. Her father must be the meanest, grumpiest troll there ever was." "Oh him," everybody chanted, "Old man Everwas, nasty piece of work."'

'There's nothing wrong with my dad!'

The forcefulness in the girl's voice took Sarah by surprise.

'I didn't say there was.'

'You said he was mean and nasty, he just isn't.'

'I made that up. I wanted to talk, that's all.'

'I'm not talking to you.' The girl looked back at the book.

'Tell me what your dad is like then, that can't do any harm. Can it?'

The girl looked at her, despair pulling at the muscles in her face. 'They said this was his fault and you're one of them.'

'I'm not, but I understand why you think that. I do know these people are not nice, very not nice. So if they say your daddy has done something wrong, then that is reason to believe he has not. And if these people say I'm here to snoop that is reason to believe I am not.'

The girl's expression morphed to hopeful. 'Really?'

'Yes of course. I would never believe a single word they say, people like that lie all the time.'

'You're not just doing tricks, to confuse me?'

Sarah shook her head. 'I saw you in the High Street, remember? You… reminded me of a girl I once knew, that's all. And then the next second you were gone. So I wondered where you went.'

The girl looked at Sarah, appraising her, her hands flat on the book in her lap. It seemed she was deliberating the hardest decision she might ever have made. Finally the girl drew in a long breath. 'Everything here is wrong, nothing is right. The tall man looks nice but he's the one that took me. The little man with the small eyes, he looks horrible but he was nice to me. You look very nice. They said you were in the street to watch me, to make sure I went in the alley. I don't believe you, you're here to check on me.'

The girl looked back at the book and did not say anything else. After a few seconds a tear wound its way down her nose and dropped free, falling onto the page.

Sarah fought a desperate urge to lean across and wrap her arms around those small shoulders. Instead she reached across for more grapes, making sure she brushed against the girl's leg as she returned. She pushed a grape into her mouth and they sat in silence.

FORTY-FOUR

Adam was sitting slumped on the floor downstairs, propped against the dining room wall. He was in shock. To this point he had managed to romanticise death by wrapping it in mortuary hues of blue and green. The reality of the man upstairs was horrifying, a body with the life literally ripped from it. The pain of that death etched all over the body. He kept hoping this man's death and the kidnapping were not related. The thought of Sarah at the hands of the same people was more than his mind could comprehend. It struck a cold fear to the very heart of him.

Brian appeared in the kitchen doorway, leaning against the frame with his arms folded. 'Whatever they came for, I'm pretty sure they got it.'

Adam tried to recall. The thin premise for them being there was the hope of discovering something useful from the Rover's actual owner, something to narrow the search. Brian thought Simon was unlikely to use a stolen car or one he was actually registered as owning.

A question burned for Adam. 'You're sure this is connected to your daughter?'

Brian stepped into the room and pulled out one of the chairs. He sat with one arm rested on the dining table he had righted earlier. 'It would be a hell of a coincidence in a village like this. Doubt it was Simon though, he already has his hands full. My guess is Simon messed something up and somebody is covering his tracks. I'd say they wanted the vehicle documentation.'

Adam thought about that. 'Surely if you're buying a car to kidnap a child you wouldn't leave your address behind?'

'Shit happens. There's not a lot of people would say no to Simon, not a big guy like that. If he offers to do the paperwork it saves them the job. Except our guy upstairs fixed cars for a hobby. Like a real hobby. He kept before and after photos of the cars, copies of all the paperwork. All in colour and neatly filed in folders, like they were mementoes. If Simon was here Friday or even yesterday, he'd have a schedule to keep to. Then he comes across some old guy who won't let him leave without the documentation properly filled out. At least that's what I'm hoping. If your eagle-eyed wife hadn't screwed things up for him, it might never have mattered. The old fella might be sat over there right now daydreaming about the Mondeo on the drive.'

'So they were after the documentation? Maybe they didn't find what they were looking for, and that's why they did what they did?'

'For a start they probably didn't kill him, not directly. And they already had what they wanted, so they either needed something else from him or were blowtorching for the hell of it.'

'What makes you think they got what they wanted?'

'The old fella's got a safe in the garage. Door's wide open and not forced. There's some decent jewellery in there, gold necklaces and rings. All sorts of trinkets. They didn't touch them. I'd say that's where he kept the original documents. If he'd printed copies then they got them as well, his neat little collection is ripped to shreds upstairs. Can't imagine him holding on to any secrets once they turned on the blowtorch.'

Adam moved unsteadily onto his knees with the intention of standing. Brian leaned over and offered his hand. Adam stared at it. It was shaking again, and he could also see a stretch of skin just back from the jacket cuff. The skin looked like melted plastic. He took the hand and Brian pulled him up. He leaned back against the wall.

Brian continued, 'Before they left they turned on the propane tank in the hallway and upstairs, and left the blowtorch on. It would eventually ignite, setting a chain reaction through the house. Combined with the fuel they splashed about there'd be an explosion and a fire. Not enough gas for something serious. Doubt it would've done more than scorch off the wallpaper and burn the curtains, maybe take out a few windows. That and fry any circumstantial evidence.'

'You said they?' Adam asked.

'Sure, two probably. Too much can go wrong with just one and three's a crowd, people might remember. Two is a good number for a clean-up. Probably blokes, statistically.'

174

Adam's whole body felt numb, he stretched out both arms and flexed the joints, looking at the dining room table. Various bits of gadgetry were lined up on its shiny surface. The broken laptop, a wrecked printer and a scanner with the glass smashed and the lid missing. Adam had watched Brian put them there, had been too busy trying not to retch or pass out to ask why. He knew enough of Brian now to know there would be a purpose.

'We should call Detective Boer,' Adam said, lifting a chair around to the end of the table. He sat down.

'Nobody's calling Boer. We got work to do.'

'Someone needs to know about the guy upstairs, he needs…'

Brian cut in, 'A good meal and a few bandages? He's dead, Adam. It's tragic, especially like that. But that's nothing we can make better. We need to think how we're going to move on.'

Adam sat back. 'Without paper copies?'

Brian nodded, looking directly at him.

And then Adam realised what Brian had in mind. 'Which means you want me to give the kiss of life to that laptop?'

Brian smiled back at him. 'He gets Simon to fill in the forms and waves him goodbye. A businessman would file the paperwork and deal with it the following morning, maybe the next week. A hobbyist files the original and sits stroking the copy. It's part of the ritual. He might have copied it straight away.'

Adam looked at the laptop. He could see the patio doors and garden through the hole in its screen.

'I need to get my bag from the car.'

FORTY-FIVE

They sat in silence for some time. The girl occasionally reached for another pack of biscuits while maintaining intense interest in the book on her lap. Sarah could feel the girl's pent-up desire to talk and had to stop herself from leaning over and lifting that stubborn child chin, to implore the girl to believe. The reality was they needed to talk.

'If you keep eating those biscuits you'll make yourself ill,' she said.

The girl ignored her. The small mouth now crunching down harder and louder each time she chewed.

'I bet you're really stubborn just like your dad.'

The girl looked up with fiery eyes and then realised what Sarah had said. Her posture immediately changed to proud. 'I'm just like my dad, mum says that all the time.'

'Why don't you tell me about your father then, that can't do any harm surely?'

The girl said nothing for a while, then defiantly, 'I'm not talking!'

'What harm can it really do, it's only words? It would be good to talk, don't you think? If you're anything like as lonely as I feel right now, you must want to.'

Lonely was the magic word. The girl's face instantly transformed and Sarah knew the first battle was over.

'You might be one of them,' the girl said tentatively.

'I am not,' Sarah said.

'They said you were.'

Sarah was about to answer when the girl held up a small hand, palm outwards and looked at her beneath a furrowed brow.

'But I've decided I can talk to you, because you seem really nice and because this is such a yuck place. This is all just so, so horrid. I might go mad if I don't speak.'

Sarah smiled at the girl's earnest conclusion. 'I tell you what then. If you think I'm doing any snooping you can tell me and I'll immediately stop whatever I'm doing that's snoopy.'

The girl nodded, her hair falling around her face. A fleeting smile as she absently brushed it back.

'Shake on it?' Sarah pretended to spit into her hand and held it out.

'Eeeaaawww, that's yuck!'

'It's pretend spit but a real handshake.'

The girl moved forward and for a brief moment Sarah felt a limp hand in hers, warm and soft. A thrill ran through her body. Then the girl leaned back.

'My name is Sarah. Is your name Andrea?'

The girl looked taken aback. 'Of course.'

'I thought so. I heard the name, earlier, it must have been you.'

The girl nodded. 'You were asleep when they first brought you. I tried to wake you up.'

'I wasn't sure, pleased to meet you, Andrea.'

The girl silently studied her and for a short time they sat in silence.

'He called my name,' the girl said.

'In the alley?'

'Yes, he said my dad sent him but I'd never seen him before. Then I felt something.' She put her hand on her neck. 'And then I was here. I had lots of bad dreams.'

'Me too,' said Sarah. 'So what's your dad's name?'

'Brian,' the girl answered. 'His last name is Dunstan but that's not my last name. Mum wanted me to have her name. She doesn't like dad at all.'

'They're not together?'

'Nooo.' The girl shook her head vigorously. 'They never have been. I only see him some weekends. When he was a soldier I hardly saw him at all. I like it now lots more.'

Sarah held on to her questions. 'Wow, he was a soldier. He must be some kind of cool dad.'

The girl's face pinched, her body rocking from side to side. 'He's rubbish.'

'He is?'

'Oh yes,' said with a relish that contradicted the statement. 'For a start he's not very good at hugs, I have to wait until he falls asleep. And he gets bored of games and my books really quickly. And he doesn't like drawing and he doesn't play. And sometimes I think he has no idea what housework is.' She tutted and folded her arms.

'He doesn't do housework?' Sarah pretended shock.

'Not at all. If I don't take his clothes to the laundry I think they would never get washed. But I don't iron them. If you fold them properly you don't need to. I got Kevin to show me. But I didn't tell him why.'

'You take them to the laundry? How, when?'

'The woman that lives upstairs takes me Saturday nights while he works.' She looked at Sarah, warily. 'You're snooping.'

'Am I? I'm sorry, I was just interested. Your dad sounds like a real catch.'

The girl beamed white teeth back at her. 'I know what that means. I think he would have to be a project. I know he wants to do hugs and stuff but it's like they are trapped inside. He's very strong and a brilliant swimmer. He takes me at the weekend. We have to go early though.'

'You do?'

'Yes, something happened to him when he was a soldier. Kevin says he was fighting terrorists in the desert and a bomb burned him. You should see it.'

'The burn?' Sarah filed the question of who Kevin might be for later, guessing at an older brother.

'Yes, it was really scary when I first saw because it was so big. It's like all over his back, it starts on his arm and stops on his other leg. Dad says he hardly knows it's there. He says we go swimming early because people don't like to see ugly things. I don't think it's ugly. I think it looks like angel wings. I like angels, do you like angels?'

She paused for breath and reached down to an empty biscuit packet, then looked back at Sarah expectantly.

'Angels aren't my thing. When I was your age my favourite was The Famous Five and stealing my brother's books because they were about fighting.' Sarah hesitated before continuing. 'I never told anyone this, Andrea, but I wanted to be a warrior when I was little. With a big sword so I could take care of people who were mean to me. But of course I never had a sword. So I pretended with my dolls and my brother's Action

Men. I also wanted to escape and go on adventures like Alice in Wonderland.'

The girl blinked at Sarah's confession. 'But no angels?' She shuffled closer. 'I love them. Mummy reads about them in the Bible but they're quite nasty in there. I make up stories, have you read Skellig?'

Sarah shook her head.

'That's brilliant, it's my favourite.' She suddenly noticed Sarah had a cut on her cheek. 'How did you get that?'

'I...I...get what?'

'You have a cut on your cheek.' The girl edged a little closer.

Sarah carefully touched her fingertips around the cut. 'So that's why my cheek is sore.'

'It wasn't there earlier, I would have noticed.' The girl sighed and tutted again. 'You should be more careful.' She crawled back to her corner and started searching through her bag, muttering to herself.

'Here we are.' She crawled back over the mattress, a packet of tissues clasped in her hand. 'It's a good job I got dad's prescription or I wouldn't have got these.' She knelt on the floor between Sarah's legs and held out the tissues.

Sarah took them. 'You're very considerate, thank you. I'm sorry I said your dad was grumpy earlier.'

The girl shrugged. 'He is sometimes but then mum is all the time. What can you do?'

Sarah smiled. 'Probably nothing. I can't imagine you ever making anyone grumpy. Now tell me, is the cut still bleeding?'

The girl's eager breath washed warm across her face, sweet from the biscuits. 'Nope.'

'Then we should leave it.' She peered at the girl as if suddenly realising something horrible, feigning shock. 'My goodness, it's yours we should be worried about.'

The girl's small fingers tentatively searched across her face. 'I don't have a cut, do I?'

Sarah shook her head. 'No, but you have a serious amount of grime and goodness knows what on there. Your cheeks look like old roads with white lines down the middle. Why don't you go and get some water.' The girl quickly scuttled over to the water and back. Sarah poured a small amount onto a wad of tissues and began dabbing at the girl's face, although to little effect.

'You have to go harder,' instructed the girl.

'I do?'

'Yes, much harder.'

So Sarah did, with the girl's eyes scrunched tightly closed and her lips pursed together. She dabbed in short hard motions that revealed a trail of pink skin and red cheeks. 'My goodness it's not a troll, it is a girl!'

The closed mouth spread into a smile. The girl waited for Sarah to fold the tissues. 'You're very pretty, are you married?'

'Why thank you,' said Sarah. 'You're very pretty yourself.' She re-applied the tissue, moving from cheeks to chin and then around to her forehead.

The girl waited as long as she could bear to. 'So?'

'Am I married? That's an affirmative.'

'Do you have any children?'

Sarah shook her head.

'Why not?'

'I think, Andrea, that I am going to invoke the snoopy law.'

The girl shook her head. 'It only works for me. Who was the girl, did she die?'

Sarah leaned back, shocked, looking at inquisitive brown eyes, a thin mouth serious. 'What girl?'

'You said I reminded you of a girl, when you saw me.'

'Oh in the street. No…she didn't die, why?'

'You just looked so sad, I thought maybe you missed her.'

Sarah folded the tissue again and wiped away the last overtly dirty smudge. 'I do, I just haven't seen her for a long time. And now I recall, I'm pretty sure she didn't talk quite so much and ask so many questions.'

'Well I need to know about you, don't I!'

'You do?' She scrunched the tissue into a small ball and tossed it into the corner, then leaned back against the wall.

'Of course, to see whether you're one of them.'

'Oh, do I seem like them?'

She shook her head absently. 'The little man kept telling me dad owed him a lot of money. He said if dad didn't pay I'd have to work for him. Which is stupid of course, I'm not even old enough to have a paper round.'

'Every word they speak is a lie, Andrea.'

'And what about you?' The girl's expression was hopeful.

180

'That's for you to decide. I like it we are talking and I would like to know all about you. But only if you think it's not snooping.'

The girl's chin lowered. 'I don't want to talk about them now or this place. Why don't you ask me something nice.'

'Nice? How about how old you are?'

'Guess!' The girl shuffled closer, her knees pushing against Sarah's leg, looking very pleased with herself.

'Six?'

'Doh! Do I look six?'

Sarah shook her head. 'Eight?'

'Saaarah!'

'Twelve?'

'Really?' She preened. 'Do I look twelve?'

'You mean you're not twelve?'

'No, but I'm almost eleven.'

'Wow, when's your birthday?'

'July the seventeenth.'

'Wow!' Sarah said again. 'I suppose that must make you almost eleven.'

'Almost.' The girl paused to weigh a question. 'Can I lean against you? I feel very tired.'

Sarah lifted her arm as the girl clambered over her legs and wriggled in beside her. For a moment she worried where to put her arm but the girl melted into her.

'Sarah?' The voice small from her chest.

'Yes?'

'If they are lying about my dad, why am I here?'

She ran her fingers through the girl's hair and lied. 'I really don't know.'

There was a short silence. 'My dad will be here soon, then they'll be sorry.'

'I hope you're right.'

She felt the girl's head move up and down against her breast. She waited for more questions but there were none. Sarah soaked in all the sensations of this child against her body. This unexpected weight that felt like the most natural thing she had ever known. She could feel the girl's heart fluttering to an even beat, her breathing, now sleeping. Sarah blinked away a hopeless tear, her eyes fierce. Staring at the wall and where she knew the door to be, then the shelf of books. Forcing herself to think. Think, Sarah, think!

FORTY-SIX

A screen with a hole through the middle, most of the keyboard missing and a crack right through the case meant the laptop was truly broken. But the files on the laptop were stored on a small disk inside, which might have survived the trauma. Adam used a small screwdriver to remove the screws on the laptop's base then carefully pulled out the disk. He plugged it into one of the jumbled cables he kept in his bag and then connected it to his own laptop. After few seconds the disk whirred to life and seconds later its contents appeared on the screen. The first hurdle overcome. He set a search running for files with images and looked up at Brian, who watched enthralled.

And then the doorbell rang.

Brian quickly stepped through to the kitchen, checking the bolts were drawn, and then back into the dining room. He closed the door behind him and swept the patio curtain closed, standing poised to one side as they both waited. The doorbell rang again, then moments of silence before someone tried the back door. Then another pause. Adam jumped as a hand rapped hard on the patio door. The hand knocked again, a faint shadow moved across the curtain and then away. They waited. The doorbell rang again and then silence once more.

Brian leaned on the table. 'How long is this going to take?'

'How long!' Adam answered. 'This is a long shot at best. I've no idea if there's even anything here.' He looked down at his computer as the search finished. The screen started filling with images. He flicked through them, the first pages full of pink flesh and women either topless or naked, often with a naked man in close attendance. The flesh gave way to another folder, this one of black and white scanned photos of a young man and a woman on their wedding day, then photos in faded colour of the same couple with two young boys, then pages of recent pictures of smiling child faces. Pictures of grandchildren talking to granddad using the webcam. There were scanned utility bills and newspaper cuttings and magazine articles. There were images of cars and parts from auction and review sites, but not one single image of a Rover or car documentation.

Then the phone started ringing. They both ignored it.

He looked up at Brian. 'There's nothing. We've got every kind of image except what we're looking for.'

Brian moved anxiously. 'Nothing? Maybe you missed it?'

Adam shook his head. 'I've got a filter here for every type of document that could be an image or could contain an image. There's a load of stuff but nothing we're looking for.'

The phone stopped ringing and immediately started again.

'You've got to find something, Adam. This guy was into cars big time. There's pictures upstairs that were in albums, copies of documentation like they were prizes. Everything but the Rover. There's got to be something and we need to find it quick. I'd bet half the neighbours have sodding keys and whoever's ringing is about a breath from deciding matey upstairs needs medical attention.'

Adam held his head in his hands and tried to think. 'If we assume he keeps copies and they're not on the laptop, maybe they're precious enough that he would keep them somewhere else.'

Brian began to look more hopeful. 'What like?'

'That's the problem, it could be anything from an external disk or a flash drive on his key chain.'

Brian had no idea what Adam was talking about but he did know what a key chain was, quickly getting up and climbing the stairs. The phone stopped ringing and stayed silent for a short while.

Adam walked through the debris of the dining room to the living room, looking at everything without really seeing anything, mentally stepping through the imagery of what he had seen in the house. Where would the images be stored? And then he saw a broken picture frame and stopped. He had seen something but where? He walked through the house trying to give the image context, searching through the kitchen and then the hall, the smell of gas and burned flesh growing stronger as he climbed the stairs. He looked through the main bedroom, stepping around Brian who was busily sifting through drawers. He checked the bathroom and then braced himself and stepped into the spare room.

He tried to avoid looking at the body, holding his breath against the nauseating smell. He edged around the hobby table to the scattered litter at the foot of a high bookcase. He bent down and sifted through magazines and old LPs on the floor. He picked up a black picture frame, the modern digital kind. The sort where you plugged in a memory card and sat watching a slideshow. He flipped it over and ejected the card and ran quickly back downstairs.

Thirty seconds later he was paging through image after image of cars and documentation. He sorted them in date order and jumped to the last of the images. There were about ten of a gleaming green Rover taken from all angles outside the house, two yellow signs in the back window he could not read but could guess what they said. He shook his head at the irony as he highlighted all the files and copied them to his laptop. He pulled the vehicle documentation full screen, the new owner details written in neat handwriting. *Simon Thompson,* an address in *Cleethorpes,* which was a place Adam knew of without knowing where it was.

The phone started ringing again.

He called Brian, failing to keep the triumph from his voice. And then something else occurred to him, a discordant note he had not dwelt on because he had not been looking for photos of people. He flipped back to the images on the old man's disk drive. He sorted them in date order and jumped to the bottom. There were lots of pictures in the webcam folder of smiling grandchildren. The image that stood out was the very last one. It had been taken three hours earlier, was badly distorted and from a low angle looking up. It showed half of one face and then all of another from the chin upwards. It must have been taken as the laptop was drop kicked, the webcam built into the lid. The picture was so blurred it contained no identifiable detail save for the fact both looked like white men with blond hair.

Brian appeared, followed by the smell of gas. He leaned in to look at the image on the screen as Adam looked up at him. The smell of gas was stronger than it had been.

'What've you done Brian?'

'I haven't done anything that wasn't already set in motion. But we have about a minute before this whole place gets busy burning.'

The doorbell rang, the sound joining the cacophony of the ringing phone. They both looked to the living room and the beam of a torch shining through the window. It pulled away as a shadow tried to peer through the curtains.

Brian's voice was now urgent. 'You need to pack your stuff and we need to go.' He released the catch on the patio and slid it open by an inch. Adam disconnected the old man's drive and left it on the table, closing the lid of his laptop as he slid it into the bag.

'Follow me out,' Brian said. 'Then run for the back fence, get over it and track back around to the car. I'll be right behind you.' Brian opened the door and Adam, without a thought, ran across the grass, ducking beneath an empty washing line he saw at the last second, high stepping through wet mud to a low mass of thick branches that backed on to the tall fence. He reached up and dropped the bag over and tried to get leverage. His foot found purchase as he heard a shout from the house that was not Brian and then footsteps right behind. Then Brian was beside him and over the fence. Another shout from behind but closer as Adam tried hoisting himself up, the beam of a torch jumping across the fence. He could hear laboured breathing getting closer, then a contained *whump* and shattering glass and a brief flare of orange that filled the night. Then he felt a hand on his jacket as Brian lifted and dragged him over and bundled him to the other side.

FORTY-SEVEN

Simon closed his eyes although it was dark already, the whiskey in his mouth a moment's distraction from the conflict of his mind. The images of flesh flickered fast, the dark within slithering wetly, whispering its sweet nothings as it squeezed free the need that washed through his veins.

He was conflicted of course. Some part of him fought. A part that clung to what he used to be. It was a wistful fight though. A fight lost before it started, this need was too much of what he had become, this dark that writhed inside.

There was no great mystery to *why*. He could place a pin on the key markers of his life, the catalogue of decisions and bad choices made over time that had gradually shaped his mind and his need, the genesis for this journey a schism in a happy childhood. He had no complaints, not really. Parents have their own agendas, their own frailties to be kept hidden. They had paid their price.

He could not recall what *she* looked like any more. Not the finer detail. Just her short dark hair, her dark eyes that turned him marshmallow inside. Her smile, that turned him inside out. Even then she had possessed some grace, tempting him with her bare child limbs as she peered shyly around his bedroom door, wearing one of his T-shirts, too big for her and reaching down to her knees.

'Can I come in?' she would ask. He could still hear her voice.

'Sure,' he would say. She would glide around the periphery of his room, plucking at comics and examining the plastic figures adorning his shelves.

'What does this one do?'

And he would tell her. 'He has vision that is like the sun. He has to use glasses to stop from burning everyone.'

She would move around the room, eventually gravitating to him, dropping restlessly onto the foot of his bed and sitting cross-legged, pulling the shirt down over her knees with a self-conscious smile.

'What do you want to do?' she would say.

He would look down at the book or comic he was reading and close it. 'What do you want to do?'

'It is up to you.' Her accent was almost too English to be English.

He knew her for just under two years from the first day she arrived to the day she had not been there anymore. So quiet at first, busily watching. There was something different about her. Skin that always looked like summer and eyes that stretched wider, seemed bigger. Those eyes had cost Jimmy Sanders his life, although nobody knew. She had been there only two weeks when she crashed through the door and disappeared upstairs. She had cried a lot, but not like that. Eventually his mother pulled the truth from her. Jimmy Sanders had spent every day at school from the first calling her a *Chink*.

Simon could not explain what he subsequently did, not then. Nothing had really mattered to him before, especially not girls. She had been explained away by his mother as the daughter of his father's friend, over from Singapore. She would be staying for a while. After two weeks they had barely exchanged more than soft grins, but for some reason an attack on her seemed like an attack on him. An invasion of his world, an encroachment on something he was responsible for. It was an instinctive reaction. He knew now why that was. But not then. Everything is instinctive when you are twelve.

So he warned off Jimmy. Most kids paid attention when Simon gave warnings. But not Jimmy. He was untouchable with a supporting cast of the disaffected. He kept up his chants and took to pushing her around. One afternoon she came home with the buttons ripped from her shirt and that night Jimmy said goodbye to his friends, walking between pools of street light with smoke trailing behind.

Simon confronted Jimmy but he would not listen. Maybe he just saw Simon for the age he was and not for what he was physically. In Jimmy's mind Simon's twelve years were no match for fifteen. Physically there was no match. Jimmy was Simon's first, silent and mouth gaping. His eyes wide with disbelieving horror right until they lost focus. The remains of Jimmy Sanders washed up on Hunstanton beach three years later. Very few missed him and nobody called her a Chink any more.

Nights in those days were about the music downstairs, the distant jukebox thump and the chime of slot machines, the endless voices merging to each other. Living above a pub was all Simon knew, these were the sounds of his every day. When sleep reached out for him it did so with gentle hands, but it was a foreign world to her.

The first time she appeared in his doorway, she was shivering and naked, although all he saw was an inquisitive face and an elbow, a fleeting glimpse of a shoulder and a bare hip. 'Do you have a spare T-shirt?' she asked.

'Sure,' he said, knowing full well she had some of her own. He stepped across and pulled one from his drawer and threw it to her. She scooped it up with a fleeting flash of flesh and disappeared. The next night she reappeared with the shirt hanging large over her slight frame. The three fish hovering just where he imagined her legs joined her body.

'Can I come in?' she asked. She always asked, each and every time.

That winter they played checkers and cards and read books to the accompanying groans of the radiator and the distant cacophony of the pub. Sometimes they would sit side by side on the bed watching TV or just looking out at the night sky. These were his favourite times. She would tell him about her world which seemed so alien to him and now so far away to her. A world of sun and warm rain that fell so hard it was like standing in a shower. And heat that she said was like a hundred hair dryers. Where all the people looked different, not like this new world where almost everyone was white and a few were blacker than the night. Her world, she said, was everything between.

Winter became spring and then a summer that stood out in his mind, especially for three weeks in which she said the daytime sun and the midday rain reminded her of home. He took to sitting on the bed in just his shorts, at first from the heat and then because she was fascinated by the stretch of muscle across his body. He liked that and the touch of her fingers as she traced the contours, although he had no clue why it should feel so good.

In those hottest weeks she did the same, wriggling out of the shirt and sitting there in just her knickers. Although he had not dared trace the shape of her body as they played cards and sat looking out of the window, every accidental touch of their legs and arms full of charge and unfathomable meaning.

188

Simon turned thirteen and she stayed twelve, still flat and lean save for the emerging shape of hips and legs, despite it taking the rest of the summer for him to actually notice. And then one day she pulled free her top, despite the sun being a distant memory and the radiators groaning their discord. And the dots connected. Simon reached across and gently held her arm and pulled her towards him. She whispered, *At last.* And they wriggled down and held each other close, getting warm with hands on bare skin. A wealth and land unknown. Both feeling within that something else must happen but not knowing *what.*

They discovered *what* the following spring and she was gone before the summer was over, taken from him one morning amid a heavy air after they fell asleep with limbs entangled.

The irony, the irony pinched Simon inside. His kindred spirit, two beating parts of a whole. The irony, he drank to the irony. *The daughter of his father's friend!* She was the dirty secret whisked away amid parental horror. Like they as children were the ones to feel guilty. What did his parents expect? Telling neither child the fragile secret lest it escape, for fear a family might be seen for what it was.

The genesis. He found her as soon as he could, when he was nineteen. His father begged and pleaded in his final moments, directing him to the sprawl of Malaysia's gateway city. Simon found her there, possessed only of a woman's charm and by a man and a child of her own. His life then shaped by choices and their consequences, a life of searching for a ghost as his needs evolved.

He submitted now to his need and drained the last of the glass, padding across the landing into the spare room. He checked the bed was neatly made and crease free, then to the bathroom. He double checked the window was secure, rinsed the glass and stepped out of his shorts and naked into the shower, his body pitted by shadow amid the weave of muscle, a body that drew endless female eyes but had never known the caress of a woman.

He washed and rinsed and towelled himself dry, pulling chinos over his nakedness, a clean T-shirt down over his wide shoulders, tight and white. He checked the bathroom window a final time then padded down the stairs, through the dining room and living room to the hallway, into the garage, the concrete cold under his bare feet, the need raging through his veins, the dark inside dancing the light fandango.

FORTY-EIGHT

A row of chimneys spewed smoke to a sky made pink by the glow of city lights beneath it, gradually growing in the horizon as they approached Cleethorpes. Adam pulled into a floodlit forecourt and refuelled while Brian hunted down a local streetmap. Then they both hunched over a small table eating sandwiches and drinking coffee, the map open between them. The address Simon Thompson had left in Peterborough was real. At least the road existed. Brian outlined his plan. He would check the house at the address while Adam searched the internet for everything he could about Simon Thompson.

Twenty minutes later they were driving towards a brightly lit pub jutting proud from the promenade. Two roads ran parallel, one rising high above the other, separated by a steep bank of grass that was home to seats, steps and a dormant crazy golf course.

Adam turned at a roundabout and descended to the lower road and the seafront, pulling into a vacant space. They both looked out at the dark void, the light picking out shallow valleys of wet sand, the distant waves crested white in the horizon. Adam wound his window down and was instantly assaulted by the buffeting air and ocean roar, the smell of the sea. He wound it back up again.

Brian buttoned his jacket. 'This is as good a place as any. Sit tight and compile as much data as you can. Make sure you keep the doors locked and if anyone gives you reason, get out of here and call Boer. He'll know what to do. Same goes if I'm not back in a couple of hours.'

He climbed out and Adam followed. Brian pulled open the boot and reached inside for his kit bag, producing a dark rubber torch that he slid between his belt and jeans. Then a pitted rounders bat that he pushed up his jacket sleeve. Adam watched, wide-eyed, but said nothing. Brian cast him a sideways glance. 'I'm only going to look. This is just in case anybody looks back. Don't worry about me.'

Adam was not worried, not for Brian. He watched him pull a small leather pouch from the bag, which was pushed into the chest pocket of his jacket. Then Brian winked, slapped him hard on the shoulder and jogged off along the promenade and up the grass rise. A small figure chased by his own shadow.

For a time Adam stood still, the buffeting breeze comforting, letting his thoughts run free. The horror of the last few hours was slowly giving way to a barely suppressed anticipation. Was this the place? He checked his expectation, trying not to hope yet that he might actually see Sarah again, that this might end with smiles.

He climbed back into the car and locked the doors. His face bathed in green light as his laptop booted. He waited for a connection to the internet but it failed. He tried moving the laptop around in the car, onto the passenger seat and dashboard, but still no signal. He looked out at the promenade and late night dog walkers struggling with flapping coats, realising there was probably little call for wireless internet in the North Sea. He deliberated while staring at the ocean, then set the laptop back on the passenger seat and reversed, starting back along the promenade.

FORTY-NINE

Simon dropped a mat onto the floor beneath the workbench and sat on it, his arms out behind for support and the soles of his feet against the wall, his legs bent. He braced himself and channelled his strength through his hips, pushing through his thighs. The door weighed 150 kilograms and sat on a metal plate and four rollers, set in two shallow gutters cut into the floor. It took over 200 kilograms of force to roll the door out and start it into the room. It was designed specifically so only he or machinery could open it. Only he, Hakan and the brothers even knew it was there.

His breath quickened and his face reddened as he pushed through his legs. The door shifted, then gradually rolled into the room. When there was a sufficient gap he pivoted around and braced his shoulder against the opening, extending his arm and jacking the concrete sideways. When it was fully open he shuffled back into the garage and squatted, regaining his breath while peering beneath the workbench into the dark of the room.

The moonlight from the garage window helped his eyes adjust, slowly defining the shapes inside. The woman was sitting on the floor, facing him with her back against the wall. On the mattress lay the sleeping girl, a small outlined shape, her hair splayed. Now he could make out the woman's features, could see she was staring sentinel right back at him.

'Go away,' she said from the dark.

'Turn the light on,' he said.

'I can't,' she replied. 'You turned off the power, you know that.'

'No, I didn't.'

A brief pause. 'Well it doesn't work now.'

He deliberated and then backed out from under the bench, pulled closed the garage curtains and went back to the hall. He switched on the garage light and squatted down again. The small room was still shadowed by the bench, so he swung it around to one side. Now he could see.

The woman had moved, was now much nearer the opening with one knee on the floor. Like a sprinter waiting, her arms loose at her sides. The garage light cut a harsh contrast with the shadow across her body.

'What are you doing?' he asked.

'You're not taking her.' Her voice was quiet and calm.

'Who says I'm here for her?'

'What else would you be here for? To apologise for the stale food, or that she even has to be here? "I'm sorry I kidnapped you but it's all your daddy's fault." You're sick.'

'It's true,' he replied.

'No it's not, Simon. It's bullshit.'

'And you know this?'

'I know enough of your sort. The lies you justify everything with, the consuming need.'

He shuffled closer.

'Get away,' she said. Her back arched as if under starter's orders.

Intrigued, he moved again. 'I don't want to hurt you, Sarah. I will not hurt the girl. I just need to talk to her. Don't make me hurt you.' His voice was edged with a genuine sadness that lost her, delaying her reaction for a fraction of a second. He was almost through the opening before she realised and launched herself forward, sweeping with her right hand towards his throat and stabbing at his ribs with the left.

The suddenness and the speed of her attack threw him, her lips drawn back from her teeth and a cold determination in her eyes. He did not see the glass in her hands until it passed through the shards of light. The glass bowl. He barely had time enough to reflex his left arm in defence, protecting his throat, the glass slicing a deep tear across his forearm, another sharp pain across his right side and again into his ribs as her momentum brought her crashing with a snarl into him.

He tried grabbing both her wrists as she repeatedly stabbed the glass at him, finally grasping them and pushing her hard back against the wall, dropping his shoulders to protect himself from the immediate jabs of her knees and feet as she screamed and fought. He squeezed her wrists until she dropped the jagged glass, now smeared with blood, both her palms supine, bloody and cut deeply. She seemed so fragile, so full of venom, shouting as she kicked and kneed him, her teeth biting into his shoulder as he moved in too close. She was no match for his strength but it was like wrestling three people at once. He filtered it, damped out the noise, the fury and the pin pricks of pain as he fought for control. Every ounce of her was invested in the fight and then he realised why.

Invested in distracting him, her mouth forming the same word over and over; *run, run, run*. He looked across at the child, now just the bundled blanket. He looked over his shoulder and to the child standing behind him, wide-eyed and rigid against the wall, next to the opening. Seeing his attention fix on her jolted her, and she scrambled out through the gap and disappeared into the garage.

Sarah immediately locked her legs around him and hung onto his body, trying to pull him down. But it was futile. He prised her loose and did what he should have done already. He brought his hand down hard across her face, but even then he pulled back from the blow. She lay motionless, a sudden peace. He spent a moment studying her, wondering and then he heard the child sobbing, frustrated as she tried to open the front door, the noise fading as she disappeared through the living room and nearer the keys, although what were the chances she would find or even reach them? He propelled himself backwards, through the opening and across the garage.

As soon as he disappeared Sarah started after him, blinking at the garage light, her face throbbing, adrenalin causing her to stand unbalanced and fall sideways, glancing painfully off the workbench. The girl screeched somewhere inside the house.

She ran through the garage and hall, living room and into the dining room. She ignored Simon with his back to her, bearing down on the girl now desperately trying to open the patio door. She focused only on finding a phone, she had seen one, was almost ready to sprint up the stairs when her eyes set on the bureau.

The girl turned to face Simon, backing against the patio door, sniffing and looking at Simon then past him to Sarah as she plucked the phone from its charger and stepped into the living room. She turned her back to him, hunched protectively as she pressed the green dial button, a tone as Simon rounded on her, not daring to look, sensing him loom, fingers pressing 999 as quickly and carefully as they dared. Knowing he was almost on her as she bowled the handset underarm through the living room, skimming across the carpet, through the door into the hallway, coming to rest by the boots and shoes. The orange screen lit up. She turned to face him but he crashed through her, pushing her down and away with his arm, catching her ribs with his rising knee, jarring her teeth and cutting her lip. She tasted blood as she rolled to her feet and ran straight back into the dining room, hearing him now in the hall.

The girl stood petrified. Sarah shouted for her to move as she gave her attention to the wooden chair. The girl jumped to the kitchen entrance. The chair sat in its place beside the bureau, the chair she had been tied to. She picked it up and spun like a hammer thrower, sweeping the chair around and into the glass of the patio door. The force made the door judder and a crack, the chair breaking apart in her hands, the momentum taking her around and despairing. She faced the door and kicked at it with the ball of her foot. The glass flexed but remained as it had. And then Simon filled the dining room doorway. She heard him and turned to face him, bending down and picking up a length of broken chair from the floor. She said to Andrea, in a low voice, 'Upstairs.' And then she ran at him.

Simon was not sure what to expect next, this certainly was not it. She came at him fast in a shallow arc, like a gymnast it occurred to him as she took a final stride and leapt straight at him. And she hit him hard. It was like catching a forty-five kilo medicine ball fired from a machine, he did it but it unbalanced him. He staggered back with Sarah's legs like clamps around him, jamming the length of chair across his throat, forcing him to take another step back and down onto one knee.

Andrea watched her ride Simon to the ground. Sarah had drilled her, what she should do. Try the front door, quick places to look for keys, the patio door and if they both failed run upstairs, open a window and scream. Sarah had repeated that over and over, first as she eased the screws from the bookshelf and then as she scratched away at the glass bowl. It had scared Andrea, Sarah's determination. At the same she realised everything Sarah was doing was for her, just as the fury Sarah invested in the fight scared her too. But then Andrea had no understanding of the consequences of failure. She flinched as Simon plucked Sarah off him and tossed her aside. Then she ran, three rapid steps onto the landing and then up the main flight.

Sarah's shoulder took the brunt of the impact as she hit the wall below the living room window, immediately turning as Simon struggled to his feet, staring at her incredulously before bounding up the stairs after Andrea.

Sarah ran straight into the kitchen. She had not been here before. It was square and minimal, small because part of it was the hidden room. She flung open drawers, looking for keys while grabbing at anything remotely sharp. Her hands smeared blood across everything she touched. Her eyes lit upon a knife rack and she immediately discarded everything else. She heard Andrea squealing upstairs, sounds that in any other house might be of joy if not for the terror permeating the noise. Sarah's short list of options were being crossed off in rapid succession.

That Simon would come for the girl had seemed inevitable. When he did, she knew it would not be the gentle Simon who had studiously cleaned her wounds. It would be the addict she would face, full of need. She could not let him take Andrea then, any more than she would let him take her now. Right now she needed him to come into the kitchen. She reached across to the knife rack and pulled out a paring knife, a boning knife and then a large carving knife, laying them beside each other on the counter as his heavy footsteps descended the stairs.

And then he appeared just beyond the kitchen doorway, breathing heavily and working hard to control it. He looked at her and she at him, the white cotton of his T-shirt rising with each deep breath, a wide band of blood stretching down his right side and soaking into his trousers. He held the girl under his left arm like a rolled length of carpet, her hair hanging down, mewling, long streaks of blood on his arm that reflected the light.

'Put her down,' Sarah said.

He gave her that same incredulous look. 'Be reasonable, Sarah, what are you really going to accomplish here? The doors are all locked and so are the windows. It's midnight. If you could stick your head outside and scream everyone will think you're a pissed-up kid. Nobody's going to care.'

'Then you should let me try.'

He smiled and took a step towards the kitchen.

'Put her down,' she repeated, pulling the paring knife from the counter, holding it loose at her side.

He shook his head. 'What're you going to do with that? You're more likely to hurt the girl.'

She flicked her wrist and the knife spun towards his bare feet, causing him to hop backwards as it clattered over the kitchen floor and into the dining room.

She reached across to the counter and held the boning knife in the same way, loose at her side.

'Put her down. In the dining room, anywhere. Just somewhere she can't see.'

Now he looked at her confused. She didn't wait for his reply.

'I know we're not going anywhere, it's not about that now. But you're not having her, not as long as I have a single breath in me. Put her down, I have something I want to show you.'

And she doubted even that. He had not once shown the slightest interest in her. He had saved her from Hakan, she was sure of that now. Everything now focused on why he had done that. She was down to her last option, not least because of all the shadowed doors it might open. It came down to one simple fact. Almost all the men who had ever seen her naked subsequently turned all kinds of stupid.

Simon gently swung Andrea down and walked her unprotesting to the other side of the door, away from the kitchen. His attention was now fully on Sarah.

She kept her eyes on him, moving her free hand to the top button of her shirt, unfastening it, then moving down as she released each button, leaving smudges of blood on the white fabric as it parted. She pulled open her shirt and shrugged the material from her shoulders, now standing in just her jeans with the shirt hanging by her waist, her torso lean and flat.

She saw it in Simon's eyes, a widening of his pupils, a dark intent that shifted across his face. He took a step towards her without knowing why, his features shaped by need. He saw her now.

She let the material fall over her wrists to the floor and Simon took another step and then another, now standing in front of her, his eyes on hers. He reached down to her hand and the knife, encircling her wrist and holding it firm. She looked defiantly up at him as he cupped her face in his free hand and ran his thumb across her cheek, then his fingers down her neck and over her shoulders and down her arm, the skin of his palm hard and warm. Gliding around her waist and then up over her ribs and across her chest, his fingers each in turn catching on a nipple. Then back to her neck and face. His brown eyes fixed on hers all the time.

197

She busily rehearsed in her mind what she would do, imagining the distance from her left arm to the kitchen counter, then to the carving knife. She pictured it, rehearsed the movement while working to veil her intentions, barely aware as he tenderly brushed her hair from her face. She closed her eyes, threw out her arm, closing her fingers around the handle, awkwardly but enough that she had a grip. She turned her wrist and the blade as she punched inwards with all her strength. The blade travelled three inches before his hand clamped around her forearm. She opened her eyes. He was still looking down at her.

He said, 'You're all kinds of resourceful.'

She looked insolently back at him, but inside she was already running from the consequences.

'You can't touch her,' she said.

'I'm not going to.' He raised her wrists as he had before, hands supine. He took both knives and leaned across her, pushing them back into the rack. 'I'm going to take her back.'

She watched as he stepped backwards out of the kitchen. She could feel goosebumps climbing her stomach and arms. She bent down and picked up her shirt as he picked up Andrea.

She listened to him walk through the living room, the house silent now, her throat sore, all of her sore. She pulled on her shirt and re-fastened the top button, flaring out the bottom, exposing her stomach and a narrowing stretch of skin to her chest.

From behind her she heard the sound of heavy concrete moving. She leaned over the work surface and examined the wall. It was relatively newly decorated, the cupboards above fairly modern. There were two of them. She pulled one open, seeing two shelves of stacked tupperware. She studied the door for a second and then on a whim pressed her palm against the inside, wincing at the pain of pushing it flat, putting pressure on her fingertips. A palm print in her congealing blood and the imprint of a thumb and four fingers. She closed the cupboard as she heard him pad back through the house.

He appeared in the doorway, holding the remains of the glass bowl and the bloody shards of glass in his hands. 'That's the problem with the light in the room fixed,' he said, looking at her in amusement. 'The bulb somehow managed to unscrew itself.' He placed the fragments of glass onto the draining board. 'How did you break that?'

She looked at the glass and replied, 'With considerable difficulty.'

'How?' he persisted.

'I used a screw from the bookshelf to cut the glass like cutting tiles. Then it was a matter of breaking the glass along the fracture, which was very difficult.'

He shook his head and held out his left hand for her. She could see the cut still bleeding along his wrist and forearm. She had been a split second from making a much deeper cut across his throat, then her world might have been a little different.

'The girl is off limits,' she stated.

He looked back at her but said nothing. She let him wait a second then stepped forward and took his hand, allowing him to lead her up the stairs.

FIFTY

A dam turned off the promenade and drove inland, the small green globe on his laptop refusing to show an internet connection. After a few junctions he turned parallel to the coastline, the late night streets empty save for occasional groups moving at a disjointed crawl. He passed a white sign with black lettering and into Grimsby, past a dormant school and then a square centred by grass, a row of shuttered shops and a glowing takeaway. The globe flashed and then stayed solid. He had a connection but carried on, looking for a stronger signal, but the globe blinked off. So he reversed back to the square and flicked off the headlights.

He searched for his copy of Simon's address, aware of the BBC Homepage slowly loading on the laptop. When he looked at the screen a young girl's face stared back at him, at the top of the screen the headline *Child kidnapped from High Street*. He clicked the link and the same picture appeared amid text, then a stock photo of Hambury on a busy day. He picked out partial sentences from the text as he paged down to an image of a green Rover, the number plate blanked, then another of a burnt-out car. The sequence of images led him to think the car was the Rover. And then he froze, giving a despairing groan as he read the text. It was not the Rover. It was the charred remains of Sarah's silver Toyota. *Oh God!* His first news of her in over a day, it weighed him heavy in the seat.

Adam sat motionless for a long time, just staring at the burnt remains of Sarah's car, fearful of reading more for what it might tell him of her fate. He only moved when the screen blanked, stretching out a finger and tapping a key. The screen blinked on. He moved to the top and started reading, sighing with relief when there was no mention of anything inside the car.

Once he had reduced the article to the bare facts there was very little detail. The when and where, a brief background of Andrea Scott and why she was in Hambury, a brief mention of parents, the fact that they were estranged but with neither mentioned by name, a short summary on the idyllic market town of Hambury. Sarah was mentioned indirectly as an alleged eyewitness who was also missing. The phrasing made it sound as though there was an unspoken implication.

He typed keywords into a search engine and found almost identical stories featured on all the tabloids and news sites, the opening gambits to a big story but no detail to create sensation. Their main thrust was the shock of a child kidnapped from a busy high street, then of the eyewitness now missing, the same unspoken implication. The light in the car shifted as he moved from site to site, soaking up every word.

Adam's first impulse when he finished reading was to find Brian. He immediately checked that thought. The fact that Andrea's kidnapping was now news changed nothing. Brian was already checking Simon's address. If Adam could tie Simon Thompson to that address online, there was potential to access a lot of data. He spent a moment thinking where he should start and then his fingers danced, images and text moving up and down the screen as his eyes scanned the page.

In ten minutes he had a myriad of Simon Thompsons cross-referenced to the east coast but none he could match to the address. His fingers hovered as he deliberated and then danced again, logging into his company's web portal, his determination and sense of urgency ploughing him past any reservations. It gave him an instant hit. The address Brian was checking was Simon's last registered place of residence. Adam searched through the DVLA, electoral roll, insurance and school records. He even ran a credit check against Simon and the address, returning a fail because Simon had no credit history.

When he was done Adam had gathered a lot of information without knowing much at all. He knew Simon's education had finished at sixteen, when he had been immediately employed by Thompson Deep Sea as a crew hand and then a watch captain, relief skipper and charter skipper. Simon had no police record, not even a speeding fine. He had a driving licence but was not listed as ever owning a car. He was not married and there were no registered dependants.

Adam felt deflated and conflicted. He had at least confirmed the address was Simon's. The right thing for Adam now was to ring Boer but he was in no hurry to talk to him. He sent Boer a voicemail, summarising Peterborough and what they found there, confirming the address in Cleethorpes was Simon's.

He still felt restless, as if there was more he could do with the information he had. He tapped a finger against the laptop and flicked back through the data. He had Simon's childhood address from his school records. It was local. He searched for the address and watched wide-eyed as the map loaded on the screen.

By his reckoning he had driven past Simon's childhood home twice in the last hour. It was the large pub right on the sea front. Another search pulled up the pub's website, a brochure page of soft lighting and smiling faces. He deliberated, drumming his fingers lightly on the keyboard. He set the laptop on the passenger seat, switched on the headlights and turned the car.

Minutes later he was parked at the back of the pub. A low wall skirted the perimeter of the car park, the long drop to wet sand guarded by a metal railing. A view out to the North Sea Simon had spent his childhood looking over. Adam pushed the laptop under the passenger seat and walked across the car park towards the pub, passing people filing in the opposite direction.

FIFTY-ONE

From the stairs Simon ushered Sarah into the bathroom and left her there, heading into his bedroom and carefully pulling off his T-shirt. He listened to the bathroom door close and the lock slide as he twisted sideways in front of the mirror. He carefully pushed at the skin, the wound jagged across his ribs. He saw pink flesh, a glimpse of muscle and bone immediately blotted by dark red.

He pressed the T-shirt against his side and deliberated. He was reluctant to stitch the wound but it was deep. With three months at sea ahead of him he could not afford an infection. He hesitated, then pulled a wooden box from a shelf and took a reel of nylon and a short bowed needle from the box. He fetched the whiskey and used it to rinse his hands, smiling to himself as he tipped a measure into his hand cupped under the wound, methodically rubbing the alcohol into the exposed flesh and the skin around it. His eyes pinched closed as he waited for the stinging to abate.

The toilet flushed as he disinfected the thread and then the needle, his ears straining for any sound as he plucked at his flesh and progressively pulled it closed. He heard a tap run and then only the dull drone of the bathroom extractor.

When he was finished he knotted the thread and cut it, cleaning the needle and returning the box to the shelf. He dabbed blood from the wound and examined the line of tight stitches. Another scar but it would do.

On the landing he plucked a towel from the airing cupboard and knocked on the bathroom door. She kept him waiting long enough for him to picture the window open and his prize gone. Then the lock slid back and the door opened. He cautiously stepped inside.

Sarah had undressed, the naked landscape of her body broken only by a small triangle of white cotton. In that instant the dark inside leapt from him, pinned her down and gorged on her body, which she saw in the flare of his eyes and the barely contained flinch of his body.

He handed her the towel and forced himself to turn away, unfastening his trousers and stepping into the shower, the beat of water against his skin soothing the rampage inside. He soaped away the blood while watching her through the screen.

She looked back at him, contemplated him, then hooked a thumb each side of her hips and dragged the material down over her narrow legs. Her skin radiated an olive sheen of faded tan, save for a small triangle of white flesh and neatly trimmed pubic hair.

She squeezed into the shower and moved close to him, the water consuming her, flattening her hair and running eagerly over her body. Her large brown eyes looked up at his, eyes that took Simon in a blink back to his childhood, the sound of the bar downstairs, a child's voice. *Can I come in?*

And back to the shower and this woman inflexible beneath his hands, her fingers searching around his side and bumping over the stitches, the devil in her smile. Without knowing why he leaned down and kissed her, tasting her lips and the water that ran from them. Aware of her palms now pressed against his chest and realising she was easing him out of the shower. He resisted at first, not willing to give up the moment, but relented, knowing his time was drawing near.

He knotted the towel around his waist and opened the cabinet, carefully smoothing a plaster over the stitches, another over the tear on his left arm. He took two more and a roll of bandage and walked through to the spare room.

It was neat and clean and ready, a soft carpet underfoot. It contained only a wooden wardrobe beside the netted window, an old wooden chair and a bedside cabinet beside the pristine white sheets of the bed. He flicked off the light and set the chair facing the door. He sat and waited, looking across the bed to the landing, watching Sarah's shadow shift beneath the bathroom door. A click and the light vanished.

Then she appeared, a ghost in the dark, searching him out and then seeing him, stepping naked towards him through diagonal shafts of light, poised and graceful. He felt giddy, forcing himself to breathe.

For Sarah it was now about playing for time and hoping for an opportunity, trying to occupy him and surviving, mentally more than physically. The voices in her head were screaming but there was nowhere left to run. She entered the room and stepped into the gap between his legs, climbing onto him. She placed one knee on each of his thighs, using her feet to balance as she sat back, the air full of shampoo and soap.

Simon reached out and she let him take her hand, watching him bind the bandage around her palm and the deep cut, securing it with a plaster. He pulled the other hand towards him and did the same.

'Thank you,' she said, flexing the fingers of both hands and looking at him, her eyes inquisitive. She reached out a finger and traced the lean ridges of his stomach and up around the slab of muscle across his chest. 'You like being clean.' A statement more than a question.

He nodded back at her.

Her eyes searched his. 'You like being tidy.'

He nodded again.

'You are a very ill man.'

'Actually, I'm very healthy.'

She leaned into him, so she could tap the side of his head. 'In here, you're ill.' Her hand dropped back to his lap, the fabric of the towel soft against her skin.

'That is what this society would say.'

'I think most would. Are you going to hurt me?'

'I am not a violent man.'

'There is something else inside though, isn't there? What will that darkness have you do to me?' She tugged at the towel around his waist, loosening it.

'Whatever my needs are, I'm not a violent man.'

She pulled open the towel, balancing herself with one hand on his shoulder as she pulled it free each side, settling back down. She brushed her hair behind her ears, watching his flesh grow as it hardened, rising against the inside of his thigh. She reached down and took hold of him, heavy in her hand as she squeezed and he thickened, using the tips of her fingers to stroke the shaft rigid.

'I want you, you know,' she said.

'No you don't, you're doing this for the girl.'

'I am, but that does not change that I want you. I want to enjoy this.'

'If you say so.'

'You know, men have been trying to fuck me for as long as I can remember.'

'I'm not surprised.'

'That can get very tiring, let me tell you. As for candidates though, who I would willingly give my body to, I can't think of anyone better suited.'

This might have been a truth for Sarah in a different life. She let her hand drift to the base of the shaft and squeezed as hard as she could, her fingers not making the full circumference, feeling his warm gasp wash across her face.

'I have one rule,' she said.

'You do?'

'Well actually it's three. You already know the first.'

'Don't hurt you,' he answered. 'The second?'

'Don't cover my mouth. I get claustrophobic.'

'What with?'

'Anything.'

'And the last?'

'Touch the girl and I will kill you.'

He smiled back at her. 'I thought you already tried that.'

'I wasn't trying my hardest.'

'Really. What would you use?'

'Anything, my nails and teeth if I had to. I just wanted you to know that.'

He let his eyes wander across her breasts and down to her hand, still holding him. And then in a fluid movement he lifted her onto the bed, setting her down in the middle.

He did not join her straight away, caution moving him to lock the door, her eyes following him as he placed the key on top of the wardrobe and came back to the bed, lying down beside her. He eased her flat with a hand that glided across her skin and looked into those wide innocent eyes.

'I will do my best,' he said, 'to not break your rules.'

FIFTY-TWO

It had been thirty minutes since the light from the window blinked out. In that time only dark had reigned. Little moved save for leaves bossed by the breeze, a cat stalking an unseen prey across the lawn. Brian waited at the back of the garden, shrouded by conifers and the bare limbs of an apple tree. A shadow amid shadows, crouched and listening to the cycle of late night sounds. His eyes moved from window to window and back to the twin patio doors. The front door was too new and exposed, too well manufactured. The garage would be easy but noisy and no guarantee of access into the house. The patio doors were older, the locks worn and loose. He hoped.

He edged slowly around, keeping low behind sparse shrubs within the profile of the fence, each step planted and sure before starting another. Then two quick strides across the patio, kneeling and easing down the handle. It was locked but you never knew. He snapped on the torch for a second, peered into the lock and then off again. Strike two, no key.

He pulled the pouch from his breast pocket and from the pouch took a thin length of metal with a half hook on the end, and a second, similar but with a paddle, like a tiny hockey stick. He pushed the paddle into the lock and turned as if it were the key. Then he slid the pick into the lock, rocking it in and out. He listened for each click that sounded a little surer, picturing the pins rising and falling. Counting off each pin as it came to rest on the barrel. Pin six and five, rafting backwards and forwards. Four, three – mentally counting the seconds he had been kneeling in plain sight. Two – so clumsy but all he was capable of these days. The nerves in his hand were so damaged he had trouble picking a coin off a table, let alone a lock.

His gaze moved to the detail beyond the glazed glass, a dining room, a kitchen and a living room, a set of stairs. One – he folded the pouch back into his pocket and pushed the door open in a single swift movement, stepping in and immediately closing it behind him again.

He stood and listened, easing into the cadence of the sleeping house, wood and metal contracting with the cooling air, a kitchen clock marking each passing second. Then with slow deliberate steps he moved to check the empty kitchen and living room. He crossed to the stairs, placing a foot on the first step and gradually transferring his weight. Testing each step as he went, easing out any groans, he patiently rose one slow step at a time.

Twenty minutes and he reached the landing, breathing shallowly. There was a white wooden balcony and a series of white doors, all closed. Light suddenly stretched from beneath one of the doors. He watched and waited, hearing no footfall or muttered voices. Minutes passed and the light went out. He kept time with the rhythm of the house, listening for a note out of tune.

Finally he stepped to the nearest door, the one with the light. He eased down the handle a millimetre by millimetre, pushing the door open by the same increments. When there was enough of a gap he eased into the room.

It was a main bedroom, neat and tidy with the curtains open and the bed neatly made, the quilt pulled back. No sleeping shapes inside. He edged out and to the next room, slowly edging the door open, stepping into a smaller space with a neatly made bunk bed pushed against a wall. The clutter of young children scattered in ordered piles about the room. The light blinked on across the landing once more.

Less cautious now he followed the light back to the main bedroom and a bedside lamp, running his fingers along the cable to the wall socket. A timer switch. He moved through the remaining rooms. A bathroom and a box room full of paraphernalia, photos on a desk showing two adult faces and two pre-school boys. He moved down the stairs to the kitchen, which was large and organised. Command central. A living room caught between clean lines and the chaos of entertaining child minds. A TV and DVD player, plastic cases stacked haphazardly, large plastic buckets of toys, a sofa and chairs. The paraphernalia of family life. An empty house. A family on holiday?

In the hallway he crouched and searched through scattered post, picking envelopes from the pile of brochures and discount vouchers. He confirmed the address again from the envelopes. Whoever lived there went by the family name of Pavlak. Which immediately raised two other questions. Why did Simon use this address and more importantly, where was Simon?

Brian shuffled the post looking for a particular type of envelope, picking a selection and ripping them open. None contained what he was looking for. He climbed the stairs two at a time and went into the box room. After sifting through the loose paperwork on the desk he moved to a row of folders lined up on the floor against the wall. He started at the left, opening the files on the desk, methodically working through the ordered bills and correspondence. The Pavlak family had lived here for eighteen months. He found what he wanted halfway through the third folder, tugging free the most recent rental statement. The house was leased through an agency in Essex. He folded the statement into his back pocket and replaced the file.

Outside Brian reversed the process with the lock, struggling with the last two pins. He was about to give up when a sound played out of tune with the night. He ducked instinctively, the boot catching his shoulder and knocking him into the patio door. Another blow caught the back of his head, a fist this time. Brian turned to face his attacker as knuckles raked his cheek. He dropped the small bat into the palm of his hand.

Another blow missed entirely as he swept the bat from right to left, imagining his attacker's shins from the angle of attack. A muted shout and Brian powered upwards, reversing the bat and hammering it hard into the attacker's face. He skipped back and took stock.

His attacker looked to be a one-time boxer, the freshly broken nose more an inconvenience for the blood that now ran from it. They rounded on each other, the boxer's stance as wide as his broad shoulders, reaching around his back and producing a thin blade that reflected the ambient light. His shadowed eyes fixed on Brian and then he made his move.

He was fast, feinting first with the knife that jabbed but did little to disguise the real threat, a thick arm that pistoned through the space occupied by Brian's head. At least where Brian's head had been. He ducked beneath and up around the arm, planting his foot and using the power that flowed up through his body to drive the bat around into the side of the boxer's head. The impact took the boxer face first into the wall and falling heavily into a rusty old bin. By the time neighbouring lights illuminated gardens and faces peered down through open windows, Brian was over the fence and jogging back to the promenade.

FIFTY-THREE

The cold night air and the smell of the sea were refreshing. He breathed deeply, jogging across the road and down the steep grass slope, along the promenade. He passed the space where Adam had parked without pausing, thinking through the likely scenarios. Adam would not have gone far. He passed cars overlooking the distant ocean, a few with their windows misted. He peered into every one, at faces sometimes asleep or unaware and sometimes startled.

He came to a roundabout and a large pub overlooking the sea, now dark and quiet, a car park around the back with a few cars visible. He stepped off the pavement and onto the road that led around. He slowed and came to a stop beside Adam's car, empty and parked close to the low wall.

He looked back at the pub as he caught his breath, the wind molesting his jacket and blowing cold across his face. He could hear a sound. Something woven amid the battering wind, something heavy against something soft, a harsh voice.

He placed a hand on the metal rail and a foot on the low wall and looked down, at the wet sand twenty feet below. Two figures stood to the left, their blond hair picked out by the low light and another shape curled small on the sand. Brian smiled and took a step back and clenched his fists and opened them and vaulted the rail.

Oddi was tired, it had been a long day. First the trouble created by the woman and now this. Hakan had been certain the woman's husband would not be a problem. But here he was. How had he found them? Oddi watched his brother at work, finding answers to their questions. He did think it better his brother not kick so often and ask more questions. But his brother was his own man and it was not wise to interrupt.

The shadow passed through the periphery of his vision, immediately followed by a dull thump on the wet sand. He turned to see a shape rolling within a centrifuge of white spray that stopped suddenly and unfolded to become a man that ran at him. Oddi threw an uncertain glance at his brother, but he was too engrossed and too far away. He turned back to the man bearing down on him. He readied himself and planted his feet. His eyes drawn to a torch now in the man's hand, the beam dancing white over the sand. Then the torch started turning in the air towards him, the beam like a Catherine wheel circling closer, *catch*. The light briefly blinded him and caught him between decisions. It glanced off his defending arm, aware of the man extending his arms as if ready to leap frog and then the hands were on his head. He ducked and turned but straight into a rising knee. White light filled Oddi's vision and Brian passed him having barely broken stride.

Baldur heard a shout that was not the moan of the man at his feet, turning to see his brother drop to a knee and sit unsteady, an arc of light rolling across the sand. His attention moved to a man that now ran at him. Baldur knew who he was at once. It was the girl's father, the soldier. He knew a lot about this man. He shifted his stance sideways, taking all in, moving his weight lightly from foot to foot. He waited.

At the last moment Brian broke his stride and slid into the sand, a short fast sweep with his leg aimed at the back of Baldur's knee. He only caught a trailing foot as Baldur skipped away and Brian's momentum took him down, immediately turning to rise but not quickly enough. The wrong decision. Baldur immediately came at him with quick kicks, jabbing at his head and then down at his ribs. Dancing in and around, not letting him stand. Brian did the only thing he could, he opened himself up and took a kick to his ribs, rolling with the impact and coming up with a hard punch to the inside of Baldur's thigh. Baldur hopped backwards as Adam crashed into him from behind, flattening him face first into the sand.

Baldur felt the weight of a knee in his back, then the weight lifted and a voice shouted *Run*. He rolled and wiped the sand from his face as he watched the two shapes running along the base of the high sea wall. He looked over his shoulder as he rubbed his thigh and watched his brother slowly climb to his feet.

'Did I not warn everyone about the soldier, little brother?' he said in his smooth American accent.

211

FIFTY-FOUR

They ran for several minutes before Adam pulled up, collapsing against the seawall, gasping for air. Brian stopped and looked back along the beach, nobody was following.

Adam had taken a beating. There were bruises already appearing beneath each eye, his bottom lip fat and bloody. He was favouring his left side and gulping in air, which at least meant cracked ribs were the worst of his internal problems. His clothes were soaked through, covered in sand and clinging wetly to him. Brian looked down and realised his had not fared any better.

Adam wheezed, 'The house?'

Brian shrugged. 'Simon's not there. It's leased, through an agency in Essex so it's probably corporate.' He looked along the beach and up at the wall before returning his gaze to Adam. 'So you decided to take a late night stroll?'

Adam did not answer until he had caught his breath. 'The house is Simon's last registered address, although that was six years ago. The pub back there was his childhood home. He works on boats from what I can see. I managed to dig up a lot of detail but it meant little, so I checked out the pub. It was closing but I talked to the landlady. Simon's well known locally and from what I could tell, well thought of, although he's not been seen much the last five years. The landlady knew his mother; it was his mother that ran the pub while Simon was a kid.'

'Where's the mother now?'

'Dead, cancer years ago.'

'The landlady have any idea where he lives now?'

'She wasn't that forthcoming. He travels a lot, apparently.'

Brian kicked at the sand and walked away, distracted, looking down the beach and out to the ocean. He walked back. 'Travels a lot, that's not good news. What about Bill and Ben our two blond buddies, what happened there?'

'They appeared out of nowhere when I got back to the car, literally picked me up and dropped me over the wall. Scared the shit out of me. They were American.'

'They didn't look very American. Did they take your wallet?'

He checked his back pocket. It was still there. 'There's more, your daughter's picture is all over the web and they found Sarah's car burnt out.'

'Empty burnt out?'

Adam nodded.

Brian started along the beach, gesturing for Adam to follow. 'We need to call Boer and give him what we have, spread the knowledge. But first we need to get off this beach and away from the promenade, find somewhere to lie up, dry out and re-appraise.' He waited for Adam to catch up. 'Preferably a hotel with an all-night bar. Can you sort that?'

'Sure,' Adam replied, deciding to come clean. 'I already gave Boer the address.'

Brian contemplated this for a second then nodded. 'We need to get him on to the letting agents as well.'

Something else occurred to Adam. 'I need my computer from the car if we're going to find a hotel.'

Brian laughed and stopped. 'What do you think our friends are doing right now?'

'I've no idea.'

'Taking the car apart for a start. You'll have to do without the computer. Ring directory enquiries or something.'

They walked on, eventually climbing a set of concrete steps that zigzagged up to the road and a section of the promenade they had not seen before, the rising bank of grass tapering as the roads levelled and joined.

Adam pulled out his phone and used his cuff to wipe the screen clear of sand and water. When the phone finally flashed to life it took five calls and eight minutes before they had a hotel and directions. He shivered as he walked, taking comfort from the fact Brian was shivering beside him.

213

FIFTY-FIVE

Simon's hand glided across her skin, a slow ceaseless movement almost soothing in its rhythm, like a collector of fine art caressing his treasure. He did this for so long she hoped it might be all. But with time the momentum increased, his need building. And then he asked her.

'Can…I?' He shifted awkwardly.

She nodded slowly and he moved onto her, easing open her legs with his thighs, gradually and very gently easing himself into her. The weight of him and the feel of him moving inside her jumped her mind back to Saturday morning, an age distant and a world apart. Adam was tall and lean and eager. Simon was so much bigger and more awkward, his arms either side of her like knotted tree trunks. She smiled up at him and grimaced inwardly, immediately desperate to escape from under him. Her focus alternated in the dim light from his shoulder to the ceiling that refused to stay still.

The friction of his body quickly wore at her constructs of sanity, handing control of her body to the processes of automation. Outwardly her hands caressed him and urged him into her, thick and invading, her legs pinned wide beneath him. Mentally she fought to keep away the gnashing teeth and jutting flesh, now hidden in all the shadows around her. She concealed her fear beneath a veneer of willingness, in the hope he would come quickly and her ordeal would be over. She had no idea for the depth of Simon's need.

His thrusting built momentum and the muscles of his back tensed beneath her hands, a final hard thrust and another and he groaned and pumped fatly inside her. The automated processes directed her hands to soothe him as he came to rest, out of breath, gasping and almost jubilant. After a short pause he rolled aside and for a time idled the back of his hand across her breasts and neck. And then he swept his legs off the bed and the key from the wardrobe and led her to the shower.

It became a routine, the soapy journeys back to the room, four, maybe five times now. Waiting as he turned or changed the sheets and climbed back onto the bed. Sated, he lay beside her, pressing a hand on her chest, feeling the beat of her heart, continuing his ceaseless exploration of her body. She could sense the tiredness inside him, longed for him to sleep, to calm her drifting sense of reality. Always hoping for an opportunity. Then the momentum of his hand would increase and she stilled her frayed mind. Her jail was these sheets and his schoolboy thrusting.

She managed to direct him onto his back, which gave her more control and freed her from beneath his body, feeding his need with the wonder of hers riding astride. A macabre rodeo she dressed with wet lips and damp hair that fell about her face, rising and falling on his flesh that stretched and now wore her sore inside, constantly trying to block out the gnashing teeth and jutting flesh now crowded around her, the gnarled fingers all reaching out, waiting their turn. She kept the terror trapped like a bubble between her chest and throat, the fear from her eyes. Each second and minute was a reprieve for Andrea.

She smelt the fresh, fragrant air, which was always the first sign. She looked to the door and window before she realised, briefly resisting before embracing that whip of cool air. It lovingly wrapped itself around her, shielding her in a vast vista of rolling green; of high trees and craggy mountains, snow-capped peaks amid clusters of cloud and blue skies, the distant sound of a galloping horse.

She sat down on the grass cross-legged, pulled her summer dress over dirty knees and plucked at daisies. A timeless place. It had been four years since her last visit and fourteen before that. She was only vaguely aware of that other world now, where her body continued to endure. At some point she heard the heavy rumble of thunder in a blue sky and a distant child voice, although she never saw other children here. So she stayed where she was, humming to herself and threading daises as she waited for the horseman.

FIFTY-SIX

Helen Ferreira stood on the pavement outside MadHatters, stationary amid the rush of commuters. She had a blue cup of tea clasped in her left hand and her phone pressed against her right ear. She was there because she was looking for the club's owner, but like his house it was locked and silent. She had even clanged up the metal steps of the fire escape, to no gain. Now she needed direction, impatiently disconnecting when she was diverted to Boer's voicemail once more.

Her frustration simmered. Getting out of bed before dawn had seemed like a good idea, especially with the press conference laying waste to much of the afternoon. Except Monday morning was starting just as Sunday had ended, chasing people who had no desire to be found. And now even Boer was not answering her calls. She sipped the tea and flicked through her address book, dialling his home number. It was the only number she had not tried because he was never there. It rang through. She silently cursed but hung on through the message.

'Francis, you're not in the office or answering your mobile. So you're either at home or dead, maybe both. If you don't ring in the next ten minutes I'm coming round with an ambulance.' She disconnected and started towards the town centre and back to the café. She was going to need something stronger than tea.

Boer used one hand to support his weight on the sink and the other to wash water across his face. Blowing to dislodge the residual drops from his moustache and swilling mouthwash. He flushed the toilet and very carefully made his way across the landing.

His study was set up in his daughter's old bedroom. Once so full of colour and life, now bookcases flanked two walls with a wide wooden desk beneath the window. The desk was home to a phone and an ancient fax machine, the case file open with a large notepad full of scrawl on top. He reached across and played Ferreira's message, lowering himself into the chair with a smile.

He dialled her mobile from memory and she answered after four rings. 'Thank God Fran, you're at home.'

'I'm feeling a little queasy today. I should have called.' He heard the sweep of tyres outside as she pulled onto his drive.

'Damn right you should have. I'll let myself in. You upstairs?'

'I am,' he answered and Ferreira disconnected.

He listened to her keys in the door and then a distant thump as her bag hit the floor, the sound of footsteps up the stairs. The landing gave its signature groan and she appeared in the doorway, her dark hair tied back in a thick ponytail. She was wearing a trademark dark blouse and a pale blue suit that stretched a little tight across her thighs. She looked at him hopefully as she leaned across and handed him the blue cup of tea.

'What's new?' she asked, leaving him to ponder the answer while she fetched the wicker chair from his bedroom. She set it down and eased into it.

'Not much,' he said. 'Not since last night. The fire crew handed the house in Peterborough to forensics. Thanks to Brian and Adam we already have the address in Cleethorpes, we're just waiting on Anne for authorisation to go after the letting agency. Trouble is she won't act until Cleethorpes is corroborated by forensics.'

Ferreira sat up. 'You're kidding me. Not even with a guy chargrilled and tied to a chair?'

He shook his head. 'She said a body in Peterborough was not evidence of a kidnapping syndicate in Cleethorpes. Said she would warn Lincolnshire the case may swing their way, but she clearly categorised the data as having no context right now. Nothing links us to Cleethorpes until forensics says it does.'

Which made an abstract kind of sense to Ferreira. Except when senior detectives like Boer trusted data, the data was usually worth paying attention to. She worked the logic to its conclusion and realised. 'Christ, she's scared they'll shift the case before she gets her face on TV.'

Boer's moustache rose wearily. 'Welcome to the fragile world of human self-interest and police politics.'

'So what're we going to do?'

'Nothing,' Boer answered. He took a sip of the tea, the now cool liquid welcome in his stomach. 'At least in regard to Anne. She quizzed how I got the data and blew a fuse when she got my answer. More, it seemed, from not having Dunstan to parade as the distraught father.'

'She's outing him live on TV?'

Boer's gaze settled on Ferreira. 'Not sure, she's got more of a thing for Sarah Sawacki. CCTV shows her sat at a table with two cups and then shaking hands with Simon. Anne added two and two and got twenty-two.'

Ferreira scowled. 'More like five. The CCTV really shows that?'

Boer nodded. 'That's how Anne interpreted it. I talked with Barry at Reading and he confirmed the two cups, said he couldn't explain that from the footage. Said his take on the handshake was that it looked accidental. Someone snatched her bag and Simon stopped them. Hopefully Anne will shift up a gear once she's had her moment on TV, then maybe she'll place the CCTV in its correct context. Tell me about your morning, Helen.'

Ferreira took a deep breath and let it out. 'Akinsanya 'Ali' Odebefemi. The number on the scrap of paper is his club, MadHatters. Of course talking to Ali to find out why his number was hidden in a child's photo frame has been problematic. The guy has completely vanished.'

Boer lightly patted a palm on the arm of his chair. 'Have you checked out Brian's ex-girlfriend?'

Ferreira paused, wary at Boer's switch. 'Don't you want to know what we have on Ali?'

'No,' Boer said. 'Tell me about the ex first.'

'There's nothing to tell. She's my next stop. From her interview yesterday you'd think Brian Dunstan was the salt of the earth. Although obviously he fell short somewhere along the line, since they separated earlier in the year.'

'If it was Brian that fell short,' he added.

'That was my assumption, Fran. What're you thinking?'

'That you should stop those damn assumptions of yours.'

'That's rich,' she retorted, 'coming from someone who had Sarah down as innocent based on her husband's statement and a pretty face.' Which came out a lot harsher than she intended.

'There's no assumption, Helen, as you well know. Just conclusions based on known facts. I'm not going to waste time trying to make Sarah a suspect, any more than I am Ali.'

She was surprised. 'Ignore Ali? He's genuinely one of the few who could have given Andrea up.'

Boer shook his head. 'Not ignore, process. Focus on the investigation as a whole and not dwell on hunches and assumptions like you intend doing with Ali.'

'Fran!' A scowl shaped her features. 'You know what I dug up on him. The mother was right. Ali has a finger in just about every pie, prostitution and porn to name just two. Kidnapping and extortion is not a great leap.'

He managed a wan smile. 'Helen, you're such a bloody Catholic sometimes. Is he under investigation for any of those or ever been charged?'

She raised her shoulders in a half shrug. 'You know the answer to that but he is being investigated by the Inland Revenue for tax evasion and fraud.'

'But not for prostitution or for contributing to our flourishing porn industry?'

She shifted in the chair and the wicker protested. 'No.'

'So does the leap from tax evasion to child kidnapping seem just as likely?'

'That's mean, Fran, I'm just trying to work an angle here.'

He stared at her over his cup, swilled a mouthful and swallowed. 'So start focusing on what is important, Helen. Check him out, sure. Just don't waste time searching for detail that isn't there. Not until what you have pulls you in that direction. Hunches are for mystics and amateurs. You'll end up missing the important detail.'

She waited on him to continue but he just looked patiently at her.

'And the important detail, oh wise one?'

'I keep telling you. Why did the girl hide that number?'

'Girls love their secrets, Fran, you always say that.' She looked at him suspiciously. 'What aren't you telling me?'

'If I knew any more I'd tell you. From what I know I only see innocent intent in her having Ali's number. So why hide it?'

'All sorts of reasons.' Ferreira smoothed an invisible crease from her trousers. 'Maybe you should be thinking about why she was hiding the

219

number of a man being investigated for tax fraud. A pretty white girl will fetch a packet for anyone who can get her out of the country. These are difficult times, people do the weirdest things.'

'They do and you may be right,' he conceded. 'I'm just asking you not to get sidetracked and lose sight of the facts. Find a link to Ali and prove me wrong but don't get lost trying to find it.'

Her dark eyes gleamed. 'Lose sight of the facts Fran, a good Catholic girl like me?'

'For that reason especially, Helen.'

They smiled at each other and the weight lifted from them both.

'You're just frustrated because you're ill. I forgive your grouchiness.'

'Why, thank you,' he replied.

They sat in silence while she drank her cappuccino, savouring the smooth taste while her eyes roamed across the bookcases. She tossed the empty cup into the bin.

'I always wondered, why does a man who doesn't believe in God have so many books on religion?'

He followed her gaze. 'That just occurred to you now?'

'Well, no,' she answered. 'I often think about it, I just never got round to asking.'

He shifted uncomfortably in his chair. 'Just because I don't believe in a God doesn't mean I didn't spend a great deal of time looking.'

'And in all that looking you never saw God in anything?

'Of course I did, there's a lot to wonder at. We look around and we all see the same beauty, Helen. You see it as a consequence of divine intent, I see the product of time and chance.'

She studied him as she thought about his words. There was something final in his tone. She saw now the man and not the aura of the detective she practically idolised. His hands were so thin, his body so frail, his skin grey. It looked like he had aged years in just one night. She could not recall seeing him this ill even when he was being treated. 'You aren't going to die on me are you? I'm counting on you at least till the end of the case.'

He smiled and lied, 'Not yet, Helen.'

'Good,' she grinned back at him, 'although I'd quite like to see your face when you do find yourself in heaven.'

He gave a short laugh. 'I might descend.' He patted the arm of his chair again. 'What time do you have to be in make-up?'

She pulled a face. 'Eleven.'

'Where?'

'Town hall, in Reading.'

'Nice suit.'

'Thanks. It didn't look this blue at five am. What's worrying you, Fran?'

He lied again, 'Nothing.'

'Something is, do you want me to call the doctor?'

'No, that's not it.'

'What then?'

'Nothing really. You know how I get if I'm housebound.'

'I do. And don't you worry about me and my assumptions, you're ingrained upon my psyche, Fran. You always eventually lead me to unemotional assessment in the end. And if you're worried about my star turn on TV, then don't. I've already been issued with instructions to only speak when spoken to.' She looked over at the case file. 'Hope you haven't been going through that all night!'

'Nope,' he answered honestly, glad they were off the subject of gods and death. 'Did you get a look at the diary?'

'Did you?' she answered.

'Barry rattled off the highlights after we covered the CCTV. Said it was remarkable for the fact there was absolutely no detail on her time in Hambury at all.'

Ferreira nodded. 'That's about the extent of it. They have a psychologist going over the detail but there's barely a word on her visits, save for a record she was here.'

'Poor kid. She knew her dad would get into trouble if anyone read what actually happens when she's here.'

'Either way, Fran, I can't see this ending well for Brian Dunstan, can you?'

'Nope. Although I doubt Dunstan's worried about social services right now, just his daughter's future.'

'Which is slipping away from us, especially today.' The frustration lay heavy in her voice.

'Yes.' Boer rapped his fingers thoughtfully against the case file. 'I can't imagine Simon would have used the address in Cleethorpes unless he thought it safe. How safe we will know when we talk to the letting agency. On the off chance I requested Lincolnshire send a list of all the

999 calls made through Saturday and Sunday. The station rang to say that arrived. There were over three thousand hoax and silent calls in Cleethorpes and Grimsby alone. I got the station to check the address against the list, but there was no match. Unless we get more data to cross-reference, the list is useless.'

The wicker creaked as Ferreira shifted to the edge of the chair. 'You're more productive than me even when you're housebound. Can I get you anything before I go?'

'I'd die for some marmite on toast?'

'Sure.' She paused at the door. 'Is that wise?'

'It could swing either way.' He winked at her.

FIFTY-SEVEN

Adam stood in front of the mirror, turning from side to side, examining his collection of bruises. There were several across his ribs and back, ranging in tone from yellow to purple, the same across his thighs and shoulders. A dark horizontal bruise under each eye made him look like a skinny American Footballer. His body ached painfully. Mentally he was still in shock, reeling from the belief he would die on the beach at the hands of the two blond men.

For all these emotions his overriding sense was of relief. He was alive and looking at his reflection. The bruises would heal. His skin would soon return to an expanse of smooth skin. He had seen Brian's burns that morning.

After checking in the night before, Brian had directed him to the room and then immediately went in search of the night porter. The first Adam knew he was back in the room was when he woke to daylight and the sound of the shower. Then Brian had stepped from the bathroom.

No amount of imagining could have prepared him for what he saw. Brian's left shoulder across to and down his right arm, his entire back down to the base of his spine, down and around to his right thigh, looked like it had been flayed, covered in lumpy red flesh with occasional patches of melted skin in a hardened sheen. It looked plastic but was not. It was so disfigured Adam had to swallow rising bile to stop from being sick.

Brian looked back at him as he pulled his clothes from the radiator, instructed him to stay put and then left. That had been an hour ago.

Adam waited, alternating his attention between the view over an industrial park and the clock beneath the TV glowing green. It was 8:26, the sounds of the hotel were of the morning, doors slamming, guests leaving and cleaners moving from room to room.

He flinched at a sound outside and the click of the lock, and then Brian swept in. He emptied two bags onto the bed. Two sets of jeans, T-shirts and underwear, two lightweight jackets. He immediately started tugging free the tags, then threw him something small that landed heavily on the spare bed.

'What's that?' Adam reached forward and picked it up.

'What's it look like?'

He weighed it in his hand. It was about the size of his phone but heavier and narrower. A solid moulded handle that curved neatly in his palm, a thick length of metal embedded within. A button sat beneath his thumb which he pressed. The blade sprung free, full of menace.

'What would I use this for?'

Brian stripped off his clothes and pulled on a fresh set of jeans. 'From the look of you this morning some last line of defence might be in order.'

'But how, how would I use it?'

'Hopefully you don't. It's the very last thing you want to use. You'll know if the time comes. Keep it stashed. If you have to, go for calves or thighs or arms. Just punch it in there. Don't go face to face with anyone. If they're half decent they'll take you out in a beat, then they might get a mind to stab you back.'

Adam felt a little indignant at the dismissive summary of his capabilities, as accurate as they were. He carefully folded the blade back into the handle, not sure where to put it. He dropped it onto the bed.

'What about the car?'

The keys landed on the bed beside the knife. 'You won't be needing those. Hope you took out the comprehensive cover.'

Adam groaned. 'What did they do?'

'No idea. It's gone. Couldn't find it anywhere on the promenade.' Brian pulled on one of the jackets, tested it across his shoulders and shrugged it off, reaching for the other one. 'I had a chat with the porter last night. Grimsby has a football club.'

Adam faintly recalled this but struggled to understand Brian's point.

'Three lions?' Brian prompted.

'They have three lions in their logo?'

Brian shook his head. 'Grimsby and Cleethorpes are part of the same sprawl. Cleethorpes is prettier, Grimsby's industrial. It was the biggest fishing port in the UK until Iceland took back their chunk of the North Sea. The fishing industry died but there was still demand, so the

Icelandic fleets used the facilities here. Now Grimsby's full of international businesses with a strong Nordic twist.'

'You mean the logo on Simon's T-shirt was three fish, not three lions?'

Brian smiled in return and Adam pulled the remaining clothes off the bed and put them on, working the logic. His logo analysis had been laborious, getting as far as international and top tier teams. Grimsby had not been one of them.

Brian had more to say. 'So we've got a Nordic influence and our blond Americans. Which is bollucks I'd say. I met a Swedish guy while I was seconded to the UN, had the damnest American accent. Reckoned he got it from watching American TV, it's all they ever watch.'

Adam mentally flicked through the inconsequential detail he had seen on his computer the night before. 'Simon is self-employed. Before that he only worked for one other company; Thompson Deep Sea. I assumed it was a family business.'

Brian moved his change and pocket junk from his old jeans to the new. 'So we could see whether Thompson Deep Sea became Nordic Deep Sea or something. They might have offices here, they might know Simon. Do you think that's something you could do if we found you a computer?'

'Possibly. It would be a case of searching the net and hoping the data is already out there. I don't have access to that kind of information at work.'

Brian blinked back at him. 'You eat yet?'

The last thing on Adam's mind was eating, the thought of it made him queasy. He answered with a shake of his head.

'Good,' Brian stated. 'The porter saved us two full English and a large pot of hot coffee.'

FIFTY-EIGHT

Internet cafés were scarce in both Grimsby and Cleethorpes. They eventually found a book store with a hand-written sign in the window, with an ancient computer set at the back in the Children's section. Accessing the internet required feeding coins into a box bolted beneath the desk, which left little room for Adam's legs.

He started by checking the news sites for updates on the Andrea story. Most had been rewritten with additional speculation, the main event was the midday press conference. He then researched Thompson Deep Sea and cross referenced the results with Simon Thompson. The only information he found was a minimal website with a single picture advertising a trawler for hire. Squinting at the image, he read the name on the bow, *Cutting Blue*. There was a UK email address in the boat's name but all the other links on the page were dead ends. He fired off an email but it was returned almost immediately as undeliverable.

He then clicked through endless pages of irrelevant family trees before discovering several stories about a Conley Thompson, who in the early 1980s had made a stand against fishing quotas by sailing his trawler to Singapore, and selling it to a maritime museum. Here again the boat's name was *Cutting Blue*, which meant that if it was the same boat it had been brought back to the UK after being sold in Singapore. He tried searching again on *Cutting Blue,* but only came back to the old website or rehashes of the story he already had. Adam had nothing that tied Simon to Thompson Deep Sea, other than his PAYE record from the night before. And there was no record of where Thompson Deep Sea's offices were or had been. Throughout, Brian sat in his co-pilot's position talking to the estate agents in Essex, unsuccessfully trying to coerce them into giving him the contact details of the house's owner.

By eleven they were standing on the promenade, the breeze tugging at the material of their clothing. Adam's hands were pushed deep into his pockets, his frustration echoed in the gloomy grey sky, the restless ocean sending drifting spray high into the air. They had a whole lot of dead ends. They had come all this way, to be within a stone's throw of Sarah and Andrea but with no way of finding them.

Brian leaned against the metal railing and folded his arms, the wind flattening his hair like long grass in a field. 'We have one option.'

Adam raised an eyebrow. 'We do?'

'We go back to the pub and wait.'

Adam took a step closer to make sure he heard correctly. 'The pub? Is that wise?'

'All depends on your perspective. It beats standing here skimming pebbles off the sea. Worst case scenario is the bad guys turn up and get pissed at us. Which is also kind of the best case scenario.' He looked hard at Adam. 'Which might not end well, so now is your opportunity to turn and walk away.'

Adam's stomach still felt uneasy. The thought of going back to the pub did not help. The chance to walk away appealed in ways that focused on not ending up like the man in Peterborough, or running through a repeat of the night before. He took satisfaction in being able to help Brian but his ability to help now seemed redundant. What use would he be? At the same time there was no way he could turn around, having come so far. With Brian's indomitable attitude anything seemed possible. He might yet make a difference.

'I can't,' he said, trying to find the right words. 'I couldn't, I could never live with myself.'

'Good,' Brian answered. 'Two are always better than one. You should know if it gets stupid your job is to run like fuck. You got that?'

Adam nodded. 'What about you?'

'I'll do my best to leave them with a lasting impression. I'd quite like some one-on-one time with either of the blonds.' Then Brian slapped him on the shoulder and walked away, along the promenade back towards the pub. After a moment of hesitation Adam followed.

FIFTY-NINE

The grass here was thick and green. Green was not the word, even lush did it no justice. Unreal was closer. An expanse that carpeted the rise and fall of earth as far as she could see. The trees behind her whispered and small clouds chased their shadows. A warm breeze caressed her skin. She gazed at the smoke rising from distant hills. She knew people lived there, had tried walking before but it had been so far.

There was a murmur, a sound within the sounds within the trees behind. A voice, but nobody was ever here. It drew her though. The sound latched into her mind and pulled her hand over hand. Someone she trusted, closing her eyes and going with the pull.

Opening them again, to the soft glow of the lamp, turning her head and blinking at reality and the girl sitting cross-legged on the mattress. An elbow on each knee and her hands pressed together, her fingers pointing upwards. The girl's mouth moved, the words almost audible, the child voice almost a melody.

'What are you doing?' Sarah asked, still half there and not fully here.

'I'm praying,' Andrea replied. She punctuated the sentence with '*Amen*' and looked at Sarah. 'You're awake!'

'Was I not already?'

Andrea stared, concerned, keeping her hands as they were.

'No, well, you looked like you were awake. But it was like you were asleep. You weren't answering me.'

'Sorry.' She looked around the room. 'How have you been, was I gone long?' She remembered now. 'I hope you weren't too upset? We did our best.'

'You were gone ages. I was upset because I thought you might be hurt or something horrid might have happened. That I might be here all

228

alone.' She looked down at the bandages around Sarah's hands. 'Then I felt bad because I wanted you here and it's because of me you're here anyway.' Her eyes were wide and guilty. 'And now you look so poorly.'

Sarah eased back into herself, leaning against the wall, the mattress familiar beneath her fingers. 'We're here because of the people who took you Andrea, no other reason. You have nothing to feel guilty about.' She pressed her hands against her stomach, recalling cramp and soreness, shifting carefully. She ached from her groin right up to her chest. She wrinkled her nose, for the first time conscious of a stench, looking across at the porcelain bowl.

Andrea shifted self-consciously, crimson blotting her cheeks, wide abashed eyes. 'I'm really sorry, Sarah, I held on as long as I could but I needed to go. It's not as bad as it was,' she said hopefully.

Sarah could not stop a smile spreading across her face. 'Phew!' She blew out her cheeks. 'For a minute I thought they'd got a horse in here as well! Who could imagine little girls could be so smelly?'

'Sarah!' she shouted indignantly, then she excitedly shuffled closer, happy now her friend was back. 'I moved the water and biscuits. It didn't seem right them being near the bowl.'

Sarah winked. 'Good idea. Why don't you move the bowl so when he comes back he will be faced with it before he can come in.' That got a giggled affirmation. Andrea made a show of taking a deep breath before dragging it slowly to where they knew the door to be. She diverted to the bookshelf and pulled out the largest hardback, placing it over the top of the bowl. 'I like Rupert,' she said, pleased with her own good idea. 'But as it's *his* book I don't feel bad about putting it there.' She returned to the corner.

'Would you like to pray with me?' she asked.

Sarah shook her head. 'I don't pray. But you can, it's nice to hear your voice.'

'You don't pray?' Andrea asked, incredulous. 'But you must pray?'

Sarah pulled her legs up but that hurt so she let them slide out a little and wrapped her arms loosely around her knees. She looked at Andrea. 'So why do you pray? Are you a bad person?'

The girl went still as she considered. 'I pray because mum tells me to. Sometimes I do bad things although I don't usually know I'm doing them. Mum says if I don't behave I'll go to hell, which is a scary place with lots of fire and Satan lives there with all the bad people.'

She paused again, giving the question serious consideration. 'I try to be good but it's not easy. I don't always do the jobs mum asks me to, or don't do them as well as she would like. And I should take better care of my sisters. And not ask for things so much. And tidy my books. I sometimes say I've done my homework and I haven't, not properly. And sometimes I make mum really angry for no reason at all. I do lots of bad things. Maybe God is punishing me?'

Sarah shook her head. 'You're not being punished. There are bad people in the world, and praying is not going to change that or get us home. Only we can do that.'

Andrea's face shifted from hopeful to dismayed, teetering on the brink of tears. Sarah immediately wished she had not been so honest.

'I really need to go home Sarah. I can't stay here forever, I just can't. I miss my sisters, my mum and dad and Kevin. I miss school. My books, the smell of towels. Writing stories, my bed and my feet on my rug in the morning. I even miss homework and Mr Evans, and he made Ian Wilson cry in class. Tell me this will be over soon, won't it? My dad will be coming. They'll have to listen to him and then we can go home, can't we?'

'Let's hope so, Andrea.'

'I know so.' Her face morphed back to pink-cheeked determination. 'My dad will make them realise he doesn't owe them money. Nothing stops my dad.'

'That would be really good,' Sarah said, not sure how to handle the contrast between the girl's expectations and the stark reality. 'In the meantime, Andrea, we have to think how we can help ourselves. Because just now it's only me and you. We have to think they might want to do bad things to us both. Things we cannot even imagine right now. We might have to fight if we want to go home and do things we might not do anywhere else.'

Andrea pulled up her legs and looped both her hands around her knees, mirroring Sarah's posture, trying to imagine the worst that might happen and what she might have to do. 'I once threw stones at boys in school because they were bullying me and my friends. That sort of thing?'

Sarah nodded. 'That and maybe worse. I think Simon might like me, in a fancy sort of way, which means I might have a chance to do something. But I have already used lots of chances.' She sat silent studying the weave of her jeans. 'Or you might have to do something, because he would never expect you to do it.'

'Like throwing stones but worse?' Andrea ventured.

'Yes,' Sarah replied. 'I'm sorry,' she added.

'Why are *you* sorry?'

'Because it would be nice to think we could close our eyes and pray and everything would be OK. But I want you to know there is nowhere I would rather be than here with you.'

Andrea crawled across the mattress and Sarah held out her hand. Andrea took it but did not ease into her as she expected. Instead she knelt.

'Can I show you something?'

Sarah nodded.

The girl looked back earnestly. 'And you promise you'll not think bad of me?'

'Why ever for?'

There was no answer, she just crawled over to her bag in the corner and rummaged as she had several times before. Then she pulled free a thin white bag and crawled back to Sarah. 'I always pick up dad's prescription. I'm not allowed to buy these really but he used to go out with Ellen, she works in Boots and is really nice. So she does it for me and I just give them to him.' She held the bag out for Sarah.

Sarah took it and looked inside, pulling out a small white box. 'This?'

Andrea giggled nervously. 'No silly, that's his prescription. At the bottom.' Sarah reached in and pulled out another box, smaller like matches but thinner. She let the bag fall to the mattress and opened one end. Five double edged razorblades slid into her palm.

'Do you think they might help, like throwing stones?'

Sarah did not say anything for some time, just stared at the blades. But Andrea knew from the look on Sarah's face she had done really good, although the look scared her a little as well.

SIXTY

Daylight shining through large windows meant the pub was light inside although it was infused with an artificial hue by the glowing lighting. The decoration was dominated by darkly painted panelling and black and white photos of the local legacy. The main bar curved round and descended through an arched doorway and steps to a smaller area, where a few tables and a games machine sat against a wall beside a silent jukebox.

Adam counted five people throughout, mostly old men who complemented the decoration and photos, either seated or leaning against the lower of the two bars. He stood in the middle of the upper bar with his arms folded, waiting to be served while looking up at a muted TV. Sporting headlines and subtitles scrolled along the foot of the screen, a large black man and a white woman silently talking sports news between brilliant white smiles and laughter. He occasionally glimpsed Brian prowling around.

He heard boots on wooden steps and a barman emerged from the cellar. If he was surprised by the bruises on Adam's face it did not register, taking his order of two cokes and a request to switch the TV to a news channel, which he did after a quick glance around the pub.

Adam took the drinks and sat opposite the TV, watching the image switch to a different man and woman behind a desk. These were more formal, the subtitles relaying news about cot deaths and the phenomenon of baby brains thinking they were back in the womb.

Brian appeared and ushered him to follow, taking them further around to a long seat attached to the wall and behind a table. Adam eased in beside him, sliding his phone onto the darkly polished surface. They sat with their backs to the wall with a good view in all directions, including a portion of the lower bar through the arched doorway. Another screen was set directly in front above the bar, the newscasters silently talking amid still images of smoke and orange plumes of flame.

'You have an exit at twelve o'clock from where you are.' Brian directed his attention to a door opposite. 'And another at ten, down the steps. Both take you out to the car park. There's another door near the toilets. If anything kicks off get out of here, if anyone gets in the way lower your shoulder and go through them. Then run as if the devil were treading on your heels. Now go and check them out.'

Adam placed his glass on the table and walked out of the twelve o'clock door. Turning left outside took him back into the car park and the long way around the building, right took him onto the promenade. He walked back in and around, down the steps through the arched doorway and along the lower bar. This door had a latch. He lifted it and stepped out into the car park, giving him a choice of going either left or right around the building back to the promenade.

He walked back inside to the toilets and a narrow hallway. Passing signs for Gents and Ladies to another door, the top half translucent bubbled glass, the bottom warped wood painted blue. He stepped onto a section of car park criss-crossed with yellow lines. Large portable bins vied for space with stacked and knotted bin bags.

Adam returned to the bar and sat back down. 'So?' Brian asked.

'Twelve o'clock is the best option, then ten o'clock, although I'd be in trouble if I fumbled on the latch. Back door is the last resort.'

Brian nodded and they both sipped their cokes. *High Street* caught Adam's attention on the screen and the image changed to an Asian newsreader framed to one side. Set beyond her and filling the width of the screen was a long desk covered in a dark blue material. It fronted an equally blue vertical panel with a large white logo that looked to Adam like a portcullis with a lion each side.

Text scrolled along the bottom of the screen as the reporter summarised the detail. Images of Hambury and a Rover and the burnt-out Toyota appeared and disappeared. There was nothing in the text he had not read a hundred times already. Then the reporter stopped speaking and looked over her shoulder, and the image switched to a close, angled view of the table. A line of people filtered behind the desk, taking seats and shuffling closer. Their faces offered shades from ruddy white to deep brown, dressed in pristine police uniform or smart civilian clothes. A man and woman sat centrally, both fidgeting and looking the least like they belonged there; the mother and stepfather. Detective Ferreira sat at the end in a pastel blue suit that blurred on the screen. Adam wondered where Boer was. The whole scene was continually washed with white light as cameras captured every face and changing emotion.

The screen shifted to a close-up of an attractive female officer, mid-forties he guessed, with short dark hair. Her mouth moved and she gestured to her right and left, the scrolling subtitles listing names and titles for those sitting at the table. A picture of Andrea appeared in the bottom corner of the screen, different from the one he had seen the night before. It showed her smiling and looking up with large eyes at whoever took the picture. Brian placed his drink on the table.

They both watched in silence as the press conference unfolded. The mother and stepfather mostly sat with their eyes down, looking at anything and everything on the desk, overcome by the spectacle and exhaustion. The mother regularly dabbed at her eyes, sore from tears. Adam had only ever seen one other woman look quite so frail. The stepfather looked guilty under the weight of so many judgemental stares.

Focus returned to the female officer, named on the screen as Detective Chief Inspector Anne Darling. He guessed she was in charge, as she was often framed on screen with the mother and stepfather. For those new to the story she sombrely detailed everything Adam had read twelve hours before on the internet.

Each officer at the table then took a turn describing an element of the investigation. Ferreira spoke briefly on the focus of the kidnapping, which seemed to be about sifting through the volume of known sex offenders and finding the missing eyewitness, Sarah Sawacki. There was no mention of Peterborough, Grimsby or Cleethorpes.

Then a head and shoulder picture of Brian filled the left half of the screen. A younger Brian with his moustache neatly trimmed. He was proudly dressed in military uniform and a red beret, a regimental badge over his left temple. On the right of the screen a list detailed Brian Dunstan as being Andrea's biological father, summarising his military career, which included all the places Adam was familiar with from the news in the last ten years. It concluded with an award of the Military Cross. The scrolling subtitles contained phrases like: *Not a suspect, Afghanistan veteran*.

Adam looked sideways and was rewarded with a wink. And then the image changed to one of Sarah. Adam watched wide-eyed. He had not seen that picture for three years. It had been taken by a local newspaper after she had been released from Culpho.

Brian almost choked on his drink. 'Christ! Could they have picked a worse photo?' Adam silently shook his head. She looked gaunt, tired and solemn, almost sinister. The subtitles repeated that Sarah Sawacki was the missing eyewitness and the last person known to have seen Andrea. The police urgently needed to talk to her.

Then Sarah's photo was replaced with CCTV footage from Delamere. They both watched as the image of Sarah jolted through the services, waiting for a cut to Simon, but the image froze as Sarah sat with two coffees. The coverage switched back to the press conference. The female officer reinforced the importance of finding Sarah Sawacki.

Centre frame now were the mother and stepfather. The mother, prompted by the female officer, started reading a short statement but faltered and broke down in tears that became sobs and then to everyone's surprise she half stood and directed an angry outburst at the assembled press. Everyone at the table shuffled uneasily as the stepfather directed her back down amid a frenzy of white light. The mother visibly shrank back, looking forlorn at the rows of shadowed journalists. Her shoulders rose and fell as the stepfather finished reading the statement. And then Chief Inspector Anne Darling made a longer statement that paved the way for questions. The only words from the mother's outburst that appeared on screen where, *Why…father…daughter…alone.*

'Bullshit!' said Brian.

Adam nodded. 'Not a single thing on Simon. Even you came out of that better than Sarah.'

'I'm not on about that Adam. Liz, the bitch. Playing the audience.'

'Was she?' Adam was surprised. 'It looked pretty real to me.'

'Bullshit,' Brian repeated. 'Guarantee that will be on the front of just about every newspaper tomorrow. Right beneath a headline of her outburst.'

'She does have a point.'

'Sod off, Adam. That woman's so wrapped in her own sense of righteousness she'd lay this at my feet in a second. Simon took Andrea because someone told him where she would be, they're the ones responsible for this.'

He fell silent and Adam did not say what he thought. They watched the Chief Inspector field questions, directing each to a face behind the table as she deemed fit. Each answered with longer explanations of what they already knew. Eventually coverage switched back to the studio.

Adam drummed his fingers against the side of his glass. 'Why no Simon?'

Brian placed his glass on the table, looking thoughtful. 'I guess if they showed images of suspects for a case like this, there'd be gangs of people laying the boot into anyone that looked vaguely like him. Giving someone a good kicking in the name of retribution, especially for the sake of a child, helps people appease their own guilt.'

'Brian the philosopher, you're full of surprises!'

'It's psychology actually, guilt and fear drives most of what we do.'

'You study psychology?'

He looked at Adam over the top of his glass. 'You think because I swear and used to be a grunt I wouldn't?'

'I didn't mean it like that.'

Brian wiped a hand across his moustache. 'What did you mean?'

'I don't know, you seem disconnected. Disinterested even. You don't seem to care about anything but you must. Or you wouldn't have talked me into being here.'

Brian considered him and answered. 'Knowing how people think is kind of handy when you've got a bunch of them trying to blow your arse over the desert. It's about figuring out what makes them tick. End of the day we're all human, just made different by the cultures we grow up in. As for disinterested and disconnected, you've got a point. I'm working on that.'

A lot more of an answer than Adam was expecting.

'So how did, you know, you get such bad burns?'

'I told you that.' He narrowed his eyes. 'An RPG.'

'I know, but how? I thought RPGs blew things up, not burned. What happened?'

Brian laughed but it contained only irony. 'It's not a bloody campfire story, Adam. RPGs do all kinds of things, especially duds. I got burnt to fuck and spent a day and night wandering the desert with bits of my best mate stuck to me. I got a pension, a medal and an honourable discharge, thank you very fucking much. My best mate's widow got a pension. His kids have no clue who their dad was.'

Brian's response felt like a slap, not because of its abruptness but for its sense of reality. 'I'm sorry, I didn't think. You…it's hard to imagine.'

'Don't worry, Adam, you're good, it's different worlds. Your one is just as alien to me.'

Adam was still curious though. 'You seem to move OK though, what's it like?'

'Medium rare skin? It hurts like a bitch and feels like old leather. I'm getting used to it. Andrea thinks it looks like angel wings.' Brian smiled. 'Trust a child to see good huh?'

Adam did not know how to add to that so they watched TV in silence, the immaculately groomed presenters profiling likely kidnappers with a specialist. White males over the age of twenty-five without a girlfriend were in the frame.

Brian was first to speak. 'I'm surprised they showed that picture of Sarah along with the CCTV. Either someone hasn't done their homework or they think they're being clever. The press will be all over her.'

'It's insane,' Adam agreed, trying not to imagine the consequences of Sarah's past regurgitated on a national scale. He ran his hands through his hair and Brian stood, collecting their empty glasses. Both their heads turned to the arched doorway as cool air ran through the bar, listening to a procession of people file through the downstairs doorway.

SIXTY-ONE

Any thoughts Andrea had that Sarah was *one of them* had long since faded, which was not to say she had not given it a lot of thought. The simple truth was in how she saw herself reflected in Sarah. Everything Sarah did was woven around an undeniable intention. She was there only for her. That meant so much to Andrea on so many levels that doubt had quickly turned to trust. She even thought she might love Sarah a little. Of course not the love she held for her mum or dad or even her sisters. That love was just there. It was more the kind she held for Kevin, who was in many respects more of a dad to her than her dad.

She could also see from the pain evident in every fragile movement that Sarah was faltering. While Andrea still firmly believed her dad would come for her, and she could not really imagine the worst of what might happen if he did not, she did know that if Sarah was too ill to help, she was too little to get free by herself. So she did the only thing she could, she invested herself in Sarah.

Andrea had a lot of love held in reserve, mostly because her dad did not need it and her mum was always too busy. So now seemed a perfect opportunity to use some of it in the absolute certainty it would help. She crawled over and ducked beneath Sarah's arm, laying her head against Sarah's chest and her hand beneath the bloodstained shirt, warm on the skin of Sarah's stomach. She knew Sarah's stomach was hurting from the way she moved and touched it. Andrea also knew Jesus healed with his hands. So she decided that was how she would let her love flow, through her hand into Sarah. Which she did, closing her eyes at first as she concentrated, willing her love from her heart through her body and into

238

Sarah through her hand. Somehow talking seemed to help as well. So she proceeded to talk about everything she could think to talk about, which was all her life that she could recall, which was about five years.

While Andrea talked, and despite her very best efforts, a nagging thought kept vying for her attention. It came from when she had been running screaming through the house trying to open windows. She had seen shelves with photos of many different faces, mostly smiling and outside, like on boats, and some with Simon. It had registered then but she had been too busy being frightened. So the thought had lodged in her mind unresolved. Later when she was by herself it occurred to her. How could a man from her 'before' life, her comfortable world of home and routine, be in a photo with Simon?

For some reason the question muddled her thoughts and made her heart a little heavy as well. She did know the world was full of puzzling questions, she also knew it was full of obvious answers. So she fully expected an explanation she could file under, *Of course that's why!*

She also thought telling Sarah about something sad might break the spell of her love, so she decided not to, despite almost mentioning it in her enthusiasm to keep speaking. She was very sure her love was helping. Talking about her before life was also therapy for herself. As she remembered these times and places she realised they were already losing clarity in her mind. Telling Sarah these stories helped make them distinct again, although sometimes she forgot some detail or why something happened, so she made it up. Which she actually quite enjoyed because it was a bit like the stories she made up at home. She even started adding bits to stories she remembered perfectly well, so she could make them more interesting. Talking and talking. All the time pressing the palm of her hand flat against Sarah's skin and thinking how Jesus did it. Pushing the occasional heavy hearted thought aside and letting the love flow into Sarah, telling all the funny stories about her sisters and Kevin, especially Kevin because when he was home, he always did funny things. Very seldom did Andrea let silence reign, lest some of what flowed through her begin to ebb away.

Sarah listened intently, only asking questions when it was clear a question was required. The girl's open affection was unexpected and very welcome. The weight of her small body was mesmerising, her hand warm and soothing against her stomach, the child's voice like a songbird's. It anchored her to reality while her mind ran through a dizzying, competing array of thoughts. With each stream of thought her mind carefully tripped along the edge of reality, trying hard to focus on what she had to do and not tumble into the unreal world of her childhood. The escape world had been how she survived as a child, waiting for the horseman to rescue her. The specialists at Culpho said the world was a composite of her favourite childhood books, the horseman a child's fixation on a saviour, the galloping horse simply the sound of her own heart beating. The unreal world was a place she could not afford to revisit. She would be no use to anyone sitting in the corner dreaming of green fields and snow-capped mountains.

Similarly her thoughts of Adam were now infrequent. For all the hours she had spent with Andrea and for all the girl's questions, talking or even thinking about him felt like it might invoke him to this place. The last place he should be. She believed Simon when he said Hakan would not waste time on Adam, but whenever she did allow herself the luxury of a memory it always wound to Adam in their ransacked flat, which only added to her mental burden. So she shut out the thoughts of her life with Adam. It was another life that existed as a video paused in her mind. Just as she did not think of guilt or for Adam's hurt in how she was managing Simon's need. She only focused on the reality of each passing second and her hope for an opportunity.

This began and ended with the blades safely hidden in Andrea's bag, a perfect hiding place it seemed. Even with the blades Sarah's problems abounded. She felt certain Simon would come for her at least once more. For now she was the antidote to his malady, although nowhere near ready or capable of sating him again. Opportunities for using the blades distilled down to two scenarios and both presented problems. First, she could only imagine Simon distracted enough with her naked, which meant hiding two small and very sharp blades would be difficult. And then given the opportunity, what would be her point of attack? What could she do to him with a razor in each hand, realistically? She knew what she might do but nothing was going to be instant or have any guarantee of success. There would be a high probability of collateral damage.

With all these myriad thoughts there was another she persistently tried to ignore, that scratched from deep inside of her. A realisation that in Simon there was an echo of herself, something of innocence prised free too early.

SIXTY-TWO

Brian set the second round of cokes onto the table. 'We have three new arrivals, three guys. A meat axe I saw at the house last night and two others I've not seen before. One looks solid and the other a thin guy. Looks like a rat on stilts. You got the knife on you?'

Adam leaned to the side and patted his back pocket.

'Right then, keep it there. This is not the time or place. If anything kicks off you're going to be too busy running. Got that?'

Adam confirmed and they waited, half on edge, half watching the TV, but nothing happened. The rhythm and sounds of the bar continued as they had. The news on the abduction started repeating itself. The three new arrivals sat around a table partly seen through the arched doorway. Brian stretched out his legs and yawned.

Adam spun his phone on the table, his hands shaking. His whole body felt light with nerves. 'What do you think they're waiting for?'

'Nothing probably. They know what we're here for and why, but they don't know what we know. As long as we're not out causing trouble they're happy.'

'So what should we do?'

'The same.' Brian's attention moved to the screen. 'They're just here to intimidate and watch. Hopefully someone will be along soon to find out what we do know. Then it'll be down to my ability to piss off a stranger in no time at all.'

Adam did not think that would be a problem. He could not believe how relaxed Brian was. 'How do you do it?'

'Piss people off?'

'No, this. Sit here cool as can be knowing there are three guys just

241

there and the two blond guys probably not far away. Or for that matter fire a gun at someone knowing they will fire one right back at you. That you may die and it might not be nice, lose an arm or leg, or God knows what. Get burned.'

Brian looked at him. 'You don't think about it.'

'That's it, you just don't think about it?'

Brian's head moved up and down. 'You put it out of your head. You just get on with it. Get through it, do your job. What else am I going to do, go home? Wait for the police to get their arses in gear? There's no point bleating about this unlucky life, you get on with it.'

From the lower bar they heard the door open, then felt cold air around their legs. The hub of conversation lowered. They both saw the shoulder and left side of a short broad man. They could see him talking to the three foot soldiers. Their eyes flicked up to Adam and Brian and then back to their conversation.

Then the new arrival turned and confidently walked up the steps. He was wearing a leather jacket, had a square face heavily creased and pinched, small dark eyes that fixed on Brian as he swung a chair around the table and faced them.

'My name is Hakan,' he said. 'Do you mind if I join you?' He leaned forward and held out his hand.

Habit almost had Adam standing. He stopped himself and decided to sit tight, to say and do nothing, his eyes on the man, struck by the thought this man might know where Sarah was right now. Brian did not say anything at first, ignoring Hakan's outstretched hand. He finally acknowledged the question.

'Sure, join us but we're in a miserable mood and I'd rather not shake hands if you don't mind.' Brian smoothed down the ends of his moustache with a thumb and index finger.

Hakan let his hand drop and sat down, leaning back into the chair. Adam fidgeted, looking across at his phone and willing it to ring.

'I was wondering why you are here in this place?' Hakan's tone was light and conversational. 'We have not seen you before.' He briefly appraised Adam and returned his attention to Brian.

'Minding our own business. Sorting a few things out.' Brian looked disinterested at the TV, which was running highlights of the press conference. Hakan turned to watch as well. Then they both turned to each other across the table.

'A terrible thing,' Hakan said. 'I can only imagine what her father must be going through. So careless of him to leave such a pretty child in the street unattended. Don't you think?'

'Unattended?' Brian answered. 'Makes her sound like a bloody suitcase. As for the father I expect he's out looking for whoever took her, at a guess.'

'Maybe, Mr Dunstan. I am sure you do not mind me calling you that.'

Brian folded his arms. 'It is my name.'

'Good,' Hakan continued. 'You say you are minding your own business. Then it seems I misunderstand your meaning. Because you broke into my property last night and attacked my employee. Then you attacked two of my colleagues on the beach. That is not minding your own business, surely?'

Brian snorted and nodded at Adam. 'That's bruises under his eyes my friend, not fucking war paint. Your two buddies started that fight. As for the guy at your house, he was impatient and careless.'

Hakan sighed and crossed one leg over the other. 'So what is it you are here for?'

Brian leaned forward. 'Well, I thought that was kind of obvious. For a start a ten-year-old girl, pretty, you just saw her on TV. And a woman, pretty as well. Then of course there's the big fella, I'd like a few words with him. Your pal, no doubt. I'd guess about six foot four, was seen by half the country driving a Rover two nights ago. Now what was his name, let me think, ah yes, Simon Thompson.'

A thin smile stretched across Hakan's face. 'You are very abrasive, Mr Dunstan. Such a lack of tact and utter ignorance, so English. No wonder you are losing this country to foreigners, when all you can do is sit in pubs and swear.'

'Is that so? Well I'll have you know we're very proud of our country's distinguished legacy of being invaded by foreigners, thank you very much. It's what makes this such a rich and civilised culture.'

'An interesting perspective.' Hakan looked around the empty bar. 'So how is the search for your daughter coming along?'

'Well ain't that the funny thing. I'll admit we were a little stuck. Weren't we?' He glanced at Adam who instinctively nodded. Brian barely paused. 'We know this Simon character is near here, but just can't figure exactly where. We know he wasn't working alone after your blond buddies fucked up Peterborough, so we got to thinking, whoever's directing things can't be that bright. So we thought to ourselves, how about we sit in that pub where Simon grew up. Maybe they'll come to us like they did the night before. And fuck me, hey presto! Not just the goons but the brains of the operation, how about that?'

'Very amusing, Mr Dunstan. You are assuming of course that I am somehow connected with your daughter's abduction.'

'Well that would be my assumption, and not desperately hard to come to either, you're here for a start. But then I'd pick you out in a crowd.' Brian theatrically appraised Hakan. 'When did you last look at yourself in the mirror mate, do you cultivate that look? Sit in bed nights reading bad guy magazines, fashion tips for the undersized crook?'

He paused and looked hard into dark impassive eyes. He kept pushing. 'And of course now we know the house down the road is yours, I guess that about seals it.'

'You really are the funny man, Mr Dunstan, and not so stupid as you look. I cannot be held accountable for the past tenants in my properties, surely? I am merely here to look out for my own interests.'

Adam was finding it difficult to take his eyes off Hakan, who sat almost totally still with a constant fixed humourless smile. The man's whole physicality put Adam in mind of a dam in the seconds before it explodes.

'I'm counting on you looking after your interests.' Brian's voice now had a harsh edge. 'How much do little girls fetch these days? White girls at that, with all the risk involved? If I were you I'd be here protecting my interests as well.'

Hakan brushed an invisible speck from his trousers and rested one hand on his knee. 'I trust you will be making your point soon, Mr Dunstan?'

Brian shifted in his seat. He actually had no point to make. He was only looking for a reaction. So he made one up, plucking at the separate strands of information and thoughts accumulated over the last day. 'My point is we already know you have a boat ready, Simon's probably on his hands and knees scrubbing the decks as we speak. What is it, some yacht he's delivering? Maybe a luxury one for some sheik or oligarch? Nice idea I gotta say, get the child out of the country on a VIP pass. Your only exposure is poor old Simon. I bet the minute he sets sail you scatter like leaves in the wind, while back in poor uncivilised Blighty we're left chasing sex offenders and reports of blonde white girls spotted in every city across Europe.'

Then something did change, an almost imperceptible shift in the air, a collective tension that made it heavier. The possible truth of what he had said dawned on Brian, sensing the realisation in Adam too. He quickly back-tracked through the detail in his mind.

Hakan leaned forward, the leather creaking. He balanced the tips of his fingers on the edge of the table. 'A very good idea, I agree,' he said. 'I might even consider it if kidnapping and extortion is a field I ever move into.' He looked at his watch. 'But I must go now, for all your entertaining conversation, Mr Dunstan.'

He did not move, sitting motionless save for a slight tremor in his shoulders, as if working to contain the forces pushing at the dam. 'You have however proven yourself to be a nuisance. I certainly cannot afford to have you running around causing trouble in this place.' He gestured slowly and proudly to the bar. 'Yes I own this as well. So I will detail for you two options which are as follows. You will both now leave. This is going to happen regardless. You will walk calmly out of here,' he nodded in the direction of the ten o'clock door, 'and climb into the car driven by my two friends. They will drive you into Doncaster, completely free of charge, where you will be at liberty to find your own way home. The only other option is the same, except you refuse to leave quietly. In which case my colleagues will fetch you and place you in the car. If you then come back...' He looked from Brian to Adam and back. 'Well, let us just say I will not be happy. Feel free to talk among yourselves, you have two minutes.'

He stepped back the chair and stood, turning to walk away, but Brian was not finished. 'You mean you're going to leave and not tell me who set up my daughter? You could at least do that, give me something to do when I get home.'

Hakan's mouth opened as if to answer. Then closed, changing his mind. 'I have no idea, of course, Mr Dunstan. But a man of your intelligence would surely find it easy to figure out.' He walked back through the arched door and down the steps, stopping to exchange a brief word with the men before leaving the pub.

Adam stared at the empty chair, not able to comprehend all that happened in the last few minutes. He felt cold inside and heavy with a sense of impending doom. Hakan and these men were not just bad guys. These were men that earned a living from selling children and were not about to give it up without a fight.

Brian faced him, placing a hand on each of his shoulders. 'Listen and do exactly what I say. You know if any part of what I just said is true we can't get into that car?'

Adam absently nodded, registering the change, a cool efficiency. There was something different in Brian's eyes.

'What're you going to do, mate?' Brian asked.

'Run,' Adam answered and started to move his legs from under the table. Brian stopped him.

'Not yet. In a few seconds they'll come up the steps. I'll do my best to stop them but you have to fucking run. Sarah, Andrea, your life could depend on it.'

The urgency in Brian's voice was seeping through his daze. 'Don't stop Adam, don't look back. Get into suburbia and run, change direction and change direction. Do not run in a straight line. When you can't run anymore, run some more. Then you hole up in a different hotel and knock yourself out. You dig up anything you can on this Hakan guy.' Brian reached around and retrieved the phone from the table, pushing it into the front pocket of Adam's jacket. 'Ring Boer with what you find. He'll know what to do.'

Adam felt as if he was floating above his own body, looking down at the scene and not part of it. 'What will you do?' he asked.

'I'm going to give them something to worry about. If it's just these three I might get my one-on-one time with the blonds and that might get me on the fast track. Your job is to get out of here. Don't fuck about with that knife. If anyone gets in your way clench your teeth and go through them. Don't stop.'

Over Brian's shoulder Adam saw two men step into the upper bar, the large one with a plaster across his nose and the tall thin one Brian had described as a rat on stilts. They stopped and watched.

Brian glanced across at them and returned his attention to Adam. 'Wait for me to stand then move behind me and go. As soon as they react I'll be into them.'

Brian smiled a broad, beaming smile that lifted his moustache up at the ends. It was a smile like a warm sun on a cold day. Adam imagined Brian commanding men; they would feel there was nothing they could not do, not with Brian at their side. He could do it.

Brian slapped his shoulder. 'You're good, Sawacki, it's been a pleasure.' And then Brian was up, walking around the table and standing nonchalantly, hands at his side, opposite the two men.

246

Don't think about it, Adam thought to himself. Stand up, smile and run. He tried not to stare at the 12 o'clock door, the strength almost leaving his legs as he stood, having to sit back down. He waited a few seconds then managed to move behind Brian. He placed a hand on Brian's shoulder and the tall guy ushered them forward, to walk down to the lower bar. The one with the plaster stepped to the side.

And then Adam ran.

SIXTY-THREE

Adam let his hand drop from Brian's shoulder and turned and bolted for the pub door, almost tripping over his own feet as he burst into the car park and the cool day and then around the corner heading straight for the promenade, and straight into a solid wall of muscle and bone. From somewhere behind he heard a shout and a loud crash.

The man Adam had run into was as surprised as he was. They careened off each other and stumbled off the wall into a heap on the tarmac. The man reacted quicker, using his weight to pin Adam to the ground. He grasped Adam's arms, rolling him face down and pulling his hands behind his back. Then he forced him to his feet. Adam had been caught after barely running five steps. *What would Brian do now?*

Adam relaxed, let the muscles loosen in his arms, let defeat show in his posture and then threw the whole of his weight back. He drove back with his legs, recalling the first time he'd met Brian. This time Adam used all the pent-up anger inside of him. The man, unbalanced, crashed back into the wall, the impact trapping Adam's arm behind his body, forcing it up and out of the joint. Then it popped back and the pain screamed from him. He dropped to one knee, the arm hanging painfully at his side but now free of the man's grip. He stumbled forward, trying to run, but immediately hands found his shoulders, a heavy weight draped over his back, pulling him down and then a fist thudded into his side again and again. He felt the blows but not the pain as he hit the tarmac face first. Then pain did explode in his ribs, trying to roll from the next kick, bringing up his good arm to defend himself, looking up at a silhouette, the man looming over him, the pub and sky beyond. And then the silhouette crumpled like a building with the foundations blown away.

Brian smiled down at him. 'Fuck me, Sawacki, you should be in Hull by now.'

Adam felt the weight pulled off him and Brian lifted him to his feet, blood running from a cut that pooled on his moustache. He turned from Adam as someone came out of the pub behind. Metal glinted and Brian circled.

Seeing the blood on Brian was a shock, it jolted him. He scrambled to his feet and ran, aware of metal clattering behind him and the sound of a body slammed into the ground. He forced himself to move despite the pain, onto the promenade and cutting right, the high grass mound rising to the main road on his left. In front of him the pavement opened out. Then he saw a blond smudge from his right, moving with increasing momentum across the car park, the tall blond gliding effortlessly with eyes focused, arms pumping, angled towards him.

Adam could only keep running, sucking the air into his body. The road was empty ahead, a vista of hope and freedom. He could see the blond was going to cut him off. He readied to run through him, aware his breathing was a ragged double beat. His feet pounding the pavement sounded like four not two. He risked a quick glance over his shoulder and saw Brian running shotgun. The blond was not looking at him at all, but at Brian. Relief washed through him, it gave him strength. He was not going to fail. He ran harder. The blond arrowed in and Brian now ran at Adam's side, his breath rasping, but somehow passing him. Step over step. The blond lengthened his stride, slowing, trying to judge as Brian veered towards him, the predator and its prey on a collision course.

At the last moment Brian lowered his shoulder and wrapped his arms around the blond's waist, swinging his feet off the floor. Both men hit the pavement hard and tumbled to a sickening halt against a bench. There was no movement.

Adam ran and did not dare look back, feeling like a tangible bond between him and Brian was being stretched. And then it was gone. He passed steps that climbed the grassy mound, knowing the two roads eventually levelled, running straight, easing his stride and trying to gain back his breath. Five hundred metres and he would be into streets lined by houses.

He was not sure what made him look back. Maybe it was the barely discerned echo of another set of feet, the smaller blond gaining ground quickly. Adam's eyes widened in horror and then fixed ahead, opening his stride, trying to power through his thighs. But at fifty metres he could hear the feet slapping behind and another fifty the man breathing easy. Adam panicked. He lost coordination, panting, his rhythm disjointed. An arm came over his shoulder and another laced around his side and he was now the prey pulled to the ground. He bounced off the pavement, the skin torn from his elbows and the breath from his lungs. A strong arm snaked around his neck and a painful weight pinned him to the ground. A voice instructed him to stand, American and smooth.

Brian's warning played constantly in his head, it was down to him now. With everything Brian had done, he had still failed. He could not let it happen, not for Brian, or Sarah or Andrea. It occurred to him and he did it without thinking. Survival willed his bad arm down, palm against thigh, the pain sharp and deep in his shoulder. He pulled his hand up the back of his leg. The blond's body was close behind, starting to turn him. Adam slid his fingers first into his back pocket and then around the moulded plastic. He pulled it free and pressed the button, the blade leapt free and without hesitating he thrust it back, thigh high, into the body behind. He jerked it free and did the same again, this time twisting the blade before pulling it away. His reward was a primal scream. The grip loosened and he rammed his good elbow around, feeling pain explode up his arm as it connected, he did not care. He struggled free. A quick look as he stumbled away showed the blond curled on the pavement. Then Adam really ran, as if the devil were treading on his heels. Up the mound as the roads levelled, across the main road and into suburbia.

Ali watched it all happen, from a distance of course. He was parked higher up on the main road, with a bird's-eye view down over the pub. He leaned against his Mercedes in his three-piece suit and long woollen overcoat. A ringside seat.

He did not know Adam, just who he was from the description. The dark stretch of Ali's lips formed a smile as he watched Brian climb from the tangle of limbs beneath the bench, going to work with his little rounders bat. That bat had been to hell with his friend, although four on one were never good odds. Not all at once.

He watched the smaller blond chase Adam down the street, two decreasing figures that eventually merged, just as Brian went down to a blow from behind. The pack descended. Ali knew what the kicks and punches felt like, that Brian knew how to take them. The taller blond pushed back the crowd and Brian was dragged into the back of a green car, a guard on each side. The car screamed away and stopped where the other blond lay on the pavement.

Ali climbed into the Mercedes and CNN flickered to life on the console, the suck of air as the doors sealed and silence. He pressed the ignition and waited for the low hum of the engine, turning the car in the road and driving down the incline. He watched the green car, wondering if it would give chase or turn around. The small blond was loaded into the front seat and it lurched forward, stopping almost immediately. It turned back along the promenade. Ali touched the accelerator and the Mercedes eased forward.

SIXTY-FOUR

Simon closed and locked the front door. He was vexed. He walked through to the dining room and stopped, staring through the patio doors into the late afternoon gloom. Most of what he saw was his own reflection and the room behind.

He had spent most of the day at the dock. Sarah had constantly been in his thoughts while he ran through tests, as excited as he could remember, the thrill of expectation, of being with her again. Not necessarily in *that* way, but just to be with her. She was more than just an echo of his past, she was perfect.

Hakan's call changed everything, angry in his barely contained way. Something had forced him to change the schedule, which meant Simon was now leaving that night.

Leaving early presented logistical problems but nothing he could not overcome. It had taken some rescheduling but the *Passing Dream* would be ready. His experience with this Ferretti was limited but he knew the range, he simply changed the testing to focus on getting out of the dock. The extended tests could wait until he was heading around Portugal.

Neither were supplies his concern. They had been delivered the week before, stacked in the old workshop on the quay. It was just a matter of loading and Hakan was organising that. Just as getting out of the dock ahead of schedule was also resolved, the amended paperwork was already filed with the harbour master. Critically, instead of knowing who would be supervising the customs checks on Wednesday night, he now knew who would be doing them that night, Monday night. These changes did not vex Simon.

His dilemma since making Sarah his problem was always going to be

252

what to do with her. With two days to spare he had simply ignored it. Now he was being forced into a decision. Hakan had given him clear instructions. He must leave her in the room and the brothers would take care of her.

The silence stretched as he deliberated, looking at his shadowed reflection in the glass. He wavered between decisions, what he should do and what he wanted. Eventually he walked up the stairs, knowing there was only ever one answer, trying to talk himself out of it. He could not leave her to the brothers.

On tiptoe he lifted back the loft door, pulled down the ladder and retrieved his suitcases. He laid them side by side on his bed, moving through drawers and packing neatly folded T-shirts and trousers and shirts. He took a packet of yellow capsules from his bedside drawer and pressed four into his palm. Stopping in the bathroom he took two plasters from the cabinet and a syringe from the drawer. Then he went downstairs to the kitchen, the capsules and the plasters on the worktop, the jug lifted from the blender. He wiped the inside and dropped in the four capsules, placing the jug back onto the blender and the plasters stayed where they were. He climbed the stairs, syringe in hand.

In his study he reached past shelves of framed photos to a basket of unlabelled bottles, checking the base of the selected bottle to make sure he had the right one. He drew 5ml of the clear liquid into the syringe.

He returned the bottle to the basket and the basket to the shelf, slipping the syringe into the desk drawer. He moved the chair within reach of the desk then stepped from his clothes and into the bathroom and the shower, then changing into fresh Chinos and a T-shirt and downstairs to the garage.

The first thing that hit him as he jacked the door sideways was the smell. For several seconds he contemplated the bowl with the Rupert annual placed on top, then carefully lifted it and placed it on the garage floor. He leaned back in. Sarah and the girl were sitting side by side, two serious faces looking back at him.

'Go away,' Sarah said. 'I can't.'

He held out his hand. 'I know, I need to talk, it's very important.' Sarah looked at him, studying his face and seeing the urgency. She said something to the girl he could not hear, brushing the child's hair from a worried face. And then Sarah crawled towards him, ignoring his offered hand, which made him smile inside.

SIXTY-FIVE

He ran and ran. Through suburbia with Brian's instructions resonating in his mind, turning left and then right, endlessly weaving with no idea where he was going, every approaching car a dread that peaked as it drew level and tapered as it passed uninterested. Running for hours it seemed. He ran along streets of houses, some behind walls and drives, others that crowded the curb. He ran along roads of shops, grocers and newsagents, stepping into the road to dodge unaware shoppers. He ran with his breath trailing like smoke, no strength left in his arms or legs, only momentum from fear. People paused, warily watching the running man with mad eyes and a bloody blade in his hand.

Exhausted beyond even fear Adam stopped at a small park, a playground beyond a stretch of grass and then a copse of brown trees. Heaving gulps of air he walked wearily to the swings, the chain protesting as he rocked forwards and backwards while watching grey darken in the sky. Some urgent need nagged but he was too spent to care.

Slowly his senses recovered as his breathing slowed and then he realised, he still held the knife in his hand. The blood was tacky now and almost dry, covering his hand as well. He cleaned the blade and then his hand using grass and the inside of his jacket and then he sat back on the swing and wept, a bubbling over of something inside that grew and boiled with his relief and comprehension – he had made it. The promise of death had touched him, its gnarled fingers had reached out and tried dragging him down. Somehow he had clung on. He cried like he had not since a child.

It was dark when he was done and ready to move on, welcoming the veil of night. He kept to side streets, walking always with an eye on the people and cars around him. He passed through an industrial park full of warehouses, emerging to a fenced car park and a flyover that ran from behind him, curving up and around on high concrete legs. He walked along a path beside the chain fence beneath the flyover. On the other side was a large brick building. He almost passed it, thinking it was a hospital. It was a hotel. He walked inside and checked in.

Once in his room he lay on the bed without removing a single item of clothing, the image of the trawler and the story of Conley Thompson now running in a constant loop in his mind, given some priority he could not fathom, trying to juggle its context with everything else he now knew. He was not aware of falling asleep, just of busily working through the different streams of thought, only realising he had slept when he woke with a start. It was as if his mind had needed his interfering thoughts out of the way as it created order from the detail, now neatly realigned. What he had to do now seemed obvious. Two words bobbed at the forefront of his mind like cork on an ocean: *Cutting Blue.*

He needed a computer. He rubbed his eyes and swung his legs off the bed. He ran his hands through his hair and left the room, the door clicking closed behind him as he jogged down the long hallway.

SIXTY-SIX

F rancis Boer knew plenty of stories about people who had known. Who had taken meticulous care of their affairs, written farewell notes, gone to bed, and never seen another day. Boer had never really known what to make of those stories and had never really given them any thought.

Until that Monday morning. A night of ravaging sickness was the forewarning. A night that made his body feel emptied. A few fitful hours of sleep and he suddenly jerked awake at four. He knew then, as if some systems check had uncovered a fatal change in the trip of his heart, the blood thicker in his veins, and then woke him to warn him. This would be his last dawn, the last day in a lifetime. It was as good a day to die as any.

When he was up and able he rested in his study with a glass of water, letting his thoughts vie for his attention. He was proud of his children. They did not talk to him or did so rarely. That was his failing, not theirs. Some men are family men and some are not. He had found every opportunity to be anywhere but home, mostly at work and never short of justification. That was probably his biggest regret. For all the effort his wife invested in changing him, he only understood the need to change when she was no longer there.

That sparked a thought in him. He lifted writing paper from the drawer and laid it on his desk. He wrote four letters, one to each of his children and one to his former wife, now living in Canada. He signed his name with love and carefully folded them into envelopes, addressing each and then slid them into the drawer.

Then he did something that went against every professional principle he possessed, despite it being the third time he had done it. He called a suspect and warned them away with detail of the investigation. The conversation was short. When he placed the handset back in its cradle he had no better feeling for whether it was right or wrong. If he was right then Sarah and Andrea might be saved. If he was wrong he could not see it would change much. It was not a spur of the moment decision. It had been growing as a thought since the night before.

Boer wrapped himself in a coat and stood outside watching east. He was rewarded with a brief flicker of pink and orange but it was overcast and the dawn was not much to speak of. Back inside, Boer's morning continued where the night had left off, racked convulsing with nausea. As if presented with this countdown to life his body was desperately trying to expel the cause of its premature conclusion, although there was little left to expel now save for the strength of his body.

Warning off the suspect did make him feel guilty during Ferreira's visit, despite it being the highlight of his last morning. If he were honest he would admit she was the highlight of his last years, wondering how she would remember him in years to come. He worried for her but only as a coach would a promising student.

After Ferreira left and the marmite toast had been cautiously devoured, he sat in the comfortable silence of the study, the steady progression of a second hand his only company. He pulled the writing paper across one more time and produced one more short letter, sealing it in an envelope marked *Helen* and placing it in the drawer with the others.

He missed the majority of the press conference, spending it in the bathroom revisiting the toast, although his only imperative was to watch the mother and Ferreira's star turn. He needed a drink, his demons straining at the leash in their last hours. He intended embracing them but not yet. First he would let his mind do what it did best. He worked the detail.

The answers to the most puzzling problems are usually the simplest. People often miss them because human minds often seek complicated solutions for the most puzzling problems. Simple solutions and a nod to all human vagaries had been his mantra for twenty years.

Once Boer started a case and began processing the detail his mind would invariably draw him towards a particular aspect. The first with Andrea's abduction had been realising she had not been picked by chance. The second had been gleaned as he flicked through Andrea's

257

stories in her bookcase, a page at random, a partial sentence in a whole page of words. The last had been the number hidden in her bedside picture frame.

Ordinarily he would then begin moulding and squeezing those thoughts until he had a hint of the truth. Then he would sit down with the people most likely to give that truth shape. Very often that took him through a maze of twists and turns to something entirely different. Sometimes it took him nowhere and more sleepless nights wondering what he had missed, always feeling he could have done more when the truth remained elusive.

For Andrea it would now fall to Ferreira to find the truth. Although he knew where he would start in giving the case substance, he had already ringed the name in the case file many times lest she miss his point.

Exhausted, he dozed, waking for the last time just before five in the afternoon. He checked the clock and cursed the irony of sleeping away his last day. The irony of a lifetime with a restless mind toiling through sleepless nights, silenced only with alcohol. The irony would have him shake a fist at the sky if he thought there was anything in the sky worth shaking a fist at.

The clock ticked past six and he decided now was the time. He pushed the chair from the desk and eased himself to his feet, weaker than he had expected, his legs attempting to buckle at any opportunity. He used the walls and door frames to support himself through the short journey to his bedroom, the journey back to his desk made more difficult by the almost empty bottle and the glass in his hand.

He cleaned the glass with his shirt and unscrewed the cap – a sound that stirred endless memories of late nights. The sound of drink splashing into the glass shifted loose a good many more.

Discovering the full meaning of the word terminal at the age of fifty-three had brought to him the realisation he wanted to live. That meant saying goodbye to his liquid friend. He had driven straight to the supermarket, bought one last bottle of his favourite and drank all but this glass of its golden contents.

He sipped it at first, like he did all drinks, but the hunger having been tempered for so long leapt free and he gulped it down. Immediately he craved another and even considered convincing Helen to stop at the supermarket. He sectioned that need and placed the glass on the table, the empty bottle on the floor beside the table leg.

The glow of the drink spread warm inside his stomach. He felt lightheaded, although it was too soon for the drink to have any effect. He picked up his pen and tapped the nib against the page, circling the name absently. Mentally he tried skimming through the detail but his mind would only remind him of his wife, smiling and exhausted, their first child pink in her arms, a picture he kept in his bedside drawer. His heart skipped to an uneven tempo and a tightness crept up on him, a tightness that embraced him and ratcheted ever tighter, a sudden fear at the realisation even though he had been waiting for its arrival, then unimaginable pain that clamped tight across his chest as if he was being crushed by giant hands. It pitched him forward onto the desk, the pen dropping onto the desk and then rolling to the floor. He fought through his failing body to cling on to dignity, for how he wanted her to find him, using the last of his strength and slowly pushing himself back into the chair, then the creak of wood and a blink of unseeing eyes, the second hand marking time. A short exhalation and then Francis Boer only existed in the minds of those that had known him.

SIXTY-SEVEN

Duncan and Brodie were waiting in a car in a layby on the A12, north of the M25. They were both unified in their purpose although not talking to each other, mostly because Brodie thought the photos were worth ten thousand and Duncan thought it more prudent they settle for five.

They had been oblivious to possessing anything worth that kind of money until that Monday afternoon, sitting in a café eating eggs, black pudding and baked beans. They were casually watching the news on a TV mounted high on the wall, another missing child. Then Sarah's picture appeared on the TV and they watched footage of her walk through Delamere.

They had of course taken a good look through Sarah's phone on the Saturday night, both impressed by pictures of her topless on some beach. They transferred the pictures to a laptop to get a better look and in the hope there might be some of her busy with her bloke. They were disappointed, so they watched a couple of movies, did some porn and then fell asleep and never gave Sarah another thought.

Until that afternoon, both avidly watching the TV while finishing their meals, then frantically searching through their bags in the car having offloaded most of their contraband the day before.

The phone was gone but the phone's memory card was still pushed into the laptop, complete with the pictures. Jubilant and relieved they set about comparing circulation figures for the tabloid press and then finding numbers to call. By five that afternoon Duncan had agreed on a price and a place to swap the money for the pictures, which is how they came to be waiting in a layby on the A12.

The journalist they spoke to had warned he might be delayed and by seven thirty he was an hour late. There had been several false alarms. On one occasion flaring brake lights heralded a driver who immediately hurried to the verge. Another car pulled up and waited with a lone driver. Brodie was on the verge of knocking on the window when a second car came to a stop and a woman exchanged a sleeping child with the first.

Then a Land Rover pulled up in front, the number plates completely obscured by muck and mud. A large man with broad powerful shoulders climbed out and walked to the back, tossing a bag onto the ground that landed several yards from the tow bar. Duncan and Brodie looked at each other and climbed out.

The traffic flashed by at implausible speeds, both of them buffeted by the backdraft, headlights and tail lights passing in a blur. They stopped several steps shy of the bag. At the same time the Land Rover's passenger door opened and another man climbed out. This man was tall and smart in a long brown overcoat, carrying something that looked like a small laptop in one hand.

'He's a Paki!' said Brodie. 'We're not dealing with no Paki!'

'I'm English actually,' the man said as he came to a stop and held out his hand. 'Now show me the pictures.'

Brodie stepped back, the memory card clasped in his fist.

'No way, Paki and English, that's twice as bad pal. Not for five grand, we want ten.'

The man in the overcoat sighed. 'Don't call me a Paki.' He stepped forward and picked up the bag, throwing it at Duncan's feet. 'There's three thousand in there. You can hand over the pictures and fuck off or my friend here will take the pictures and keep the money. Which is it?'

They both looked at the broad man. He looked to Duncan to be the result of cross-breeding humans and Rottweilers, including a collar-like tattoo around his neck. 'Three is good for some photies Brode, what would we have said to that this morning?'

Brodie looked for a moment like he might protest but they were out of their league and they both knew it. He handed Duncan the card and picked up the bag, opening it and flicking through the stacked notes as he walked back to the car. Duncan took three steps towards the man and handed him the card. He was about to turn when the crossbreed made a sound not unlike a growl.

'Wait there a second my bonnie friend.' The man opened the laptop and slid the card inside. Duncan waited, watching the man intently browse the images. Finally the man nodded and turned and both men climbed into the Land Rover and back into the flow of traffic.

Duncan and Brodie divvied up the money there and then and immediately began planning what they would spend it on, quickly deciding it would probably involve a top class hotel and hookers.

SIXTY-EIGHT

S arah followed Simon through to the dining room, expecting him
to climb the stairs, but he veered into the kitchen. She followed
him to the doorway.

'What?'

He glanced at her as he pulled the jug off the blender, dropping three
tomatoes into the jug along with the contents of two cracked eggs. She waited.

'I have a problem, Sarah.'

'You only just realised?' She stepped in and leaned against the
worktop, watching him slice half a cucumber into sticks, collecting a
handful of mushrooms, carrots, a peeled banana and a small spring
onion, tipping them all into the jug.

'You are my problem, Sarah.'

She knew that, of course, had been deliberating the converging paths of
her future as best she rationally could. Although she knew Andrea was being
sold into a *magical* new life, all paths for her came to premature conclusions.
The green glow of the microwave clock said it was seven thirty.

'Well, that's easily resolved,' she replied.

'It is?' He ladled in a spoonful of powder from a large tub of whey.

'Of course, you let us go. I promise to tell the police you have been a
kind and considerate host.'

One corner of his mouth upturned and he shook his head, adding
milk to the concoction. 'Hakan wants me to leave you here for the
brothers. You don't want that.'

She had no idea who the brothers were but the tone in Simon's voice
sent a chill down her spine. She tried to keep the tremor from her voice.
'I thought you were good for a few more days?'

'I am,' he lied. 'But there's no point delaying important decisions.' He sprinkled chilli powder into the jug and set it on the blender, fastening the lid and turning it on. They both stared at each other, waiting out the percussive noise. It stopped and he peeked in, starting it again and retrieving two tall glasses, placing them on the work surface. He turned off the machine and poured two equal measures from the jug, taking both and holding out one glass for Sarah.

'If you think I'm drinking that you're insane,' she said, folding her arms.

He stepped closer, still offering it to her. 'It's full of nutrients, carbohydrates, proteins, fibre and even a little fat. It's good for you.'

'But you made it.' She kept her arms where they were, looking right back at him.

'I did make it. It's all clean if that's your concern, I am a very hygienic person.'

She half laughed. 'That is not my concern. I don't trust you. Why something like this now?'

'Why not? I want to discuss your future with you. You should take the drink as a good sign. If I was going to do you harm I would not be feeding you such healthy concoctions.'

She blinked back at him and he sighed. 'You think it is drugged, is that your problem? You watched me make it! Why would I do it now when I could have laced the water you have been happily drinking.' He shrugged his shoulders and drained the offered glass, wiping froth from his top lip. 'The other is yours if you want it. The chilli fuses all the tastes. It really is quite nice and you must be ravenous.'

She looked from him to the glass and then back to him. She was starving and could not face another biscuit. 'You mentioned brothers?'

'I did,' he said, placing the remaining glass on the counter beside her. 'My problem is that I ship out in two days and you were not part of the original equation.' For a moment he looked lost and uncertain. 'I don't think I'm ready to say goodbye to you just yet.' He fell silent, what he wanted to say caught in his throat. 'I know what the brothers will do to you. I will not let that happen.'

The last statement completely threw her. Not just his compassion and her relief in finding the unlikeliest ally, but in her instinctive empathy towards him. She saw the boy he had once been and had to check herself from reaching out a hand to him. She broke the moment by taking the

264

drink, watching him with wide eyes over the top of the glass. She took a cautious sip. The drink was unbelievably delicious.

'So what are you going to do?' She drank more of the thick liquid, the taste sending her mouth into spasms and then powerless to do anything but greedily gulp it all down, wonderfully fresh and spicy and cold into her stomach. 'Wow!' she said. 'Who'd have thought!'

He nodded acknowledgement. 'What am I going to do? The answer is simple. I'm taking you with me.'

'What about the girl?' she immediately returned.

'The child is going too. That is indisputable.'

'And where are you going?'

He took the empty glass and rinsed it with the other. 'We are going to the one place you will cause me the least trouble, the wide open ocean. First to the Atlantic around Portugal, and then through the Mediterranean, Suez and then the Arabian and South China Seas.'

She wiped her mouth with the back of her hand. 'What happens then?'

'I pilot private yachts and cruisers for a living. I deliver them to their owners. I test them or sail them to wherever they need to be. What happens after? In four months I will anchor off Hong Kong's Gold Coast and hand over the boat. With you, I hope. After that I don't know,' he said truthfully. 'We can work that out along the way.'

'And Andrea?'

'I hand her over sometime before. Hakan radios the coordinates. Probably not for a few months. The yacht is a convenient mechanism for transport. The owners never know and are incredibly wealthy, it sometimes helps.'

'Helps you sell little girls into slavery!' She tempered her vitriol and he shifted uncomfortably. Quiet descended as she contemplated a thousand questions and scenarios.

'You know I'll do everything I can to stop you, whatever that may be. It isn't going to end well.'

'Life generally doesn't. And you never know, we might come up with something inventive.' He shrugged his large shoulders hopefully.

Sarah now felt overcome with too much information and incredibly weary. 'But why?'

Simon stepped across and took her hand, which she let him do. 'Why risk so much and take you against Hakan's orders? I'm trying to figure that out myself.'

He reached into a drawer and pulled out a pair of scissors, cutting through the bandage around her hand and carefully lifting it away. He did the same for the other hand, his attentive movements soothing, directing her to the sink where he cleaned the cuts with tap water and soap. Neither were swollen which meant no infection. He dabbed her hands dry with a towel and retrieved the plasters, smoothing each across a palm.

Sarah now felt exhausted and barely able to think. Curling up right there on the kitchen floor seemed unimaginably appealing. She struggled to string together a cohesive thought and was losing the ability to command her body. She knew why but was unable to physically react.

'You drugged me! How?' Her pronunciation drawn out. 'You drank it too?'

He smiled and looked at her with soft eyes, lifting her unprotesting into his arms. 'I weigh 110 kilos, Sarah, that's 230 pounds. I have a body fat ratio of 17%, in bare feet I'm six foot four. I'm good for a while yet.'

'You rambled,' she slurred as he carried her upstairs.

'I did gamble. But then you're unbelievably stubborn and resourceful. I need you quiet and out of the way for a few hours.' He carried her into the study and sat in his chair, Sarah curled on his lap. He moved her head so it rested on his shoulder, exposing the length of her neck.

She fought heavy eyes and managed a last, 'Why?'

He did not answer aloud. He cleared the syringe and carefully pushed it into her neck and the liquid into her. Her eyes stayed closed. He felt her body relax, watching her in his arms, the rise of her chest. *Why?* That was simple. She was the perfect echo of a memory and a time and no one would take her from him again.

His own thoughts were starting to fray. He dropped the syringe into the drawer and carried Sarah's body into the bedroom, lowering her into the largest of the two suitcases, shifting her legs and folding her in. He padded the back of her head with a fresh towel and folded another beneath her chin, now increasingly struggling to coordinate his own movements. He gave up and returned to the study. He set the alarm on his phone and sat in the chair, his eyes heavy and closing. He would fetch the child later. Then it would simply be a matter of clearing customs and that would not be an issue. They were methodical and efficient but also people he had known all his life.

266

SIXTY-NINE

Helen Ferreira sat at her desk in the station, sipping water from a small plastic cup. She was taking a break from the tedium of paperwork, her frustration palpable.

With all the manpower now available to them, it was being wasted interviewing sex offenders and raking through Sarah Sawacki's past, looking for some oblique context for why she bought two coffees in Delamere. Deciphered by Chief Inspector Anne Darling, this meant Sarah was involved with Simon. With forensics still holding onto the Peterborough crime scene, Darling's only concession to any of Boer's information so far had been to notify Lincolnshire that Dunstan was thought to be on their patch.

Despite Ferreira's frustration there was also a part of her that empathised. For all the Chief Inspector's articulate speeches and drive, she was the figurehead of a system that was bureaucratic and slow, that focused at the beginning of any investigation as much in protecting itself against recriminations as it did the investigation. Chief Inspector Anne Darling was simply covering all the angles and her own back.

Ferreira tried imagining what Boer's focus would be now the press conference was over. How would he move forward and keep outside the Chief Inspector's radar? Having resisted all afternoon she reached for the phone, secretly disappointed he had not called to comment on her star turn.

Then it hit her. A realisation she would never be able to explain. It slapped her hard like an unexpected wave, stunning her for a few seconds. Disorientated, she placed her cup on the desk with shaking hands. She sat back and closed her eyes, then opened them again. The world was just as it was and a little different. She pulled her keys from her bag, moved her bag onto the desk and looked for the keys, knocking a stack of papers onto the floor and finding the keys under the bag. She rested both her hands on the desk, took a deep breath and counted to ten. Then she walked quickly out of the station.

She did not go straight there. Instead she drove home and changed. She pulled on her favourite loose jumper over a white T-shirt and jeans. Comfortable and smart. She ran a comb through her hair and tied it back. She left a note for Ricky, telling him not to wait up, and then slung her coat over her arm, her bag heavy over her shoulder, and drove to Boer's.

He was sitting slouched in his study in his chair. From behind she was still hopeful he might be asleep. That he would laugh at her foolishness. The reality was apparent as she circled around. His chin rested on his chest, a hand each on an arm of the chair, his skin lifeless, his body a waxwork effigy of the man that once was. She checked for a pulse all the same.

She moved around to his desk with her hand on his shoulder, taking in all that was on his desk. The case file lay open with a much used notepad on the top, several pages of printed addresses underneath. She ignored them for now, instead picking up the whiskey glass and sniffing it. She wrinkled her nose and stepped back to look on the floor, knocking the empty bottle over with her foot as she did.

She rinsed the glass in the bathroom and left it there, slipping the bottle into her bag. Then she checked the drawers and found the letters, the envelope with her name on top. She dropped it unopened into her bag and flicked open her phone and called in Boer's death.

Boer's children were scattered and from recollection, only the oldest daughter was still occasionally in contact. She leaned across him and pressed down the top of his old address book. The lid sprang up. She ran her finger down the lettered index and stopped at R, tapping the numbers into her phone and waiting through an international call tone. It occurred to her when she heard the distracted female voice that this was one of the few calls that anyone had answered that day. Boer's ex-wife was called Rebecca and took the news of his death quietly, and with gratitude that Ferreira had made the call first.

With her phone back in her bag, Ferreira set about sifting through the sheets of Boer's scrawl. Words were circled and joined to others with arcing lines of ink, *Dunstan* headlined one page above the address in Cleethorpes, detail of the letting agent, notes from Adam's voicemail after Peterborough and Boer's conversations with Brian. Another page was full of large lettering amid random doodles; *beach, blonds, short, tall, American?* A set of small wings, more pages of random thoughts with no context by itself. Little that would make any sense to anyone other than Boer and Ferreira. Endless sheets devoted to the scrap of paper found in Andrea's picture frame. Boer had fixated on it.

It was easy when you found evidence to give it more importance or read into it more meaning than it was due, simply because you wanted it to be the one thing that made the difference. Except Boer had found that vital detail so often. If he thought it important it was pointless thinking it was anything else. Boer also never worked on hunches or instinct, had spent four years drumming that into her. The most obvious paths he seemed to ignore, although she knew he never did. He simply left the obvious to mortals. What he did have was an eye for the flaws of the human psyche. She considered this was because Boer was flawed himself, that he saw his own weaknesses reflected in others, probing into the subtle cracks of human nature and often prising free the truth while all others looked elsewhere.

On this occasion he saw something Ferreira could not see or even comprehend. The scrap of paper had led Boer to a name he circled over and over, the page almost worn through with dark ink. If she did not know Boer so well she would immediately dismiss it as too obvious. There was too little substance. Everything for the stepfather had checked out. She had studied the transcript of his interview and paid keen interest before and after the press conference. The guilty more often gave themselves away because they hid their guilt behind reaction. The stepfather had shown her nothing today but a man struggling to face a harsh reality.

But Kevin Smith was the name Boer had circled. Ferreira picked up the notepad and puzzled aloud, as if Boer might explain himself. She then spent the time as she waited flicking through the case file, shifting backwards and forwards through the pages, unearthing his mobile used as a bookmark between pages of Sarah's past. The display on the phone listed no missed calls. She pushed it into the pocket of her bag and resumed her study, but there was no other detail she did not already know.

Presently a strobing blue light made itself known across the hallway. She took one last look around the room, pondering whether to take a keepsake from his bookshelves. Her eyes skipped along the shelves and settled on a book she sometimes pondered from the wicker chair. A leather bound pocket Bible. She pulled it out and opened it. It was the type that zipped closed but the zip was broken for the wad of Boer's notes wedged inside. She was already looking forward to going through it, sliding the Bible into the side pocket of her bag with his phone. She then ran her fingers through his hair, something she had always wanted to do, then kissed him on the forehead and walked downstairs.

Ferreira opened the door to the paramedics and watched as his body was lifted into the ambulance. Then she waited in her car for the square vehicle to pull away, the flashing lights chasing along the houses either side of the street, a few faces peering from windows.

If she left now it would be ten before she arrived. The best time to question suspects as far as Boer was concerned, the last hours before midnight. It made them pliable and more prone to error. Ferreira was inclined not to because she wanted to go home and quietly cry. She did not because finding Sarah had been important to him. She called family liaison and arranged to meet them at the house. There were rules, of course, about interviews, the when and where. This early in an investigation they were rarely refused. She arranged for an officer from the local station to attend as well. She made herself comfortable as she passed through suburbia onto the A34, trying to alter her mindset, working on how she would approach the questioning and not looking forward to it one bit. She could not stop thinking it would be a complete waste of time.

SEVENTY

Adam placed both hands palm down on the reception desk, waiting patiently for the receptionist as she searched through her handbag. Eventually she fixed a smile beneath green eyes and gave him her attention.

'Do you have a PC with internet access I could use?'

She kept smiling. 'It's broken. We provide internet wireless in the rooms,' she stated as if that was the answer he needed.

He drummed his fingers on the counter. Behind her was a door that opened to a small office. 'I don't have a computer, do you have one there I could use? It's important. I'd only be a few minutes.'

'I'm sorry, the office is off limits to guests.'

'Do you know what's wrong with the internet PC, when's it likely to be repaired?'

'It was reported yesterday, there should be someone out this week.'

'This week!' He almost shouted. 'Where is it?'

'The computer?' She directed his gaze to a single desk pushed against a trellis that separated the restaurant from reception. On the desk sat a screen and keyboard. He walked over to it, ignoring her protests.

The computer was on but it had frozen, the mouse pointer stuck in the middle of the screen. None of the keys or the mouse worked. He ducked under the desk and pressed the power button, keeping it pressed. The lights blinked off. He pressed power again and waited for it to boot. The fact it had frozen meant there was a problem but it might take minutes or days to happen again. He shuffled the chair closer and waited for the login prompt. When it appeared he pondered the password, tapping a finger against the keyboard. He tried the name of the hotel in

271

various levels of capitalisation. All failed. He looked around reception, did the same for the name of the group that owned the hotel. That failed as well. He was certain help would not come from reception. He flipped the keyboard and smiled, a sequence of eight numeric and alpha digits were sellotaped to the base. He alternated between reading and typing and waited for the desktop to appear.

His plan was simple. He needed information on shipping insurance but was not authorised to access it. Usually companies accessed it via a paid service. Importantly for Adam, these included companies he also ran security reviews for. The shipping terminals were often remote accessed, and the passwords staff used were weak because they were used by so many. His most recent review had been a month before. He was betting they had not even read his report yet, let alone changed the passwords.

Accessing the shipping terminals was as simple as navigating to a central website, selecting the company from the list and remembering the password. Two minutes later he had the terminal glowing in front of him. He was about to enter the final password when the computer froze.

He silently swore and re-booted but he had barely logged in and it froze again. He resisted the urge to shout, holding it in as he waited for the computer to reboot. He was navigating to the website when it froze for the last time. He held his head in his hands, it could take all night like this. He needed to start doing what he was good at, which was finding ways through barriers. He stepped back across to reception.

'Where's your nearest superstore? One that sells big TVs?'

The receptionist finished typing and looked past him. 'Out of the doors behind you, straight on, next to the shopping centre. It's a five-minute walk.'

Eight minutes later he was back in his room catching his breath. The new laptop's box and packaging were discarded on the bed. It took as long to click through the laptop's welcome screens as it did to buy it, clicking past the final screens and connecting to the hotel's Wi-Fi, then going straight into the central website and then the shipping terminal. Another ten seconds and he had access to shipping. He smiled to himself as he splayed his fingers on the desk, breathing in deep and out again. It all came down to this one search. He typed in *Cutting Blue*, pressed return and waited on the results to appear on screen.

His heart sank. There were fourteen *Cutting Blue*s and none of them were registered to addresses in the UK. He cross-referenced them against *Simon Thompson*, but all returned a negative. Twelve of the *Cutting Blue*s were flagged as commercial and two private.

He scuffed back from the desk, shocked at the failure. He had been so sure *Cutting Blue* would be registered in the UK. He scooted back and cross-referenced against *Iceland* and when that failed, *Singapore*, clutching at straws. He felt like crying. He stared up at the dusty ceiling for inspiration, running a hand through his hair, trying to think in abstracts while skipping through everything that had happened that day. And then he realised, it was obvious. He opened another browser and searched for the website he had seen the night before, clicking on the link and watching it load. Hakan's pub on the seafront. It had sunny pictures showing it on the promenade, of tables and customers laughing, the bar gleaming. He paged down to the bottom. His mouth moving as he silently read the small characters that spelled the name of the management company: *Ragnorline Holdings*.

Barely able to contain his jubilation he flicked back to the terminal and typed in the name. It failed. Without pause he shortened the search to *Ragnorline*, his heart tripping, certain he was close. It returned an immediate hit: *Ragnorline GmbH, Cutting Blue, registered in Hamburg*. The words *Grimsby Dry Dock* glowed bright on the screen as the last insurance location.

He sat back and processed the information. The address in Hamburg was no use to him. He closed the shipping terminal and ran a search he did have authorisation for, against all UK properties insured against *Ragnorline*.

The search listed twenty-one addresses. He sat blinking at the lines of dark text. Jackpot. Seven of the addresses were in Grimsby. He studied the list, barely able to comprehend the goldmine of information he now had. The local addresses were warehouses in the main, the one pub and two residential properties. All were owned by a mixture of Ragnorline companies. Logic led him to consider the residential addresses as the obvious ones to check first, also the easiest. He already knew one of them was a non-starter; it was the address Brian checked the night before.

He searched for the other address, *Eve Hill Way,* the map revealing a curved cul-de-sac beneath a grass square. For a while he just stared at the image, dizzy with expectation and hope. He jolted himself from the reverie, thinking on the best way to get the information to Boer. He copied the addresses into an email to himself that arrived on his phone as he plugged the laptop into the wall socket. He would leave it charging in the room in case he needed it again. He forwarded the email as a text to Boer's number with a brief explanation and called a taxi as he headed back down to reception.

SEVENTY-ONE

He couldn't see anything, just a dull light at the fringes of the thick material covering his eyes. He was sitting, his hands tied either side of him behind a chair, likewise each of his legs to a chair leg. He moved his jaw and it popped and crunched back into place. He moved it around cautiously, tensing the muscles in his arms and legs as best he could, running through a systems check. A dislocated jaw and bruises seemed to be the worst he had sustained. There was nothing covering his mouth, so they were not worried about noise.

A cold draught drifted across the bare skin of his body. They had removed his shirt and his feet were bare. He was only wearing jeans. The stabbing pains marched up and down his back, but they were the constant. He tested the bonds around his wrist and ankles. Rope could be loosened, the fibres with careful attention would stretch, could give you space to work. Leather and most fabrics were the same. Given time and some inattention when applied, there might be hope. With plastic cuffs pulled tight there was no hope. He moved his hands within the confines of the plastic. It dug into the skin of his wrists and cut. With some movement he drew blood and used it to lubricate and slide the cuffs to the base of his hand. But that was it. If he had no thumb on each hand he would be home free.

So he stopped wasting energy and made himself as comfortable as he could. He slowed his breathing and tuned into the environment, immediately closing down the fear. Panic would get him nowhere.

There was practically no sound, just an occasional klaxon of lorries reversing, drifting in and out on random eddies. The draught came from somewhere out front, carrying with it a thick stagnant smell of refuse and ocean.

He opened his mouth and shouted loud, using the sound to get a feel for the space. It was not big, but there was resonance, maybe another room out front. He was in a smaller space. He didn't know what time it was, but did know time was a premium. Time passed, an hour, maybe two.

He heard a sound, a metal door and shuffling feet, two or three people. There was no point pretending to be unconscious or trying to buy more time. It was a matter of getting on with it. So he faced forwards and did not move.

The metal door closed and he heard a single low voice, an American accent, smooth and rich like melted chocolate. A single pair of shoes came towards him. The sound again confirmed the thought he was in a separate room. The shoes stopped a few steps in front of him.

'Hello, Brian, my name is Baldur. We will spend some time together.'

The shoes moved to the right and the voice continued. 'I guessed three months ago it might come to this, but nobody would listen to me. A deadbeat, a has-been. That is what they said. He does not even care for his daughter.' The shoes paced around him, returning to the original spot in front. 'A drunk and no kind of father. You can understand why they would think that, can't you Brian. And such a beautiful little daughter who idolises him, she really does. And all you can do is wallow in your own self-pity, a once proud man defined by his life in the army. Incapable of living a life outside of it. No place even with your army friends working the circuit and earning good money. There's not much call for soldiers with bodies crippled like yours, is there Mr Dunstan? What use is an ex-soldier who cannot even fire a gun?'

Brian swallowed hard. The words hurt as much as anything that would follow. He said nothing.

For a while there was silence. Then wood dragged across concrete, not a chair although something similar and then something more than silence – intent. The pain crashed against his left shoulder, compressing across his chest, something thick and solid with hard edges. It knocked him sideways, forcing him to use what little leverage his feet gave him to stop himself from toppling over.

'On second thoughts,' the voice said, 'I want to see you.'

He sensed a body move close.

'I want to see you realise there is nothing you can do for your little girl, to see the anger in your eyes. So many chances wasted.' The material was pulled from his face. Light beat against his closed eyes and another moment of intention and a crushing pain against his other shoulder, just as hard.

'Open your eyes Brian, it is about time.'

He did. Blinking and focusing, both his arms dead at his side but not enough to douse the constant needling pain of his back.

'There we are, remember me?'

Brian did of course. Baldur was the tall blond, lean and positively glowing with pink-cheeked health, moving around like a dancer pre-performance. Brian checked through the space; his blindfolded assessment had been mostly accurate. He was in an average-sized room, probably once a workshop, the brick walls partly covered in a green moss. A room much bigger and higher opened directly in front. Rusted rails like small train tracks led to a heavy door at the end, the door newer and too small for anything that might use the tracks.

Brian could see the smaller blond at the far end by the door, sitting on the edge of a wooden chair, watching, one leg straight out as if it was the cause of some pain. Brian had not done that. He briefly thought of Adam and smiled, sensing Baldur move around behind and then a blur and then a pain exploded across his thighs. He cried out.

'You have caused me so many problems, you and the woman. I told them we must not underestimate you. Men like you work from a different moral code. One minute you do not care, the next you fight to the death.' Baldur circled.

Brian tried to shift his legs, they weren't broken but he couldn't feel his toes. He looked up at the man, staring intently back at him. 'You just going to hit me with your stick, or get on with it?'

Baldur came around and stood in front of him. The stick was a length of wood at least three feet long, four inches by four inches in diameter.

'Settle down, we have little time as it is.' Baldur looked from his watch to Brian. 'Ninety minutes, in point of fact. Not a long amount of time but more time than you have life.' He looked around the room as if reminiscing. 'We use this place occasionally. Not so much now people know not to misbehave. It is a very good location because the high tide cleans away any mess, as long as we don't get too much on the walls, of course.' He smiled at Brian's impassive face.

'Do you believe in God, Brian?'

Brian groaned and shook his head.

'You should not be so dismissive. It is an important question people must ask, especially a man in your position.' He moved around the chair. 'Well, you should know that I do, my faith is very strong.'

Brian nodded but did not say anything.

'Why are you nodding, Brian?'

'I agree, you fit the profile, borderline psychotic and deluded. You'd get on with my ex.'

That earned him a wry smile and a hard blow across his chest. It caused his lungs to spasm, struggling to choke in breath. And then immediately another blow hard against the side of his head, the edge of the wood dragged across his cheek leaving a thin trail of splinters and blood. He slumped forward, convulsing, bloody drool from his mouth dripping into his lap and to the floor. Baldur walked away into the adjoining room. The hushed sound of victorious voices as Brian gasped for air.

When Brian eventually sat up Baldur returned. 'That was from my brother, you will spend time with him soon. Although of course you must know your friend has already met with a very painful death. A shame really, I cannot see he was here for any reason other than chance. Although a noble effort on your part to get him to safety.'

He had no idea what had happened to Adam but thought the boast unlikely, not without some morale-sapping memento on show. Either way there was little he could do about it now. 'Are we moving on to bedtime stories soon? Your TV accent is really making me sleepy.'

Baldur wordlessly propped the wood against the wall and scooted Brian's chair around 180 degrees, to face a gnarled old workbench. To one side was Brian's kit bag and laid across the surface were the tools he had packed into the bag.

'Did you think you would be fighting an army, Brian? We are spoilt for choice here. Would you like me to cut you with this knife or yours, or maybe I should hit you with these on my hand.' Baldur ran his fingers over a set of worn knuckle dusters, the knuckles filed to points. 'Or this little bat here. Or this rubber baton, maybe this chain. These sharp things you have welded into it, they are razor blades?'

'Wilkinson, they stay sharp longer,' answered Brian.

'But whatever for?'

'You wouldn't understand, a nonce like you, only brave with children and tied up people.'

Baldur smiled at him. 'Humour me.

So Brian did. 'You run out of bullets, the guys you're shooting don't wait for you to get more. So you improvise.' He let his eyes fall on the hilt of his knife on the bench. 'How about you cut these plastic ties. Then we can get to seeing whose side God is on.'

This earned him a jolly laugh. 'Very good Brian. I'm obviously in far better shape than you, younger, and I do not drink. I have never smoked. It would be a poor match and besides, why trouble myself when you're quite obviously going nowhere.'

Baldur's phone started vibrating in his pocket. He walked back into the other room and talked in hushed tones that became urgent before returning. He looked at his watch and moved Brian's chair back around.

'I think we shall have some fun with your tools when I get back, but I have to see a man about a woman now. A busy night indeed!'

He retrieved the length of wood propped against the wall and turned to Brian.

'My purpose, Brian, is to bring people before God and wash away the undeserving. I think you count as the latter. You now have time to think about your little girl and what will happen to her in the next months and years. That poor little body, passed from pillar to post, all those things that will be asked of her. All those tears and years wondering why her father betrayed her.'

Baldur weighed the wood in his hands. 'And you incapable of doing anything for your child but die here.'

Brian watched Baldur's arms swing around and the wood arc towards him, at the last second turning from the blow. It caught him across the face, rocking his head against the opposite shoulder, something breaking and dislodging inside his mouth.

Baldur threw the length of wood onto the floor and walked away. Brian used his tongue to search the inside of his mouth, moving his head carefully from side to side, spitting blood and broken teeth.

SEVENTY-TWO

It was ten when the taxi pulled away, leaving Adam standing on the pavement next to a deserted playground. He looked from the playground to the square of grass and to the shops. A brightly lit takeaway glowed in the darkness. It looked familiar, reminding him of where Sarah had grown up. He walked across the grass and directly into Eve Hill Way.

The house owned by Ragnorline looked empty. All the lights were off, no car on the driveway, a garage with an alley at the side. He walked across the road and down an alley diagonally opposite, watching the house while leaning against the wall in shadow. He hesitated, knowing what he had to do but trying to talk himself out of it. *Don't think about it!* It was easier said than done. He took the battery from his phone, lest some random alarm shrill to life when he least needed it. Then with his heart beating fitfully he stepped from the shadows, walking purposefully across the street and down the alley beside the house.

The garage tapered on the left and became a fence and then a tall gate, an identical gate opposite it. He peered over the top and was rewarded with brilliant white light that he immediately stepped back from, turning to the gate he was interested in. He grasped the handle and pushed. It stuck. He put his shoulder against the gate and got ready to push and lift.

'What're you doing?'

The voice startled him, he jumped so hard a scream almost made it from his throat to his mouth.

'Christ!' he said, turning to see a girl. She was about twelve, slight in jeans and a short jacket, a fur lined hood pushed back from long dark hair. She had a pretty face. 'You made me jump!' was all he could think to say.

She studied him, her eyes appraising, her face earnest. She repeated the question, her tone firmer. 'What are you doing?'

He stammered on an answer. 'None of your business.'

'It is my business and I know what you're looking for.'

With a sudden sense of horror he thought she was about to proposition him, but realised she was working at an entirely different level. He turned to look at her properly. 'Do you, what would that be?'

She answered confidently, 'You're looking for her. You're just the sort of guy she'd be with. Although I thought you'd be a little, a bit more polished.'

Adam's heart started beating afresh. 'Her, who is her?'

'The woman on TV, I saw her while making my tea. Knew straight away who she was. She was here the other day checking them houses.' Her head indicated *them houses* were somewhere behind her. 'Soon as I saw you from my bedroom I knew who you was.'

He breathed deep several times, trying to calm himself. Sarah had been here. 'And I am?'

'Her bloke, like I said.' She nodded at the gate. 'But you won't find her in there, that's Simon's place. He's cool.' She paused as if realising something, 'Unless, you know…' She shifted her weight from foot to foot. 'Unless she wants to be there.'

He shook his head. 'This Simon, you know him?'

'Of course, Simon's a legend, everyone knows Simon. That's how I know.'

'Know what?'

'That your misses ain't in there less she wants to be. Wouldn't blame her if she was. Anyway, you're too late. He left already.' For a flicker in the low light he saw sadness in her face.

'When?'

'About an hour ago, I saw the car. Had his suitcases although I knew already he was going. Only it was meant to be Wednesday, so I guess there's something to do with the boat.'

'The boat?' Adam was still busy trying to process this new information, the conversation spinning way beyond his ability to put it all into context.

'He sails boats for rich people. If he was going Wednesday and he's gone today, it must be something with the boat.' She looked at Adam as children do when they know something the adult does not.

And he sensed curiosity alone had not brought the girl there, she was protective of Simon. He looked at the closed gate. There was no way he was leaving without checking the house.

'You didn't see the girl then?'

'What girl?'

'The girl who was on the TV, at the same time as my wife.'

She shrugged. 'Don't know anything about no girl. Just that I'd seen the woman. Who's the girl?'

'It doesn't matter if you haven't seen her.' He let his eyes settle on the gate and then back to the girl. 'I know she's here so you obviously don't know Simon that well.' He made ready to walk past her, not really sure what he was doing.

'What do you mean, I know Simon better than anyone!'

'You don't or you'd know my wife was here.'

'But she isn't.'

'Yes she is. Why else would I be here, it just goes to show.'

Her mouth worked and her eyes shifted between hurt and fierce. 'She isn't and I can prove it.'

He stopped. 'How?'

'I can get in, it's easy.'

A thin sliver of dark moved inside him and a little guilt. 'Don't believe you. You're just saying that because you want me to think he's your friend.'

Her young face moved in on itself indignantly. 'Simon's cool, we're good mates, better than anyone around here.' She looked genuinely hurt. 'He's my friend. Get out of my way.'

She brushed passed him to the gate, pushing and lifting, stepping into the garden and disappearing inside. He heard her voice, calling 'Come on!'

He stepped through and followed her. 'But you can't look about too much. Just to prove your misses ain't here and that's it.'

He followed and she turned impatiently. 'You got that?'

'Yes, of course. Just a quick look around and then I'll know you're right.' He looked at the back of the house. He had no idea how she was going to get in. It had modern patio doors and double glazing at every window. He doubted Simon kept keys under pot plants.

'Wait here,' the girl directed. She put one foot on a shallow ledge protruding from a small greenhouse. She pushed up and stepped quickly onto the sill of the garage window, both hands on the edge of the garage roof, lifting herself and turning to sit as if she had just pulled herself from a swimming pool. She shuffled across to where the garage and house met, her head level with the bottom of the bathroom window. She leaned over and banged the frame with a fist. She studied it and then banged again. Nothing. She banged again. Small sounds in the night.

It suddenly dawned on Adam she might actually be knocking for someone to open it. He took a half step back, ready to run, but this time whatever she was looking for happened. She pulled at the bottom edge of the window, opening it to an angle. Standing she used a hand on the gutter and stepped over onto the bathroom sill then disappeared inside. He doubted a monkey could have made it look any easier.

Moments later the curtains covering the patio doors parted and she reached up, retrieving keys that refracted light, and then unlocked the doors. She pushed one door open and waved him in. He took eleven steps and found himself standing in Simon's dining room. She closed the door and looked at him jubilantly. 'See, I told you it was easy.'

'That looked dangerous, why don't you just knock?'

Confusion set in her eyes. 'He's not here, what'd be the point?'

'No.' He shook his head. 'I meant why do you have to do that at all if he's here? Why don't you just knock? He could open the door. It would be a lot easier.'

She looked at him a little uncertain, as if she was about to tell him something she should not, without knowing why. She walked into the kitchen and he followed.

'He says it wouldn't be right if I knocked and he let me in. He says if I want to climb in it's up to me, my choice. It doesn't work all the time. Sometimes he locks it and I can't get in. That's when he has to study. I understand.'

An unease started to grow at the pit of his stomach. 'When was the last time you did that?'

'Last Thursday.' The girl leaned back against the kitchen counter, folding her arms across the jacket. 'I like to come. I like to be with him, he's a legend. He makes me feel...' She faltered. 'I don't do nothing I don't want to. He makes me feel nice, he's interested in me. And he helps with my homework. And he's big, you should see his muscles,' she said with an awe only a child could muster.

In the low light now she looked even younger. Or was it his own guilt playing tricks on his eyes. He looked around. 'Small kitchen?'

She looked as well. 'I guess so.' She drifted into the dining room. 'Not sure what you're expecting to find. It's empty like I said.' She moved into the living room and he followed. 'Through there is the garage.' She nodded towards the hallway. 'And then upstairs there's the bedrooms and his study. Where'd you want to look first?'

'The garage?' he answered.

She walked into the hallway, shuffling through the keys, flicking a switch and then unlocking the door. He followed her in.

It was practically empty. Probably the neatest garage he had ever been in. On the left there was a work bench and a wall full of tools on hooks. A large plastic mat lay beneath the window at the far end. Apart from a broom, a bucket and a stack of magazines that was it. Even the concrete floor looked like it had been scrubbed. He tried to take in the detail, trying to imagine Sarah here and getting a sense for her in the space. But he could not. He wandered to the end by the window.

The girl fidgeted impatiently. 'Seen enough?'

He ignored her and reached down to the stack of magazines, yachting magazines. Which set his hands shaking as he took the one on top, last month's. He flicked through the pages of glossy pictures, text and advertisements. There was nothing that jumped out, no folded pages of significant information, no handwritten notes. He dropped it back onto the pile. 'What about upstairs?'

'Go through then,' she said tartly, now the lady of the manor. 'Don't turn on any lights,' she added.

Upstairs was no different. Sparse rooms drained of colour by the night. 'That's his bedroom there.' She flourished a hand. He looked inside, slightly more clutter but neatly stacked on shelves or on a simple dresser. The space was dotted with pictures of people and smiling faces. Simon liked the outdoors.

Adam moved along the landing to a spare bedroom, containing a wardrobe and a chair. The bed was made with hardly a crease to be seen. 'That's for guests.' She said. 'And his study is there.' He peeked into the box room, taking a good look. More pictures of Simon on boats, some with Hakan and the two blond men, others with people Adam did not know.

'Seen enough yet?' her voice impatient.

'No, I'm still looking, thank you.' Her cheeks flushed and her hands alternated between playing with the keys and being thrust deep into her jacket pockets, impatient for him to go now the euphoria of showing off was over. Realising he had glimpsed something of her that nobody else had seen, which felt like her secret was about to be broken.

Adam made himself look through each room although some part of him was afraid of what he might find. All were exceptionally tidy and the house was obviously empty. It looked like it had been empty for weeks, let alone having been a prison to Sarah and Andrea. Although he was not exactly sure what he should be looking for or what he had expected to find, possibly some proof with which he could definitely ring Boer. All he had confirmed was that Simon lived there.

'Has Simon been here all weekend?' he asked.

She hesitated. 'No, he went out early Friday and didn't get back till Saturday night. His boss was over. He's horrid, not at all like Simon.'

'And that's when you saw my wife?'

The girl thought for a moment. 'Nope, saw her earlier. Not sure when 'cos she was looking at them houses. Me and my mates was going to watch a movie. Like I said, she wasn't coming here. As you can see.'

'And you're sure Simon has gone?'

The shadows shifted across her face as her head moved up and down. 'I saw the taxi, can't get no surer than that. Just he's gone early is the only thing.'

'Do you know how long he'll be away?' He turned to face her.

'Dunno, last year he was gone lots of times. Sometimes weeks, others months. Year before that he was gone four months in one go. The boats are for faraway places. I think he flies back. Can we go now?'

He walked into the bathroom. 'Do your parents know you come here?'

'Course not, although I doubt they'd care. It's nicer here and quiet.' She followed him in. There was a different quality to the air, thicker, as if someone had showered recently. The girl reached over the toilet to the window and grabbed hold of the handle, making sure she had his attention. 'You have to leave it a little open and then close the handle. It sort of locks it. But it will open if you hit it right. He always leaves it like that for me when he goes away, although once last year he forgot. I couldn't come over at all. Even by myself it's better than sitting at home listening to them two get pissed up.'

Adam's eyes were fixed on her serious face but his mind was elsewhere. Something he had seen now registered. He walked back into the study. The girl followed, watching him for the first time do something with purpose. He reached up to a shelf and pulled down a magazine, this month's, with a yacht in full flight on the cover. He started flicking through the pages, stopping at *Tide Times* which had been marked with the corner folded over. There were two glossy pages full of charts and abbreviations and times that did not initially make sense. He scanned the section headed *England – East* but neither Grimsby or Cleethorpes were listed.

'Which of these is nearest?' he asked.

The girl leaned against his arm, intently tracing a finger across the different regions. 'Immingham,' she said after a while.

He read across the page. He knew nothing about boats or anything related to them. The next high tide was not for another five hours. 'Simon left an hour ago?'

'About that. Maybe a bit more. But it was just him and his stuff.'

'All the same,' Adam said, 'it would be good to catch up with him. Maybe ask him if he's seen my wife. He might help. Where do you think he was going?'

She looked up at him with wide incredulous eyes. 'He sails boats.' She walked out to the landing and hoisted herself onto the window sill. 'You can't do that from any old place.'

'The Marina?' he offered.

'No,' she said, shaking her head while struggling to pull her phone from her pocket. The light from the screen partially illuminated her face in the low light. 'The dock, his boats are big.' She thought for a second, a flicker of realisation. 'The dock has a gate. If he's looking at tide times it's not for here. Tide times don't matter for the dock. S'pect he'll leave soon else he'd have gone tomorrow.' She looked out the window into the dark above the alley. 'You could te…' She stopped mid-sentence and did not finish it.

Adam looked from her to the magazine, putting the magazine back on the shelf.

'Have you seen enough now?' She pushed herself off the window sill. 'I think so.'

She had morphed back to a child again and now looked smaller, wordlessly leading him down the stairs. While she opened the patio door he took another look in the kitchen. It was clean and sparse just like the rest of the house, a worktop, a knife rack, a microwave and kitchen cabinets. Something was missing but he could not place it. He followed her outside and the girl locked the patio doors, pushing the keys into her pocket.

'I hope you find her. She seemed nice,' the girl said.

'I will.' He looked down at her. 'You should get home.'

She did not nod or confirm, just walked out through the gate, waiting for him and making sure the gate was closed. She followed him up the alley. The dim street lighting seemed harsh in contrast.

Something occurred to him. 'Why is Simon a legend?'

'Dad says we used to have loads of problems with some gangs that came from over St. Luke's. Mostly kids but organised by adults. Everyone being bossed to pay money, shop windows smashed. Half the houses in the street were broken into. People were at their wits' end. Simon said he would deal with it. Dad says a month later and it all stopped. Says there's not been a single break-in around here for three years. Anyone here will tell you it's down to Simon.'

He imagined Simon valued his privacy. 'I wanted to apologise,' Adam said. 'I feel bad for making you show me around.'

She shrugged her shoulders. 'You're fine. I wanted to.' And then she turned and walked away. He walked in the opposite direction, only looking back as he stepped onto the kerb by the corner store. The street was empty.

SEVENTY-THREE

It was gone ten by the time Ferreira parked and negotiated the jostle of remaining press, ducking beneath the police cordon and walking self-consciously up to the house and the two constables outside. Andrea's stepfather ushered her in from behind the door, a genuine if tempered smile beneath his heavy eyes.

He asked polite questions about the drive as she avoided his gaze while removing her shoes in the hallway, then padded in her tights behind him through the kitchen into the dining room and to three faces around the long wooden dining table.

The mother sat opposite, beneath a large wooden crucifix, her mood thunderous and laced with frost. The stepfather scooted a chair in behind Ferreira and took a seat next to the mother. Both the family liaison officer and the constable sat on the left with lush curtains drawn behind them. Their jobs were to serve the needs of the family and witness the interview. They looked like they might have taken the brunt of the mother's displeasure, offering Ferreira cool nods and pursed lips.

She replied with apology in her smile and dropped her bag onto the floor beside her chair, the bottle from Boer's study clonking against the table leg. She flushed as she pulled free her notepad and pen, placing them square in front of her. She took a long deep breath, feeling very alone. Nervously, she began.

'I am very sorry to disturb you tonight, especially at this hour.' They both looked back at her, the stepfather open and waiting, the mother frail and tired despite her impatience. 'But one angle that is taking up a lot of our time is why Andrea specifically was targeted.'

'I would have thought that obvious,' the mother immediately

answered. 'Andrea was the only child on the street left to wander alone.' She breathed in as if to say more but did not.

'Well actually, it is not that uncommon to see children without chaperones in the High Street, regardless of the rights and wrongs, Mrs Smith. And while I certainly empathise we consider the chances of someone waiting on chance, well, it is unlikely given the planning we know went into her abduction.' She let that hang in the air. 'So what I would like to do is focus on who might have known, who knew your daughter would be standing outside Boots at that time on Saturday?'

The mother stared with eyes that shifted from questioning to exasperation that for a moment Ferreira thought mocked. 'I think I already made that perfectly clear, Detective. You're best talking to Andrea's father about that.'

'You did, Liz – can I call you that?

'I prefer Beth.'

Ferreira amended. 'Beth then, sorry. You have said Brian is the best person for us to talk to but you also told us there was no aspect of your family you did not know about. So which is it?'

The mother looked as if she had been slapped but immediately came back. 'One day you may have children, Detective, and you will understand. Of course I know all about my children's lives but what she does at her father's is beyond my control, unfortunately.' The stepfather reached across and grasped her hand.

Ferreira looked at their hands linked on the table and to the stepfather, still struggling to see Boer's logic. *Why was she even here?* She looked at the mother. 'I'm sorry Beth. I didn't mean that to come out as it did, it's been a long day this side of the table too. Please understand my main concern is to move our search for your daughter forward. We have to move beyond our emotional feelings or any sense of blame and look at the facts. Knowing who knew could be a key element to finding her.'

Ferreira's apology went unheeded.

'Don't you think I know that, but I cannot tell you more than I already have. If there is anyone that knows, then it is quite simply her father. And to be quite honest, Detective, the sooner you find that *loser* the sooner you will find Andrea. That's where you should be focusing your efforts, not here.'

Ferreira's mouth opened and closed. She was right. Her whole purpose for coming here was Boer's, not her own. As much as she had thought through the angles during the drive, she didn't really believe she should be there. She needed a time out.

'Possibly so,' Ferreira said. 'But I'm here now and there are details we need to discuss. First, do you mind if I use your bathroom? I could do with freshening up.'

The mother gave a wan smile. 'You know where it is. Kevin will make you a tea. White, two sugars I recall. I'm sure these ladies could do with a drink as well?' She looked down the table at smiles and nods.

Ferreira picked up her bag and made for the hallway and the stairs, angry at herself for faltering. Interviewing was what she enjoyed most; it came as naturally as throwing a ball against a wall. Except now the wall was no longer there. She had to step back and embrace impartiality, start feeling for those subtle flaws of human nature. Boer had always made it seem so easy.

SEVENTY-FOUR

The dreams of closed-in spaces became vast horizons of yellow and shows of lightning streaking across the sunset and endless ocean. Her mind eased back to consciousness, her senses busy processing the new environment. She was aware of being in a different space before her eyes fluttered open.

Cool air breezed across her face, carrying the smell of oil or fuel. A gunmetal ceiling and a dim bulb enclosed in wire mesh. She was lying on a comfortable mattress. She slowly sat up, thick-headed as if woken from a deep sleep. She felt a little hung over, sore and bruised and battered but serviceable. She felt rested even. Andrea was not there.

She panicked, swinging her feet onto a bare metal floor, staring directly at a door. She tried the handle but the door was locked. She looked beneath the bed in vain hope.

The room was very small and angular, like it was the corner of a much bigger space. *Where was she?* Where was Andrea and why had they been moved? The answer to the last seemed obvious now. Simon's plans had changed. *But why?* Snippets of their conversation in the kitchen replayed in her mind. She was on a boat. She shouted out load and banged hard on the door and kicked it. She stepped back and kicked beside the handle, angry and frustrated at still being trapped and powerless. She kicked again and then again, each time harder, the sound echoing dull and brief. The door stood solid.

She stopped and listened for any discernible sound or movement, pushing thoughts of where Andrea might be from her mind. *Were they moving?* There might be a slight sideways shift but she doubted that. She felt sure if they were in the North Sea she would feel something.

She sat on the bed with her elbows on her knees, her head in her hands, trying to calibrate and calm her thoughts, to think clearly. She had to get out of this room. Her mind raced through the detail, trying to calculate meaning and consequences from her conversation with Simon, weighing her options and constantly worrying for Andrea. She was not sure how long she had sat like that but started suddenly at a noise outside. Then the door silently swept open and Simon looked in at her. 'You're awake.'

She felt immediate relief at seeing him. He was not with Andrea.

'You're an absolute rotten bastard,' she said, moving off the bed.

He smiled uncertain as she stepped lightly over to him, on tiptoe reaching both hands up behind his neck and pulling his head down. She pressed her pelvis against his thigh and kissed him fully on the mouth, his mouth stiff-lipped then softening. Once she was done he stood back and looked at her.

'What was that for?'

She idled her hand down his arm. 'A promise of what could be if you stop locking me in small rooms.' She looked hopefully up at him and he studied her face for intent. Then he ushered her through the door into an area the size of a tennis court, a communal space with a shallow sofa and cupboards. There was another angled wall and a door like hers in the opposite corner.

'Andrea's in there?'

He nodded.

'Show me,' she commanded and watched as he unlocked and opened the door. Sarah stepped in, her relief so great she almost punched the air. An identical room, Andrea lay asleep curled in a ball. It struck her straight away. 'Where's her bag?'

'Back at the house.'

She turned and burrowed her eyes into his. 'But all her stuff's in there. Everything she still has!'

'I know. That's why it's back at the house.' He directed her out of the room. 'She won't be needing it.' He locked the door and put a hand on each of her shoulders. 'It's a zero risk right where it is.' He manoeuvred past her, climbing the steps. He waved for her to follow.

She contemplated Andrea's locked door then carefully climbed the steep steps and emerged onto the main deck and the open night air. The change was glorious. She breathed deep the sea air and welcomed its embrace of her body and face, looking out across a wide expanse of water to a distant container vessel amid busy cranes and varied bright lights.

Simon directed her through an outside bar with a covered sofa and a mounted TV in a clear plastic case. Glass stretched almost the whole width of the wide deck with sliding glass doors in the middle. She could see a high tower brightly reflected in the glass as Simon rattled keys. She turned to look. The tower was beside the dock entrance, which looked like an enormous version of a canal lock.

'This is huge,' she said with more than a degree of natural wonder.

He slid open one of the doors and wordlessly directed her into a sumptuous living area with thick carpet underfoot, curving white leather sofas facing each other from both sides of the space, the carpet giving way to marble set in an abstract mosaic and a gleaming dining table surrounded by chairs. The sound of keys again as he locked the glass door then walked her through to more steep steps that went up and also down to a lower level.

She had a brief moment to look around. She was high up, as if looking from a second floor window through floor to ceiling glass, the glass stretching all around her to a curve at the front. Outside to the left she could see a floodlit quay, at the right the expanse of shimmering water. Simon directed her down the steps.

They descended to a passageway walled in polished wood. Simon followed her along the corridor to a narrow door and into a large bedroom, bigger than the main bedroom in her flat and more luxurious than any hotel she had ever stayed in. A low king-size bed sat directly in front of her. All the surfaces were the same polished wood or mirrored, all the colours were tones of burgundy red or complementing contrasts, the time marked by an old-fashioned brass clock, the second hand busy tripping around.

She sensed Simon had not followed her into the room, turning to see his body framed by the door.

'There's an en suite everything through there,' he said. 'Including a glass-sided shower that looks out over the water, which you will find much more appealing when we're in the Mediterranean. I'll be back soon. The guy doing the loading must be on an hourly rate.'

'You can't touch her.'

'I won't,' he said and swept the door closed. She listened to the keys turn, wondering at the logic of locks on a boat. Immediately she began a very thorough investigation of her new environment, beginning with confirmation the door was locked. When she was sure there was no way

293

he could see her, she pulled two blades from the back pocket of her jeans. The blades were wrapped in a strip of material from the red blanket. She had taken them in the hope of an unexpected opportunity, and was very glad she had.

Her problems remained though. She had repeatedly drawn a blank on effective methods of attack, even trying them in her mouth. They did balance on her tongue but were too big, the edges cutting into the roof of her mouth when she swallowed or tried to speak. She wrapped them in the red material and pushed them back into her jeans.

SEVENTY-FIVE

Getting to the dry dock took Adam from suburbia into an industrial estate, over a level crossing and past endless giant warehouses interspersed by whole tracts of land given to row upon row of cars. His destination was a colossal wall of concrete. It ran a long street's worth either side of him and up to a plateau way above his head, a row of sheds the size of houses butted to the edge. He had not known what to expect, imagining all kinds of security. Even requesting the dry dock as a destination seemed improbable. The driver had simply nodded his head.

He walked to the end of the wall, the night air full of sea and the busy sounds of industry, of lorries reversing above all others. He came to a narrow road on the right, a three-storey building on the opposite corner with the top floor illuminated. He continued around the concrete structure, realising it was a giant wedge. Parallel tracks ran from the sheds, descending at a gradual gradient, down through silt near the base. At the far side a boat was silhouetted, mounted on scaffolding. Although small, from where he stood it seemed like some distant beached behemoth. A trawler with long winch arms protruding like insect antennae.

Adam's stomach fluttered. He was contemplating whether to walk back around or across the sloping concrete, when a door opened from the building behind. A man in a luminous jacket and hard hat emerged. Adam's anxiety turned to relief at the sound of a friendly voice.

'You OK there pal? You're looking lost.' The man was at least sixty, a face that looked like rock shaped by weather.

'I am, I was looking for the *Cutting Blue*?'

'You found her right enough.' The man gave him an appraising look and nodded at the distant trawler. 'And I'll admit we do sometimes get the odd visitor that's interested in her history.' He gave Adam another up-and-down look. 'And I gotta say you don't look like any of them.' He had a smile on his face.

'Well, I was actually looking for Simon Thompson. I don't suppose you've heard of him?'

The man laughed. It was genuine and told of a lifetime of smoking. 'Now would I know Simon Thompson? Well, like a lot of guys here I crewed with Conley a lot of years, many of them on that very boat. Knew Conley's boy too, I crewed with him sometimes as well. He's all grown up now and spends his summers working on that boat, and damn glad of his company I can tell you.' He nodded across at the boat. 'Does all the work himself. How he managed to sail her back from Singapore is the stuff of legend around here.'

Adam nodded cautiously. The man had come alive, as if recounting an all-time favourite story. The man caught his breath and continued.

'Although if you're looking for Simon this night, you're skulking around the wrong boat.' He turned and pointed beyond the building. 'Simon cleared customs an hour ago. He's waiting over there for the dock gates.'

Adam squinted but only saw the top half of an illuminated tower distant. 'Where's there?' he asked.

'Over there lad! You can't miss the bloody thing. Bigger than a damn house, not even a yacht to my mind but impressive there's no doubt.' He ushered Adam back to the road. 'Head along there till you come to the warehouses on your right. You can wend through them, don't mind the noise, that's just the generators, or carry on till you get to the road then follow that to the right. Either way you'll find yourself on the Royal Dock. *Passing Dream* is birthed at the far end.' He looked back at Adam. 'You got that?'

'Think so. Warehouses, big boat, far end.'

The man smiled. 'You got it.' A thought occurred to him. 'How'd you say you know Simon?'

'I don't,' Adam answered, thinking quickly. 'My wife wants to charter a yacht next summer. Simon was recommended although he's been hard to find.'

The man looked at him with amused eyes. 'Your wife often get these sudden impulses in the middle of the night?'

Adam laughed to buy himself a few seconds. 'Well, she asked me to do this last year. Now I'm on an ultimatum and left it to the last minute, and the clock's ticking.' He shrugged and grinned at the man. 'Wouldn't be here now if he wasn't so bloody hard to track down, he doesn't advertise at all.'

Nodding knowingly the man winked at him and walked past. 'Doesn't need to. And don't let the look of him put you off either, that lad's only got eyes for the ocean.'

Adam watched the man head across the concrete towards the shadowed trawler, stepping over the first set of rails. He started jogging along the road.

SEVENTY-SIX

Simon had been right about the shower. It was the size of a bedroom. The floors were a warm brown slate and the walls gleaming black tiles. Three giant shower heads faced a wall of glass that overlooked the dock. There were shutters that whirred down at the press of a button, although when she realised she opened them immediately. After days in a tiny room the wide expanse of the dock was a luxury. She stood beneath the warm water in the dark, looking out in awe at a luminous halo of light over the distant container vessel, the kaleidoscope of colours shimmering across the water.

Sarah was not idly wasting time. She was ready. Having ferreted through the space of the bedroom she had not found one thing that might aid her. The drawers contained his neatly folded clothes and brochures for ports of the world and their facilities. In the one used wardrobe Simon's two suitcases were stacked with books beside and on top, the bedside table also home to his books. There was not even a roll of tape that might be useful to her. Even if there had been, hiding anything in plain sight was impossible because of the mirrors.

So she worked through the different scenarios, imagining them both in the room and how she might leverage the space to her advantage. The bed was where her options began and ended. She had laid and sat and knelt at every angle, increasingly aware of the time and a need to place the blades. She tried the ledge inside the bed's frame, but found she could not relocate the blades with the repeated ease she needed.

So she decided the foot of the bed was her best option, one blade either side of the left bed post, resting on the ledge. Almost each time she rocked forward she was able to thumb the right blade up against the

298

frame. No matter how often she practised, the act of moving for the second blade threw her off balance. She eventually consigned the spare to backup, thinking how she might use it as she stripped for the shower.

SEVENTY-SEVEN

Ferreira let the cold water run across her hands and splashed it up over her face. She knew her problem of course, she empathised too much. This family were not her kind of Christian, but at least they had faith. She heard Boer chuckle to himself behind her. The sound was so distinct she almost turned to check. Instead she reached across and pressed a towel to her face, squeezing shut her eyes and breathing out. She needed to get a grip. *But where to start?* Of course Boer had told her that as well, she just had to do it. She had read through the stepfather's interview. He was close to Andrea, that was evident from the dialogue. Boer had seen more.

On the landing she stopped and checked herself in a full-length mirror, sighing inwardly. She was about to start down the stairs when she sensed she was being watched. She turned to see the older of the two girls, standing in a bedroom doorway, with big inquisitive eyes and a shy smile.

In the dining room a cup steamed beside her empty notepad. She nodded her thanks to the stepfather and scooted her chair forward, picking up her pen and pulling closer the pad.

She looked across the table at the mother. 'So Beth, for the record. You said you have no knowledge at all of what Andrea does while with her father?'

There was a slight pause. 'Well, I...not the detail. She takes swimming kit which comes back wet. She takes books that I know she reads because she tells me all about them, pencils and a drawing book that come back with more pictures. I know she watches DVDs because she will tell me about those as well, in the smallest detail.'

Ferreira's pen busily scribbled, her posture indicating that every word was the most important.

'But apart from that.' She paused. 'No, I honestly do not.'

Ferreira finished her shorthand, took her time with the punctuation and looked at the stepfather. 'And what about you, Kevin? Do you know anything about her weekends? Maybe she would confide in you where she might not her mother?'

'Are you trying…?' the mother cut in.

Ferreira quickly turned to her. 'I am not saying anything, Beth. Children's minds are wondrous thing, as you will know. They have a lot to tell and that is not always to one person.'

'And how would you know, Detective?' she asked imperiously.

Ferreira looked back at her matter of factly. 'The force expects detectives to be degree educated. I did psychology and enjoyed it. I have a diploma in child psychology as well.' She focused back on the stepfather. His eyes were kind, bright in a square face that was soft around the jaw.

'Does Andrea confide in you, Kevin?'

He shifted, uncomfortable at suddenly being the centre of attention. 'Well, I…not much.'

Ferreira looked down at her pen poised and then back at him, waiting.

'Well Andrea and I are close, there's no doubt. And I have to say I do forget she's not my daughter, although she's very loyal to her father, in fact she idolises him.' He stopped and Ferreira thought about asking if that ever made him jealous, but let him continue.

'So yes of course she tells me things she wouldn't tell her mother. But I always pass the information on.' He looked sideways in need of confirmation. 'Don't I?'

The mother nodded. 'We have an agreement. If she tells Kevin, he tells me. As much as it often infuriates me, I don't act on it, at least directly.' They both joined hands again and the liaison officer shifted in her seat.

For just a moment Ferreira was sure guilt had flared in his eyes. 'So what you're saying, Kevin, is that Andrea does confide in you. But there has been nothing about her time with her father. Because of course, if she did, by proxy Beth would also know and therefore so would I.'

He nodded tentatively and then fell silent, moving uneasily. He looked away from Ferreira's stare and then the mother realised.

'What?' She turned on him. 'Spit it out Kevin.' She let go of his hand, her elbow on the table to face him. He moved his hand to his lap and took a deep breath and held it. He looked at his wife and then at Ferreira and breathed out. 'I guess there's no point holding on to secrets now, if any of them can help.'

The shocked silence in the room was broken by the mother, half caught between standing and sitting. She sat down. 'Secrets? Kevin, what on earth are you on about?'

He tripped on his words. 'I can't, I can't see how it can help you.' He directed this at Ferreira. 'I guess it's not up to us now to decide what might be helpful.'

Ferreira smiled encouragingly at him, the mother now still, her stare fixed on him.

'Just tell me what you know, Kevin. Anything Andrea might have told you.'

SEVENTY-EIGHT

The deafening noise of generators fell away and Adam emerged onto the quay, a wide expanse of water away to his left, a long low ship at the far side with cranes busily lifting containers that looked in the distance like small blocks of Lego. He could see the dock tower illuminated in the centre horizon like a lonely version of Big Ben, and to his immediate right a line of shuttered brick workshops a road's width from the water's edge. The whole scene was whitewashed by floodlights, the light and long shadows tripping over the concrete and out across the sparkling water.

At the end of the quay was a very large boat, sleek and darkly reflective. The furthest workshop and the one nearest the boat was open, the light glowing from inside, creating a moving shadow, which Adam assumed was Simon.

Full of apprehension, he made his way behind the nearest of the workshops, into the gap between the back and a fence. He stepped cautiously over gravel and refuse blown into the gap, could hear distinct noises as he moved closer, the sound of heavy boxes being moved and stacked. It seemed to take an age as he nervously made his way behind the line of square buildings, finally coming to a stop beside the last workshop. He heard the sound of a trolley wheel away.

The rear wall was brick with a peeling window frame above. It was devoid of glass but out of reach. He looked around but there was nothing to stand on. The fence would be too noisy and was too far from the wall. He ran his fingers over the wall; some of the bricks were corroded and crumbling, leaving holes he might use to climb. He tried a few, managing to push in his foot and reaching to find a handhold to pull himself up.

The trolley bumped back and the stacking resumed. He waited still and quiet until the wheels rolled away again.

During their honeymoon cruise he had great fun one afternoon climbing a fake rock face, this looked vaguely similar. He wanted to know what was being loaded and importantly how long it might take. So he rehearsed the movements in his mind as he waited again for the heavy rattle of the trolley to fade. Then he manoeuvred his foot into the lowest hole, just below waist height, took a deep breath, and threw himself at the wall, pushing up through his leg and searching out the handhold, clamping into the hole, fingers scrabbling and sticking and pulling, immediately throwing up his other hand and getting his fingertips onto the ledge. He hung suspended for a second with his feet blindly searching for leverage, then pulled himself up to the window.

Silently elated, he worked at catching his breath and keeping quiet, while taking in the scene. The workshop was twice the width of a normal garage, opening at the front on to the quay. Stacked across the floor into just about every space and at least head high were boxes of all sizes, mostly sealed in transparent plastic. He tried reading the wording. Those he could fathom were not just the staples of water and tinned food, bleach and toilet rolls, but electrical supplies and plumbing, engine parts, filters and refrigeration, a load of supplies for a long journey. It occurred to him as the trolley reappeared that it would take some time to load all of it onto the boat.

He ducked down beneath the window and waited on the trolley, hanging with his arms burning and his legs aching. He carefully lowered himself and slowly made his way around the building between interludes of stacking, keeping close to the fence, moving beyond the boat and to a series of worn concrete steps that dropped down into the water.

As he peered over the top step back towards the boat, Adam was already trying to figure how he would get onto it. And if Sarah and the girl were there, how he would get them off and past Simon to safety.

SEVENTY-NINE

The heavy metal door slammed closed and silence reigned once more. Brian immediately started counting down from ninety, as he did deciding which hand to choose. His right hand was stronger, he was right-handed, although intricate movements were a problem amid the static of tortured nerve endings. His left hand was fine but weaker. It was not even a debate, just some way of preparing his brain for what was to come.

He turned his left wrist within the confines of the plastic and placed the thumb on the flat of the chair, taking the stretch of the plastic to its limit. Once the thumb was in place he tested the movement and finished the ninety-second count. He started another and without finishing violently pushed down through his left shoulder, angling the thumb and not stopping until the plastic cut deep into his skin. He shouted out load, the pain jarring through his entire body, the thumb out of joint. He got it wrong. A few seconds and the ligaments popped it back and he shouted louder and doubled over, a mixture of pain and frustration.

It came down to one single simple fact. He could not be in the chair when the metal door next opened. He placed his thumb on the flat of the seat, pushed the joint flush with the edge of the chair and shifted his weight. He closed his eyes, breathed out and pushed down hard again, harder and quicker. A different kind of pain, he got it right. Something gave in his hand, a sensation like a solid branch snapping. He screamed at the ceiling, this time tinged with jubilation that quickly faded, knowing the real pain was now to come.

He dared not stop and think. His thumb was now pushed back away from the hand, pointing back towards his wrist. He could feel it. It needed to be flat across the palm. If his hands were closer he could quickly lift the sheered bone over, scream some more and get on with it. But his hands were fastened each side of the chair. There was no easy way to do it. So he used the plastic to cut into his wrist and the blood to lubricate the skin, pulling up through the narrow diameter of plastic, the plastic tie moving up over his wrist, shifting the thumb back across the palm.

Brian knew pain, had even come to welcome the battle. He might even tell you of times that equalled this pain. Those times would be few, little competed with moving a fractured bone across the break. Desperation pushed him on, his face red and spit on his lips and eyes bulging, fixed madly on the door, moving his wrist in small motions side to side and gradually upwards. Tears ran down his cheeks and his voice high pitched and distant and pleading as the plastic moved, over the joint and swelling flesh, the thumb slowly shifting and grating. Then at last the plastic freed and his hand slipped through, stopping at the ridge of knuckle. His vision was failing, his brain searching for escape, his determination keeping him conscious. He used blood from his wrist again, already thickening, to shift the plastic over the ridge of knuckle, now the widest part of his hand. The plastic slid and his left arm swung free and he blacked out.

EIGHTY

Ferreria turned to a fresh page of her notepad. She drew two circles, writing into the first: *Andrea* and the second: *Secrets*. She joined them with a curving line and looked up at the stepfather. He was looking right at her, lest he glimpse his wife's eyes burrowing into him. And then he spoke.

'At first I did pass everything on to Beth because when you have a little girl in your care who's not your own, well, it's difficult for a man. You worry about secrets between the both of you because it's so easy for them to be misconstrued. You can see it in people's eyes, as if they're waiting for the slightest hint something ugly is hidden. So at first I passed on everything to make sure there was no confusion at all. And I still do, in the main. Now we have our own two it doesn't seem so important.'

His eyes never left Ferreira. 'So sometimes I judge there are things that are best kept from Beth, she can…she can care a little too much sometimes. Especially where Brian is concerned. And nobody could ever accuse Beth of not caring about her children.'

All four of them waited as he searched for more words. 'So yes, Andrea does sometimes confide in me and I do sometimes keep that to myself.'

The mother without moving loomed over him. 'Like what, Kevin?'

'Mrs Smith, if you could please…' began Ferreira.

She did not listen. 'What, Kevin, tell me, what have you done?' Her voice rose in pitch. 'What have you not told me that has caused this?' Her eyes glistened. She turned back to the table, her frustration becoming tears. She reached beside her chair and tossed tissues onto the table, falling silent again as she wiped away the tears, as keen to hear what her husband had to say as everyone else. He started talking, still fixed on Ferreira.

'It's not much really. Andrea asked me questions about what I was like before I met her mother. Did I wash my own clothes, did I cook? Did I iron and tidy the house, buy food? That sort of thing. Did I like to drink, how much I drank.' The stepfather gained confidence as he spoke. 'So I told her. And of course I guessed she was comparing the answers against what her dad was doing, so I pitched my answers. She was just trying to suss what was normal and what was not.' He stopped and tapped the pad of his index finger on the polished table, studied it and then turned to Ferreira. 'And the more she told me, I realised she had started doing some of this stuff for him. Cleaning the house. Asking me how to…asking if she could borrow some money so her dad could wash his clothes.'

Sitting beside him the mother sounded like she was about to choke. The words came out in a rush. 'You gave Andrea money so Brian could wash his clothes! How do you know it was used for that? Buying drink more likely. You fool.' She almost spat. 'I've been struggling to make ends meet and you paid to do his washing! Keeping the truth from me.' She dabbed at her eyes.

Ferreira waited. 'And?'

'I knew Andrea wasn't giving him the money, she was washing the clothes for him. She wanted to know how to work the machines in the laundrette and then I started hearing about the neighbour she goes with, a woman who lives upstairs. In the last year I think I heard most of what goes on. How often he works and that he leaves her by herself Saturday afternoons, and Saturday nights. And yes I deliberated a great deal on the rights and wrongs. What was I to do? If I told anyone I can only imagine what social services would do. And in my heart of hearts I can't believe it would be for the best. It would destroy Andrea not to spend time with her father.'

'Or she could see her father for what he really is!' The mother's spit peppered the side of his face, which he wiped away after a moment. 'You're just as much to blame as he is.' The words peppered him again. She collected herself as if suddenly remembering they were not alone. She sat back in her chair.

Ferreira made a mental note and turned her attention back to the husband. 'So did you know Andrea waited for her father outside Boots?'

He moved his head from side to side. 'I promise you, I had no idea. I knew she waited for him in the afternoons. I knew she often picked up his prescription or he would leave it to the last minute or forget completely. That would really worry her. The when and where wasn't the nature of what she told me. It was probing, not conversational. She was trying to work things out. I half admired her and of course I worried like hell. I gave her a phone so she could ring if she was scared or something happened. She mostly forgot it and lost it completely in the summer. I think the phone was for me more than her.'

Ferreira flipped a page and continued writing. Then looked back up when she had finished. Kevin shifted his gaze to the wall.

'And you knew none of this?' directed at the mother.

'Obviously the man I married is not the man I thought I knew.' Her anger brought colour to previously ashen cheeks, her eyes dug holes in his flesh but he refused to look sideways at her.

Ferreira made sure she had her attention. 'But you didn't know any of this?' she repeated.

'No!' snapped the mother. Their eyes met mid-blink and there it was, the subtle flaw in the perfect veneer. A lie.

Ferreira picked up her tea with hands that suddenly wanted to tremble, calming herself by thinking how Boer would prise open this flaw. The mother had lied. Ferreira now realised why Boer had endlessly ringed the stepfather's name. Not as a suspect, but as the one most likely to lead her to the truth. She studied her notes longer than necessary, euphoric and wary. Then she looked back to both parents. Both were now separated by a chair's width and no longer holding hands, the crucifix looking down over the empty space between them. The mother's arms were folded on the table, looking at the reflection of something in the table. The stepfather still fixed on the wall beside Ferreira.

She took Boer's lead, could almost hear his voice in her mind. Knowing now how she would prise open that subtle flaw. 'Tell me what you know about Brian,' she asked the stepfather.

309

EIGHTY-ONE

He jerked conscious at a sound, his panicked eyes immediately going to the door and seconds of anticipation. It stayed closed and the cause of the sound stayed outside. He looked over his shoulder and judged the distance and angle to the gnarled workbench. He had no idea how long he had been out. His left arm hung loose at his side, his hand throbbing with a vengeance, his back busy with its needling dance. He needed to turn the chair.

Turning was near impossible. He tried jumping the chair around but gave up almost immediately, instead he rocked precariously onto his feet, stooped and managing to shuffle around in very small increments, the chair legs scuffing and unbalancing him, his free arm knocking against the chair. Finally he faced the bench and immediately started rocking from side to side, each sideways movement rewarded with a small step forward. A modernist hunchback gradually moving from the view of the metal door.

He stopped with the top of his head pressed against the wood, eyes on the floor. He swung his free arm up onto the surface, searching blindly, each bump and contact causing a schism of pain which he ignored, using alternate movements between the ball and heel of his feet to shuffle sideways, the sweat dripping from his nose and chin, tracing his path on the dusty floor. His senses were on constant alert for any sound, aware of each passing second, his fingers bumping over the metal of the knuckledusters, the bat and across the fabric of his kitbag, to their destination. He struggled with four fingers to get a grip on the blade. Each time he managed to lift it, the weight caused the knife to fall. So he gave up and used his hand to drag it over the edge.

310

It clattered onto the concrete and just under the workbench, forcing him to spend precious seconds scraping with his fingers to pull it into the open. Being able to see the knife helped, picking it up was an ordeal. His reach was restricted by his right hand, still tied to the chair which was now set square on the floor. His outstretched fingertips just reached the cold metal. He rocked perilously onto his feet again, scrabbling frantically then grasping the hilt between his fingers. He would hold a special reverence for his thumbs from now on, the knife held precariously in four fingers. He lifted it carefully and levered the serrated edge under the plastic at his ankle. He applied pressure and his grip slipped.

The knife clattered to the floor again and he used his fingertips to claw it back. Lifting and levering the serrated edge three more times and dropping the knife each time, trying to temper his anger and frustration, but each time the required pressure was becoming more familiar.

He heard a sound at the metal door, a padlock or key into a lock. He manoeuvred his fingers around the hilt and lifted the knife as rusty hinges protested. He positioned it against the plastic tie and steadily twisted. The plastic gave and snapped and his fingers lost their grip. One leg and a broken hand now free as the door creaked open. He clawed at the knife, trying to scrape it closer as he heard feet, which paused and then came towards him, uncertain at first and then at a run. He focused, blinked away the sweat that rolled into his eyes. He rocked forward, concentrating with life and death in every movement.

He held his breath, fingers searching for purchase, the footsteps quickening. He held the knife in four fingers, pushing it up and into the plastic, with just the right amount of angled pressure. The footsteps close now, a loping run favouring one leg. He mentally adjusted. The plastic gave and snapped and now he had a broken hand and two legs free as the shoes made the opening.

Not enough time for the remaining hand. Brian was already moving, the movement fluid. Starting with the blade clamped between his teeth, he set his feet, trusting his aching legs to keep him upright, the chair clasped in his right hand as he stepped forward with his left leg, stepping into the swing. The chair came up and around as Oddi turned, a defensive arm raised as the chair crashed across his shoulders and head. Brian's foot raked Oddi's shin and immediately swept the back of his leg, forcing him to the ground. Brian jabbed with his foot again but was blocked with a hard forearm, but not the second strike of the chair. The joints splintered and broke free, another strike and it broke apart. Brian ignored a knee to his calf and fingernails that gouged his ankle, punching down with the remaining length of chair attached to his wrist, straight into Oddi's centre mass. Brian shifted his weight and body, the opening now at his right periphery, kicking the ball of his foot into exposed ribs, Oddi curled foetal at his feet, Baldur coming at him fast.

One-armed and tiring, Brian needed an advantage. He pulled the remaining length of wood through the plastic, ignoring the splinters that snagged his forearm, dropping to one knee and pounding the wood into Oddi, into his torso, neck, chest, face and head, fending off arms and legs frantically trying to ward him off or kick him away. A final vicious stab to Oddi's stomach and he discarded the wood, taking the knife into his right hand, ignoring Baldur now only three strides away, the strike timed for the reaction he hoped it would have. Oddi gave a final weak kick as the knife plunged through ribs into a healthy heart, his shocked wail quickly turning to a despairing moan as Brian immediately turned and defended a ferocious kick with crossed forearms. The kick carried Baldur off balance, giving Brian the chance to push up and run him into the bench, the impact hard and jarring and causing them both to shout out.

An impasse. Baldur was wedged between the bench and Brian, his back to Brian, neither able to move. All of Brian was now invested in pinning him against the bench, both gasping in the frenzy before sudden death. Brian's strength was failing, his grip loosening, trying to twist an arm up around Baldur's neck. Baldur managed to pull his arm free, slamming his elbow immediately back into Brian's shoulder, and with more space into the side of his head, trying to turn. Brian returned each blow with a blind punch into Baldur's back and ribs, a war of attrition he was never going to win, adrenalin now a distant memory.

An elbow exploded against his ear, causing a hum inside his head and then a second, smashing across his cheek, catching his nose and blood into his throat that he choked and coughed into Baldur's hair. Another blow scuffed his shoulder into his neck and another into the side of his head and almost a ten count. Brian managed two last punches, steeling his mind against the next two seconds. Baldur realised victory, using his strength and the bench to push back and spin around.

Two seconds. The first second Brian invested in grasping blond hair in four fingers amid a wall of pain he would never know, his right fist managing a single last punch. The next second was the time it took for him to fall backwards, buckling his knees to create the right angle, Baldur spinning around and forward, except Brian was no longer there.

One second of free fall. Two synchronised movements. Brian held Baldur's hair with his left hand and pushed up under his chin with the other, turning the head back against the body's movement as Baldur spun around. Baldur's neck muscles tensed in reflex but momentum and gravity were now his enemy, the sound of gristle and cartilage stretched and snapped and bone shifting over bone, cutting and tearing through the complex tangle of nerves connecting body to brain. A cry cut off. Brian hit the floor and Baldur landed heavy on top of him, a dead weight.

Brian immediately pushed the body one way and rolled the other. Sitting up and gasping, he tried to stand but his legs failed him. He spat blood, wiped more from his face and shuffled back, kicking out at the head lying at an unnatural angle to the body, releasing his barely contained fear and anger. He spat again and studied the face of Baldur.

Green eyes stared back at him, unblinking. Not technically dead yet, just paralysed from the neck down. With no pumping heart to push blood to neurons, no lungs to fuel oxygen into the blood, it would be minutes before starved cells began to die. He'd be unconscious after two or three, technically dead after five. Brian wondered as he watched if Baldur could hear or was aware. Not that Brian had anything to say to him, he just wondered.

He turned his attention to the matter in hand, his thumb, swollen and oddly angled in his palm. His medical training dictated that the pull of ligaments made setting a bone easier than breaking it. This break was a good way back to the wrist, the skin broken with the bone now pushed through. He was beyond verbalising pain so he breathed deep and grasped the thumb. Lifting it and using the natural pull to set the bone amid barred teeth and a low, drawn-out growl.

He was not sure if he had blacked out, he blinked and his thumb was roughly normal amid purple bloated flesh. He climbed unsteadily to his feet and stepped around the blood pooling from Oddi. He pushed a foot against his ribs and the knife sucked free from the vacuum of wet flesh. He cleaned it on Oddi's trousers and cut strips from his top. He cut a small splint from the chair frame and bound it to his thumb and wrist. He then searched both dead men. Both were completely devoid of any identification or personal possessions. No phone, receipt or loose change.

313

He reclaimed his rounders bat and searched for his trainers. They were gone, along with his T-shirt and jacket. He checked Baldur and Oddi for shoe size; one was too big and the other too small. He pushed the bat between his belt and jeans, dropped the long chain of blades, the knife, the rubber cosh and the knuckledusters into his kit bag. He hauled it over his head and onto his back as he surveyed the scene.

You're alive! How many times had he thought that? He had lost count. This time it was different. He was fighting for one thing only, the chance to hold Andrea and say sorry. Not for the here and now, but for the last two years, the endless love she invested. That is, if Andrea would forgive him? Which he felt quite certain she would. He took a final look at the bodies and walked through the metal door into the open.

Outside he was immediately assaulted by the sea air, refreshing against his shirtless skin. He stepped from concrete onto sandy scrub, the sea rolling to a stop a few feet away, then walked around the building to an open area with discarded fridges and shopping trolleys. A silver car and a dark figure leaned against it. They saw each other at the same time. The figure by the car hesitated for a second, reached inside his jacket and pointed something at Brian that looked very much to him, in the dark, like a gun. A Walther he guessed in that fraction of a second. Then it spewed fire, the casing ejected in an arc and a single 9mm bullet cut through the air.

EIGHTY-TWO

'What do you want to know about Brian?' the stepfather asked.

'Tell me about him, anything at all,' Ferreira said. 'What's he like as a man and a father, what do you think of him?'

The mother sighed and shook her head. 'Is this necessary?' She flicked her hair behind her ears.

'Yes, Beth. Maybe you two know something about Brian that we don't, it may be important. Maybe you're right about Brian. Humour me please.' She turned back to Kevin. 'What are your impressions?'

'Well, for a start, he's not someone I'd want to get the wrong side of. He's a hard kind of man. You meet them sometimes. They just don't know how to deal with people. He's not the sort of guy I'd ever spend time with. He's just different, I suppose. I've known him for seven years on and off. We never saw him for long periods. We used to exchange the odd word in lay-bys at weekends as we handed Andrea back and forwards. He only moved to Hambury after he was discharged.'

Ferreira flipped over a page. The stepfather continued. 'The army was his whole life, he lived for it. Now his whole life has been turned upside down, his whole sense of worth.'

The mother pressed the palms of her hands flat on the table. 'I really don't need to listen to this. I'd better check on the girls.'

Ferreira reached across. She could not touch the mother's hand but pressed hers onto the table in the same way. 'Please, Beth, this is important. Check them in a minute.'

The mother lowered herself back down and placed her folded arms back on the table.

The stepfather addressed Ferreira. 'Brian is struggling, what can I say? I hoped for Andrea's sake things would sort themselves out. I offered him some work but he turned me down flat. Said…well, he said he should probably keep his distance. To be honest I think the injuries are not his problem, as bad as they are. It's not being in the army that he really struggles with. It must be a hell of a shock being a civilian now, going from being the best of the best, surrounded by like minds, to nothing.'

The mother was growing increasingly agitated, visible most in her shoulders. Ferreira took her time catching up with the notes then paused to drink her tea. She reached down to her purse and pulled out the scrap of paper Boer had found in Andrea's picture frame. Four pairs of eyes followed its journey to the centre of the table. The stepfather briefly studied it and looked away. The mother picked it up with trembling fingers.

'This is Andrea's writing. A Hambury number?' she asked, puzzled. 'But Brian doesn't have a phone now, of any description.' Her face twisted. 'I absolutely forbade Andrea from calling him, she would have plummeted us into more debt in no time. She would have spent her whole time on the phone trying to call him. Just imagine what that would do to the child.'

Ferreira looked at the stepfather. He looked at her. He did not say anything, just shrugged, the meaning implicit. *I'm already in the shit, why not!*

The mother saw it as well, immediately shaking her head disbelievingly from side to side, lifting her chair further away from him. She crossed her legs and folded her arms. 'Pray tell, do!'

For the first time in a long time Kevin looked at his wife, relaxed now as if he had seen into his own future and accepted it. Ferreira had seen the reaction in interviews before. She tried to recall the statistics, it was often the least guilty who confessed first because they felt the guilt more. Everyone in the room waited for him to speak.

'Don't be so high and mighty, Beth. You've become obsessed with chipping away at the man. As if you'll only be satisfied when he's finally erased from your life. As if you are embarrassed by the fact you were fancy free when you were younger, and Andrea is the living proof. I should have stopped it a long time ago. But…but you're a hard woman to face up to.'

He reached across and picked up the scrap of paper, confirming to himself what he already knew, dropping it back onto the table. 'It's Brian's boss's number. Ali's his name. I give Andrea my mobile on the Saturday nights she's here. She calls Brian while he's working. I guess the paper is how she remembered the number.'

That was about all the mother could take. She gave a low scream and launched herself at her husband, the liaison officer and the constable scrambling too late to their feet and knocking their chairs over in the process. The mother rained blows that bounced off his shoulders and arms and the side of his head. The words forced from her mouth each time a blow hit home.

'What...kind...of...man...have...I...married?'

EIGHTY-THREE

Simon finished the last checks and powered down the console, turning in his chair to look down at the quay, the trolley moving backwards and forwards. Another hour and he would start the engines and complete the final preparations, in two hours they would be in the North Sea heading towards Scotland. In three nights all navigation and tracking would be powered down. They would be skirting the Irish Atlantic coast. He was nervous and excited, which had nothing to do with getting his cargo out of UK waters undetected.

He dropped down the steps to the lower level and walked along the narrow corridor, unlocking the bedroom door and stepping inside. Sarah was sitting cross-legged on the bed, wearing only a pair of his red shorts, a book open on her lap. The shorts were impossibly large on her.

The bare expanse of her flesh quickened the fluttering inside him, not the dark slithering, but a giddy sensation he barely recalled. He stepped around the bed towards her and tipped the book to see the cover.

'Why are you reading the end?' he asked.

'Because it's not my kind of book,' she replied, looking up at him. 'I just wanted to know what happens.'

His eye skimmed the page. 'It's one of my favourites.'

'What happens to him?'

'It's not about him,' he answered. 'It's about her, he's just her guardian.'

She closed the book and he drifted his fingers across the skin of her back and shoulder. She sent a tentative smile up to him. 'Why don't you shower and I'll finish this, then you can explain to me your favourite book.'

His fingers paused on her shoulder. 'What are you doing?'

'You can see what I'm doing.'

'No, why are you being like this?'

She let her head rest back against the headboard. 'Because if I don't try and do something normal I'll go mad and I really mean that. It's not something you ever expect to do, to run away with a…a kidnapper and that's the best light I can paint you in.'

'So you're coming, of your own free will?' he asked, his voice hopeful.

'You mean I have a choice?'

'You know the choices. I meant you are here rather than fighting me.'

'What is there to fight with? I go where the girl does. You know my intentions. I'm hoping to show you the error of your ways. What will you say to Hakan?'

She watched him pull off his shirt and walk back around the bed, unable to pull her eyes from him, the natural poise of a predator with few peers. He stopped by the door that led to the shower.

'Hakan thinks you're still in the house. He'll need machinery to get into the room, and for that he needs the brothers. How long before he finds out depends on his priorities. I would say a day, maybe two. By then it will be too late. He won't be thrilled but what matters to him is delivering the girl. He's not worried about that.' He unbuckled his trousers. 'He practically owns me.'

'How so?'

'My father. He built a number of obligations that became mine when he died. Hakan took them on.'

'Obligations?'

He smiled ruefully. 'Money type obligations, they sprout legs and arms and lots of attitude, especially if they originate in Asia. Read the end of the book,' he said and walked into the shower.

She looked at the pages but did not read the words. There had been half an opportunity as he leaned over to check the book, but she needed more than half an opportunity. She slipped the spare razor back into the book, listening to the sound of water as she struggled through the last twenty pages.

EIGHTY-FOUR

The harsh discharge of the gun filled the night air, sending seagulls flapping and squawking in alarm, the noise rolling out to sea. Brian could see the man was young, in his early twenties. He took a step towards him.

'You never know, mate, maybe the bullet will get me on the way back down.'

'Stop!' The man's voice was buffeted by conflicting eddies of air.

Brian did. 'Put it down for Christ's sake! Do you know how old that is? If it's the P38 you're talking 1940s, that's older than your granddad. Very latest we're talking 1970s. I bet the recoil really fucking hurt, didn't it? Pull the trigger again and you're likely to break your wrist. How many times have you fired it, a couple in the woods? Probably not even that. You didn't even mean to fire it did you? The safety's on the left side, do yourself a favour.'

The young man stood still and Brian took a step that went without reply. 'I know you weren't issued with that by this lot, this lot are far too professional. Guns attract the wrong kind of attention.' He rested his right hand on the handle of the bat. 'So you probably bought it from some bloke in the pub, or even stole it from your granddad. Did you check the magazine, made sure you've got more bullets in there? Cleaned it yet? It's easy to get blockages, especially if it's been sitting around for fifty years.' He took another step. 'How'd you think Hakan will react when he finds out you're carrying a gun? Not happy, I'd guess.' He took another two steps.

'Stay where you are.'

Brian stopped. He could see the whites of scared eyes. 'Look mate, I really don't want to hurt you. But think about your two blond buddies,

320

where are they? Would I be taking a stroll if they weren't all kinds of mangled inside? That's what you've got to think about. And I mean proper mangled. If you thought they were hard fucking cases, and there's no disputing they were, I've got to be all kinds of nasty. What is there, eight, maybe ten yards between me and you? If the recoil doesn't break your wrist and the gun doesn't blow up in your face, you'll only have time for one more shot. Then I'll be all over you like some avenging fucking angel. One shot, that's all. Even if you hit me and not a seagull up there, I'm still getting to you unless you land one between the eyes. And I don't figure on that happening. Either way you're screwed. So put the gun on the ground and fuck off.'

The man kept the gun levelled at Brian, took two sideways steps away from the car, stood very still for several seconds and then lowered the gun to the ground and turned and ran. Brian watched the soles of his trainers fade into the night.

He picked up the gun, a Walther P1 from the weight of it. He stripped it and removed the chambered round, the gun was of no use to him at all. He was next to useless with his left hand even with a thumb. With his right he stood more chance of hitting his foot. He threw the parts into the sea, thumbing each of the rounds from the magazine and throwing them in as well.

There was a mobile in the car's glove compartment along with a chocolate bar, which he devoured as he studied the mobile. He guessed it was Baldur's. It was locked with a pin. He tried several obvious sequences, but each failed. After five attempts it refused to let him try again. He pulled out the battery, put it back and waited for the phone to flare to life, but it remained locked. He dropped it on the passenger seat and cursed himself for not getting the car keys with the gun. He ran, carefully, barefoot across the sandy scrub, onto mud and to the road, the hard surface cold beneath his feet, following the coastline with lights shimmering in the middle horizon.

EIGHTY-FIVE

The water slapped the concrete below his feet. His head was level with the top step, studying the repeated routine of the trolley. He could lean sideways over the water and see a low platform at the back of the boat. Already piles of boxes had been lifted down. There was no other obvious way onto the boat.

The trolley stopped and more boxes were offloaded and then the wheels circled around. Adam waited for the tall figure to disappear inside the workshop. He climbed the few steps and jogged to the boat.

He jumped with only a moment of hesitation, landing on both feet but off balance, his hands on the floor as he bumped awkwardly into boxes. He steadied himself and looked around. Directly in front of him was a large enclosed space beneath the main deck, big enough for a small car and partially filled with boxes. To the right of the space was a set of rising steps. Keeping low he climbed to the main deck and a flooring of neat slatted wood, a covered sofa and an outside bar with a TV boxed in clear plastic. Just beyond this was a wide expanse of glass and two sliding doors. He looked at himself reflected in the glass, a dark shadow crouched, the illuminated dock tower rising behind him.

He edged to the glass panel but it was locked. He looked around. A walkway led around both sides to the front, and steps to his left dropped steeply into the boat. He shuffled across and as carefully and as silently as he could, climbed down, into a wide area of sparse grey metal, a communal area for crew with doors set into angled walls. Another door opposite led further into the boat, a workshop. He walked through into the engine room and past two giant cylindrical shapes lying horizontal on a frame with masses of intertwined cables and tubes. It looked like

322

something mislaid by NASA over anything he might imagine to be on a yacht. There was no way forward so he walked back through.

He had one foot on the bottom step when the obvious suddenly occurred to him. He moved back to the angled metal doors, going to the one on the left first. It was unlocked. He opened it. Inside was a single bed that had been made, but the neat order of sheets had been disturbed. Someone had been on the bed. The other door was locked. He considered the logistics.

This area had to be soundproofed. It would have to be with this kind of luxury and those engines. He fetched a large wrench from the workshop, then back to the door, took aim and with only the slightest hesitation, brought the wrench down hard on the metal handle. The noise was brief and harsh and followed by a startled yelp from beyond. A child's yelp, he thought as he hit out again, causing the door to jump ajar. He pushed it open and stepped inside.

It was a small space, identical to the other. In this one a young girl was sitting on the bed, her hair tousled, wearing a pink T-shirt and jeans. She was pressing herself back against the wall, exhaustion in her eyes, a wild echo of the smiling face and the girl she had been.

'Andrea?' He took another step and she shuffled back to the end of the bed, putting one leg to the floor. 'It's OK Andrea. I've come to take you home.'

'Who're you?' Her eyes moved from his face to the wrench and back to his face.

'My name is Adam.'

Her face briefly flickered recognition, then back to unsure, backing into the corner. 'Adam? Sarah's Adam?' Puzzled to herself, 'You can't be. Adam's at home. Sarah said.'

'It's me Andrea. I'm here with your dad to take you home.'

'Don't believe you! Where is he then?' Her mood was now defiant, her eyes warily on the wrench.

Adam laid it on the floor. 'Daddy's searching somewhere else. We've looked all over for you.' Adam had no idea where Brian was, trying to think of ways to win the girl over fast, uncertainty still in her eyes. He lowered himself to one knee, making himself smaller.

'Andrea, we don't have much time. You need to trust me. I know your daddy. He has angel wings on his back, how many people know that? Would I know that if he didn't tell me?'

'They're not real wings,' she said dismissively, but her fear had evaporated in an instant. 'Is he really here? He did come to get me, I knew he would.' Her mood effortlessly shifted to jubilant. 'Are they ever going to be sorry.' She stepped towards him. 'Can you take me to him? He needs to help me find my friend. Sarah's gone.'

'You've been with Sarah?'

'Yes, of course. We've been together all this time.' The muscles in her face shifted as she tried to recollect the span of *all this time,* and failing.

'When did you last see Sarah?'

'She said something horrid was going to happen and we had to fight. I couldn't do much.' She raised her hands at her side, demonstrating it was only her size that prevented her from fighting. 'I did help and I gave her the razors. I've been worried about her, she was getting more ill.' She tapped the side of her head to demonstrate her point. 'In here. They've been horrid, horrid people. They did bad things to her. I could see, although she said she was fine. I could see, I tried to help make her better.'

Adam reached out and held her shoulders as gently as the rising panic inside him would allow. It startled her a little but she could see his intent. 'When was the last time you saw Sarah?'

'In the house.' She paused, looking around at this new room. 'He came for me. He gave me a drink and said I was going on a journey with Sarah, and then I woke up here.' She absently pushed her hair behind her ears. 'You will find her won't you?'

'Yes, but you need to listen to me and do exactly as I say. I think your daddy will be here very soon. I cannot leave without Sarah, you understand? I'll find her and we will come for you.' She nodded wide-eyed.

'So I want you to hide down here.' He led her out of the small room into the communal area. 'Hide anywhere.' He pointed towards the workshop. 'Anywhere, but stay down here because Simon is outside. I will come back for you. I have to find Sarah.' She nodded again. 'And proper hiding,' he said. 'So if they come down and see that door they will think you have escaped and gone outside. So you have to stay quiet unless it's me,' he thought for a second, 'or Sarah or your dad. You got that?'

'Yes,' she said, dazed, surveying the room with serious eyes. There were lots of small drawers and cupboards. She trotted into the workshop.

Adam watched as she peered beneath the bench and disappeared into the engine room. He felt guilty leaving her there, but leaving without Sarah was not an option. He considered the wrench but decided against it, climbing the steps back to the main deck.

EIGHTY-SIX

Ten minutes and distant lights became distinguishable as roads and industrial buildings. Ten minutes after that he jogged beneath street lighting and over a roundabout, passing a petrol station with an impossibly high canopy, then a two-storey glass building set behind a narrow car park, empty save for a dark Mercedes parked at an angle.

He checked the number plate and slowed, breathing hard as he jogged around to the back of the building, along a path skirted by bare trees that opened to grass leading down to the water and slatted wooden quays. Row upon row of yachts were parked like cars, a dizzying array of masts and lights all creaking to the swell of the restless ocean.

He stepped onto the grass, put two fingers to his mouth and whistled, the sound harsh and short in the night. He listened intently but nothing was returned. He peered through the thick glass at the back of the building, only discerning silhouettes made by light from the front. Not even a glowing computer screen. He tried the double doors, both were unlocked and swung heavily as he stepped inside, into an office, open plan over two floors, the ground floor given to a reception and administration. The only sound was a faint repetitive noise, as if the wind was playing with paper left by an open window, or deft fingers flicking through the pages of a file. He whistled again, this time low.

'Up here,' Ali answered.

Brian climbed the spiral stairs to a corridor flanked by desks. Ali stood at the end, hunched over a desk with a soft glow illuminating the front of his body. He was dressed in dark casual clothes. If not for the machete holstered against his thigh, he might have been checking paperwork before going for a meal.

Brian approached, relieved and on high alert at the same time. 'Fancy seeing you here.'

'Fancy that,' Ali answered, intent on his task.

Brian looked around. The space was devoid of any other people, and the only light was on the desk.

'Guess they're going to need a new alarm.'

'Looks like it,' Ali said.

'What about CCTV? They can make out all kinds of shit on those things.'

'Not without power they can't,' Ali answered, flicking through a stack of papers, pausing at each page, his eyes searching and moving on.

'No power's going to draw attention.'

'It did already. He'll be back in fifteen, if I'm still here he'll get twice as much.'

Brian debated the obvious, still cautious. 'How'd you get here?'

Ali shifted a thick folder to one side and pulled across another, flipping it open. 'A detective rang this morning at five, seemed to think you were the ace up his sleeve and thought you needed help. He gave me an address just down the road. Had to choke the pub out of the guy they had sentry inside.' Ali's fingers walked through the stack of paper. 'Imagine my surprise, Brian, when this detective told me I was in the frame for your daughter's kidnapping, considering we spoke Saturday night and there was no mention of *kidnapped* or *missing*.'

'You're pissed at me?'

Ali stopped at a page, studied it and moved to the next. 'Pissed at you doesn't come close, my friend. You knew this on Saturday and said nothing. That hurts, that really fucking hurts, after what we've been through.'

'You were pissed at me then, you're always pissed at me. On Saturday it was one guy and you were a breath from kicking my arse onto the street.'

'You need to realign your perspectives, Brian, stop feeling sorry for yourself and making life miserable for everyone around you. Business and friendship are two different things.'

Which was all Ali had to say on the matter and Brian was in no state to argue with a six foot six Nigerian with a machete strapped to his thigh.

'How'd the pub lead you here?' Brian asked.

'I watched them put you in the car. They dropped off one of the guys from the pub. We had a chat.'

'You decided against coming to get me?'

Ali chuckled. 'It was a toss-up between going after Andrea or you, and you can look after yourself.'

Brian leaned over a desk and plucked a headed sheet of paper from a tray, studying the header. 'The marina,' he realised. 'You know which boat she's on?'

'*Passing Dream*,' Ali answered. 'Our problem is Grimsby's got a marina, a harbour and a dock.' He closed the last folder. 'Except it's not in the marina.' He turned and for the first time faced Brian. 'Christ!' he said.

'The two blonds,' Brian said by way of explanation. 'Now in the company of their good lord.'

Ali laughed, a deep basal sound that echoed in the space. He took two steps and draped a massive arm over Brian's shoulder, directing him towards the stairs. 'You, my friend, had better hope we find your daughter before that boat sails. I shall not be pleased if we have to tear Europe apart looking for her. And then when we're done I will teach you a few hard lessons about friendship.'

EIGHTY-SEVEN

Simon knotted the towel around his waist and padded into the room. Sarah placed the book face down on her lap, her bare legs stretched straight out in front of her.

'Sit there.' She pointed to a space to the right of her feet and laid her hand on the book.

'Why that exact spot?' he asked, amused, exaggerating as he looked at the ceiling and pulled up the mattress, peering beneath.

'Because I want to know about you,' she replied. 'How…what makes you such a gentle man and at the same time a monster.'

He stepped onto the bed, a brief flicker of hurt as he lowered himself to sit cross-legged. 'We have thirty minutes before I have to go,' he said, reaching and tugging the book from beneath her hand. 'You must first tell me what you thought of the ending?'

She watched his hand as he lifted the book from her lap, trying to avoid looking at the blade that fell onto her shin with a barely audible sound and to the bed against her skin. She moved her leg a fraction and felt it slide cold beneath her calf. 'Angels aren't my thing,' her voice a little uneven. 'Why is the woman so important?'

'It's about what she becomes, and then her child in later books.' He dropped the book onto the bed and rested a warm hand on her ankle. 'I have the others, you might like them.'

She looked at him looking at her, searching for some hint he had seen the blade. He could only have seen and might even have heard. All she saw was love.

'Tell me about those obligations you inherited,' she said.

'They were my father's, passed on to me.'

'That doesn't sound very fair?'

'It all depends on your perspective of fair. Fair is two people who agree terms. My father died because I killed him. His ideal of fair was not mine.' Simon lifted both palms and looked at them, and then at her. 'I killed him and inherited his obligations. Every action has a consequence.'

'You killed your own father?'

He laid his hand back on her leg. 'He deserved it. He made me what I am. My father died because his ignorance took something precious from me and that shaped what I would become. My mother played her part too. You'd never wish for anyone better to stand at your side, nor a worse enemy. Nor anyone more insecure, desperate for someone to notice the woman she was. I spent more nights in her bed than any man, for her peace of mind she said. I can't stand the smell of women and their perfumes.'

'You killed your mother as well?'

He shook his head. 'I didn't need to, cancer did that for me.'

From somewhere, which Sarah was sure came from inside her own head, she heard a child cry out.

'What did they take from you?'

'My sister,' he answered. 'They told me she was the daughter of my father's friend. In fact she was the child of my father's mistress. They put us together and never said a single word, for fear we would let slip the flaw in their married illusion.'

'She was your sister and they never said anything?'

He shook his head.

'What happened?'

'What do you think? We fell asleep together and were made to be the guilty ones. She was sent back to Singapore.' It was the first time Simon had told anyone.

Sarah shuffled closer to him.

'We are not that different, you and I.' She climbed her hands up onto his knees and let her mouth drift up across the skin of his chest, up around his neck, trailing damp hair across his shoulders.

'I wish you would let the girl go,' she said. 'We two are meant to be together.'

'You know I can't,' he replied.

'I will persuade you, you know, in the weeks to come.'

330

EIGHTY-EIGHT

The sound of lifting boxes and bumping wheels was temporarily quiet, replaced by the light breeze and soft staccato of waves against the hull. Adam watched the stationary figure, a cigarette glowing, his shadow made long by the workshop light. He ducked down and edged along the narrow walkway.

He stopped at a sealed door in the bulkhead and struggled with the handle, managing to lift it out before swinging it open like any other. He moved inside, cautiously standing again and carefully moving through a kitchen to a space entirely fronted by curving glass. A darkly sleek console dominated the space. A leather chair faced a row of blank screens built into the console, a small round steering wheel and an array of neat dials and switches, a complementing leather sofa to the side. From here he had an elevated view of the quay and the service road, the warehouses looming in the middle distance.

He walked back through the kitchen into the main area, a mosaic set into the marble floor, the illuminated dock tower visible through the glass doors. He could hear a sound, like voices, too faint to discern but definite.

He climbed steps that rose another level through a hatch, to the bridge above and the open air. It was a near duplicate of the console he had already seen, an audience of sofas set on both sides. A canopy flapped above, but that wasn't the sound he had heard. He went back down to the main deck and slowly down again another level, to a narrow corridor of polished wood. The sound was more distinct here, definitely voices, although too quiet to tell if one was Sarah's. He moved towards a narrow door, pulling the knife from his pocket without even knowing he had.

331

EIGHTY-NINE

With her hands resting on Simon's knees she was too far forward to easily reach behind her for the blade on the bed, and too far back for the one tucked between the bed frame and mattress. So she shuffled back and wriggled the shorts down over her knees and kicked them free. She felt the blade beneath her fingers as she pressed a palm behind her for balance and opened her legs wide for Simon.

'I have decided you may kiss my body. You can start there,' she said, tapping a finger against the inside of her thigh. He smiled and leaned forward as the door opened.

She immediately registered it was Adam without giving any thought or time to why, her mind too busy calculating opportunity. At the same time Simon glanced over his shoulder at the intrusion, which blocked her view of the door with the exposed flesh of his neck. The thick mass of muscle and ligaments that shielded his carotid artery. The perfect opportunity. Without pause and in a smooth motion she rocked her weight forward and swept her hand around towards the exposed flesh.

Simon saw the man in the doorway and was aware of Sarah's sudden movement at the same time, reflexively ducking his head into the blow. The blade sliced across the curve of his jaw and up to the bone of his cheek, Sarah immediately cut back, left to right, with a second blow that hit hard and bit deep into the other side of his neck. Simon was only aware of her hand punching into his neck, not of what she held in her hand, just the cold intent in her eyes. He caught her arm as it came back for a third strike and clubbed the side of his fist into the side of her head.

332

It spun her almost right around, over the edge of the bed, and unconscious before she hit the floor. A single blow that removed her as a threat, and more importantly for Simon, it meant if this was Hakan's men come for her, they would have to get past him to get to her.

He rolled off the bed to face the intruder, feeling something warm on his shoulder. The blade had cut through skin and muscle and the surface of the artery, but not through it. He appraised the man in the doorway, only one man. Quite a tall man, lean with dark hair and bruises on his face. He was holding a knife. He was not one of Hakan's men, simply because Hakan would not send only one man against him. And then the man did something that took Simon by surprise, mostly because it was the very last thing he should have done.

As the door swung open some part of Adam's mind was already conditioning itself for what he was about to see. Seeing Sarah naked with another man was part of the inconsequential detail he stored for later processing. It was Sarah but it was not, she saw him but never took her eyes from her prey. He watched her arm strike twice, two fast pendulum blurs before she was knocked aside with no effort.

Seeing Sarah discarded like a rag doll overcame him with a dark vengeance, a blood lust and fury that inhibited his sense of self-preservation as Simon rolled off the bed to face him. Adam now stood face to face with his nemesis. The same man he had seen in ceaseless CCTV images, the man responsible for the here and now. A giant with a crimson slash across his face and blood oozing from a deep cut on his neck, seeping over his massive shoulders and chest. Adam did not need to think, he did not need to think about not thinking, he just did it. He ran at Simon.

He had seen Brian do something similar on the beach. It was no more than three strides across the room and having made the first two he slid to the floor and stabbed hard as Simon tried to hop sideways. The knife sliced through the towel and into the muscle and sinew of Simon's thigh, the blade glancing off bone. He wrenched it out and plunged it in again and this time slashed, hoping to cut something important as Simon's fist slammed into the side of his head.

The blow knocked Adam sprawling across the floor, almost shutting down all his cognitive processes. He looked up unfocused at a dark shape that filled his vision and got bigger. Hands laced through his hair and lifted him to his feet. A rising fist powered into him just below his chest and the join of his ribcage, compacting his diaphragm and paralysing his lungs. He gasped and then another punch. This one was like concrete slammed into him. The pain was instant and so deep it felt like Simon could wrap his fingers around his spine. Nothing had ever hit him so hard and nothing ever would again. Something inside him tore and he reeled backwards against the door frame, sliding to the floor. He looked down at himself, blinking and making out the familiar profile of his body. Hardly a blemish on the T-shirt but he knew inside he was broken.

Simon took a hesitant step closer to the man crumpled in the doorway, no longer a threat. He assessed his own injuries. Blood flowed freely from the wounds in his leg. He pulled the knife free and dropped it to the floor, then dropped to one knee, struggling to orientate himself, leaning forward with a fist on the floor, shaking his head as if trying to clear a fogged mind. He could feel the blood on his neck now, touched a finger to the cut, now torn wider, could see his own blood spurting across the room like a sprinkler in summer.

Adam coughed, more a spasm than a real cough, feeling something wet on his chin. He looked down and this time saw blood. He was sure it was not Simon's, could see the big man's eyes on him. He was leaning on one thick arm like some great Athenian mortally perplexed, his blood pulsing over the dresser and walls. Adam coughed again and again, his breaths short and gasping, the infrequent drum of his heart. White filled his vision like snow on a cold vista, not even sure now he was breathing. He felt nothing any more, had no sense of fear or regret.

A small shadow rose from the far corner amid the haze and then a sound like a wounded animal, demented and woeful. A wail and a battle cry and utter sorrow. The shadow climbed across the bed and descended on Simon, fists pummelling an oblivious torso. As Adam's eyes failed, Simon slumped to the floor. And then as Adam's heart stopped beating he contented himself that he had saved Sarah. The sorrow in her cry was for him. And then his love and loyalty for Sarah, along with all the things he ever hoped for them both, died with him.

Sarah had no strength with which to do anything but lay prone on Simon, staring at Adam's body. She knew it was Adam but her mind struggled to place him there. *He should not be here!* Everything had been about him safe at home. She kept blinking and expecting to see someone else. Each time she opened her eyes it was still him. He was bruised and bloodied but there was a peace in his face that she envied. *Why was he here?* It consumed her thoughts, running on repeat with time and urgency suspended.

Then a sound outside swiped her back to reality. Andrea! She pushed herself off Simon and tried stepping over the wide swathes of blood on the floor, but it was everywhere. She caught her reflection in a mirror, a naked red devil. She pulled her jeans and shirt from a drawer, trying to avoid looking at the door and Adam. She heard another loud sound, like a door banging somewhere near.

NINETY

It took Andrea several minutes to find the perfect hiding place because at first she did not notice it for that very reason. There had been lots of possibilities but they were too obvious. She even briefly contemplated the narrow spaces beneath the engines but could only imagine what would happen if they fell on her.

So she wandered to the cabinet attached to the wall and idly opened it, finding inside a space she was not expecting. She was not sure what was meant to be inside, maybe something big with flashing lights. Instead it was empty save for a coil of tubing protruding from the back. She would be able to sit sideways inside with her knees pulled up. So that is what she did.

At first the metal protested as she got comfortable, or as comfortable as she could. When she pulled the doors closed they made a click that made her think she might be locked in. Realising, as she repeatedly pushed it open and pulled it closed, the click was what kept it closed, although it was difficult to really know because when she did it all went very dark.

When she thought about it, it was amazing she could even get in the cabinet. She never would have a few days before, not even with wild promises. Now she was getting used to the unusual. And then her mind started to wander. How long would she have to wait? How would her dad know where to look? He might not look in the right place, or she might not hear him and would never be found. The thought of that almost had her climbing back out. But she stopped herself. Her dad would call out. He wouldn't just look.

Her thoughts drifted and settled on the persistent niggling question.

That face in the picture in Simon's house. She was now very sure it belonged to a man who sometimes came to church. He had a voice like a movie star and talked to them all and sang. She remembered him because he made her mum laugh, and that was not an easy thing to do.

Then she heard the scream. It was the most frightening noise Andrea had ever heard. It felt to her like it came from somewhere close but distant at the same time. It cut through her resolve like a sharp knife, a sound demented and sorrowful, all her fears at night and of the day in one horrifying second that propelled her out of the hiding place with a sob, tumbling onto the floor, wild with fear, scrabbling through the workshop, feet and hands sliding, aware only that she needed to get away.

She tripped up the large steps on to the main deck, looking for an exit, seeing the steps down to the platform. She almost jumped straight down, scraping her arms as she stumbled. Then she despaired at the stacks of plastic-wrapped boxes and the impossible height of the quay. Panic pushed her to climb from stack to stack, to the top of the highest stack and to consider she might be able to jump to the quay.

She almost made it, landing hard on her knees on the rough concrete. She bounced into the boxes that closely lined the edge and with no hold slowly lost ground, desperately scrabbling with her hands for something to hold on to. She slipped over the edge with a desperate whimper, hitting the platform shoulder first, the momentum rolling her over the edge and into the water with hardly a splash.

Andrea did not panic straight away because she was a good swimmer. She was proud of that because her dad had taught her, managing to pull herself to the surface several times despite her shoulder being really painful. The water though pulled at her from all directions as it slapped backwards and forwards between the boat and pilings, and mostly it pulled her down. Already she was exhausted beyond anything she had ever known, splashing towards the boat and pulled back under, struggling to the surface a little further away. Not sure each time whether she would ever breathe again. With no strength left in her body she desperately gulped for air too early and slipped for the last time beneath the surface.

NINETY-ONE

The constable pulled a chair around between the mother and stepfather, the mother now on the far right of the table pouring loathing across the room at her husband. He remained much the same. His cheeks were flushed and his eyes were animated, but otherwise the same.

Ferreira was angry with herself. Not from the drama being played opposite, but from only now realising what Boer had seen in pictures of Andrea, the similarity to Sarah. Ferreira's realisation came from the girl upstairs and a child's lack of comprehension. Andrea's eyes carried something more. An awareness beyond her age, as if she already knew some of life's burden. The burden of trying to support her father with only a browbeaten stepfather to help. The anger Ferreira felt took the edge off the guilt, for what she was about to say. She had calculated the odds though and was fairly certain she would be close to the truth, despite it being entirely speculative.

'So can you tell me, Mr Smith, about your affair?'

She sensed the mother go still to her right and the constable set herself again. Kevin's head snapped up and his eyes flared and then immediately back to passive, staring back at the table. 'I don't see…how did? How has that got anything to do with this?'

'Tell me, Kevin. It might be important.'

'There's not much to tell. I met an old friend by chance and we got to talking and didn't stop. It was an antidote for the way Beth and I have become. It wasn't even an affair really. We met a few times for coffee, had a few phone conversations and then one afternoon we ended up in a hotel. It was a real wake-up call for me. The act of being unfaithful

338

really brought home how much I had to lose, how Beth and I were caught in the endless cycle of getting more for ourselves and not enjoying what we had. Our children were growing up right in front of us and we were missing it.'

He swallowed hard and started again. 'It was only then I found out Beth was already seeing someone, a…' He pulled his gaze from Ferreira and looked across at his wife. What he saw froze him. Ferreira did not turn at first but the shock on his face told her something was wrong, and then she turned and looked at the mother.

She had expected her to be convulsed with anger at the confession but instead she was pushing back into her chair, had backed herself against the wall with a wide-eyed fear pulling at the muscles of her face. As if her Satan was climbing from the table and crawling towards her.

The stepfather finished the sentence, eyes still fixed on the mother. 'It was only then that I found out Beth was already having an affair, with an American evangelist at her church.'

Ferreira only really heard *American,* one word that branched out through everything she had lived and experienced through the last three days. Every conversation with Boer and restless hours in bed working through the details. A mental rolodex of recollections and images, puzzling and random facts all suddenly sliding into place, each now connected and illuminated in her mind like lights across every limb of a giant tree.

'An American, a tall blond American?' she said, breathlessly to herself, repeating it out loud. 'A tall blond American?'

'Yes,' Kevin answered. 'Hair like snow and a voice like he's from the movies. Really knows how to thump out a sermon.' He was still unaware of the context, looking from his wife to Ferreira. 'How do you know all this stuff?'

Ferreira was too shocked to say anything. She just stared stunned at the mother who looked like she might topple sideways or dissolve into the wall at any moment.

NINETY-TWO

Andrea gulped more water, reaching for the lights and the surface, drifting away and down. Her hair snagged on something painful that jerked her sideways, then the material of her top was pulled and she felt herself lifted, coughing and spluttering into the air and then from the water. She heard a shocked male voice and then felt herself carried up steps and carefully laid on the quay. A concerned face peered down at her as she retched onto the concrete, gasping for breath and retching more. After a few minutes she could breathe more easily. Her shoulder really hurt now and her lungs felt like the rest of her body, raw and all used up. She sat up, pushing wet hair from her face, looking at her rescuer. She had never seen the man before.

'You all right there, nipper?' He crouched down beside her.

Andrea nodded, coughing some more and now very cold. 'Thank you.'

'Where the hell did you come from? One minute I'm loading boxes, the next I hear a kid crying for help.' The man's concern was genuine. 'I only checked to make sure I wasn't going mad. Where's your mum? Did you fall in or something?'

Andrea was slowly coming to her senses. The man was tall and a little like Simon, although he was not so big and smelt of cigarettes. Now wary, she pulled in her legs. 'I was on that boat, a man took me. Why're you here?'

He puzzled and turned to look at the *Passing Dream* and then back at her. 'You were on the yacht?' He never got an answer.

Andrea decided as he looked away that even if he had saved her he must be working for *them*. So she jumped to her feet, her body protesting

340

at every movement and started running. She immediately sensed he was not chasing, risking a look over her shoulder. He was watching, caught between a step and a stride with his hands on his head.

Her wet clothes were making running difficult, as if being exhausted and cold was not enough of a problem. She forced herself to keep going because she knew the scary scream and Sarah were part of the same thing. She did not know how it could be Sarah, but she knew help was needed and intended getting it. There were lots of very big buildings ahead. Initially she headed towards the warehouses because they looked safe but diverted back to the road when she heard the loud noise of the generators, determined to get as far from the boat as possible and find someone who could help. She followed the road around and realised too late the brighter light was from headlights as a car emerged and passed her. Three surprised faces stared at her as she ran in the opposite direction.

Then she heard screeching tyres and doors opening, footsteps chasing after her. She tried to run faster, to reach the main road ahead and the distant people. A hand clamped around her waist, another covered her mouth, lifting her off the ground with her legs still running.

She bit a convenient finger as hard as she could. Frustration and anger bunched the small muscles around her jaw as she made a real effort at biting it off. It earned her a shouted *Fuck!* And she was dropped to the floor. She knew she was caught though. There was nowhere to run to as two more figures rounded on her, one of them the short horrid man. She gathered all the air into her lungs and screamed as loud as she ever had. A brief shrill sound that was cut off as Hakan's hand cut across her face and she slumped unconscious to the ground.

NINETY-THREE

It was enough.

Brian stopped mid-stride, his attention fixed on the direction of the scream. Any other child and he might have missed it, faint amid the cacophony of industry. Except he would know Andrea's scream anywhere, it reminded him of her mother's laugh.

Brian held the small radio in the palm of his hand, pressing the call button twice and then once again as he ran towards the scream. He passed a long line of cranes poised over a large container vessel, protected by concrete bollards and a high chain fence, then the natural deterrent of water and the dock. Against the far quay he could see a darkly sleek pleasure boat, large in context to its surroundings, although from where he was it looked no bigger than a fingernail.

As he ran he watched a small car chase its headlights towards the distant boat and then disappear behind it. He ran harder. The cold air on his skin was no relief from the sharp needling pains across his back, the biting throb of broken teeth and a broken hand almost inconsequential.

He came to a junction in the road that fed the quay. Buildings on the left blocked his view so he moved slowly around until he could see the car, pressing himself into the shadows as he clicked the call button four times, two sets of two separated by a short pause. Two clicks were returned. Direction and status confirmed.

He watched and calculated. Save for Andrea getting loose to rip a scream, he had no reason to believe Hakan's world was anything but ordered and rosy. A scenario that forced Hakan to abandon the boat was a long way down Brian's list. At the top was the assumption they were getting ready to leave. Judging by the stacks of boxes on the quay, leaving was at least an hour away. He had time.

He could make out two shapes in the car but nothing else. He thought about moving around to see if Andrea was in the back, but that would involve traversing a wide open expanse or the narrow gap behind a row of shuttered workshops. He stayed where he was, waiting and constantly working through the scenarios.

The first he knew something was wrong was when he heard Hakan's angry voice invading the night air. And then he saw the squat broad figure emerge on to the quay from the back of the boat. Hakan was animated and agitated, lifting one of the boxes and hurling it down at something or someone either in the water or climbing off the boat. He leaned forward and hoisted hard upwards, sending a small shadow tumbling across the quay.

Brian caught his breath, quickly realising it was a woman as she picked herself from the ground. She stumbled into light and he could see her shirt was open, fastened with a few buttons pushed through the wrong holes. Her body was smeared with something dark across her chest and face, so much that the whites of her eyes stood out. Blood? There was too much for it to be her own. Her movements were awkward and stiff. She was practically thrown into the car, Hakan violently angry, turning back and hurling himself at a tower of boxes that he kicked until it toppled over, onto the boat and into the water. Something had seriously messed with his plans.

Brian re-prioritised as Hakan's voice faded and he climbed into the car, the door slamming closed as it turned, the engine screaming as it came towards him. He glimpsed Andrea's hair low in the back seat as it passed, shouting a short loud instruction to the radio. The car turned left at the junction and Brian sprinted after it, watching it fade as it headed down a decline towards lights and streets. He put everything he had into the complementing movement of arms and legs. The car grew smaller and then turned and disappeared. His bare feet slapped against the road, his gasped breaths almost desperate. It took precious seconds before the Mercedes overtook him. The door opened as it stopped. Brian jumped in and the Mercedes accelerated away.

343

NINETY-FOUR

In the dining room the mother pulled her feet on to the chair and wrapped her arms around her legs, watching Ferreira with feral eyes.

Ferreira spoke directly to her, 'You don't like your ex-husband at all, do you?'

She blinked.

'How did you find out?' Ferreira asked.

'About what?' The mother's voice was low and dry and quiet.

'About Andrea, Beth. About how little time she spent with her father, that he left her home alone Saturdays. Did you hear Andrea talking to Kevin?'

She used exaggerated movements of her head to vigorously enforce her denial.

'How then?'

The mother did not answer, blinking rapidly as if she expected another reality to suddenly appear at any moment.

Ferreira changed tack. 'You knew, Beth, I know that. You discovered something, it made you angry, but you didn't act because you knew you had something valuable. Something you could really damn Brian with. I bet even telling social services wasn't enough for you. You wanted him humiliated. To crush what Andrea held for her father, to snuff out how she felt about him. You just weren't sure how. Were you? Then the American, your preacher, came up with the idea, didn't he? What did you tell him Beth? Tell me because we can find Andrea. Tell m...'

'It was his voice.' The mother cut in, her eyes were on Ferreira but she was looking at a memory. 'It was his voice. I wanted to wrap it around me. I would have told him anything. I did tell him everything.' The mother scratched at her trousers with clawed fingers. 'His faith was so strong, it flowed from him, he was so sure. He listened to me and all I could do was tell him all about Brian, how Brian made me feel when he walked out. Talking to him unravelled it inside me. He came once or twice a month and I...'

She glanced at the stepfather. 'I just couldn't stop myself. I so wanted Brian to suffer, I hate him. This is all because of him. He left me in the middle of the night. Can you imagine, me and my baby? He couldn't give me the life I wanted! It wasn't that he couldn't give me that life, he just wasn't man enough. I hate him, the loser. I showed him. You can see what I've done for myself, what I've made of myself. While he walks in the dirt with the low life. Couldn't give me the life I wanted, well I made my own life. I showed him.'

Ferreira waited for her to expand but she started repeating the Brian mantra. So she interrupted.

'How did you know Beth? How did you know to tell the preacher? Who told you about Andrea being left alone?'

'Nobody,' she answered, her eyes searching through all the empty spaces in the room.

'They must have, Beth. You knew all about Andrea, she told you didn't she?'

The mother angrily turned on Ferreira. 'Andrea told me nothing, the ungrateful little cow. All she told me was lies to protect her good for nothing father! She made EVERYONE tell me lies.'

'Tell me, Beth, it's important. It wasn't in her diary, there was nothing written about her visits to Hambury.'

That earned a single nod and then the mother told her.

'Not the diary, it was all wrong. That child can't keep a secret to save her life, she'd have to tell someone, somehow. Then I realised.'

'Realised what?' Ferreira leaned in closer.

'Realised if she didn't write it in her diary she would simply write it somewhere else. That child thinks she's so smart, just like her father. Well I'm smarter, I can tell you. I searched and searched and then I found it. Andrea wrote her diaries as pretend stories. She changed herself to be a boy and thought nobody would know, stupid little cow. Of course she added angels but she would, it was all right there, all the detail anyone would ever need. He said they were perfect.'

'You gave Andrea's stories to the preacher?'

'Of course not, he came here. I showed him, he read them. He came a few times a month.' She smiled fondly at the memory. The stepfather moved in his seat, sinking his head into his hands.

Ferreira kept pushing. 'What did he say Beth?'

'He said God would punish Brian, that he would wash him away for me. He would make it very public, for everyone to see.'

For the first time and only for a second she looked uncertain. 'He said it might look bad, at first, but it had to be to really hurt Brian. He would bring Andrea straight back to me, it would all be a misunderstanding explained. Except Brian would be hanging in the wind, everyone would see him for what he is.' She looked like she enjoyed that image, nodding and smiling to herself.

'That was it?' Ferreira asked, disbelieving.

'He just said I must be strong, he would bring Andrea straight back to me. Andrea would see Brian for what he was.' She rocked back and forwards on her chair.

'You believed this man, Beth? You bartered your child's safety for a vendetta? You trusted this man with your own daughter?'

The mother straightened her back, the imperious tone back in her voice, an echo of the day before. 'Why would I not, Detective, he is a preacher.'

Ferreira lost it a little. She was seldom given to violence but barely stopped herself from slapping the woman, for fear she might not stop. She forced herself to fold her arms. 'He didn't say it would be like this though, did he Beth? He didn't bring her back to you did he?' The liaison officer moved uncomfortably and Ferreira collected her temper, taking a step back and a deep breath.

'Where is he, Beth, where does he live? Where can we find him?'

The mother stared at her with saucer eyes and slowly shook her head.

'You don't know?' Ferreira's voice rose in pitch. 'How did you contact him? How is he connected to your church? Can we contact them?'

There was not a sound in the room, all eyes on the mother. Ferreira tried imagining how she would make sense of all this to the Chief Inspector. Then the mother started speaking, little more than a whisper.

'*Suffer.*' Her voice sounded like tyres slow over gravel.

Ferreira leaned in, trying to make out the word. 'What was that?'

'SUFFER YOU BITCH!' The mother's hands clenched and opened,

346

the skin on her face tight, her eyes filmy and her lips pulled back to her gums. 'SUFFER, I wanted him to suffer, you bitch! I wanted to humiliate him. Make him suffer, he should suffer, he should suffer like I did, you nosey little bitch!' She climbed off the chair and stepped closer. The constable was a half step behind.

'All that child ever does is worship him and he left me! The humiliation! He left me in the middle of the night, I WANTED HIM TO SUFFAAA!'

The constable eased her back into the chair and the stepfather looked at Ferreira with his head still in his hands.

'Who runs the church Kevin? I need names and numbers right now. Who would have booked this American preacher?' She held up three fingers, which his gaze shifted to. 'I need it in three minutes. You got that?'

He slowly nodded and pushed himself upright. Ferreira carried her bag out to the kitchen counter. She flicked open her phone, finding no missed calls, but as she scrolled down to the Chief Inspector's number she saw the top of Boer's phone in the side pocket next to his Bible. It was flashing a dull blue light. She pulled it out and cursed him. He had left it on silent. There were a series of texts from a mobile number she half recognised. The texts contained a sequence of addresses in Grimsby. They were signed by Adam Sawacki, he had given the addresses context.

Adam? She walked through to the reception room, scrolling through the addresses, into the room where she and Boer first interviewed the mother. Boer had seen something even then. She checked her watch. It was twenty-three minutes into Tuesday morning. Ferreira flopped onto the sofa and rang Chief Inspector Anne Darling. Already she was figuring how quickly she could wrap up here and get to Grimsby.

NINETY-FIVE

All she could smell was fish. It was cold here as well, sitting with her legs and arms bound to a chair. *Same old same old,* she thought and a childish giggle sounded not far away. She was in a warehouse, wide and mostly empty with metal struts beneath a high ceiling. The far end was open to the night and a lorry was reversing in, a large blue container set on the back. Her chair rocked awkwardly, straddling a gutter in the floor that opened to a large drain beside her.

Hakan was not happy. He was screaming and shouting, his arms making dramatic and exaggerated movements. Pointing and raging at her, although for all she knew he was miming. She could hear nothing in this real world, a blissful silence like being underwater.

Andrea was standing away to her left looking hopelessly miserable. That was all Sarah would change if she could. That Andrea would not see this. But a man knelt behind her, one arm around her body, a hand on her head forcing her to watch. Hakan wanted Andrea to see. Two other men stood guard between Andrea and the reversing lorry.

Sometimes and more frequently now Sarah was spared the trauma of reality, closing her eyes to see green fields and blue skies, the wind heavy with the scent of spring. She could hear in this place and was quite happy to stay but for the sound of the horseman, now dragging her back to the real world. It was all wrong, he was supposed to save her.

In this real world there was a box on the floor near the drain, quite large, like musicians carried. She did not know what was inside, but knew it would not be nice, not a musical instrument. Hakan gravitated towards it. She wished he would hurry up. She was tired of it all, tired of struggling in the face of man's ceaseless need.

The sound of the horseman was deafening as Hakan opened the box with a flourish, a magician revealing the rabbit under the hat. Except this was a chainsaw. How inventive, she thought. It had a red base that he gripped as a handle and a long blade with jagged malevolent teeth. She smiled wickedly which caused him a moment's indecision, then he pressed a button and the teeth were lost in a blur.

Beyond Hakan she could see Andrea now struggling violently and silently screaming. She forced herself not to look at the girl. Hakan stepped closer and she felt the tiny percussive vibrations against her skin. Just three more steps. She willed him to take them.

The lorry came to a stop and a man jumped from the cabin, walking to the rear, a giant black man with a metal clipboard in his hand. He walked towards Andrea with long sure strides, his long coat trailing behind.

As Hakan's men realised and converged on him, Sarah saw the black man was not carrying a clip board after all. It looked more like a sword as he moved like a vibrant shadow cutting fast arcs through the air and through the men, who circled and spun and fell away, first one then two, the machete glinting in the light, now smeared dark. Then it was just the black man, rounding on Andrea. Andrea screamed at him and the man holding Andrea turned her, a child shield between him and this wraith. Then the man's nerve failed and he turned and ran, but not as fast as the glinting metal, spinning end over end, burying itself in the man's back. His legs buckled and he pitched forward, sliding face first to the floor.

Andrea stood motionless for a second, as if looking for something she could not see, and then she ran and leapt into the black man's arms. He looked across at Sarah and turned the child to look the other away.

Sarah turned her attention back to Hakan. His mouth contorted, unaware as he approached his grand finale, the chainsaw dancing its jig. She was so happy for Andrea but now Hakan must hurry. All she wanted was green fields. Her gaze fixed on those blurring teeth that would take her there, then drawn upwards to dust falling through a shaft of light from high above, following its trail up to the angled struts in the ceiling, to a shape within.

She blinked and blinked again, trying to see the shadow within the shadows, a leg and the curve of a spine. She saw bare flesh, a crouched man with a surreal tattoo on his back, the sparkle of his eyes. She closed hers, she smelt the trees and the grass and opened them and the shape was gone.

Hakan stepped forward and raised his arm and she braced herself for the bite of angry teeth, a pain that would be a threshold to eternity beneath blue skies. But the pain never came. Hakan was now held by some invisible force, wide-eyed with a new necklace of laced blades, her old friends Wilkinson and Sword. Tears of blood welled on his neck.

The chainsaw fell away, skittering across the floor before coming to a stop. Hakan stepped forward into the light and behind him she was sure she could see the horseman. He winked at her with eyes that had seen more than a lifetime and pulled the chain tight and hard to the right, a malicious snaking tail of blades that whipped across Hakan's neck. Sarah smiled and closed her eyes and felt the rain of another world warm upon her face.

Andrea Scott Found Alive

London (Reuters) - Tuesday morning police raided seven locations in Grimsby that culminated in the recovery of the missing child Andrea Scott. There were several related fatalities that were not the result of the raids, police said.

Sarah Sawacki, the witness police have been seeking, was also found unharmed with Andrea. Several tabloids today have stirred speculation around her role in Andrea's abduction, revealing a history of criminal convictions. There has been wide condemnation for topless pictures of Mrs Sawacki published by a number of tabloids.

Chief Inspector Anne Darling who headed the investigation into Andrea's abduction made the following statement: 'It is a great relief to us all that Andrea has been recovered unharmed. It is an excellent example of collaboration within this force and our ability to react and act on information decisively and quickly. Our investigations are of course ongoing and will be undertaken with the same efficiency and attention to detail.'

A separate press release by Northampton Police has confirmed Andrea Scott's mother was last night taken to hospital, nobody was available to confirm whether she was in custody.

D etective Sergeant Helen Ferreira fished her ID from her bag and slid it across the counter. The woman waiting the other side studied the photo and started copying the detail onto a sheet of paper.

Ferreira leaned against the counter, looking across the small room at Andrea. The girl was sitting on one of the chairs, fidgeting and writing in her book while listening to music through headphones. When Ferreira flicked through her recollections of these Saturdays it seemed she stretched taller before her eyes. Today Andrea was excited and with good reason. A stark contrast to when she first saw her five months before.

She had made Cleethorpes that night in just over two hours, waiting then amid the mayhem of legalities and the raids, anxious to hear news that Andrea was safe. They found four bodies in a warehouse, blood in a house and nothing overtly sinister at the other addresses. It was only when they began figuring why the girl was still missing that they discovered Sarah and Andrea were already in Grimsby Police Station. It seemed they had walked in off the street just as they had started knocking down doors.

Separating Andrea from Sarah had resulted in a violent and hysterical reaction from the girl, so they were given blankets, hot drinks and food and left in an interview room, with the door open and a constable outside. That was how Ferreira first saw them, two sets of haunted eyes, both sitting on the floor in the corner of the room, Andrea holding on to Sarah as if some feat of gravity might suddenly render them separate. It was only after Sarah's subsequent interview that they learned of the hidden room in Eve Hill Way and of the luxury yacht in Grimsby dock.

'You're free to take the child, Detective.'

She turned to say thank you but the woman was already making her way to a photocopier. So she took her ID and stepped across the room.

'Come on then,' she said and held open the door as Andrea hastily packed her book and headphones into her rucksack.

'Let's hope your dad's remembered!'

Andrea flashed a fleeting smile and a faux scowl as she considered the possibility. The supervisor for her visits had reported him late twice and a no show once.

They stepped from the council building to a bright March morning, the air cold and the sun climbing a clear blue sky. They crossed the road with Ferreira's hand on Andrea's shoulder, then along the High Street, not yet busy. They crossed the market square into a weave of side streets, passing the library and through its car park. And then they were on the verge of the park. Throughout the short journey Andrea's excitement had grown in a babble of questions and each stride that was almost a skip as she kept up. It had been three weeks since her last visit and this would be her first unsupervised since her abduction.

'He is here!' Andrea's faith was vindicated as she bounced and skipped back.

Ferreira squinted at two figures standing by a bench next to the canal, framed by a red and white narrow boat passing behind. 'Go on then.'

Andrea ran across the park, a receding figure with her rucksack bouncing on her back, an outward image of a happy child that belied her struggle. A child who now saw her mother less than she did her father, her de facto parent was her stepfather. Andrea merged with the two figures by the bench, first a leaping hug at Brian and then a much longer one with the other figure. Although Ferreira could not make out any features she knew the other figure was Sarah Sawacki.

Brian hugged Andrea and watched her attach to Sarah and then squat beside her as they sat on the bench, their bond tangible just from watching them together. He turned his attention to the detective making her way towards them, a little self-consciously. Andrea had spent a lot of time these last months completing her statement with Ferreira. So far their own statements were holding up, partly because they were *mostly* the truth, substantiated by Andrea, largely because the police and media were busy hunting for two men who were already dead. Whenever he thought of the two blonds he imagined them washed out to sea or their bloated bodies floating at high tide in the brick workshop. A detail he was not about to share with the police, lest some bright spark decide he had used excessive force escaping execution.

He had stayed away from Boer's funeral although he did go to Adam's, watching Sarah beneath her large umbrella in the rain. He felt guilty, of course, just like she did. Except for him death had been a companion for so long, they were on easy terms. He kept his distance though, despite the chaos being stirred around her. Then in December she had turned up at the club, asking about Andrea, but in reality she was looking for help.

Ferreira came to a stop, glancing at Sarah and fixing her attention on Brian. He was looking smarter these days, easy in a shirt and jacket, his hair and moustache neatly trimmed. 'Andrea's officially returned to your care. If we get to court there'll be a review of her statement, otherwise I'm done too. Your time with Andrea is now between you and Kevin. Take care of her. We could do without the paperwork.'

'I'll do my best,' Brian hesitated, 'and thanks.'

Andrea climbed off the bench and gave her a hug. 'I'm going to miss you.'

Ferreira hugged her softly back, her attention now on Sarah, looking at each other and exchanging shallow nods in greeting.

Sarah seemed different to Ferreira each time she saw her, her clothes and style evolving over the months. Always it looked effortless, these days a lot darker. Today she was wearing jeans and a silk shirt, a long coat and stylish boots. Thin silver chains shimmered at her wrists, her eyes given greater emphasis with dark liner, her fringe cut straight. Her hair, peroxide with dark highlights, normally down past her shoulders, but today held up with two wooden pins.

'You need anything at all, you call. Anything,' Ferreira said.

'Thank you. Your number is committed to memory, Helen.'

Sarah stayed seated and Ferreira let go of Andrea. She said her goodbyes and walked back along the towpath towards town. She had a backlog of work stacked high on her desk, but today, she thought, she might just blow her time in the library, working on a project that increasingly consumed her spare time.

Sarah relaxed into the restless attention of Andrea and the breeze rippling across her shirt. She embraced this rare moment of normality, comfortable as ever these last months in Brian's company. She had struggled of course. She still did, constantly reconciling his involving Adam, against what might have happened if he had not. The truth was she felt at ease with Brian, secure even. She knew this might be psychological, an unconscious correlation with her childhood desire for a saviour and being saved by him. It might also come from a shared sense of being damaged. It was what it was. She felt better now in her own skin. She was learning to look after herself and that had started with not looking like a victim.

You're always going to get looked at so fuck them off with that first look.

That was Brian's considered philosophy. It had been an evolution but he was right. Her clothes were a large part of that, the part she struggled with the most. Her hair was key too. It had taken a while to find the right mix. Right now she loved it. It was the first layer in her mental armour.

And how she needed it. The topless photos were the least of her problems despite the puritan reaction they had stirred. Her life had been picked apart with the blanks filled in with make believe. She was being painted as some homicidal harlot, complicit in Andrea's abduction, now free to roam the streets. A modern day witch, the whole thing played like a sinister pantomime on the national stage.

But for all she had faced and was now readying to confront, she had no right to be scared, never again. She wore Adam's bravery like a medal on her heart. She missed him terribly, woke each morning and went through the heartache and guilt all over again. She constantly saw him in the crowd and felt him beside her, but he never was there. She felt like a fraud at her inability to grieve. It felt trapped inside. She lay in bed at night and willed tears onto her cheeks but the great gasping sobs of release had so far refused to come.

She jumped as Brian scooped Andrea up from behind and lifted her squealing over his shoulder, making as if he would throw her into the canal. It looked like he actually might. She smiled and walked over to them, taking Andrea's hand when she managed to scramble to the ground. At least Brian was trying, which made her like him a little more. Sometimes it felt like she had gained the one thing she had always feared – a family – although dysfunctional didn't even come close.

ACKNOWLEDGEMENTS

I want to thank Peter Hanson, Louise Brady and Timothy Taylor for their invaluable generosity in reading a raw script and telling me what didn't work. Also to Nikki Smith and Karim Chafia who complained a lot less about a later draft because of those that went before them. A very big thank you must go to Nina Jervis for not missing a thing. And to Renata Santos I offer my eternal gratitude for investing so much at every stage.

Above all this book would not exist if it were not for Katherine Priddis. She shaped its early stages and researched much that would make a child's world. Her clinically accurate appraisals of each new chapter were equally feared and welcomed.

For taking a story and turning it into a book my thanks go to Daniel Goldsmith Associates and their whole team. Special thanks go to my editor Katie Green for her invaluable wisdom. Any failing in the storytelling is entirely mine.

This book's cover art is so much more than my fuzzy concept thanks to John Wood the photographer, Monika Trzpil the model and Caitlin Tanner for make-up effects. You can see more of the stunning images on the Chasing Innocence website.

This book is thriller fiction but in researching the nature of lost innocence I read a number of harrowing non-fiction accounts. It is for these survivors and the many anonymous victims that this book is dedicated.

Finally my gratitude goes to Helen and Ricardo Ferreira for kindly lending me their names. And to Moby for creating music that plugs directly into my creative soul.

J.P.

If you enjoyed Chasing Innocence then please rush out and tell everyone. If you didn't then tell me what I got wrong and then tell everyone to read it anyway.

johnpotter@chasinginnocence.info

For more about Sarah Sawacki including news on upcoming publicity, the next book and additional images from the cover shoot, please pay us a visit.

http://www.chasinginnocence.info

Creative Crow is a small, author-run publishing company. Every penny of profit is invested in bringing entertaining books to a wide audience.

http://www.creativecrow.info

Lightning Source UK Ltd.
Milton Keynes UK
UKOW051650280312

189773UK00003B/21/P